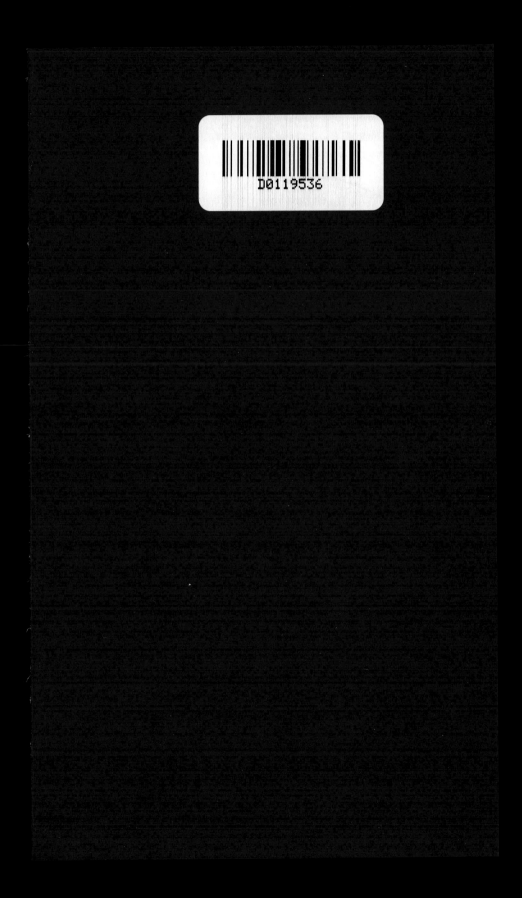

DREAM
DETECTIVE

DREAM
DETECTIVE

Chris Robinson

with

Andy Boot

LITTLE, BROWN AND COMPANY

A *Little, Brown* Book

First published in Great Britain in 1996
by Little, Brown and Company

A CIP catalogue record for this book
is available from the British Library.

ISBN 0 316 91466 5

Typeset by Palimpsest Book Production Limited,
Polmont, Stirlingshire
Printed and bound in Great Britain by
Clays Ltd, St Ives plc.

Little, Brown and Company (UK)
Brettenham House
Lancaster Place
London WC2E 7EN

FOREWORD

Chris Robinson first contacted the Regional Crime Squad in 1988 with information concerning an IRA atrocity. It was treated with scepticism at first as the police have many approaches from people claiming psychic powers who are either attention-seeking, misguided or whose information proves inaccurate.

I was, however, asked by the Regional Co-ordinator to monitor Chris' dreams, which I did, sometimes on a daily basis, until I retired from the police in 1995. As a senior police officer and experienced detective, I had always concerned myself with hard facts and usable evidence. Because of this, Chris did not find me an easy contact to report to, but over the years Chris has convinced me of the genuine belief he has in his powers.

Despite the vagueness of many of his dreams, we have worked together on a number of investigations and Chris has been able to offer helpful information in relation to major crimes and terrorist activities.

ALEX HALL: Ex-Detective Chief Inspector, Regional Crime Squad.

AUTHOR'S NOTE

Go outside on any night and look up to the sky. If it is cloudy you will see very little, but on a clear, dark night you will see thousands of stars. Take a powerful telescope, look through it and you will see much more, but on a cloudy night you will still see very little. We know the reason – clouds of water vapour. We sometimes get very clear messages in our dreams and at other times it is just a mess. Maybe something gets in the way of the messages in just the same way as the clouds do with starlight. We know a little about light and how it behaves, but we have almost no knowledge about how or why we dream – or for that matter about any other kind of psychic ability. I ask that you keep an open mind as you read this book and form your conclusions at the end. Remember, we used to think that the Earth was flat.

In the early months of the dreams I almost cracked up. Without the support of Detective Inspector Paul Aylott, Chief Inspector Alex Hall, and Detective Inspector Chris Watt and their superiors who remained open-minded, I probably would have. The Rev David Bolster from St Andrew's Church helped me enormously then and is still doing so now; thank you all. I would also like to thank all my friends and family who are too many to mention; but especially Penny Thornton, Dr Keith Hearne and Gary Jones who gave me the most valuable professional help. Most of all I would like to thank my friends who now dwell in the next world for coming to me with the information about events due to happen. Thank you Yvonne, Keith, Trevor and Robert, may God bless you. I look forward to joining you one day in the realms beyond this one . . .

Chris Robinson

INTRODUCTION

I first met Chris Robinson over the Easter of 1994. At that time I was promoting a book about psychics who have been used by the police to solve murders. The publisher had despatched me to Wire TV, a cable company operating out of Bristol, where I was to take part in a talk show about psychics and the police.

It was an awful night: very stormy, windy and rainy, making urban Bristol seem like the back end of hell – in some ways, the perfect setting for discussion about the so-called supernatural. It didn't make matters any less doom-laden when you consider that the studio was located in the middle of a shopping mall – and is there anything more dark and creepy than a deserted mall? It was like something out of a George Romero zombie movie.

The people from the television company, however, were very pleasant, and their production offices – across the road from the mall – were warm and full of people willing to make tea when you came in out of the rain. This was where I first heard of Chris. One of the researchers said to me, 'We've got a guy called Chris Robinson appearing. Have you heard of him?' I had to admit that I hadn't. Underneath her desk was a small cardboard box, perched on a pile of phone books. 'We've set a little test for Chris,' she went on with a sly smile.

Puzzled, I said nothing until Chris arrived from our hotel – he had reached Bristol earlier than I had – with another of the guests on the show, parapsychologist Robin Furman.

Straight away Chris impressed me. He was casually dressed, and very open and friendly. Many of the psychics I have come across like to project a vaguely mysterious and otherworldly aura. The ones with the most to offer are usually more natural. Chris already seemed to fit into the latter category. We talked about many things that had nothing to do with psychics, and then I took the plunge and asked him about the theory that all ghosts are nothing more than 'tape recordings', impressions of things past trapped in buildings and locations. Chris told me that he felt this was untrue, as he'd been having conversations with ghosts for years, and you can't conduct a two-way conversation with a tape recording . . .

We also talked about football, and he told me that he'd had a dream the week before about the West Ham–Luton FA Cup Quarter-Final. Luton caused an upset by winning 3–2, and, interestingly, Chris's son had dreamt the name of the Luton scorer – hat-trick hero Scott Oakes.

Then came the time to open the box. The researcher asked Chris what he'd dreamt about the box, and Chris got out his dream diary, flipping to the entry for a few nights before. The page was filled with disjointed phrases and scrappy line drawings. The phrases were coherent in themselves, but resembled a stream of consciousness, jumping from one subject to another with little apparent connection.

I was looking over Chris's shoulder, fascinated. There were phrases to do with dentists, razor blades and teeth. Chris explained that he'd had a dream about cutting his mouth with razor blades, blood everywhere. He'd also dreamt about going to the dentist, which he usually did only when he actually needed to go himself. There was also a reference to 'yellow pages' in the diary, and I remembered that the box was standing on a pile of old phone books.

When the researcher opened the box, inside was a baby's teething ring, of the kind that is made up of brightly coloured plastic keys. The symbolism of a mouthful of razor blades, and trips to the dentist, in relation to a baby cutting its first teeth was obvious. The researcher asked Chris if she could use that on the show.

He refused. That made me take even more of an interest in him. Most psychics would be more than pleased to have such an obvious piece of symbolism used as a direct 'hit'. Not Chris: he told the researcher that it wasn't accurate enough for his liking. Unless he'd actually dreamt of keys, or a baby, he didn't want it included on the programme.

This was definitely impressive. If such an obvious piece of dream symbolism wasn't good enough for him, then what was?

After the show, on our way back to the hotel, I made sure that I got to talk to Chris. He told me about his life: he'd had the odd precognitive dream, but not until 1989 had he started to get them with any regularity. He was a down-to-earth man, trained as a television engineer, and had in the past run his own business as a television repair man and had also run a chain of video hire shops. He'd been an entrepreneur, in his own words a 'ducker-and-diver', for most of his life. Now he was unable to work, as the dreams were so frequent that they kept him in a state of semi-consciousness through the night. He no longer slept properly.

Things began to get even more interesting as he told me of some of the terrorist and homicide cases he had worked on. Back at the hotel he showed me press clippings, and letters from the Ministry of Defence and the Metropolitan Police relating to his dream premonitions. Most importantly, he showed me his current dream book. Over the years since 1989 Chris has built up a vast archive of these dream diaries, written at night. Extracts from these will feature heavily in the course of this book, so perhaps now is the best time to explain what they are.

Every night Chris keeps a notebook and pen by his bedside. Throughout the night, while he is dreaming, he writes in this book by the method known as automatic writing. This is performed when the subject is not conscious of what he is doing: usually in some kind of trance state. It is believed to be the unconscious mind that guides the hand, bypassing our everyday conscious mind. As a result, the subject has no idea what has been written down until he or she is conscious again – in Chris's case, when he wakes up.

Consequently Chris's notebook is a confusion of half-sentences, phrases describing vivid images, and some line drawings and sketches. Often the dreams are couched in symbols. It took Chris a little while to work out what these symbols mean, but they form a definite code, with the same images and symbols recurring time and again. Interestingly it became apparent that sometimes it is not the dream itself that provides the code, but rather what is written about the dream.

I found all this fascinating, and when Chris told me that he wanted someone to help him write a book about his experiences, I offered my services. At that time I had no idea that Chris was used by the security services, and that every chapter of this book would have to be vetted before it could be offered to the publisher. I didn't know that the police were willing to endorse everything that Chris says in this book.

Chris Robinson feels that it is time for these things to be recorded, and that whoever – or whatever – is guiding these dreams for him wants him to tell people about it. I know that he has a phenomenal accuracy rate, and that the police have never before endorsed a psychic.

Chris Robinson: Dream Detective describes how this psychic came to be endorsed, and how he gets such incredible results. The events in the book all happened, and my accounts are based on Chris's memory and on research of subsequent news reports. It should, however, be pointed out that all conversations are dramatic reconstructions, pieced together from memory. They are not verbatim reports of actual conversations, as there are no transcripts from which to work. I have been asked to point this out by both Chris and Alex Hall, his liaison officer with the Bedfordshire Police Force.

PART ONE

THE LEARNING PROCESS

CHAPTER ONE

Chris Robinson's strange experiences with dreams really began in 1989, although he is somewhat reluctant to discuss them in great detail. Over the years he has encountered a lot of scepticism and downright hostility towards his premonitions, and so he prefers to use in this book only material for which he has written corroboration. The fact is that until January 1990 he didn't keep a dream diary – all his automatic writing was done on scraps of paper, which have since been lost.

So the purpose of this short chapter is to fill you in on what happened before Chris started to take records. I think it's important as, despite his own lack of documentation, there are others who will endorse what he has said. Some of what follows cannot be proved without records – not at a distance of over half a decade. But what can be corroborated from other sources is more than enough to introduce you to the world of Chris Robinson.

Back in 1989, Chris was in his late thirties, and in the middle of a period of upheaval in his life. Following the collapse of his video business and subsequent court cases concerning the circumstances of that collapse – circumstances in which Chris was an innocent third party caught up in other people's private wars – Chris was living in a caravan in a mobile homes park in Bedfordshire doing odd jobs. He had just become a father again – his daughter Lauren was born in January of that year.

Some nights Chris's sleeping pattern was disturbed by the child's feeding: one night, Chris was woken by what he thought was the child crying. Then he realised that he could hear a voice in the room. A voice he recognised. His grandmother's voice.

But his grandmother had been dead for several years.

When she was in hospital for the last time, Chris had gone to visit her. All his relatives knew that she was dying, but they were keeping it from her. They asked Chris to do the same.

'I told them – if she asks, then I'm going to have to tell her, 'cause I can't lie to her,' he said to me. 'So I went to see her in hospital, and I was on my own. And she said to me, "Christopher –" and I knew it was trouble, 'cause she only called me Christopher when she knew I was trying to fool her, "Tell me the truth. I'm not coming out of here, am I?"

'And I said to her, "Look, you know I can't lie to you, Nan. Why are you asking that?"

'So she said, "I keep seeing your grandad, down at the end of the bed. He keeps asking me to go with him."

'And I said to her, "Well, Nan, the only thing I can say to you is this: next time he comes to see you, and asks you to go with him, I think you'd better go."

'I knew it was the last time I'd see her, so I kissed her, and we both cried a bit. And then I went. She died that evening. In fact, from what one of the nurses told me, she was probably dead before I'd even reached my car.'

Chris could hear his grandmother's voice clearly, as though she were standing next to him.

'Christopher,' she said, 'someone is trying to steal your car.'

Chris's car wasn't outside his friend's house, where he was sleeping – he'd left it at home, back at the caravan, five miles away. His car was a Porsche 924 Turbo, his pride and joy. He'd bought it as scrap and had spent much time, love and money on restoring it. The first time he took it to his friend's house, hooligans had broken into it. Since then, he'd taken the bus when he visited her.

Chris found himself talking to the voice in a half-dream state, accepting it as fact that he was talking to his dead grandmother.

'Nan, the car's five miles away. There's no buses, Lorraine hasn't got a car, and by the time I get a taxi or walk there, it'll be long gone. No, it's lost. Anyway,' he added, wanting to get back to sleep, 'it's insured.'

'Don't worry, Christopher,' his grandmother said, 'I'll do something about it.'

Chris fell back to sleep and thought no more about it. The next afternoon, as he reached home, one of his neighbours came out to see him.

'Is your car all right?' she asked.

Chris was surprised. He hadn't been to examine the car, which was parked in the mobile homes' small car park, but had noticed it as he passed by and everything seemed okay. He'd almost forgotten about the dream.

'Are you sure your car's all right?' the woman continued. 'Only something strange happened in the middle of the night. There was a blinding light, and a voice. My husband got up, because it frightened the life out of him, and he looked out of the window. There were these blokes trying to break into your car, so he chased them off. He spent the rest of the night sitting up, guarding it.'

Chris went and checked the car: it was perfectly all right. He thanked his neighbours, and went into his caravan, where he sat down and thought about it. Had it been his grandmother who had saved his car?

The more he thought about it, the more he became convinced. He went down to his local church and prayed to his grandmother and grandfather, thanking them. He was convinced that they were responsible. At the same time, he had no idea that this was the beginning of something. He simply put it down to a strange coincidence, something that could never really be explained.

The next incident didn't occur for several months.

Chris was flying over water. There was a man below him, in the water, and obviously in some distress. He was calling up to Chris for help. Chris knew that the man was going to die. He flew down to help him but, as is the way in dreams, they ended up talking inconsequentially. The stranger had fallen off a boat that Chris could see in the distance, sailing away from them. At one point, the man – who hadn't identified himself, and who bore no resemblance to anyone Chris knew – said, 'It's all right for you – you're going back to your body in the morning. I'm not.' He then began to rant and rave about wreaking revenge on the boat's owners, who had left him to die.

It was shocking and frightening, waking Chris with a start. He told his friend, who – none too happy at being woken – told Chris to write it down and go back to sleep. Chris found an old letter by the side of the bed, scribbled down a few details, then went back to sleep.

Two days later there was an item on the news about an ex-soldier who had fallen overboard from a ferry bound for Sweden and had drowned. Chris knew immediately that this was the man in his dream. He was shocked by the revelation, but at the same time excited about what it could mean.

'It's all right for you – you're going back to your body.' These were the words that have stayed with Chris ever since.

After his dream about his grandmother, he had mentioned the dream to two policemen whom he had been assisting with an investigation concerning some ex-colleagues. He had also told his friend Trevor Kempson, a *News of the World* journalist.

A week later the same boat was involved in another incident. Chris had already had a feeling that something terrible was going to happen to the boat, and had told the policemen (who have, unfortunately, asked not to be named): it wasn't a dream, more a vague notion, something half-remembered and grasped.

The boat was carrying a consignment of beagles to Sweden, something that it did every week. Only this time it was different: nearly all the beagles died, suffocating through lack of oxygen. This was a regular run, and such a thing shouldn't have happened. Chris could remember the ex-soldier's vows of revenge. Could it be that – impossible though it sounds – he had returned as a ghostly presence and scared the dogs to such a degree (remembering that dogs – like cats – are particularly sensitive) that they panicked and used all their oxygen in manic barking?

Chris was disturbed by this. What did it say about his dreams that he knew something was going to happen – and then it did?

The night after the incident concerning the beagles had featured on the news, the soldier appeared again in Chris's dreams, and told him that he was going to set the boat alight. The next morning Chris was on the phone to his police contacts, telling them what he had dreamt.

Ferries work on a 'sister-boat' system: as one boat leaves, say, Harwich, its sister will be departing for Harwich. This time the incident occurred not on the boat from which the soldier had fallen, but on its sister-boat. About halfway across the route, at the point where the coastguard felt sure that the soldier had drowned, the sister-boat caught fire.

It didn't take long for the police to pay Chris a visit. What was going on? A spontaneous fire in a linen cupboard – how could Chris possibly have known?

The summer went on, and a few dreams came and went. Having no proper records, Chris can't recall the exact details now, but the dreams were jumbled and confused, with elements of precognition among them. At this time Chris wasn't too sure what it was that he possessed, only that it both excited and worried him.

The police, on the other hand, were becoming extremely interested. Two officers took over the job of dealing with Chris and, if not monitoring him, then at the very least keeping an eye on his dreams. For reasons of security they prefer to be known simply as Frank and Steve.

'Let's face it,' Frank said to Chris, 'we knew where you were when all this happened. You couldn't have pushed that bloke overboard, you couldn't have killed the dogs, or set fire to the ship. So how the hell did you know about it?'

Everybody – including me – has always asked Chris the name of the soldier. His reply is that the man was just there – only once did he mention his name, in passing, referring to himself as Robert. Otherwise, the soldier never bothered with names, sticking instead to an 'all right, mate?' approach, as the exchange of names didn't seem significant.

Chris had far more important things to talk about, as became obvious on 30 September 1989.

CHAPTER TWO

Chris stood in the middle of the deserted street. He had flown here. Now he was facing the mysterious soldier who had lurked in his dreams for some time.

'You know why I've brought you here, don't you?' the soldier said calmly.

It was the strangest dream yet.

It was an ordinary Saturday night for Chris. He watched television until deciding to go to bed at half-past ten. He's always told me that he needs to have between eight and ten hours' sleep a night, otherwise he spends the rest of the next day feeling like a zombie, unable to function properly. Part of this he puts down to multiple sclerosis, from which he has suffered for years and which is currently in remission. He has also had a heart condition – mitral stenosis – since childhood and, despite several major operations as a child and young man, the condition remains.

This was not to be a night of restful sleep.

Chris was just drifting to sleep when he felt himself begin to leave his body. He described it as though something were pulling him out of himself . . . it was the strangest of sensations: everything told him that it couldn't be real, yet at the same time it was the most intense and real feeling he had ever had. It was like the difference between watching a film of a rollercoaster ride, and actually being on one: everything seemed to be somehow heightened.

Chris could feel himself float up from his body, as though gently sucked upwards by something from above. At first the sensation terrified him, and he could feel his own resistance straining at the upwards pull, trying to drag him back. But the gentle pressure continued, and he found himself beginning to enjoy the upwards motion, his fear starting to disappear and be replaced by a calm acceptance.

As the fear lessened, so the movement upwards became easier. He allowed himself to be pulled along, and it seemed as though his acceptance was all that was needed: from a feeling of floating, he found himself instantly pulled up with a shock. Suddenly he was sitting in the branches of a tree that overhung his caravan. He was sitting next to a British soldier, dressed in uniform. Chris recognised him immediately as the man who had fallen into the sea and drowned – but he'd never seen him in uniform before.

Chris looked at the soldier, and then looked down. He could see the roof of his caravan underneath the branches. As he looked around, he could see all the other homes in the park, which was dotted with oak trees like the one in which he was sitting. The park was sprinkled with lights, and the greenery of rural Bedfordshire disappeared into the black of night. Chris had been living here for three years, and had never seen it like this before.

Chris turned around to ask the soldier what was happening – but he had gone.

Later Chris told me, 'I remember thinking what a strange dream it was. I realise now that it wasn't a dream at all. It was a totally different state: not dreaming, nor waking, but something that lies in between.'

For Chris it was already an unusual dream: he was fully aware of who he was and felt as though he was awake. It was as though he had climbed the tree and was looking around, rather than merely dreaming about it. There were a sharpness and clarity that were unusual for a dream – at least, for the dreams that Chris usually had.

It seemed as though he was sitting there for ages, just looking around. Then he felt that pulling feeling again, just as he had when he was lying in bed. Wherever it wanted to take him, he was keen to find out. He stretched his arms out like wings, and toppled off the branch.

Instead of falling, as he had half-expected, he found himself flying through the air. He'd had flying dreams before, but this was different. In other dreams Chris had no idea of who he was: his identity was lost, and he was flying in the same way as you view a video taken out of an aeroplane window. There was no direct involvement. This was quite different. He could feel the wind plucking at him as he flew, could feel the currents of air around and beneath him, buoying him up. This time he was experiencing everything involved in the physical act of flying, and knew that it was *really* happening.

In previous dreams he had been aware of the flying only at the point when he was about to awake and knew that it was all a dream. The difference now was that if this experience was a dream, then being alive was really the dream, and this was reality. The sensation of being alive was more heightened than anything he had ever experienced.

Chris felt himself flying. It was a westerly direction – this much he knew from the landmarks that passed underneath him, places he drove through every day. Once past them, he watched the fields and hills unfold below him. Over trees, rivers and houses, villages and towns he flew, some of which he recognised, and could therefore confirm the direction his guided flight was taking. And guided it certainly was, as Chris had no control over what was happening. Somehow, recognising a few landmarks made him feel a little more comfortable about what was happening.

He had no idea how far he flew, or for how long. Eventually he felt himself begin to descend towards a small town, which he could pin down only as being somewhere in the West Country. He landed softly on the pavement of the town's main street. It was deserted. Chris looked around for any signs of life – after all, it was still early for the Saturday night revellers you get in the centre of any town. If he had fallen asleep quickly, then it must only be about eleven or half-past . . . if normal time scales applied.

Here he was, at a point that seemed to have been planned for him, rather than by him.

Chris isn't the type of man to scare easily. All his life he's battled against obstacles. He is also naturally laid-back, to the point where some people wonder if he really cares about anything. He does: but he's seen too much to let anything really bother him. Because of this, he's prepared to turn any situation to his advantage. Rather than be scared of what was happening to him that night, he maintained a curiosity about what would happen next.

When he looked around again, the soldier was standing in front of him. His uniform had changed, and he was now in full dress, as though ready to go before the Queen at the Trooping of the Colour. Chris wondered what the soldier wanted. He'd featured in Christ's dreams since that night when he had fallen off the ferry. Yet Chris still didn't know who he was, and if he was some kind of symbolic or fictional dream figure of the kind that sometimes populate the landscapes of the night, then there was little Chris could recognise in terms of origin – he looked like no-one Chris had ever known. Come to that, Chris didn't know anyone in the army at all: so why a soldier?

Chris wanted to ask him who he was, but this question went unasked as the soldier suddenly said, 'You know why I've brought you here, don't you?'

Chris looked at him in silence for a moment before shaking his head. 'No, of course I don't – I don't even know who you are.'

'Come with me,' the soldier replied abruptly.

If Chris thought he was going to get some idea of what was going on, he was very much mistaken. Instead, he was given a tour of the town. The buildings were mostly fairly old, made of stone rather than brick, with a few new developments scattered about. The weirdest thing was that the town was totally empty. And despite his attempts to catch sight of a few road signs, Chris couldn't make out where it was, and the soldier was less than helpful. When Chris asked him where they were, he didn't answer. Instead, he led Chris up the steps of a cheap hotel-cum-bed-and-breakfast. They walked in through the front door and up the stairs to one of the rooms.

Chris had the strangest feeling about this: although he was following the soldier, he seemed to know where they were going and could easily have taken over the lead.

This disquieting thought was put to the back of his mind as the soldier sat down on the bed and began to speak in weary, measured tones as Chris stood and listened.

'There are five men in this town,' he began, 'who are not what they seem. They're posing as building workers, but in fact they are an IRA cell. They're over here doing reconnaissance work, because they've got a bombing mission planned. They're working on a site near here, and they've got guns and explosives stored nearby for future use.' He looked up at Chris, and continued with emphasis, 'It's important that you remember all this.'

Chris nodded, listening intently. The soldier went on to tell him all the technical details involved in making a bomb, details he found hard to follow. His attention kept straying: would he remember all this? And where, exactly, was he?

Chris woke with a start and sat up in bed with his heart thumping, the sweat pouring off him. He looked at the clock: five in the morning. He felt on the edge, not knowing what to believe, or how to feel. It was a strange and frightening experience, but also exhilarating. He felt as though he was discovering a whole new world, but didn't know what it held. His mind was racing, and he had to do something to ease it. The dream was so clear and vivid, as though etched on his memory with battery acid to make sure that it was permanent.

Although he was extremely agitated, and had to do something about the dream, the question remained: what? The first thing was to write down all that he could remember.

As Chris was writing, he thought about where he had been. A distant memory of a holiday made him think that it might have been Gloucester. It certainly reminded him of that part of the country. But as he went to write down the word 'Gloucester', a voice behind him said, 'No – Cheltenham.'

Chris looked round in shock: there was no-one else in the room.

He turned back to the piece of paper, shaken by the sudden mystery voice, and wrote down Cheltenham. As he scribbled the name down, something else came back to him: in the part of the dream when he had been flying, he could remember seeing some satellite dishes. The only dishes of that type in that part of the country were at GCHQ, the secret government listening post. None except those who work there really know what goes on inside GCHQ, but it suddenly struck Chris that this might be an ideal terrorist target.

My God, he thought, these terrorists I've been told about are going to bomb GCHQ, and I know that people will be killed. I must do something about it – I must tell someone. But who on earth can I tell?

Although he had already had contact with two officers concerning his dreams, the first person Chris thought of was Paul Aylott. He was a Detective Inspector based at Dunstable, the nearest town to the mobile homes park. Chris and Paul Aylott had first crossed paths three years before, when Chris was down on his luck and living in a boarding house that was also used as a brothel. Mistaken for the man who ran the brothel, Chris was approached by a businessman who wanted him to procure a couple of prostitutes in order to set up the local Tory MP, who was also a business rival. Chris had agreed to go along with him, then promptly contacted the police. Paul Aylott was the officer who had dealt with the matter. The plot was foiled and the businessman not seen again.

After this, Chris had kept in touch with Aylott, and the two men had become friends. This had been useful, as strange things seemed to happen to Chris with alarming regularity. All his life he has been plagued with the strange coincidences that the psychologist Carl Jung termed synchronicity. It sometimes seemed that his life was a complex web that wove in and out of other people's, connecting them in the strangest way. Although no criminal, Chris was for ever 'helping the police with their enquiries', simply because his life seemed to touch on a number of strange events.

Aylott always used to say, 'It can only happen to you', whenever Chris found himself caught up in something. So it came as no surprise to him when Chris phoned and told him of what he had dreamt. Paul Aylott was only too well aware of Chris's contact with Frank and Steve, and so accepted that what Chris was saying to him that morning was no concocted story. It was obvious that Chris found it deeply disturbing, and Paul agreed to a meeting later that morning.

At quarter to twelve Chris met Aylott in the car park

of the Do-It-All superstore in Dunstable Road, Luton. Aylott was in his car, waiting, when Chris arrived.

'What's all this about, Chris?' he asked genially as Chris got in beside him, clutching the sheets of paper on which he had scribbled down his dream. Chris hesitated for a second – did it all seem too incredible? 'Go on,' urged Paul with a grin, 'spit it out.'

Chris began to tell him about the dream, taking a deep breath and not stopping until he had told Aylott everything, from being pulled up into the tree to hearing the voice behind him as he scribbled down what he could remember. When he had finished, Chris hardly dared ask Aylott what he thought.

Aylott looked at the pieces of paper in silence for some moments, then said slowly, 'If this is true, then I suppose I'd better eat it all, right now. It's top-secret stuff, isn't it?'

'Yes,' Chris replied nervously, 'I suppose it is. But I think that it's true, and the IRA really are there.'

There was another moment of silence, and then both men burst out laughing. It all seemed so absurd, even though Chris knew it to be true, and could tell that Aylott believed him.

'Leave it with me,' Aylott said when they had both stopped laughing. 'I'll file these, and notify my boss. It's all I can really do with any information – of any sort.'

Chris shrugged. 'Well, it's more than I could have hoped for, isn't it? I know how cynical you lot are towards psychic stuff. I'll tell you what, thought. I'm not going to leave it at that. This is really bothering me. I'm going to tell Chris about it as well.'

This referred to Detective Inspector Chris Watt, who was based at Scotland Yard. His path had crossed with Chris's during an involvement in a fraud case some few years before. Both men had stayed on friendly terms, and Chris Watt lived only a few miles away, near Watford.

Aylott agreed with Chris that two heads would be

better than one when it came to making sure that people listened. But he did have a warning.

'You do realise that if this really happens, or we find these guys before something actually happens, all sorts of people are going to be jumping on my back, and on Chris Watt's. They're going to want to know where this information came from, and I'll tell you this for free: no way are they going to believe it came from a dream. I'm going to have to tell them it was you who passed this on, and it could get a bit rough.' He smiled. 'But I guess we'll have to cross that bridge if, and when, we come to it.'

That bridge was reached in eight days.

Chris Robinson is still trying to cross it.

When Chris contacted DI Watt about the dream, it was suggested that he go and see someone who understood the mind and the way it works – perhaps an accredited psychotherapist and hypnotherapist. Chris wondered if they thought he needed psychiatric help, but was assured that this wasn't the case. In fact, there were two valid reasons for Chris to see a therapist. The first was that a professional opinion on Chris's state of mind would come in useful later, if accusations of mental instability were thrown at him. The second, and perhaps more important reason, concerned the therapist's skills. It was hoped that, under hypnosis, Chris might be able to recall more of his dream and so give the police more details with which to work.

There was such a therapist based in Luton, not far from where Chris lived, and the appointment was quickly made for him to visit the next day. By the time he arrived at the therapist's office he was far from relaxed. Not only was he nervous about what might happen, he was also under a growing conviction that he was being followed. A car seemed to have trailed him into town from the mobile homes park, and while he was walking around town it seemed as though a few faces kept popping up in shop windows wherever he went. Perhaps it was paranoia – but perhaps not.

Fortunately for Chris, the therapist, Jim, was not at all surprised when Chris told him his dream. He assured Chris that he had heard of such things happening before, and he believed that some precognition was possible. Whether or not Jim really believed this was beside the point – Chris immediately felt more relaxed and confident.

Jim asked Chris what he really wanted from him. Chris replied that there were aspects of the dream that were unclear, and he wanted to try and get a better grip on them. For instance, although everything about the dream seemed to scream Cheltenham, there was something about the hotel that gave him a vaguely uneasy feeling: for some unaccountable reason, Chris felt that it might actually be in Wales. It was as though the dream had compressed both places into the one spot in order to give him as much information as quickly as possible.

This highlights – both for Chris and for those who have studied his dreaming – the problem of interpreting the dreams and their symbolism. The symbols in Chris's dreams later became very complex and personal, but even at this early stage, when they were much more literal, there were things that didn't quite add up. In fact, the hotel was nowhere near Wales, and whatever had made Chris feel that Wales was involved was an intrusion from his subconscious. This was to be one of the initial problems for Chris: the sorting of dream detritus from the true messages that he was somehow receiving.

After a cup of tea to calm his nerves, Chris lay back in a reclining chair. Jim dimmed the lights and began to talk Chris into a relaxed hypnotic state . . . Three-quarters of an hour later they were finished, and Jim handed Chris a tape. Chris couldn't remember a word of what had been said, but handed the tape back to Jim with the suggestion that it would be better if he sent it directly to DI Watt at Scotland Yard. But, as soon as Jim took it, Chris reconsidered: Watt lived within easy driving distance, and it might be quicker to drop the tape off at his house the next day.

Chris thanked Jim, left the office in Luton, and walked back to his car. He had parked it near the police station, and by one of those strange quirks of fate to which he was prone had bumped into Paul Aylott on his way to the appointment.

But was that purely coincidence? For as Chris walked the short distance to his car, he again felt he was being followed. He was sure he could see someone turning every corner just a few yards behind him. In the few minutes it took him to reach his car, he became a paranoid wreck, aware only of the tape he was clutching.

He got into his car and began the journey home, the tape beside him on the passenger seat. The paranoia was increasing: it was much greater than he had felt that morning.

The journey seemed to take longer than usual, as though time had become elastic. It took what seemed like an eternity to get out of the centre of town, as every set of lights seemed to turn red as he reached them. Every time he stopped, he looked over his shoulder. It was impossible to tell for sure, but had that same car that was three back been the one he had seen that morning? Was it the one that had pulled out of the car park when he had?

As he drove out of town and headed into the country, Chris found his sense of unease growing. In his rear-view mirror he could see a car gaining on him. Then it seemed to settle into a speed like his own, so that it stayed at a uniform distance – just hovering, waiting . . . It was hanging back, waiting to see what he would do. Chris speeded up a little, and the car gained a little.

He felt a sudden rush of blind panic, and an overwhelming belief that if he went straight home he would be killed, and the tape lost. He didn't know if it was a premonition or just fear, but he trusted his own instincts enough to follow them. He knew that he couldn't afford to go home.

As soon as he made that decision the feeling subsided, almost as though his instincts knew he had made the right decision. He looked back over his shoulder: the car was still there, but it seemed to be dropping back again. Perhaps it wasn't really following him after all?

He kept driving, and kept glancing back over his shoulder. The feelings might have subsided, but he didn't want to take any chances. The car hadn't gained any more on him, but it was still there, maintaining a discreet tail. At least, that was how it appeared.

Now they were well away from town, and the autumn evening was turning to twilight. The country road was deserted, with only the occasional passing car to give any sign of life. There was little in the way of lighting, and as Chris looked in his rear-view mirror, the headlights on the tailing car loomed ominously.

If he wasn't going straight home, then where the hell was he going? Chris considered this for a while, still driving aimlessly. Then he made a decision: Chris Watt lived not too far away – it would be a simple task to drop the tape in tonight instead of tomorrow morning.

It was some distance from Luton to Watt's house, especially taking into account the detour through open country, and it was nearly ten o'clock at night by the time Chris arrived at the semi-detached house in a quiet suburban street. He parked a little way down the road and walked slowly towards the house. There had been no sign of the car tailing him, and now he felt a bit foolish.

Halfway up the drive he stopped. Should he really bother Watt at this time of night? On consideration, he decided: why not? I've come this far . . .

'What on earth do you want?' Chris Watt asked in surprise when he answered Chris's knock. His tone changed when he saw Chris more clearly. 'Are you all right?'

'I think so,' Chris replied. But he was white with fear – a reflection on how he had felt that evening. He asked Watt to come back to the car with him, as he wanted to talk about the tape in total secrecy. He didn't even want Watt's wife to hear them.

When they were sitting in the car, Chris handed Watt the tape, and told him about the car that he thought had followed him out of Luton. He explained that the tape might contain further evidence from his dream that had emerged under hypnosis.

Watt took the tape. 'Leave it with me,' he said quietly, 'I'll give it to someone in SB.'

Chris knew that this was how serving officers referred to the Special Branch, the police department dealing with matters that touched on security and intelligence. Quite what was going through the policeman's mind concerning the tape was one thing – but Chris now knew Watt was taking the matter seriously enough to pass the tape on. That was important, as Chris firmly believed that the soldier had come to him in a dream to warm him of a serious IRA threat.

He apologised to Watt for being so paranoid, and for calling on him so late.

'Don't worry,' Watt smiled, 'go home and get some sleep. I'll be in touch when I know what's happening.'

Chris's dream happened on 30 September, and the interview with the hypnotherapist was conducted at the beginning of October. A further week passed by, with no word. Then one evening, as Chris was driving home around six o'clock and listening to the news on his car radio, he heard the following:

'Police in Gloucestershire have arrested a number of suspected IRA terrorists in a raid on a hotel in Cheltenham. A cache of guns and explosives has been recovered.'

So the hotel was in Cheltenham, after all, not Wales. Not that Chris had time to think about it right then: he was far too busy trying not to crash the car, as the shock of what he had heard made him temporarily lose control.

Had it been as in his dream? And did this mean that somebody had been following up his dream evidence?

A thousand other questions filled Chris's mind: was the soldier real? Had Chris seen into the future? Read the minds of the terrorists? How was that possible? Why was he the one who had received this message?

He put the car into gear and drove home as fast as he could. As soon as he was inside the door he grabbed the phone and called Paul Aylott.

'Is Paul there?' he asked, shaking from head to toe as Aylott's wife answered. She told him to hold on, and there was an anxious wait while she went to fetch her husband. What would Chris ask him? Would Aylott know anything?

Paul came on the line. 'It's me,' Chris said hurriedly. 'Have you heard the news?'

'Heard it? I nearly crashed,' Aylott replied. 'I was on the way home from work and heard it on the six o'clock news.' It was another one of those little coincidences.

'Look, is it because of what I told you? And the tape I gave to Chris Watt?'

There was an awkward silence. Finally, Paul said, 'I can't say anything about it to you at the moment. I just can't – I don't know what to say.'

He seemed keen to get off the phone as quickly as possible.

*   *   *

Chris wondered what would happen next. It was both exhilarating and frightening at the same time. He told me that he had never been so scared in his life, but never as curious as to what would happen, and where this new force in his life would take him.

'The one thing you've got to get across,' he said, 'was the total feeling of fear, and the total feeling of wonder and exhilaration. And the exhilaration is so strong that it cancels out the fear. I suppose it's like climbing a mountain: I've never done that, but there must come a point when you're halfway up, when you look down and think "What the hell am I doing here?" And there's no way back other than the way you've already come.

'But you want to go on – you've got to. Because now you know that you're not mad. You've told people, they've written it down, and then you've gone back to them afterwards and they've said, "Look, it's written down, we know you're not making it up. We can't understand it, but we know it's there."

'But that doesn't really make it less scary.'

To this end, Chris went to his local church and discussed the matter with Reverend David Bolster, vicar of St Andrews, Slip End.

Chris asked the vicar if he were mad, or if it were a case of possession by evil spirits. Bolster replied that evil spirits might be involved, but that was unlikely considering that Chris's dream was designed to do good. He couldn't refute the evidence, but couldn't offer an explanation either.

The two men did, however, keep in close touch over this period, and the Reverend Bolster had a hand in some of Chris's later dream exploits.

But for now there were other, less spiritual matters to be attended to.

CHAPTER THREE

Following the incident of the Cheltenham dream, Chris got together with Chris Watt, Paul Aylott and the Reverend Bolster. All four men knew they were on to something important, but none was quite sure what it actually was. What they needed was some kind of corroborated and irrefutable proof.

It was suggested that Chris keep a proper diary of his dreams, rather than scribbling things down on scrappy pieces of paper that could easily be lost.

Chris didn't like the idea at first. This was partly because of the dealings surrounding the collapse of his business, when all the paperwork had led to a maze of legal tangles. But it was more than that: he felt a vague unease about writing things down that were specifically to do with the dreams. What would be revealed if every night's dream was written down? What was Chris opening himself up to? He might have been halfway up a mountain with no wish to turn back, but that didn't make what lay ahead any the less scary.

Trevor Kempson, perhaps sniffing a possible story for his newspaper, came in on the project, and the five men eventually agreed that Chris should start his dream diary on 1 January 1990. Chris had started to get himself used to the idea of writing everything down, and he was now looking forward to the day with considerable excitement.

So much so that he began three nights early.

Christmas is a period when people traditionally drink

too much, and over-indulge, and this is exactly what Chris was doing, with the result that he began his diary without any qualms. Perhaps this was for the best, as he got an immediately startling result, although – perhaps due to the over-indulgence – the first few months of diary entries run in reverse order: the pages must be read from right to left, instead of the more usual left to right. This was not without its own perverse sense of logic, for if an ESDA (Electro Static Document Analysis) test were carried out on these pages, they would reveal that the pages were written in order, and that nothing was added at a later date.

The first surprise was that Chris woke up to find that he had already written quite a lot on the first page. This both astounded and shocked him: the idea was to keep the diary by the bed so that he would be able to scribble down his dreams as soon as he awoke. Instead, he sat up in the morning to find a page covered in writing. Either he had written it during the night, then forgotten as he dropped back to sleep, or else . . . well, Chris couldn't even, at this stage, consider the idea that he had written it while actually asleep.

The first thing written related to Chris being in a submarine, with someone shooting at him. There were also the phrases 'Parcel In Paper' and 'Something Sent To The Police', with the letters 'SA' and 'SN', one on top of the other, and surrounded by a box. Chris was puzzled – what on earth was that supposed to mean? It would be some time before things like this became understandable and Chris became aware that they were a sort of code that he had to learn to crack.

The next entries related to trains: he dreamt he was a train driver, and he was in the cab of his train. Then something happened: through the window of the cab, his face was covered with something that was burning him – it stuck to his skin, and he couldn't pull it off. He was filled with terror, frightened beyond any capacity for thought . . .

And then it changed, and he was walking along a track in Wales – a steam railway where he used to go when he was a child, on holidays with his nan. It was a coal train, and the driver would sometimes let kids ride in the cab. And his nan was there.

It changed again, and the train driver (now separate from Chris) was trying to pick the burning substance from his face, and was in great pain and distress. Then Chris could see people on an embankment, or sea wall, planning something, although he couldn't hear what.

It seemed to Chris that the steam train was there because it was his only experience of riding in the cab of a train, but the fundamental of the dream was that he was with the driver of a train, and the train was somehow attacked, injuring the driver's face.

Two nights later, on New Year's Eve, a train driver in Wales was injured when drunken New Year revellers threw rocks from an embankment near Cardiff and shattered the windscreen of his cab. The glass smashed into his face, and he was blinded by the flying fragments.

In effect, Chris had seen this attack two nights previously, and had experienced the driver's pain and distress. However, at this early stage Chris was still inclined to put this down to coincidence. It would need a great many coincidences, or something really incredible, to make him truly believe that a continuous process had started.

That was exactly what the night of 30 December had in store for him.

There were cameras and people everywhere, although Chris didn't know where he was. He was standing under a gantry with a television camera on top of it, and he had written down 'German not Japanese', and 'Telefunken'. Did this refer to the make of the cameras, or was it a reference to where he was? Certainly it could have meant the cameras, as Chris had a number of different cameras

– still, movie and video. All of them were Japanese. Were the words an attempt to differentiate from his own collection?

Then there were two things side by side – a line drawing of two objects that looked like the crash barriers that used to be scattered around football terraces. By the time Chris woke up, the significance of the drawing was lost to him. There was also some writing about the girl he had been standing with. She had been raped by her father, and there was a newspaper involved – the *News of the World* (the paper for which Trevor Kempson worked).

It seemed like nothing more than a confusing jumble of images, and that's the way it would have stayed, were it not for the fact that cameras and the crane occurred again on the night of 31 December. This time the number 120 was written next to the line drawing of the crash barrier-like objects, with the phrase 'Camera up in air. Broken.'

Why did the same dream occur two nights running? Perhaps because it was leading up to a real event: on the night of 31 December, at the coming down of the Wall in Berlin, there were several camera crews filming the exodus to the West. Two of the crews were German, and had their cameras up on gantries shaped like the objects Chris had drawn. They were too close, and the cables became entangled. One of the cameras plunged down to the ground, falling into the crowds below.

One hundred and twenty people were injured.

Also in that night's dreams came the first appearance of Terry Waite, who would later regularly haunt Chris's dreams. The Archbishop of Canterbury was seeking an audience with the Queen to discuss Waite's kidnapping, and there were bees in the same room, buzzing around a honeypot. At the time this seemed inconsequential, but it would return later.

★   ★   ★

These dreams were exciting and frightening at the same time. Chris had begun his diary three days earlier than agreed, for no real reason, and in those three days had received premonitions of two events that had actually occurred. It wasn't enough, by any means, to present as proof that something truly remarkable was happening. Not yet. It did, however, allay any last lingering doubts about whether or not he was fooling himself. Something really was going on: now he needed to find out what.

The new year began with Chris in a space ship, and the crew worrying about the loss of CFCs in their ship. It was floating aimlessly out in space. A few days later it was announced that the space shuttle currently in flight had problems with the cooling system, and had to return early from its flight . . . it was only after it landed that the truth came out: the ship had been brought back under manual control, and for a while it was touch-and-go whether or not it would be able to make the trip home.

Another segment of that night's dream related to Chris's wife Bessie's flight home after visiting her family in the Philippines: 'Don't worry. She is not going on today's flight but next week's.' In fact, she did re-book her flight and stayed an extra week. So already it was clear that the dreams were not just foretelling major events: there were things in them that mattered only to Chris.

The whole affair has been a learning curve from day one, with things sometimes not becoming apparent until some time after the event. For instance, the dreams of 2 January yielded nothing that would make any sense, apart from the fact that Prince Charles cropped up in connection with a man who had a broken right arm. Chris watched the news carefully for the next week, but there was nothing that related to this. However, some four months later, Prince Charles had a polo accident and broke his right arm.

Was this a coincidence? Or was it proof to Chris that the area of time covered by his dreams would be more than just a few days? At several years' distance, and with the benefit of hindsight, it's easy to make connections that may be in some way spurious. The point is that later events showed Chris that matters could evolve in his dreams over a long period of time. Could this have been an early intimation of that? Certainly Chris believes that now: the information builds over a series of dreams and a period of time.

On Thursday, 4 January 1990, Chris dreamt that he was with a group of journalists who went to visit a prisoner. When they arrived, he found that the prisoner was Myra Hindley. At the top of the page he wrote the words 'Cookham Wood' and 'HMP' with a box around it. He also wrote about a man with a child, and lesbians and prisons, with boxes around them. There was also the time '4.15 p.m.'.

This meant nothing to Chris at all, and he forgot about it until he picked up a copy of the *Daily Mail* dated 31 January. The lead story concerned a letter from Ian Brady, in which he detailed the full extent of Hindley's involvement in the murder of Leslie Anne Downey. The story went on to mention that Hindley was serving life in Cookham Wood prison, in Kent. This followed on from an interview she had given to journalists . . .

Chris was shocked. He hadn't known about the visit to Cookham Wood – more importantly, he'd never heard of the place in his life. Yet, four weeks after his dream, a connection had occurred. It could be put down to coincidence, except for the fact that he had never even heard of the place.

Trevor Kempson was receiving faxes of Chris's dreams every day, and when Chris phoned him, Trevor referred back to the pages from 4 January and was astonished. He told Chris that, given the nature of the story, it was possible that the journalists had visited Hindley within days of Chris's dream.

Now, several years later, Chris tells me that he considers it possible that he may have heard of Cookham Wood at some point – if Hindley had been there for some time, and it had been on the news, then it may have buried itself in his subconscious. However, he was not consciously aware of the place at the time.

More startling events were to overtake this.

Chapter Four

In his dream Chris was standing in Bedford police station, the headquarters of the local force. He was talking to a police officer, and they walked into a meeting where the police were discussing a bomb explosion. A man had been injured, and parts of his body had been blown away. It was all connected to a triangle – the sort that is used to set up balls on a snooker table. The name of the policeman Chris spoke to was J. Branscombe.

The next day the local paper came out and Chris bought a copy as usual. The lead story concerned a man who had an argument at a snooker hall. He went home and built a bomb to blow up the hall. Unfortunately, he wasn't the expert he presumed, as the bomb detonated in his hand, severely injuring him. The name of the officer in charge of the investigation was John Branscombe.

Aylott and Watt found this particularly interesting. Could Chris be of some use to them in their investigations after all? If nothing else, it proved that the Cheltenham affair wasn't a one-off event.

The possibilities were to become apparent sooner than they thought, for on 8 January 1990 Chris had the dream that began his long-term involvement with the police.

Chris was in a car, accompanying a woman who was setting out to kidnap a baby. They stopped at a hospital by a river. The tide was out. Chris could see this, and he could also see a bridge. On the bridge were police from the Metropolitan force. The baby was now missing.

The dream went on: Chris could see the baby being taken, despite the watching police. The woman ran through the double doors of the hospital and put the baby in a carry-cot pulled out of the car boot by a man. She put the baby on the back seat, then they got in the car and drove away.

The dream changed again: Chris was now standing in the car park of a police station, talking to a Detective Inspector called Peter Ireland. He was telling Ireland about everything he had seen.

Then he woke with a gasp, and glanced at the clock. It was seven o'clock. Looking down at the diary by his bed, Chris could see that he had written down key words from the dream, including the name Peter Ireland.

For a few moments he sat there, his mind racing. He knew that a child was about to be kidnapped, and he had a rough idea of what the locale would look like. But there was nothing definite. He was left with the sure knowledge that it would happen, but no way of preventing it by himself.

At ten past seven he called Paul Aylott. Although none too pleased at being dragged out of bed at this time in the morning, Aylott considered it serious enough to drive over to the caravan straight away.

When Chris had told him everything he could remember about the dream, Aylott looked perplexed. 'So what do you want me to do?' he asked. 'Put a guard on every hospital on a river when the tide's out? What are we supposed to do when the tide's in, then? Not bother to look?'

'No, no, we're not supposed to be doing that,' Chris replied, 'but there is going to be a kidnapping from a hospital somewhere where there are Metropolitan Police, and where the tide comes in and out – so it can only be along the river in London, can't it? If it was further up or down it'd be Thames Valley or something. It's got to be that central stretch in London.'

'So how are we supposed to stop it?' Aylott asked.

'I don't think we can. I think I'm supposed to be able to trace the baby when it's snatched. It's a baby or a little girl, but I just feel that it's a new baby – only a few hours old.'

'All right,' Aylott sighed. 'I'll put it on the log at the station, and I'm sure that if a baby gets kidnapped they'll want to talk to you.'

There was more than a hint of irony in his tone, and he left to log-on at the station when his shift began, and to record what Chris had told him.

Nothing happened for the next couple of days: Chris's dreams were quiet, and there was no story breaking about a baby being kidnapped. Then, on 11 January – a Thursday – Alexandra Griffiths, a 36-hour-old baby, was snatched from her mother at St Thomas's Hospital, in south-east London, overlooking the River Thames.

All hell broke loose, and no sooner had Chris seen the story on the news than there was a knock at the door, and Chris was greeted by two policemen with the words, 'All right, where have you hidden her, then?'

It was not the last time that his dream premonitions were to place him under suspicion. His caravan was searched, and he was questioned about his whereabouts that day. The officers felt that Chris had so wanted his dream to come true that he had driven to London and taken the child, just to make it so.

But the baby wasn't in the caravan, and Chris had witnesses to prove he had been nowhere near London. Despite the heavy-handed behaviour of the police, Chris could see their point: 'If someone tells you there's going to be a baby snatched, and then it is . . . well, you're going to decide that you want to talk to them, aren't you?'

Chris went to see the Reverend Bolster again and told him what had happened. The curate was, understandably, appalled by what had been going on. Like Trevor

Kempson, Paul Aylott and Chris Watt, he had been receiving copies of Chris's dream diary on a regular basis. He told Chris that, as far as he was concerned, it was either God or the Devil who was sending messages via his dreams; and, as the messages were primarily designed to help people, then they must be messages from God.

Chris returned home with a renewed sense of purpose. It was obvious to him now that he must try and help find the baby. There was just one problem: how could he direct the dreams so that he would receive messages that pushed him in the right direction? It was not until much later that he discovered that he could actually ask questions before going to sleep by the simple expedient of writing them at the top of the page. Right now, all he could do was hope.

On the night of 14 January the dreams gave him images of a high street, with clocks that showed a series of incorrect times. He was standing in a village on the side of a hill, standing behind some shops, then in a cottage. He had a very clear picture of this village as it looked when approached coming down a hill.

When he awoke Chris puzzled over this and tried to match the village in his dream with any he might actually know. The only place he could think of was a village called Berkhamsted: the view of the town as you approached it on the road from Aldbury, with the canal on one side, and the main street of the village.

It didn't all fit, but it was the best he could come up with. He phoned David Bolster and told him about the dream. Bolster was decisive: they must go there.

At the time it seemed like a wasted journey, as they found nothing, and there was nothing in the village itself that inspired Chris. It appeared to have been a dead-end.

But the next few nights gave the lie to this, for Chris dreamt again about the baby. It seemed well, but was seen in a variety of strange situations. On one occasion it was in a boat, but there was no water around, and the boat was covered in chains. He dreamt of an empty lock on the canal, and then the area of London known as Camden. Most bizarrely of all, he dreamt of being on the London Underground, and of Farringdon and Oxford Circus stations. It must all mean something, but what?

It was early days, and cracking the dream code was still difficult. However, Chris and David Bolster worked on the dream diary, and through word association came up with the notion that the baby might possibly be in a village called Farringdon, in Oxfordshire. They resolved to visit Farringdon as soon as they could, as Bolster had work commitments that prevented them going immediately. They would see if the village resembled Berkhamsted in any way, or tallied with the images in Chris's dreams.

They were in no particular hurry to go, as the current theory splashed across the newspapers was that the baby had been taken to Australia. Chris wondered about this as he went to sleep on the night of 23 January. He did dream about Australia: he was in the King's Cross area of Sydney and ended up on the beach, which was littered with rubbish. When he awoke he could only take this to mean that the theories about Australia were – literally – rubbish.

On the evening of 26 January, two days before Chris and David Bolster were to visit Farringdon, baby Alexandra was found in the nearby village of Burford. She was being kept in a cottage that lay at the back of an antique shop. In the window of the shop was a model boat, a large wooden carving suspended by chains. Burford stands on a hill, with a river running at the bottom of the village. It is only four miles from Farringdon.

Chris was relieved that the baby had been found safe and well, but more than that: if it had taken the police just a few days longer, then he would, in all probability,

have passed within a few feet of where the baby was
being kept.

And he was beginning to learn more about interpreting
his dreams. The juxtaposition of Farringdon and Oxford
Circus underground stations was fairly obvious with
hindsight, but another, more inscrutable symbol had
wormed its way into the dreams: the empty lock and
being in Camden had appeared on the same night as the
boat in chains. Camden Lock is an antique market in
London. The boat was kept in the window of an antique
shop, the baby being kept in the cottage behind.

Paul Aylott had been informed of the dreams as
they occurred, and the police had been considering
Berkhamsted as a possible site. The kidnapping was
Chris's first encounter as a psychic with the press, as
Tony Snow – a reporter from the tabloid *Sun* – had
met Chris and David Bolster in Berkhamsted, and they
had spent an afternoon looking for cottages on a hillside
near the canal.

When the baby had been found, Chris had travelled
to Burford, just to look over the village and see how
much it matched his dreams. While looking around he
bumped into Tony Snow.

'Well, you weren't right,' he said, 'but you were
bloody near. You said a cottage on the side of a hill,
and this village is just like that place we trudged around
last week.'

One night, in the middle of all this excitement, there was
a programme that Chris wanted to watch on television.
But it was on fairly late, and so he set the timer on his
video and went to bed. The programme was about ghosts
and the supernatural. That night Chris dreamt about a
man called Mr Green, who lived in a haunted house.
The dream was a complete, self-contained story. In its
coherence and logic it was quite unlike a usual dream.

The next day Chris wound back the tape and sat down

to watch the programme. It was about a man called Mr Green, who lived in a haunted house. Chris watched it with both a sense of dismay and hilarity: it was exactly as it had been in his dream. This suggested two things to him: first, that he was now able to watch anything he liked just by dreaming about it, and – less flippantly – that the dreams were probably not just random trawlings. In some way they related to his own future, and to people and events that he would have some kind of contact with. He decided that if he hadn't wanted to watch the programme, then it wouldn't have entered his dream.

Chris is a believer in destiny. His experiences since 1989 have convinced him that his life led up to the point where he was ready to receive these dreams. All his adult life he has experienced strange coincidences, whereby his path has crossed those of people who have either led him into contact with the police or were policemen themselves. When he first started to have dreams that related to forthcoming crimes, he knew exactly who to get in touch with, and they knew him well enough not to dismiss him out of hand as a crank.

He reasoned that the only way to get a good result from his dreams was to involve himself, so that the dream would touch him personally in some way. If, for instance, he had wanted to know more about the kidnapping, and had wanted the information more clearly, should he have gone to St Thomas's before dreaming?

It was a question he resolved to answer as soon as possible.

Baby Alexandra had been found on 26 January. On 27, Chris went to Burford and bumped into Tony Snow. He also talked to police involved with the case. He stayed overnight, and on the Sunday he found the boat

hanging in the window of the antique shop. He felt
sure that he would have had a clearer vision of things
if he had become more closely involved. That was the
way forward.

CHAPTER FIVE

Dr Keith Hearne is a parapsychologist whose speciality is dreaming. In the 1970s he put forward a paper that laid out his research into the matter of dream transference. Through the study of experimental subjects he was able to ascertain that some people can dream the same dream in unison and pass messages through their dream states. It was a discovery that was hailed as a breakthrough.

Since then Dr Hearne has been one of the country's leading parapsychologists, so it was natural that he should study Chris Robinson. The contact came about through Chris Watt, who had been checking into possible avenues of investigation since the Cheltenham incident. Watt had made contact with Keith Hearne through the Society for Psychical Research, a London-based body that has been at the forefront of research into the so-called supernatural and strange and anomalous phenomena since the end of the nineteenth century.

Chris Robinson had been in touch with Hearne since October 1989, and had been phoning him every morning to read him his dream diary. Hearne came to visit Chris and ended up staying for days on end, recording the dreams as they happened, and studying Chris as he slept, observing the way he wrote in his sleep.

Hearne has been keeping an eye on Chris ever since, having described him as potentially the most important subject in the field. He has been working on a paper about Chris for the last five years, and still no end is in sight. When the paper eventually emerges it will be possibly the most important paper since Hearne's discovery of the early 1970s.

Hearne was studying Chris when the next major event occurred.

February started with some terrible dreams about the rape of young women. There was nothing definite in the dreams, but they seemed to tie in with the arrest and charging of Russell Bishop over the rape of a 7-year-old schoolgirl at Devil's Dyke, outside Brighton, on 8 February. Nothing specific in the dreams could be used to help the police, and all they succeeded in doing was make Chris feel ill-at-ease with his dreams.

There had also been an accumulation of data concerning planes, which built up to the night of 9 February, when Chris filled a whole page with references to 'plane', 'end', 'die', 'child on a plane', 'gone to airport on way home' and 'CRASH'.

He happened to be talking to Paul Aylott the next morning, and said, 'I think there's going to be a plane crash, and there's going to be people die. I don't know how many, but I've got the number ninety-three for some reason. I still don't get all this stuff about chemicals, though. I just know that it's going to come down in a bunker.'

'A bunker?'

'Yeah, like on a golf course. And I think it's going to be Valentine's Day. There's Asians on the plane. Two of the people will die later. But the clue to it is really these bloody chemicals.'

'So where does that come from?' Aylott asked.

'Don't ask me,' Chris said. 'Just you wait and see. Valentine's Day.'

It was actually on 15 February – the Wednesday rather than the Tuesday predicted by Chris – that Aylott and Chris next spoke.

An Air-India plane had crashed in India, on a golf

course, killing ninety-three people. It had left Bangalore on an internal flight, and had exploded coming in to land over the town of Bhopal. That was the link with the chemicals: Bhopal was the scene of a chemical works explosion in the late 1970s that had left many dead and the inhabitants of the town with long-term health problems.

If Aylott had ever had the slightest doubt about Chris's veracity before, then this occasion finally convinced him. Whereas previously Aylott had come into the picture later on, this time he had heard the dream directly from Chris before anything had happened. He had been told that the plane would crash on a golf course, that ninety-three people would die and that the accident would be linked to chemicals.

Paul Aylott was now more than just a friend in the police force: he was one of Chris's staunchest defenders.

Despite its connotations, this dream premonition was nothing compared to what was to happen on the night of 16 February.

Chris was standing in a street. It was nowhere that he recognised and the street itself was out of focus. But the location was unimportant: what mattered was that the soldier was there again, for the first time in several months.

'Look,' he said, 'I want you to listen like last time. There's going to be a bomb. Now what I'm going to do from now on is give you postcodes.'

'What?' Chris was stunned. If he had postcodes, then finding the locations of any bombs would be so much easier. 'What is all this about?'

'There's three bombs,' the soldier continued, intent on getting his message across. 'Three in BT, but they're in two parts. Two there, one here. The bombs have been made and they're here: LE1.'

Chris took all this in, worried at the back of his mind that he had no idea where LE1 actually was.

LE1 is the centre of Leicester, and BT is the postcode for Belfast. The soldier continued to talk, but Chris could remember little more when he awoke, and the sparse writing in his dream diary didn't reveal much: 'DANGER', 'clean up mess' (inside a box), and 'danger' yet again being the only clues to what had happened in the night.

Things were getting just a bit too strange for Chris now: postcodes were a new one on him – he had enough trouble remembering his own code, let alone knowing where these others might be. There was only one thing to be done: he phoned Paul Aylott straight away.

'There's going to be another bomb,' he began. 'It's going to be under an army vehicle – a Land Rover, I think. And it's going to be at LE1 – wherever that is.'

The dreams of the following night reiterated this: 'LE1' appeared again, this time inside a box. The letters 'ALR' appeared, each one boxed. 'Packets', 'BT' and 'Telephone Engineer' (an obvious association of ideas) appeared, linked by a drawn line. The words 'council house' were written, with 'bombs made here' directly underneath them.

The intensity of the message was staggering: it blotted out everything else in the dreams that night. Chris could see the house clearly, and when he woke he drew a map of the layout, pinpointing the lounge, where he was sure the bombs were made.

His soldier's claim that the three bombs were in two parts was also explained. It seemed to Chris that the bombs were being posted from Belfast: the timers and other electrical parts were sent to the council house through the post, and the explosives were added there. One of the bombs had been sent, and two were in Belfast waiting to be despatched.

Chris phoned Paul Aylott again. He was told that he

should come in and make a statement – but not until Tuesday (it was now Sunday).

On the Sunday night, Chris dreamt only of submarines coming into dock – the next day a consignment of 'W'-class subs arrived in Britain to be broken up for scrap. It was another small and interesting outcome, but had no real bearing on the bomb in LE1 – and this was really beginning to worry Chris. If, as he believed, this was a genuine premonition, then the bomb could go off without anything being done to prevent it. People might be killed or injured: something that could be prevented, if only he were able to talk to someone.

He spent the whole of Monday in an agitated state, worried in case something terrible occurred. Yet at the back of his mind, something reassured him that it wouldn't happen that day. It's hard to imagine the strange mix of emotions that coursed through him during that Monday: concern and fear on the one hand, yet on the other a hope that he might yet be able to help avert a disaster.

There were no dreams on Monday night: there was very little sleep, as Chris lay awake worrying about what would happen the next day.

On the Tuesday Chris kept his appointment, and went to Leighton Buzzard police station, where he made a statement in front of Frank and Steve. The statement was simple: a bomb would go off in LE1 – wherever that was. It would happen today – or if not today, then tomorrow. The bomb would be under an army vehicle. This was what he had been told in his dream. But the important part was LE1.

'Or it might be LE1,' Chris shrugged. 'I don't know. That's only what I'm being told.'

His statement was two pages long and by the time they had finished, and Chris had checked and signed it, they had been in the room for two hours. He left the station between half-past three and four o'clock, got in his car and drove home.

At ten past five a bomb exploded under an army Sherpa van in the centre of Leicester. There was a television newsflash and Chris immediately phoned the police in Leicester.

'Look,' he said, 'I've just been in a police station giving a statement that a bomb was going to go off in Leicester. Please – what's the postcode where the bomb went off. I must know.'

The voice on the other end of the phone replied that the postcode was LE1. He took Chris's name and address. He also took the names of the policemen who had been with Chris all afternoon, and Paul Aylott's telephone number.

'For your information, Mr Robinson,' he said, before hanging up, 'LE1 is a very small area in the centre of Leicester. Very small.'

Chris put the phone down. 'I felt freaked,' he told me years later, 'and totally exhilarated, too. Because no-one had been hurt in the bombing – there were a few minor cuts and bruises, but not what you could call casualties. That was a relief. But I thought: now we're going to get postcodes. This is brilliant. Now we can crack it.'

But not everyone was as happy as Chris. Not everyone believes in the powers of precognitive dreams: particularly the Royal Ulster Constabulary and the Special Branch.

Within two days representatives of these forces arrived to interview Chris. The interview was held at Dunstable police station. Chris was questioned for over five hours in two separate sessions, both of which were taped.

The questions were always the same: how did he know about the bomb? Did he have any connections with it? Why had he reported it only a couple of hours before it went off, not before? Why was he saying that

the premonition came in the form of a dream? Who
was this soldier?

The truth was that Chris had as little idea at this stage
about what was going on as the officers interviewing
him. Six months before he had never had an experience
like this, and now he was dreaming about bombs. All he
could do was tell them, again and again, that it just came
to him in a dream, and that was all there was to it.

The persistent interrogation, with the same few
questions hammered at him over and over again, was
designed to break Chris down: to try and find some
inconsistency in his story, some flaw that would break,
that would reveal what – in their minds – was really
going on.

Of course, the truth was that Chris Robinson had
started to have precognitive dreams, and such things are
just not supposed to exist.

Each interview was taped, and two copies were made.
One of the interviewers told Chris, 'One of these is for
us, but the other is for another agency who is interested
in you.'

'Don't I get a copy?' Chris asked.

'No way – you'll never see or hear these tapes
again.'

'Fair enough,' Chris replied – what else could he say?
But he did wonder who this other agency might be.
And he noticed that, as he left the station, there were
several lingering looks after him from officers who had
obviously heard about the interviews.

He asked Paul Aylott to find out what was going on,
but Paul was non-committal and tried to get rid of Chris
as soon as possible. Chris then tried asking Frank and
Steve: neither policeman would speak to him at first,
but eventually he did manage to speak to Frank, who
sounded distinctly nervous on the phone.

'What's all this about?' asked Chris.

'Look, I don't want to talk to you,' Frank replied.

'That business with Leicester – there's no way you could have been involved in that, so how the hell did you know about it? I don't know what to say, and I really don't want to talk about it just now.'

Chris put the phone down, not knowing what to think: his friend Paul Aylott seemed to want to maintain a cordial distance while this investigation was going on, and now Frank and Steve were so spooked by what had happened that they didn't want any further contact with him. Things couldn't get worse than this, could they?

They could.

Over the next few days, as he went about his daily business, Chris noticed that he was being followed. What's more, it seemed that his followers wanted him to know that he was being tailed, because their actions were none too subtle. The same car – a green Volkswagen – would start to tail Chris when he left the caravan park in the morning, heading into town. Whether he went to Leighton Buzzard, Luton or Dunstable (all towns within about a half-hour drive of his home), the Volkswagen would always be there, one or two cars back in the traffic, always parking just round the corner. Sometimes Chris would get out of his car, round a corner and the Volkswagen would be sitting there. Empty.

Then there were the people who followed him on foot. It was just like that first occasion, when he had the dream about Cheltenham. He was sure that he was being followed, as the same faces kept appearing, again and again: behind him in supermarket queues, at the bar in pubs, buying spare parts in car-repair shops. The difference was that, whereas previously they were keen not to seem to be following, this time they were blatant about it. They would smile at him if they caught his eye, bid him good day, and then follow him right out of the shop.

How much of this could he put down to paranoia, and how much of it was real? Certainly, because of the complications when he lost his business, Chris was inclined to be paranoid about these things, and he admitted as much to himself. After he'd reported the Cheltenham bomb attempt and thought he was being followed, he was able to dismiss that as paranoia. But not this time – people who said hello to him and used the same car all the time? They *wanted* him to know he was being followed.

He sat down and tried to think about it calmly. It was impossible for him to have travelled to Leicester, planted the bomb and returned to give the interview at Leighton Buzzard station in the time scale they had to work on. Therefore they – whom he assumed to be either Special Branch, the Anti-Terrorist Squad, or even MI5 or 6 – were not working on the theory that he might be one of the actual bombers. Instead, they must be following to see if he had contact with anyone who could possibly be involved.

But if that were the case, why would they be so blatant about it? He reasoned that they were either trying to pressure him into making a mistake, or . . . or what? It had him confused and worried.

It was also bad for business. By this time Chris had returned to his old trade as a television and electrical engineer and was repairing televisions both on-site and in the back room of the caravan. He also bought a few old sets, which he renovated. It wasn't good for trade to have a green Volkswagen roll up after you'd arrived at a customer's house. Chris's wife Bessie was working as a waitress at a local hotel, and what would happen if they started to follow her so blatantly? So far, she had been shielded from the hassle that Chris had received over his dreams.

In the meantime Chris and Paul Aylott had decided that, if they were getting postcodes in the dreams, the time had come for action. Paul told Chris that there was a computer program that contained the postcodes for the entire country overlaid on area maps. Chris needed no more prompting: he went out and bought the program. Now he was ready for the next postcode – which was just as well, as the next code had already arrived.

Back on 22 January, the letters HX had been written on the dream diary page. At the time Chris had been totally baffled by this, and had dismissed it as something that just hadn't quite come out right. But, using his new computer program, he was able to establish that HX was Halifax. There were also elements of the dreams that suggested that the target was to be a government building: he had repeatedly seen the front of the Social Security offices in Luton, but all of the entries for that had a box drawn around them. From his study of the dream writing, Chris was beginning to understand that a box drawn around a word or phrase meant that it did not actually stand for that precise thing, but for something like it. In this case, he assumed that the attack would be on a government building, and that the Social Security offices appeared in his dream because they were a government building with which he was familiar. Yet at the same time there were references to Chris's friend Gary: where did this fit in?

All this material went off to Paul Aylott, who asked Chris what the connection was.

'I don't know, do I? I just know that there's something to do with Gary and his dad mixed up in this.'

There was a bomb in Halifax: it exploded in the letter box of an Army Information Office, next to the forecourt of a garage owned by Gary's father. The building was leased out to the army by the same man. It left Chris with a sense of failure: he had been unable to decipher enough of the dream to tell the police when and where the bomb was to go off – yet there was enough to say for sure that he was receiving premonitions about future events.

It was a question of balance: but when would he

achieve it? He was impatient, yet he knew that it would
happen soon, for as well as the material concerning
the future, he had also received messages from what
he considered spirits, who were guiding him. On the
night of 22 January, when the postcode for Halifax
first appeared, Chris had also written the following in
his sleep:

> Christopher, I have shown you many things. The
> time will come when they accept you and the gifts
> that I bestow through you. They have seen but
> cannot believe. Your faith will see you through.

Chris had sent this to David Bolster and had asked him
for help and guidance, as he had also seen a Christ-like
figure, who had spoken to him. Chris was hardly the
world's most religious man, although he did believe in
God, and once again he was left confused by his dreams.
He asked Reverend Bolster if this really did come from
God, and if he was doing the right thing.

Bolster considered for some time before replying, and
when he did he told Chris that he believed the dreams
did indeed come from God, and because they were
continuing after Chris had prayed to receive more, then
God must be willing to reveal more to Chris. There was
a purpose to all this, but what it was must remain – for
now – a mystery.

The night of 22 February saw the beginning of recurring
symbols in Chris's dreams, one of which was to become
more important as the years went by: dogs.

For most people, dogs are household pets, objects of
affection. But for Chris Robinson dogs mean one thing
alone: they are a symbol of the IRA.

That night Chris dreamt once more of the Halifax
bomb, and the connection that it had with his friend
Gary. The dog was there, not specifically connected

with anything, but lurking in the background. It was not the most auspicious or obvious of entrances, but it wasn't difficult for Chris to associate the dog with danger and fear.

Later Dr Hearne psychoanalysed Chris and took him through regression therapy in an attempt to establish the basis for many of the symbols in his dreams. His theory is that Chris's subconscious uses dogs as a symbol for terrorists because he is – quite literally – terrified of them. No-one in his family has a dog, and he has never owned one himself. When he was a child he was threatened by a dog, and since then dogs have been associated with fear in his mind.

The month of February ended with a premonition of a train crash. On the night of 27 February Chris dreamt that he was on a train running towards a junction where the line was closed. It was a commuter train and the passengers were unaware of what was about to happen.

Chris phoned Paul Aylott when he awoke, and said, 'Look, there's going to be a train crash in Penge. I don't know when, but the line's going to be closed, and the train will be derailed.'

Aylott made a note of it, but commented that there was little he could do about it. Later in the day Chris saw his friend Gary Simpson and mentioned the dream to him. And that would have been that – except that, on the night of 28 February, Chris received a phone call from Aylott.

'Have you seen the news?' Aylott asked.

'No – why?'

'Because there's been a train crash in Penge.'

'Well, what did you expect? What did I tell you?'

'Yeah, but even so, it still amazes me.'

Chris put the phone down and pondered on what his last dreams of the month might mean. Washing machines and radiators: there he was, sawing the top off a radiator and repairing a hole in the pipes of a washing machine. He also had the words 'water' and 'WATER – leek' written on the page. Why had he spelt 'leek' that way?

The answer became obvious within the next day or two, when torrential rains caused flooding in parts of Wales. Not only had he been repairing potential flood risks in radiators and washing machines, he had written about a water leak with a double meaning: 'leek' being the vegetable with which the Welsh are associated, and also an obvious misspelling of the word leak. If nothing else, this showed that his subconscious had a sense of humour.

CHAPTER SIX

During March Chris obtained a fax machine, thanks to his friend Gary Simpson. For some time he had needed one in order to get his dreams distributed as fast as they were written. Taking photocopies and throwing them into envelopes, or hot-footing it down to the local copy shop in order to send a fax later in the morning, was no good: what was needed was a machine of his own, whereby he could fax the dreams to either Paul Aylott or Keith Hearne as soon as he awoke.

It was now that one of those coincidences came to his rescue again. Gary Simpson, a friend of Chris's, had a fax machine at his home. Chris approached him with an offer to buy it. Gary declined, as he needed the machine for his work, but a few days later he turned up on the doorstep in the evening, clutching a brand new Mitsubishi fax machine.

'Here,' he explained, handing it to Chris, 'I've got this mate who works for an office equipment company. He's heard about you, and wants to help in some way. I've told him how genuine you are, after that business with my dad's garage and the train crash. If you can make use of this, he can let you have it for two hundred pounds.'

'Can I make use of it?' gasped Chris. 'Give it here.'

Within a month he had paid for the machine, and the machine had more than paid for itself.

The dream was odd: it was more realistic than many of

the dreams Chris had been having lately, and all the more scary for that.

Chris found himself standing behind a wall on a dyke. Although he had never seen this particular wall before, he had seen many like them when he was in Holland. So he knew that he must be somewhere in the Lowlands. And he wasn't alone: he was in the middle of a group of men, obviously soldiers of some kind. There were four of them, and they were dressed in black, talking in quiet, cautious voices. They were also keeping their heads down – Chris did likewise, and wondered how long it would be before they would notice he was there.

They didn't: it was the start of another kind of dream. Now he was able to take part as a detached observer. It was as though he were part of a virtual-reality game, where he could move about with the inhabitants of this dream world, yet not be seen.

So did this mean he was like a ghost, moving in the real world? Had his spirit astrally-projected to this point?

All such questions flew out of his mind when he moved in closer and heard what the camouflaged men were talking about.

'He's a large fish,' one of them said.

'Yeah, and about time he was caught,' another replied. They laughed softly among themselves.

As Chris followed them, they drove across country. It seemed as though they had been picked up from the dyke by pre-arrangement, as a car was waiting for them. Throughout the short trip they kept talking about fish, and landing or netting them.

They drove into a large city. By now Chris was convinced that they had come to 'make a hit' and eliminate somebody. He knew they were secret service agents of some description, but had no idea who they worked for, or who their target was. But one thing had become clear. The operation was to do with arms being smuggled and supplied to the IRA.

The car drew up at an anonymous block of flats in the suburbs of the city. The men got out of the car, now silent and moving with great stealth. They slipped into position outside the building, two of them keeping an unobtrusive watch while the other two entered. It was the middle of the night, and there weren't that many people about. Chris tailed the two look-outs as they signalled to each other and followed their companions. Inside the block they took the emergency stairs at the back of the building, in order to avoid being seen by too many people: a minimal risk, but one that had to be considered nonetheless.

They reached the second floor and gathered in front of an apartment.

'Is he in?' one of them muttered *sotto voce*.

Another of the men shook his head briefly. The first one nodded at this. They were keeping verbal contact to a minimum.

The large fish was not at home: they had to wait.

In dreams time is a strange phenomenon. It can stretch out or be compressed in the most bizarre manner. The study of REM (Rapid Eye Movement) in dreamers has shown that dreams that appear to take several hours can, in reality, pass in a matter of minutes. And so it can sometimes seem in dreams themselves. Chris knew that he and the security agents had been waiting for the large fish for hours, yet it seemed as though it were only a few minutes.

The action seemed just as brief. The four men were positioned outside the apartment – in hiding as much as was possible, although cover was scarce. Then they heard the lift clank on the ground floor and the motor whir as it began to move upwards.

Chris could feel every sinew in their bodies grow taut as they prepared themselves. This could be the man they were waiting for.

The hall and landing in front of the flat were

in semi-darkness: they had taken the precaution of removing one of the lightbulbs in the hall, so that there was a reflected illumination from further down the landing, but in front of the flat was shadow. There was enough light for them to kill by, but not enough for anyone coming out of a lighted lift to see his assailants.

The lift seemed to take for ever to reach the right floor, and Chris could feel the bitter taste of tension in his mouth. All four agents drew handguns, screwing silencers on to the ends.

The lift stopped and the doors opened. A man in late middle-age, dressed in a shabby suit, stepped out. He looked incongruous, as this was a block that clearly only wealthy tenants could afford. He walked down the hall, taking a few steps out of the light and into the dark.

The execution was an anti-climax. As he approached his door, the four men stepped out of the shadows, weapons poised. Two kept watch around the hall while the other two lined up the man.

'What –' he began, looking bewildered and blinking in the half-light. He got no further: one of the agents squeezed his trigger twice, and the soft 'phuut' of a silenced pistol sounded in the hall. Both shots went into the man's neck, blood spurting from an arterial wound.

As the target slumped to the floor, the four men began to withdraw. Chris tried to go with them, but found he could not move, his attention drawn to the man on the floor.

Then he awoke, in a cold sweat . . .

He looked at what he had written.

> [Fishing]   Large Fish
>   Caught
> [Follow to exterminate]   [Landing]
> Shot in head.   [No witness]

It was exactly as he remembered the dream. Yet the strange thing was that there were two pages of further dream writing that seemed to indicate a bomb in Kent, perhaps in a pub. The final sheet also contained a map with a compass direction on it, but nothing relating to an actual town or place. Chris could remember nothing of these last dreams, yet he must surely have had them. It was the beginning of a process that was to lead him to the conclusion that what he wrote was equally as important as the dream to which it related.

At that precise moment, however, all he could think of was the graphic dream of death. And the disturbing recollection that this was not the first time he had dreamt it; the vague memory that he had seen someone being shot in the head a few nights before. He hadn't written anything about it, but could remember the phrase 'blown away', as though someone was saying it. He wasn't sure, but it seemed as though that had happened more than once.

Not for the first time, Chris found himself emotionally and mentally drained by his dreams. He felt in need of more sleep, but knew that he would only dream again. For the first time it struck him how alone he really was in this experience. Reverend Bolster, Paul Aylott, Dr Hearne . . . they were supportive and fascinated by his dreams, but they didn't experience them, they didn't know how much they took out of him.

He sank back, exhausted, on to the pillow. He wanted to fall into a deep, dreamless sleep. But for him, there was no longer any such thing.

Over the next couple of nights Chris had uneasy dreams. In one of them, he dreamt about the smuggling of mercury detonators of the type used in nuclear weapons. There were also intimations of forthcoming problems between Iran and Iraq. Were the two connected in some way? And did they have anything to do with the shooting he had seen on the night of 23 March? Certainly the next night had seen him write 'shooting in the street' and '[Bullet] in [head]' in his dream diary.

On 26 March he wrote '[Holland]' beside more references to shootings. The fact that the country was in a box suggested to him that it would be somewhere near Holland – Belgium, perhaps. In the same way the box around the word 'head' a few nights before suggested that the assassination victim would be killed by a bullet somewhere near his head . . . like the neck, for instance.

Something big was brewing, and somehow Chris knew that it was connected both with the Middle East and with a man being shot in either Holland or Belgium. But how could he approach Paul Aylott with this? It seemed to an outsider to be nothing more than a series of half-remembered facts and sheer conjecture. In some ways that's all it was: but driven by the conviction and memory of what Chris had seen in that dream.

It *was* something big. And at the very end of March it all fell into place.

On 28 March five people were arrested at Heathrow airport after the security staff made a chilling find in a hangar there. A routine security check uncovered a cache of forty kryton triggers stored in an ordinary suitcase. These triggers, manufactured in the United States, form part of a sophisticated electronic triggering system for a nuclear device. They are high-speed electrical switches, which send impulses within microseconds, detonating the conventional explosives used to trigger the critical nuclear mass in a warhead. They have no other purpose, and are useless on their own. Whoever was in possession of these items had only one intention: to link them to a nuclear device.

One of the five arrested was an Iraqi businessman,

Omar Latif. The others included an Iraqi-born natu-ralised Briton, a Lebanese and a British couple. Special Branch officers, immediately alerted, soon arrested a sixth man in Lancashire.

The krytons were bound for Iraq, where Saddam Hussein had, two weeks previously, ordered the execution of journalist Fazad Bazoft for allegedly spying on missile bases.

This explained part of Chris's inter-connecting dream – but only part. The really amazing confirmation was to happen the next night.

On the night of 29 March weaponry expert Dr Gerry Bull was assassinated outside his apartment in Brussels. Bull was on his way home in the early hours of the morning when a crack team of agents ambushed him in the hallway. He was killed by two shots in the neck, delivered from a silenced 7.65mm automatic. The Canadian-born arms smuggler was known to be working for the Iraqis and was one of the few men who could have blown an undercover operation that had been going on for the past eighteen months. His murder was no casual robbery, for when his body was discovered he still had £16,000 in his wallet.

In a plot that resembled something from a thriller novel, MI6 and the CIA had staged an undercover operation that had seen the kryton triggers bought by Omar Latif substituted for fakes. Bull was the only man in the whole Iraqi chain who could have spotted the substitution and blown the operation wide open. The discovery of the kryton triggers at Heathrow was an unexpected development and did not halt the operation to eliminate the arms dealer. Possibly it was decided to continue with the plan as Bull was known to have sold and traded arms with the IRA, and it would still be useful to MI6 to have him out of the way.

It is this connection with the IRA that may have brought him into Chris Robinson's frame of reference.

Chris believes that all his dreams are connected with things that touch on his life, and the fact that he had already had dreams concerning the IRA was enough to make Bull a subject of his dreams.

Gerry Bull was a 62-year-old ballistics genius who worked for anyone who paid him: he was working for both Iran and Iraq at the same time, and he also did outside jobs. As such, he was a ripe target for any number of secret service organisations. But the fact remains that he was working for a country whose activities had featured in Chris's dreams over the period leading up to Bull's death, and that his description and the manner of his execution matched those of Chris's dream.

This was not the end of Chris's dreams relating to Iraq, for on the night of Gerry Bull's death, Chris had a dream in which he was watching a large computerised missile system that was connected to a jet plane flying over the Iran–Iraq border. On the pages of his dream diary he wrote '[Navstar]', which was the most up-to-date missile system he had heard of: the boxing of the name indicated that it was close to this, but not quite there.

Shortly afterwards the scandal broke surrounding the Iraqi supergun, a computerised missile system that used parts made in Britain. But that wasn't all . . .

> 'Hang my camera on the wall,
> Please take care it must not fall.
> Put it there for all to see
> Complete with film and wait for me.'
> I can [FREE] [WAITE]

It was the night of 1 April, and Chris awoke from his dreams to find that he had written this on the sheet of paper by his bed. Then he remembered his dream: he had been lying in bed when a man approached him and said these words. He seemed to be familiar, but wasn't anyone that Chris actually knew.

It was only when he looked at the sheet with the writing on that he remembered who his visitor had been: the journalist Fazad Bazoft, held pending execution by Iraqi dictator Saddam Hussein. Bazoft had been accused of spying on military installations, and it was generally believed that he would either be expelled from the country or have his sentence commuted to a lengthy spell in prison.

Chris now knew otherwise. The spirit of Bazoft had visited him that night and had spoken that rhyme, in which he gave intimations of the possible freeing of hostages in the Middle East (with particular reference to Terry Waite, the Archbishop of Canterbury's envoy), and also of the manner of his execution – he was hung by the neck, just as a camera is hung around a neck . . .

Chris was actually in Holland that night, staying at the Kraznapolski Hotel with a *News of the World* reporter called Garry Jones. They were investigating a story that had nothing to do with Chris's psychic abilities, and in fact Jones was openly sceptical to Chris about his dreams.

'Wake up,' whispered Chris, knocking on Jones's door at three in the morning.

'What is it?' the reporter replied testily, unhappy at being woken in the middle of the night.

'They've just executed that journalist bloke – Bazoft,' Chris whispered. 'I've just seen it.'

'Don't be stupid,' said Jones, now fully awake. 'They're not going to kill him. It's common knowledge that he's just being made an example of . . . They wouldn't dare. Now go back to sleep, for Christ's sake.'

But the Iraqis had executed Bazoft. In the middle of the night, Dutch time, just when Chris had dreamt about the visit from the dead man's spirit. When Garry Jones heard this on the news the next morning he was no longer a sceptic.

Despite being vindicated, Chris was disturbed by what had happened: although he had been visited by the spirits of dead men before – indeed, his first contact had been with the drowned soldier Robert – it had never been someone who had been in the public eye in any way. This presented Chris with a distinct problem, as there were two ways of looking at such a contact. First, there was the positive approach, that such a contact was opportune and everything Chris could have asked for: after all, here was a man who had made international news. If Bazoft could tell Chris something of importance, then it would make everyone sit up and take notice. It could prove to the world that Chris was genuine.

Then there was the negative side. Bazoft had been murdered by a despot seeking to keep his weapons-potential secret, paranoid about spying. As a victim of such a fate, Bazoft and his family had the sympathy of the world. For a psychic in rural England suddenly to claim that he was in contact with the spirit of the dead man, and that he was being told by him about the freeing of hostages, could bring down the scorn of that same world. It could, in fact, be counter-productive and guarantee that Chris would never be taken seriously or treated with anything but contempt.

So what should Chris do? Bazoft had said that he would keep back some stories for Monday – 2 April. Chris had also written WATCH THIS SPACE inside a huge box.

It seemed that he had no option but to wait.

In the event, Bazoft's promise seemed to be something of an anti-climax. There was certainly more writing in Chris's diary during the early days of April than at any other time, yet most of it could be seen only as hints of forthcoming events, with nothing really solid to grab hold of.

Chris's view is that these days were in some ways an

enigma. Whoever – or whatever – was guiding his mind through the watches of the night had decided that Chris must have more information; but, in order to have that, he must be able to decipher a more complex code.

There were small things that might be seen as victories, but nothing quite as mind-blowing as being visited by a freshly deceased spirit. There was a prison riot at Sandy Mount in Scotland that could possibly have been foreseen by Chris's dreams, but otherwise they seemed to be nothing more than a jumble. Except perhaps for the inkling that there was something amiss, with another bomb attack . . .

On 6 April Chris dreamt that he was back in northwest London, where he had lived as a child. He dreamt of Roger Moore in his 1960s television role as *The Saint*, and of the car that Moore drove in the programme: a white Volvo sports model. There was also a bed with weapons hidden underneath it, and a fire that started on the roof of a building.

Chris awoke puzzled: he hadn't been back to that part of London for some time, and certainly hadn't seen any films or television programmes featuring Roger Moore. So what did it all mean?

The next morning he took the piece of paper, and followed his usual procedure for trying to make sense of the cryptic clues contained within his dreams. Laying the two pieces of paper side by side, he would look at what was written on the dream sheet, which lay on the right. On the left, he would write word associations and ideas, or memories triggered by the dream sheet.

This morning he had the following:

[ROGER] MOORE
[Sports car] Darts.   [BED]
                                       Hidden under
                                       weapons

[FIRE]

The word 'fire' with a box around it he now knew to mean danger, following past experience. A box, of course, meant something 'not quite' like the word within, and fires were considered dangerous by the subconscious. Likewise, the words 'Roger' and 'sports car' weren't quite accurate.

Chris sat for some time, puzzling over what they might mean. It baffled him completely, until a dim and distant memory of his childhood came to him. When he was a small boy, he and some friends used to have a car-washing round in their local area, and they would spend the weekend washing cars for a few shillings a time.

Although he had seen Moore as the Saint, driving his sports car in the dream, the boxes suggested that this shouldn't be taken too literally. Quite rightly, as one of the cars that Chris washed regularly was that of Roger Moore, when he lived at 58 Gordon Avenue in Stanmore, north-west London. He particularly remembered Moore, as the actor would always tip the boys well when his car was washed.

Gordon Avenue is situated at the back of the RAF base at Stanmore.

Then the significance of seeing Moore as the Saint hit Chris fully . . . The clue lay in the car Moore had been driving. In the series, the Saint's name had been Simon Templar, and his car had the personalised number plate ST1. ST1 was, Chris thought, the postcode for the RAF base at Stanmore. He soon found this to be incorrect, but the link had been made in his mind.

Suddenly, a strange and meaningless dream took on a whole new slant. Was it another coded warning from Robert about an IRA attack? Looking at it this way, Chris could see that 'hidden under' and 'weapons' could refer to a bomb being hidden in a storeroom. What the word 'bed' within a box meant was still a complete puzzle. There wasn't enough information.

Chris could only hope that the attack wasn't imminent, and that some more information would be coming his way. If only he could ask questions, instead of being a passive receiver.

Fazad Bazoft was visiting Chris again in his dreams, with messages about planets colliding and problems with the Hubble telescope. There was nothing definite, but it might have been a garbled attempt to explain the problems that the Hubble was having with the alignment of mirrors in its attempt to study distant planets. It was frustrating to Chris, who was waiting in vain for more information about a possible attack at RAF Stanmore.

Bazoft was not the only dream visitor. One night, at the end of Chris's bed, sat a dishevelled man in late middle-age. He seemed to be familiar, and it was only a matter of seconds before Chris identified him as Dr Gerry Bull, the arms expert whose death he had so graphically dreamt about a few weeks beforehand. Bull started to tell Chris about the ongoing war between Iran and Iraq, a skirmish that had been going on intermittently for some years. He tried to explain how it would increase in magnitude, to a point where Saddam Hussein would try to take over an oil-rich country and increase his power base.

Bazoft would alternate with Bull in these dreams, which continued for most of the month. Again and again they reiterated that the conflict between Iran and Iraq would escalate to such a degree that other countries would be drawn in.

Chris didn't know what to make of this, as it was a subject that was starting to fill the news at night. Was this an example of his own subconscious starting to churn over worries about war? Was it getting in the way of any messages that he was supposed to receive? Or were the two becoming so mixed that neither made any sense?

The only event at that time that Chris can put down

to premonition is the death of Greta Garbo, which he dreamt of on 15 April. He saw her spirit leave her body while she lay in a hospital bed. It walked to an open window and flew off into the night.

That same night Bazoft said to Chris, 'I am still with you.' Quite frankly, Chris was beginning to wonder why, as Bazoft had little to say that made any kind of sense. It was not until 21 April that he got the kind of message he was waiting for.

[sign. Kill all dogs]

This was not the first time that dogs had appeared, but whereas previously they had been representative of killers, this dream was a little more specific. They were connected with a map that Chris had drawn in his sleep, which showed a fenced-in enclosure with a building marked with an X, arrowed with the word 'here' beside it, and the phrase 'Building or work shop' written above. The enclosure seemed to be on a main road. Underneath was written 'Two the road side by side', and 'Men in uniform asleep'.

What could this mean? The enclosure might be part of RAF Stanmore, which consists of two separate enclosures, one on either side of the main road. Did this map show the half in which the bomb would be planted? Certainly Chris thought so: on the piece of paper on which he tried to make sense of the dream images he wrote '2 bases side by side', and drew a rough map of the RAF base as he remembered it.

There was also an instruction on the dream sheet to 'tell David Bolster'. But tell him what? It was still early days for Chris, and he found that sometimes the dreams slipped away before he had a chance to record anything that wasn't already written.

Chris phoned Reverend Bolster and talked to him about the dream. He told him that he feared another attack, yet there wasn't really enough evidence for him to give to Paul Aylott with any sense of conviction. Bolster told Chris what he always did: how the dream premonition worked he didn't know, but in some way it was a gift from God and one that Chris must use as he saw fit.

That was all very well, but there were some things that came to Chris in dreams that made him question his very sanity. On 7 April, just a fortnight before, he had been visited by a Christ-like figure, who had dictated the following message:

God said I come not this day to teach man charity nor yet to teach man as to what is right and wrong between men. These things were revealed before. I come to produce a new race and show them how to fulfil the former commandments, to do unto others as they would be done by. To return good for evil, to give away all and fear not. Before these things were preached I come now to put them into practice. By this shall man know who are the chosen of the Lord Jehovah. You are a chosen one. One who has shown his worth before me. You live in heaven and dwell on earth.

Chris had been so preoccupied at the time with the possibility of messages relating to RAF Stanmore and another bomb attack that he had almost forgotten about this. Perhaps it was this that he had to tell Reverend Bolster?

'It's possible that there are demonic spirits who are trying to deceive you,' said Bolster after careful consideration, 'but I think that the majority of what you are receiving is in some way useful information. I think that someone is telling you it's your duty to record and report what's happening to you.'

In other words, Chris should tell Paul Aylott about the dogs, regardless of how little evidence he believed

the dream contained. It was a view that was confirmed
when, a few days later, Chris started to dream of Holland
and Belgium being somehow connected with the dogs.
Although he didn't know it at the time, this tied in with
MI5 and Anti-Terrorist Squad investigations into an
IRA arms and explosives-smuggling cell, which operated
from the Continent and was instrumental in supplying
many of the explosives used in mainland IRA attacks
during that year.

The next four nights contained nothing of any real
consequence. Terry Waite featured again in the dreams,
but there was no real indication of when he would be
released. It was not until the night of Monday, 30 April,
that things really began to move.

Chris was driving through Stanmore, and he stopped at
a shop. He parked his car around the corner and walked
to the shop. The strange thing was that, although he
went in, he didn't know what the shop sold, or what
he wanted to buy. Instead, he kept looking out of
the window, from where he could see the entrance
to the RAF base across the road. There were dogs
standing outside the base, at the sentry posts. Both dogs
had guns.

He woke up in a cold sweat. There was something
about this dream that was more chilling than all the
others, as though there was a stronger intensity to
everything he had experienced: a greater sense of being
there, a stronger stench of fear in the air.

He knew why he felt this when he looked at what
he had written. First, there were two small maps, one
of which showed the position of his car, the shop and
the entrance to the base. The other showed a junction,
and had the words 'stop at junction' written underneath.
There was also the phrase 'go to shop – message', with
'[TAPE]' written beside it.

Could this be a message to him: should he go to the

base and warn them? Is that what the shop represented: he would be trying to sell the RAF his 'wares' – in other words, his dream. If so, then the appearance of the word 'tape' would become highly relevant in view of future occurrences.

The overwhelming feeling of the dream was one of immense urgency. 'Stanmore' was written inside a box – but this was a box drawn in squiggly lines, with the name of the base underlined. Next to it were the words 'ATTACK', '[RESTRAIN]', and '[KILL]'. They were written with such force that the paper was deeply impressed, the sheet underneath containing a deep gouge.

Finally, at the bottom of the page, Chris had drawn a container of some kind, with a cartoon bomb inside, fuse smoking.

This was just too much to keep quiet about. First the dogs had been recurring for several nights, and now the messages about Stanmore had returned with a vengeance, linking them to the dogs. Whatever was going to happen, it was going to be nasty. Chris felt that this was his big chance really to achieve something with his dreams. Previously he had foretold bomb hits, but hadn't been able to stop them. Now he might just be able to do that.

He called Paul Aylott, after faxing him the dream pages for 30 April.

'So what are you going to do about it?' he asked the policeman.

'What can I do?' Aylott replied. 'I can only pass it on. It's not up to me what happens next. Besides, be fair – there's not much hard detail, is there? I mean, like dates or something.'

'Yeah, but couldn't they increase security?' asked Chris.

'Maybe they already have heavy security. I don't know,' Aylott said.

It was not a satisfactory conversation. When Chris got off the phone he felt deeply frustrated. Ever since the dreams had started he had wanted something like this to happen. All his dreams had foretold some kind of event, and he wanted to be able to change the course of events, instead of just observing them. But was that possible?

It is a vital question, with overtones that go beyond mere action. If what Chris was seeing was the future, then would it be possible for him to change it? For instance, he could see dogs with guns hanging around RAF Stanmore, and had dreamt of the planting of bombs. If that was the future, then was he able to alter it? If he could change the course of events, and prevent a bomb being planted, would he dream about that? And if he had been destined to stop it happening, would he have dreamt about it in the first place: if it didn't happen, would it be there for him to dream about?

Chris was now presented with a set of moral and metaphysical questions that could have left him tied in knots. But that's not the sort of man Chris Robinson is. He loathes terrorists and the way their random violence affects innocent people: it runs contrary to everything in his nature. Whatever the philosophical arguments, he knew that his conscience would not let him rest without trying to prevent the bomb.

CHAPTER SEVEN

If the previous months had been astounding, then May was going to be a different kind of month altogether. It was the busiest month of all in the world of dreams, with more information and detail coming through than ever before. It was also another step in the learning process.

But, first, Chris had to gain support for what lay ahead.

The first day of May was a beautiful spring Tuesday, with a crisp, sunny morning greeting Chris as he made his way towards the Vicarage. Having spoken to David Bolster a few days earlier, Chris now wanted to see him. The problems that the dreams presented to his faith were questions that he needed to address.

Chris Robinson is not a religious man in the conventional sense. He is a Christian, but like most of us only follows a particular religion because he was born into it. He went to church to pray and thank his grandmother after the near theft of his car, and approached Reverend Bolster when the dreams began, but he had no strong religious conviction other than a general belief in God.

Now he was becoming close to Reverend Bolster. The other men to whom he faxed his dreams looked at them in a detached manner: Paul Aylott and Trevor Kempson were concerned only with the facts that they could draw from his dream diaries, while Dr Hearne was concerned with them only as pieces of data for analysis. David Bolster, on the other hand, was a man of God, and thus concerned with the idea that Chris was in contact with a world that lay beyond death.

He greeted Chris at the door of the Vicarage and showed him into his study. The two men had a cup of tea, while Chris poured out his latest dreams and the questions that were still coming to him concerning the nature of what he was seeing. Usually, David said very little and just sat there listening to Chris; today, there was something he had to say.

'I've been thinking about what you've been saying, and I've made a few notes about it,' he said, rising from his seat and rooting about among the papers on his desk. 'I've been doing some studying, and I think that I may have some answers for you.'

Chris was keen to hear more and waited while David found his sheet of paper, covered with a crabbed script. Without a word, he handed it to Chris, who read it eagerly. It said:

1. The dreams are right, not wrong.
2. Don't question why, or why me?
3. He (God) uses your past stories. He knows you. (Psalm 139)
4. Very few answers will be given this side of his Kingdom Reign. Don't look for answers, because you might pick up the wrong answers. I am concerned you will pick up wrong answers.
5. There is a gift of the spirit known as 'testing the spirits'. I want to exercise it for you. It is not infallible, but I do exercise it regularly, and scripture is very helpful in testing. *But* will you listen if I tell you?

Positive
1. Your witness. 2. Solve crimes. 3. Prevent crimes.
4. Show you how to pray (e.g. Terry Waite to negotiate).

5. Angelic ministry (ferry drowning, girls in fire).

Warnings/Danger
Not all dreams may be right. Be careful. Not
everything is purposeful. Look keenly only at
those dreams which have a positive lead already,
e.g. Stanmore.
Only fax the barest minimum to the police.

Reverend Bolster believed that the dreams came from
one of three sources: God, the Devil, or from within
Chris himself. Chris could concur only with the first and
last ideas: by this time he believed that his precognitive
dreams fell into two categories. First, there were those
that came from within himself. These were the ones
where he found himself in strange locations witnessing
events. Often these locations resembled places he had
visited in his youth. Bolster believed that God could
be using Chris's past experience as a reference point
in order to relay messages to him, and he had found a
relevant scripture passage to explain it. Chris wasn't too
sure that he agreed on that point, but was interested in
it as a possible explanation.

However, he had no doubt that there were some
dreams that were motivated by God. When he was
visited by the spirits of Robert, the dead soldier, Fazad
Bazoft and Gerry Bull, then he had no doubt that they
were sent by a higher power in order to pass on messages
that would be of some use.

As for the Devil . . . Well, it was possible that some
of the nightmares Chris had suffered from were due to
interference from the Devil or from demons, but Chris
remained ambivalent towards this.

'Only fax the barest minimum to the police' . . . This
went against everything that Chris's instincts told him.
Besides, he now had another contact in the force. As well
as faxing his dreams to Paul Aylott at Dunstable police

station, Chris now had to send faxes to John Branscombe, Head of the Regional Crime Squad, based at Hatfield. By one of those strange coincidences, Branscombe's name had come to Chris in the dream concerning the man who had blown his own hand off in a bungled bomb attack.

Chris left Reverend Bolster feeling in a more optimistic frame of mind than he had known for some time. He would still fax everything through to the police, but he would take notice of most of what David had suggested. He resolved not to worry about the information he was going to receive, but instead to concentrate on deciphering whatever he was given.

There was going to be a lot to work on . . .

On the night of 1 May Chris felt renewed, and a stronger pull from his subconscious than ever before. It felt as though he had taken some kind of powerful stimulant, which shot him through the ceiling as soon as he fell asleep. He felt more alive and alert than when he was actually awake, and he was soon flying through the air.

He landed beside the sea, on a tourist beach. It was a beautiful day, and there were children running across the sands, laughing and building sandcastles. It was an idyllic scene. Chris could feel the sun on his face, and the joy of the children.

But there was a cloud on the horizon. In the distance Chris could see a crowd of youths, shouting and screaming their way along the beach. They got closer, and Chris could see that they were fighting among themselves. Some of them were wearing football scarves.

Before he knew what was happening they were upon him, scattering the crying children and smashing the sandcastles. The idyllic beach scene became a scene of bedlam, with blood and bodies everywhere, and only the thin blue line of the police to stop further mayhem.

And then he was awake.

★   ★   ★

Chris was puzzled by the dream, and even more puzzled when he looked at the sheet of paper by his bedside. There was a lot scribbled across the paper, much of it relating to things that he couldn't even remember. Some of it referred to a Porsche, but not in any kind of context. Chris was inclined to relate this to his own subconscious, as his own car was a Porsche. There were also several references to coins, which baffled him. However, there were several things that related to the dream as he remembered it:

> [Foot Ball] = Place
> [Pool]
> Sandcastles on road/Fight in street
> Children playing.   [Hooligan]

The words 'football' and 'pool' equalling 'place' puzzled him most. Did this mean that the location where the riot would take place was contained within this cryptic clue?

One thing was for sure: if Chris was going to crack this, he would have to be patient and wait at least until the weekend. After all, a riot involving football hooligans only takes place after a match, and most matches occur at the weekend. The chances of trouble following a midweek evening match were very slight indeed.

Although the rest of the week was busy, Chris made sure that he kept an eye on the news, and was not surprised to see on Saturday that there had been trouble with football hooligans in the town of Poole, in Dorset.

'Pool' equals 'place'.

Poole. A simple example of wordplay. Chris was amazed at the simplicity of the code, and also at its sudden appearance. But that wasn't all: referring back to his diary for that day, Chris saw that he had also written 'low door – go under to get in'.

Chris was not that familiar with Dorset, but had once holidayed there as a child. The only place he could really remember was Durdle Door, at Lulworth Cove, where there are a series of caves that can be explored only if you bend almost double. Was this the meaning of 'go under to get in' and 'low door'?

Perhaps this was stretching the interpretation of a wordplay code a bit far. It was hard to say; if the new codes were going to be based on wordplay and word association, then they would be highly personal to him. Time alone would tell how well this worked.

Meanwhile, the rest of the first week of May had been full of incident, with further warnings of IRA bomb attacks and more clues to an attack on Stanmore – still Chris's main concern, as his premonitions about this were deeply disturbing.

On 2 May he dreamt that he was trying to explain to people how he was able to fly. He was also talking about spoon-bending and levitation to a journalist. This came true eleven days later when Uri Geller was featured in the *News of the World* discussing exactly the same techniques that Chris had been talking about in his dream. On a less flippant level, Terry Waite appeared again. In his diary Chris wrote '[Terry]', with 'still working, still waiting' beside it. But that told only half the story. Chris still had a clear memory of the dream. He had been sitting with Terry Waite, who had told him that he was alive and well, and that he hoped he would be the last of the hostages to be released. Since he had been sent to negotiate the release of the other hostages, he would feel he had failed if he were to be released before them.

Chris told Reverend Bolster, as usual, but didn't pass the message on to Lambeth Palace: earlier, when he had first received messages from Terry Waite, he had contacted the Archbishop of Canterbury, but had been treated like a madman. There was no point in continuing the contact.

Interestingly there was a similar 11-day gap before Chris received confirmation of his message, when the *Daily Mail* reported on 13 May that news had come through concerning Waite: he was alive, the first time that his survival had been confirmed.

On 3 May the first bomb message of a crowded month came through. Although the actual dream was a jumble, the evidence was self-explanatory.

> Bomb warning.
>
> Base.   [Holland] Germany.
> [Explosion] NO.

There was going to be a bomb planted in an army base, either in Germany or near Holland. But there wouldn't be an explosion. Somehow the plot would be foiled.

Chris switched on the television as he waited for Paul Aylott to answer the phone, but replaced the receiver when he saw a news item telling of the discovery of an unexploded bomb at an RAF base in Germany. It had been discovered at 2 a.m. – while Chris was still sleeping.

Another item on the Teletext service caught his eye: there had been a power failure on the London Underground system that morning, at Moorgate station. Looking at the sheet of paper in his hand, Chris could see the words 'electric train', with '[tube]' and '[power fails]' next to it.

Two items to be confirmed as soon as he was awake was something he had never experienced before. It was getting to the stage where he was almost too excited to get off to sleep at night.

There was another bomb warning during the night of 4 May. 'Time is ten past four,' Chris wrote in his diary. Again, the dream was garbled, but he could remember that his soldier was there, explaining to him that he would be giving times as Greenwich Mean Time. As

British Summer Time was now in operation, Chris took this to mean that the bomb would go off at ten past five. But a.m. or p.m.? And on what date would this occur?

Chris was certain that the bomb would use a digital clock and delay timer, and that it would originate in Holland – 'same as other dream'. '? – Bomb – Explosion,' he wrote the following night, the second night running that he had dreamt of this bomb.

On 6 May another pattern was established. For the third night running he dreamt of a bomb. From this point on, he would know that three nights in a row meant that whatever he was dreaming about was imminent . . .

[Radio Set] [TV on front] [Phillips make] Warning.
Wires if short out.
Bang – Explosion.   [Bomb]
Add two wires to complete circuit.
                          [Terrorist group]
                          Wires in device short out.
                          Printed circuit board.
4.15 – 4.30 = TIME

Chris woke in a cold sweat. Robert had come to him once again, intent on warning him about three impending bomb attacks. Two of these would occur in the same place, and Robert was insistent that Chris pay close attention. People would die. The first two bombs were going to be in a bed.

What kind of a bed? A flowerbed, or one you sleep in?

Try as he might, Chris couldn't remember if he had been told. But he did remember more about the third bomb. It would be under a vehicle, possibly a Forces vehicle. Once again, detail eluded him. There was, however, one part of the dream that remained with him vividly. Could this be a clue?

Yet again Chris found himself in a shop in his dreams.

But this wasn't like the shop near RAF Stanmore: this one was all too familiar. It was the CIVIC store in Wembley High Road, where he had been employed many years before. The shop was a radio and television retailer, and Chris had worked there as one of the repair men.

He could only take this to mean that the bomb would be in Wembley High Road, under a vehicle of some kind. Would this be the bomb for which he knew the time?

He faxed the information as usual, feeling frustrated that he was getting so close to something important, and yet a few vital details still eluded him.

Yet while this occupied his waking hours, his dreams had something more horrible in store . . .

He didn't recognise the airport: it wasn't one that he could ever remember using. Yet he seemed to know where everything was situated as he checked in and made his way to the boarding gate. The majority of the staff and passengers were Asian, and the weather was sultry. He didn't know which country he was in, but it was somewhere in the south-eastern corner of the globe.

The plane was a 747, and he boarded with all the other passengers, making his way to his seat near the back. Settling back, he waited for the plane to taxi to the runway.

Then chaos descended: a sound so loud that he literally couldn't hear it − it made his eardrums ache and his jaw crack. And the light was so bright, so intense that even when he shut his eyes the glow burned through his eyelids. Burned through so brightly that he had to open his eyes.

The bomb must have been planted in the toilets at the front of the plane. He knew this by the direction of the blast, and the way it shattered the heads of two people sitting near him, their skulls blown backwards by the blast, sending a spray of blood and brain over him. He tried to scream, but the smoke from the rapidly spreading fire caught in his throat, making him choke. And now that his ears had cleared from the shockwave of the blast, he could hear the thundering roar of the flames coupled with the excruciating screech of rending metal as the plane juddered to a halt.

He woke in terror, sitting bolt-upright and staring into the quiet Bedfordshire night. The silence around him was overwhelming, with only the soft breathing of his sleeping wife and the rustle of leaves outside the window.

Yet he could still see the after-image of the fire.

Chris didn't look at his dream diary – not straight away, as he didn't want to be reminded of what he had just witnessed. Instead, he got up and made some coffee, showered and dressed. By the time he had calmed down it was just past nine in the morning. He drove over to visit David Bolster straight away, and told him what he had seen.

'I don't understand why God should show you these terrible things,' David said sadly, noting Chris's obvious distress.

Chris shrugged. 'I think it's because no-one really believes me yet. It's like I'm being shown things that are so far away that I can't have anything to do with them. Yet I know they'll happen – what more proof could anyone want?'

Together they prayed that this would be one dream that would not come true.

It was not to be: four days later, on Saturday, 12 May, a Philippine Airlines plane was taxiing to the runway at Manila Airport when a bomb exploded in the lavatory at the front of the plane. It decapitated the passengers sitting near the centre of the explosion, killing them instantly. Another five passengers were killed, and eighty were injured. There were 230 people on the flight. Responsibility was claimed by the NPA (New People's Army), which also admitted it had screwed up: the bomb was supposed to go off at cruising altitude, leaving no survivors at all.

Chris had faxed his dreams to Paul Aylott as usual, mainly because there were mentions of dead soldiers on the pages, and also the phrases 'face in door' and 'across the road'. Although meaningless in themselves, they triggered memories of dreams where he was in Stanmore and Edgeware. He had also been in a car driven by a dog, which he knew to mean it was being driven by an IRA cell member, and Chris wanted to record what he had seen from the car, in case it might give some clue to what was going on concerning Stanmore.

On the same sheet of paper Chris had written:

> Airways [747] Crash warning. [Head off]
> [open – toilet – no door] Blood on face.
> Asian people.

Paul Aylott rang him. 'What's all this about a plane crash?'

'I saw it. It's going to happen.'

'Well, can we do anything?'

'You tell me,' said Chris.

On the morning of 12 May, Aylott rang again. When Chris answered the phone, he said, 'How did you know that was going to happen?'

'You tell me,' Chris repeated. 'I just had a dream, and there it was.'

'If I had any doubts about it being luck before . . . Christ alone knows I haven't now,' Aylott said. 'What you're doing flies in the face of everything we've ever been taught.'

It was the first time he had ever expressed any doubts he might have had to Chris. Their relationship had

always been based on Chris's assumption that Aylott
simply took the dreams at face value. But now it would
seem that there had been a grain of scepticism.

No longer. It confirmed what Chris had said to David
Bolster. Perhaps this was God's (or whoever's) way of
proving Chris's validity to others.

On the nights of 10 and 11 May there were strange
hints in Chris's dreams about the IRA bombers he had
dreamt about so frequently. One seemed to indicate
that a soldier with Northern Ireland links would be
a victim, and the other somehow connected the IRA
with gypsies, as Chris saw travellers changing sites in
a familiar north-west London landscape. But there was
nothing definite.

One dream that was a definite premonition happened
on Sunday, 13 May. Sandwiched between eight or nine
dreams came one that was startlingly clear.

Chris found himself standing by a railway line. It was
a rural area, and he recognised it as the stretch of track
that runs between Chorleywood and Rickmansworth
on the Metropolitan Line out of London and into Hertfordshire and Buckinghamshire. It lay only about forty
minutes' drive from where he lived, and he was familiar
with the area. There were four people with him, and
they explained that they were going to die on this stretch
of line. They were resigned to it, and didn't seem in
any way distressed. They explained that it would be an
accident that occurred in the course of their work, and
that this was to be the spot where it would happen.

Then, in the manner of dreams, Chris found himself
watching the rape and murder of two young girls,
helpless to do anything to aid them or to stop the
crime. The sudden cut from one scene to another was
deeply disorientating, and the futility of having to watch
made everything else seem garbled.

Chris woke up sweating again. Another night of

deeply disturbed sleep. It took him some while to calm down, and then he was able to fall back into a kind of repose. It was in moments like these that he pondered his current situation. Bessie still had her job as a waitress in a hotel. With tips, her income was pretty good. Chris's income, on the other hand, had taken a nose dive. Since the dreams had started, his sleep had been heavily disturbed, and with his other medical problems this left him tired and unable to concentrate for long periods during the day.

And it was not just the sleep: much of his days seemed now to be taken up with matters relating to his dreams. If he wasn't puzzling over the meaning of his dream diary, then he was discussing his problems with David Bolster, or talking to Paul Aylott or John Branscombe. He was still in contact with Chris Watt at Scotland Yard, although Watt had taken a back seat of late. In short, the dreams had taken over Chris's whole life. He had neither the time nor the energy to carry out repairs or renovate old television sets, and the way things were going he would have to start signing on for unemployment benefit. To someone who had always made his own way since leaving school, the idea was anathema. Circumstances, however, dictated otherwise.

The problems that disturbed him in the quiet watches of the night always vanished when he looked at his diary pages the next morning. This time he was astounded to see that he had drawn a map showing where the railway accident would take place, complete with an X to mark the spot on the line between the two stations. There were also some notes relating to the murders he had seen, with a rough sketch map of the area where one body would be found. He felt that the murders were not connected, though similar.

All three premonitions were proven within a week: on Wednesday, 16 May, at 2 a.m. four London Transport track engineers (despite its rural setting, the Metropolitan Line is part of the London Underground system) were killed while taking part in routine track maintenance. An 18-ton trailer wagon containing equipment and sleepers rolled over a 5-man gang as they worked on the line one mile east of Chorleywood. The brake had slipped loose on the wagon, and before the men had a chance to clear the track it was upon them. One man scrambled to safety, but the other four were crushed by the rolling stock.

Chris's map shows the point where the accident took place, just before a road crosses the line via a bridge. In some photographs of the accident scene, the bridge is visible along the line.

Four days later, two stories appeared in the press. One concerned the murder of student Joanne Parrish in France, the other of teenager Elaine Foley somewhere along the River Thames – exactly where is not known, as the disguised body was dumped on a British Rail luggage van and conveyed along the line. The reporting of both stories described their injuries in similar terms, and this made Chris wonder about the nature of his premonitions: although he had seen both killings, had he really been at the scene of the crime, or had his imagination constructed this from the newspaper reports he would read in the future?

In some ways it was an academic argument, but one that interested him greatly, as he was still keen to get at the root of his suddenly acquired gift.

When we talked about these events before this book was started, Chris dwelt on this at some length. Was he really seeing the events as they happened, or was he seeing a reconstruction of them? Had he read about them, or seen them on the news, so that they were in his future field? If so, was the dramatic reconstruction his imagination's way of feeding him these facts from the future? After all, he had no more detail to offer on these murders than that contained in the newspaper reports.

At the same time his dream about the trackside accident covered totally different ground. Admittedly, everything he had seen was in the newspaper report he later read, and the film of the accident scene was on the local television news. Yet he had spoken to the men involved, before they died.

Chris has no doubt now that some of the dreams relate to events that happen in his own future field, and others come from a different source. It took some time to come to terms with the fact that there was no one simple answer, but Chris has learnt by experience not to make any kind of judgement. And, because of the dreams in which he has spoken to soon-to-be dead spirits, he has evolved a theory about the nature of time and events.

This will be detailed in a later chapter: for now, events were about to overtake Chris Robinson.

Monday, 14 May, brought Chris the realisation that the symbol of cups meant dead people, so that if he saw four cups, then it would mean four dead people. Four dead people on a rail track: the Chorleywood incident, still two days away, was being impressed upon him, as he made a safety check on an electrical tube in his dream. The men were killed during routine safety work, and the Underground system is commonly known as the Tube: another example of word association.

It was the night of 15 May that the bomb warnings came back with a vengeance. Things were pointing towards Stanmore and Wembley, as the information built up, both through direct vision and a more personal symbolism.

Chris was on a train going to a Nazi death camp. It was so clear that he drew a map of the compound, writing 'Zyklon [B] [Gas]' and 'Jews/Train/Escape'. Then things changed, and he was in the old CIVIC shop in Wembley, where he had worked as a young man. He was looking out of the window at a Hillman Imp, with the registration 666 FXX. Someone was looking under the car, saying that they couldn't find a bomb there.

When he woke up Chris was confused by the dream. There was an urgency to it, yet at the same time there were aspects that seemed to muddle the issue: where did a Nazi death camp fit into it?

He decided that the only solution was to go out and forget about the dreams for a while. He had to clear his mind, so that he would come back to the diaries with a fresh outlook. Perhaps then he would be able to make sense of them.

It was a pleasant day, though not too warm. So Chris drove his camper van to Northampton, some forty miles away, and spent the morning at the Billing Aquadrome, a camp site and holiday centre five miles from the town centre, doing everything but think about the dreams.

When he returned to the camper, he pulled out the pages he had scribbled on during the night. There were four sheets, more than he had ever before produced in one night. This alone showed that something vitally important was contained within the disjointed sentences that he now had to try and make into coherent sense.

The make of car and registration number were in boxes, so the bomb would not be under that particular make of car. Instead, it was meant to stir a memory that would assist him. This was followed by:

> [Sex in a car] – who did it?
>   Where is car now?
> ?   Found under [car]
> [Bomb]   Driver's seat – look for it!!!

On the following page the name of the electrical store Dixons was written in a box, followed by a series of boxes referring to stock returns and faulty equipment.

The last page began with a sketch of a lorry, with the words 'weight important – no HGV required or got'.

Then came 'Spray in another colour', '[Green] + white' and '[Brown] + white'. The last item was '[car] repair'.

For some obtuse reason, it was the last part that made the whole thing click into place. Back in 1968 when Chris worked in the CIVIC shop in Wembley High Road he bought a Hillman Imp whose registration number was 666 FXX. The car was blue, and didn't work. Chris had to repair the engine while the car was parked round the back of the shop. Once he got it going, he resprayed it green.

'[Sex in car]', if it referred to the Imp, meant Stanmore, as Chris had enjoyed many youthful exploits in the back of the Imp when it was parked on the common at the back of the RAF base.

The name of Dixons could have been another reference to CIVIC, as the old shop was now a Dixons store. Chris used to park the car outside the shop while he was at work, and believed that the reference to someone looking under his car for a bomb meant that the vehicle under which a bomb would explode would be parked in this place. But what type of vehicle?

The drawing made this obvious. It would be a van or lorry – and a small one. 'Weight important – no HGV required or got' was the clue: if a van or lorry weighs under three tons, the driver doesn't require an HGV (heavy goods vehicle) licence.

So the bomb would be planted under a small lorry or van in Wembley High Road, and in order to find it a search would have to be made underneath it. Only one thing remained to be explained: the Nazi death camp.

It was then that the name of Henry Jacobs came to mind. Chris once knew a Mr Jacobs at around the time he had been working for CIVIC. Henry Jacobs lived in Dalkeith Grove, Stanmore, but had been born in Belsen, and had often told Chris about the horrors of the Holocaust.

Another personal reference to pinpoint an area.

Chris was appalled. He rushed to the public telephones and rang Paul Aylott, gabbling out his story. He had such a sense of urgency that the words poured out in a torrent, and Aylott had to slow him down, make him go over the story again.

'And you're sure about this?' he said finally.

'Yeah, of course I am. If it's not Wembley, then it's certainly north-west London. Look, Paul, I know I'm being a nuisance ringing up like this, but it's just that—'

'No, you're not being a nuisance,' Aylott assured him. 'I'll pass all this on to "them", and see what they say.'

'Thanks, I really appreciate that,' said Chris, knowing that 'them' meant some nebulous branch of the secret service or Special Branch.

'That's okay,' Aylott replied. 'And look, don't worry about it, okay?'

Chris said goodbye and hung up. He returned to his camper and lit a cigarette. He was trying to give up, but the pressure was too great at the moment.

Don't worry? It was easy for Paul to say that. He didn't live with it, couldn't possibly know how much anxiety it caused.

Chris switched on the television and was greeted with the lead story on the lunchtime news: the deaths of the four workers at Chorleywood in the early hours of the morning. On top of everything else, this was just too much, and he ran back crying to the public phones, from where he dialled Aylott's number, all the while thinking that he should have done more than just pass the information on by fax: he should have contacted the transport police (who are responsible for all railways), or gone there himself, instead of taking the camper out . . . Anything.

'Why didn't you do something?' he asked Aylott when he was put through.

'I passed it on – that's all I can do.'

'But what about what I've just told you?'

'I've passed it on . . . Chris, I can't make them do anything, I can only tell them what you tell me. And I do that, believe me.'

Chris hung up and returned to the camper. He felt drained, and could only hope that the mysterious 'them' would take notice of the Wembley and north London warning.

He fell asleep, and slept until twenty-past five.

At 5.12 p.m. on Wednesday, 16 May, Sergeant Charles Chapman locked up the Army Recruiting Office in Thurlow Gardens, Wembley, and walked to the Sherpa van he used for transport. He checked underneath for bombs, as all army personnel had been instructed, but could see nothing. He got into the van, turned the ignition and was killed by a bomb explosion.

The van was under three tons, and didn't need an HGV licence. It was parked outside Dixons (formerly CIVIC) in the High Road. Sergeant Chapman had checked the vehicle but found nothing, as the man in Chris's dream had done.

Several days later it was reported in the press that police were seeking to interview tinkers seen near the van in the early afternoon. Even this tied in with the travellers seen in Chris's dreams.

Chris Robinson had been right in almost every respect: his precognitive dream had foretold the event, and he had warned the authorities.

Still Sergeant Chapman died. Did this mean that – no matter what – the events he foresaw would simply have to take place? It was a question that would worry him in the future, but not now.

Chris woke at twenty-past five. After a cup of coffee and a cigarette, he turned on the early evening news, hoping to find out more about the accident on the

Chorleywood line that had upset him so much earlier in the day. What he saw did more than upset him. The first news reports were garbled, as information was still coming through: a bomb had exploded in Wembley, and a soldier was believed to have been killed. The bomb was under a van.

Even now, years after the event, Chris can't find words to describe how he felt. He knew he had been right, he knew he had done everything that it was possible for him to do, and yet – and yet there was a feeling of immense devastation. Failure. He had tried to save lives, yet still they had been lost. He cried: tears of bitter frustration and rage. Rage at himself, rage at those who had seemingly ignored what he had told them.

Tears streaming down his face, he ran from his camper, across the road to the public telephones at the Aquadrome. Fumbling in his anger, he dialled Paul Aylott's number. Right then, he hated Paul. He hated the police, and whichever spook section of the secret service was taking his messages. Most of all, he hated himself for feeling so ineffectual.

Aylott was still in his office, and picked up the phone to hear Chris screaming at him. It was an incoherent burst of justified rage. Aylott, whom Chris describes as one of the nicest men he has ever known, stayed calm. He waited for Chris to finish, then said, 'Okay, mate, just calm down. I know how you feel, I really do. I feel upset about this myself, but all this will get neither of us anywhere. The best thing you can do is go home right now, and try to calm down. I know you're not going to believe me right now, but I did try and help. I put through everything you said, but there just can't have been enough for anyone to tell when and where.'

On reflection, Chris would agree with this, but right then he could think of nothing other than feeling useless: without any kind of result, his gift was futile.

Calmer, if not happier, he apologised to Aylott for

railing at him and walked back to the camper. He occupied some time by checking the engine, then decided to watch the seven o'clock news and find out what had happened in Wembley.

The bomb had been at a Territorial Army recruiting centre, and another soldier had been injured in the explosion. It was almost painful to watch, knowing that he could have stopped it, had he been listened to and the dreams understood. And then came the revelation that made him gasp . . .

'This is the second IRA outrage in seventy-two hours,' the newscaster continued, 'following on from the attack in Eltham, south London.'

Chris sat forward on the edge of his seat. Second attack? He hadn't watched the news for a few days, or seen a newspaper, so this was startling. As he listened, he discovered that a bomb had exploded outside an Army Education Centre in Eltham, injuring seven people. The bomb had been planted in a flowerbed . . .

Chris's mind reeled. Flowerbed? That made alarm bells and warning sirens scream in his mind. A bomb in a flowerbed, or – a bomb in a bed? Quickly he scrabbled around the camper, desperate to find the ring-binder that he used to keep his dream diary in when he filed the papers. He flipped back to 6 May and there it was: '[BOMB]', on top of a sketch that had a rectangle labelled 'bed', with lamps at each end. At the time he thought this meant that a bomb would be planted in sleeping quarters, but the lamps were like the display lanterns you get in ornamental gardens. Were there lamps around the flowerbeds at the Army Education Centre in Eltham?

In his low state, Chris felt more confused than ever. Why did the symbols have to be so ambivalent, so loaded with meaning? Why was it not possible for him to get simple, clear, direct messages? If the dreams came from God, as he believed that many of them did, then surely

He would want Chris to make use of the information and help people. If this were the case, then surely He would give the information to Chris in a simple way, that could be understood by anybody.

Depressed by his inability to prevent the death of Sergeant Chapman, Chris wondered if he were the one at fault. What if everything was being, as it were, transmitted correctly, and it was he – the receiver – who was at fault? As a trained engineer, Chris wondered if the dreams came like television and radio signals, and he was tuned into their signal. Perhaps it was possible that his aerial – the part of his brain that received the signals – was not quite correctly tuned?

The idea of a psychic as a human radio television receiver is one that has occurred to other people: the writer and researcher Colin Wilson once referred to Dutch psychic Gerald Croiset as a 'badly tuned TV set', and the late Brian Inglis posited the theory that we receive a narrow band of information signals in our brain, and that psychics are like televisions whose aerials have gone haywire, picking up signals that the rest of us cannot detect. This fits with Chris's big worry – that his haywire aerial wasn't picking up the signals clearly enough for him to relay the correct information.

What if it was his fault that Sergeant Chapman had died? What if it was his fault that the information was coming out confused? Chris spent the evening wallowing in guilt. He felt that he wasn't making full use of the gift that he had been given, felt depressed and useless.

But he is not the kind of man to feel that way for long. If nothing else, he has resilience, and a life full of setbacks has taught him to never give up, just to find a way around things. He was feeling a little better when he went to sleep at around ten in the evening. He produced several pages of dream writing, but the really important move had been made before he went to sleep: Chris had decided that he would work on cracking the dream code, and that he would take a more direct hand in making sure that his dreams were acted upon.

No matter who he had to cross.

CHAPTER EIGHT

In many ways, it was the first great test of his powers, and of his faith in them.

Thursday, 17 May, Chris parked his car about half a mile away from the RAF base at Stanmore. It hadn't changed much in the years since he had worked around these parts. He had been having the dreams for eight months, and had long since overcome his initial wariness to embrace them wholeheartedly. It was well over a month since he had started to dream about a bomb attack on Stanmore. He had reported all these dreams, just as he had reported his dreams about the Wembley bomb.

No-one had seemed to do anything about that. He wasn't prepared to let that situation arise again.

But was he doing the right thing by driving here? He decided that it couldn't do any harm, as he had already reiterated his warnings to Paul Aylott. The faxes had also gone to John Branscombe and Chris Watt. If, between them, they hadn't passed anything on to a higher authority he would be extremely surprised.

If nothing else, this was making him feel better: after the death of Sergeant Chapman two days earlier he had to do something to alleviate his conscience.

He walked from his car to the turning that led to the base entrance. It wasn't as long a distance as he remembered, and he stopped, his resolve wavering. The entrance appeared too soon for him to gather his courage. He had deliberately parked some distance away, so that he would have the walk in which to psyche himself up for the encounter that he knew would come. Now he stood on the corner for a few seconds, bracing himself.

For all his doubts, Chris knew that he would not be able to rest easily with himself until he had at least tried to tell someone in authority at the base about his dreams.

He gulped down a breath and walked up to the barrier to be greeted by two soldiers in combat uniform, machine guns slung over their shoulders. They watched him approach in a distant, non-committal way. They had no real interest in him. If anything, his approach seemed to irritate them.

'Can we help you?' one of them asked, with a bare veneer of politeness covering his boredom.

'I'm not sure,' Chris replied nervously. 'My name is Christopher Robinson. I'm a psychic, and I've had a dream telling me that your base is going to be bombed by the IRA.'

Whatever he had expected – probably hostility, if he thought about it – he was greeted with looks of blank incomprehension from the soldiers. They seemed young, only in their early twenties, and looked at him as though they thought he was either a madman or a practical joker. There was a silent pause, filled with embarrassment on both sides. Finally, one of them said, 'Is this a joke?'

'Do you think I'd joke about something like this?' Chris replied, trying to keep his voice level. He didn't want to sound like the lunatic or joker they expected. 'I tried to warn the people in Wembley about the bomb that killed Sergeant Chapman. I told policemen in Dunstable, Milton Keynes and at the Yard. But no-one listened. This time I've decided to come and tell you personally. That way someone might listen.'

The two sentries exchanged glances: Stanmore was only a few miles from Wembley, and the events of the day before had made them understandably nervous.

There had been an immediate stepping-up of already tight security, and neither of the young airmen felt in a position to take responsibility for the man at the main gate. If he was telling the truth, and another bomb was to be planted, then let the responsibility for dealing with Chris be taken by a superior officer.

Their attitude changed. No longer distant or bored, they were, if not friendly, then polite. One of them asked Chris to follow him into the look-out post just behind the main gates. The other sentry followed behind them. They kept Chris covered: it was a precautionary measure, in case he had been sent as the vanguard of an attack. To Chris it seemed vaguely ludicrous. They thought he would create trouble, but that was precisely what he wanted to prevent.

The look-out post was a squat concrete building, and when Chris entered there were three other people inside: two men in military police armbands, and a woman in RAF uniform. He couldn't tell her rank, but knew enough to recognise, from their armbands, that the military police were both sergeants. One of them searched Chris, while the other called through to the base commandant's office. They hardly uttered a word, communicating with each other in the barest of sentences. Obviously they wanted to give nothing away that Chris might be able to use in some way. Another security measure.

The search finished, and Chris straightened up. The MP conducting the search seemed almost disappointed that he had found nothing on Chris, and now spoke directly to him for the first time. His voice was low and harsh.

'You should now consider yourself under arrest. You will not be allowed to leave here until you have been interrogated further.'

It was a strange situation in which to find himself: he knew the names of none of the people in the room, and the rank of only two of them. The small building was now crowded with five people – one of the sentries had returned to his duty on the main gate, unwilling to leave it unmanned for long.

Normally, like anyone else, Chris would have been terrified at the prospect of being under arrest in a military base. But not this time. On the contrary, he was overjoyed. This is great, he thought: if they arrest me, they have to start filling in forms, and there will be a record of my actually having been here. Then there will be no way they can deny it.

If only the atmosphere hadn't been so cold. Chris had every faith in the story he had to tell – he knew it was the truth – but how would it sound to RAF officers hearing it in a room like this?

Although the MP who had searched him had seemed hostile, the others seemed almost apologetic about the whole thing. Chris was on his own, with no weapons and no place to conceal them. As he filled out the form registering Chris's arrival and arrest, the sentry who had remained said to him, 'I'm sorry about all this, but it's got to be done. We don't have any choice in the matter, it's all procedure.'

'That's all right by me,' Chris replied. The fact that he seemed almost happy about the turn of events seemed to confuse them. Chris continued, 'This isn't quite what I expected, but now that it's happened I'm quite pleased about it. You can't say now that I didn't try to warn you.'

Forms filled, superiors alerted, they sat in an embarrassed silence for more than ten minutes before another two men arrived. They didn't announce themselves, and from their uniforms he couldn't tell what rank they were, but from the way that the others smartly saluted he could only assume that they were fairly high-ranking.

Their attitude was markedly different from that of the airmen he had first encountered. They took him across a concrete yard to an ante-room in an outbuilding, where he was offered tea in the great British tradition. If this was an attempt to create a friendlier atmosphere, then it certainly worked, as Chris felt more comfortable in the company of these two, who almost fitted the 'dashing RAF officer' archetype. They were interested in what he had to say, and told him that they would tape-record the interview. Chris was more than happy with this: if nothing else, it would represent another record of his visit to Stanmore.

One of the officers – and neither of them, despite their friendliness, volunteered a name – offered Chris a biscuit and switched on the tape recorder. Chris felt at ease with them, and trusted them to believe that he was telling the truth as he saw it, regardless of their own personal opinions. Hopefully they would concur.

'Now that you're here,' began the other officer, who had remained seated, 'and you've been formally arrested, we're duty-bound to inform the civilian police force, and you can only leave here to be released into the custody of the Metropolitan Police Force. We've been in touch with the local station, and two officers will be down shortly to collect you. In the meantime, why don't you tell us what this is all about?'

It may well be that it was up to the local force to deal with Chris as they saw fit, but at least the RAF were giving him the chance to tell them what he had seen in his dreams.

The previous night's sleep had been fitful, but despite this Chris had managed to write three pages of dreams. Most of them related in some way to Stanmore, not surprisingly, since this must have been on his mind virtually all the time.

In the strangest part of the dream, Chris had been sitting in the back of a car that was speeding through London streets. The car was being driven by a dog, which meant that it had something to do with the IRA. Chris was convinced that this car was the one that would carry the IRA bombers across London. He didn't know the make of the car he was in, or the number of the licence plate: he did, however, know the area in which the car was travelling, and he could clearly see the number and make of the car in front.

Chris wanted to tell someone about this, but knew it would sound like crazy ramblings to the two officers sitting in front of him. Instead, he opened his dream diary at a relevant section, and began to explain what was in front of them.

The first section read:

Two cups the same, 1 dirty and burned, 1 clean and new
   Full of milk.
                     Large machine gun beautifully made
Fast warship [LAUNCH]   They are catching up
                           with us
Illuminate target   Are we lit up.   Sex case.

Then there were two sketches of wristwatches, only one of which had a strap. This was followed by:

Wrecked car bomb. Inside car.   Steering wheel.
   Very serious problem.   Car like Dick's.

To most people, including the RAF officers, this would appear as rubbish if just read from the page. So Chris attempted to explain to them the series of symbols he had been taught by his spirit guide, Robert. Some of the things, like the references to 'wrecked car bomb', were fairly obvious and straightforward; some, such as the reference to 'car like Dick's' were personal and needed only a little explanation. Other symbols, however, Chris was only just beginning to learn himself, and he could see that the RAF officers sitting across from him exchanged a few glances that varied between disbelieving and simply bemused. They became even more confused when he explained the significance of postcodes, and how he used the postcode computer program to locate where the bombs were likely to explode.

He explained to them that he was sure the attack would be on Stanmore: he was born in Bushey, Hertfordshire, and had lived round this area of London and the suburban outreaches all his life. From other dreams in the diary he was able to explain to them that references to Bushey and to Holland were occurring again and again. There were symbols and landscapes in his dreams that were unmistakable. He knew from news reports that the IRA used Holland as a base for its operations. He also knew, from information picked up from friends in the police, that there were investigations into the transportation of arms and explosives from IRA cells in Holland to Britain.

When he reached this part, Chris chose his words very carefully: he didn't want to get his friends into trouble, but he had to do all he could to persuade the officers that he was speaking the truth.

The atmosphere in the room was filled with a strange kind of tension. Like all psychics, Chris is sensitive to mood and atmosphere, and he could feel the pull between his own efforts to explain and the bemused and confused scepticism of the men he was trying to convince.

He moved on to his next piece of evidence. There are some government buildings, mostly Forces administration buildings, that might also have been IRA targets, but Chris believed that the base was more likely to be the target because it was split into two sections: Headquarters Fighter Command, as it used to be known, was on Bentley Priory, on the north side of Uxbridge Road;

the second section of the base was actually on the road itself. This meant that, unlike other buildings used by the government, security was hard to maintain because of the wide spread of land involved. Although security would be as tight as possible, it was virtually impossible to cover every inch of ground on the two widely spread sites for every minute of the day.

Going back to an earlier dream, Chris had seen the Queen riding on a horse. This worried him: it could refer to the Trooping of the Colour, which took place in June. But, at the same time as he was having this dream, and on the same pages of the dream diary, there were continual references to 'a house', 'a horse', 'having a', 'adjust hold'. The letters 'h' and 'a' cropped up continually. Early on, he had learnt that this repetition meant that a postcode was being given to him. There was no postcode that used the letters 'ah'. But there was one that used 'ha'.

The postcode for Stanmore he now knew to be HA3.

That very morning, as though to reinforce his resolve, Chris had stronger feelings than before when he awoke. He was sure RAF Stanmore was the target. He still had vivid recollections of his dreams from the night. This was fairly unusual, as the dreams usually became vague memories on waking. The dream diary was usually necessary as an aid to the memory, and was Chris's only reference to some of the dreams. Also, he was sure that he had heard Robert's voice as he awoke, telling him to go and warn the base. Now.

So it had been an easy decision for him to make. But, he told his interviewers, whom should he approach? He had no real working knowledge of the rank structures and hierarchy in the RAF. He knew he would have to get advice. So he had phoned Paul Aylott, and told him that he was going to Stanmore himself, unless Paul could reassure him otherwise.

'Look, don't go,' Aylott had said. 'I'll try and get in

touch with someone. It'll be better if it goes through official channels. You know what it's like with this sort of thing by now – they'll think you're some kind of nutter if you just turn up out of the blue.'

Chris put down the phone knowing that Paul was always as good as his word. Yet there had still been a feeling that nagged at him, telling him he should do something himself. It was as if Robert had entered Chris's waking life and wouldn't rest until Chris actually took action.

Without even thinking about it, he had got into his car and driven to Stanmore, parking about half a mile from the main gate. He had with him his passport as proof of identity. He drove past the side of the base in Uxbridge Road, then up to the main entrance in Common Road. Unsure how to go about his task, he stalled for time by turning left along Clamp Hill and then left again back into Uxbridge Road, passing the entrance to the South Base again. He couldn't make up his mind which part of the base to try first.

He could see that the officers in front of him were more at home with the familiar descriptions of the roads around the base. It seemed silly, really, but he had taken pains to tell them this detail simply because it had reassured them. He knew intuitively that a return to – as they saw it – common sense would make things easier for them to assimilate.

Then he told them that as he drove past a second time, a voice in his head told him to go back to the second entrance, as that was where the majority of the personnel worked. Yes, he thought, that would be a good idea: if I stop here, then I'll only be taken over there anyway. So Chris had parked in Bushey Heath High Street, and walked back to the base entrance.

Seeing that he was losing the officers again, Chris decided to pull out all the stops: he told them how he had felt when he had heard of Sergeant Chapman's death the day before, and how he had thought about this as he walked up to the base. He knew that if he had acted as decisively on that dream, there was a chance that the Sergeant might have been saved. That had given him the determination to see this through, no matter what they thought of him. He just wanted them to listen.

And now he was sitting in this office with two senior officers listening intently to what he had to say, recording it all on tape. He continued his story, telling them that as far as he was concerned they were about to be attacked by the IRA.

One of them asked again what 'car like Dick's' meant.

'Dick is a friend of mine,' Chris replied. 'He's got this really knackered four-door saloon, which is dark green. In my dream I was in a car. I don't know what this car was, but the one in front was the same shade of green – but I can't be sure if it was the same make. I think it was a Peugeot, but that's not like Dick's. When I was sitting in the car I could see two road signs. One was for Wood Lane, and the other for Green Lane.'

'Aren't there two roads around here called that?' asked one of the officers.

Chris shook his head. 'No, that's not it. There are a couple of roads called that, but you couldn't see them from the same point, as I could in the dream. Anyway, they didn't look like these roads. They were too built up, too much like city roads. No, those names have got some other significance. Find that car, and you've nabbed some terrorists – maybe even stopped the attack.'

In all, Chris spent about three hours at the base, going through his dream book with the RAF men and pointing out the relevant entries, discussing what he felt was going to happen at the base. He'd taken the whole of his diary with him as proof of the dreams. But it didn't really prove anything: a determined hoaxer would simply have written out a whole book of 'dreams' before leaving home. It did seem to convince them, however, that this was something more than a casual joke, and Chris felt that there had been a change in attitude when he told them about the cars and the two road names. He couldn't pick up what it was, just that they suddenly seemed more receptive.

At the end of three hours Chris was released into the custody of two uniformed constables from Wealdstone police station. They didn't go directly to the station: first, they went back to Chris's car. The constables asked for the keys, and as he had nothing to hide Chris handed them over gladly, and waited patiently while they searched his car, looking for bomb-making equipment. He had expected something like this, but why they thought he would go to the base and take the equipment with him if he was a genuine bomber was something he still can't work out.

Of course, they found nothing. To Chris's amusement, they seemed disappointed by this and took Chris to Wealdstone station, where he was put into an interview room to await the arrival of a Detective Inspector who would question him.

The room was small and cramped, with no natural lighting, only a harsh neon strip. Chris sat in silence after a few friendly attempts to engage in conversation the uniformed constable who stood in the corner. It was a long wait, and not particularly comfortable.

Eventually a plainclothes policeman entered the room. He wouldn't give Chris his name when asked, and Chris found his manner to be bordering on hostile. This immediately put Chris on his guard: even now, after several years, he still can't understand why the man wouldn't give his name. It was obvious from the way he was treated that he was a Detective Inspector – the one Chris had been waiting to see. It was equally obvious, right from the beginning, that he thought Chris was the perpetrator of a hoax in very dubious taste. The first thing he did was tell Chris that he had found his name on the police national computer. Chris Robinson was down as a bank robber. This was totally untrue.

'I think you're wasting my time, son,' the DI said, leaning across the table. 'I'm going to nick you for something if it takes me all day. I don't like you at all.'

The feeling was mutual.

It was fortunate for Chris that the DI's partner, Detective Sergeant Holmes, was the opposite. He was quiet and understanding, and listened to what Chris had to say while the superior officer just snorted. He even laughed at Chris's weak and nervous joke about the DI's name being 'Watson'. Perhaps it was just part of their routine – the 'good cop/bad cop' routine you see on every police television show. Chris couldn't look at it this way at the time, and was glad when the DI told him he was going off to the base to listen to the taped interview that had been recorded earlier.

Chris was left in the hands of Holmes, who questioned him while the other officer was absent, with the uniformed constable still impassive in the corner. They went over Chris's story time and time again, with Holmes looking for discrepancies that he just could not find. Chris showed him the relevant parts of the dream book.

'But how do you know you're writing it down correctly if you can't remember the dreams that well when you wake up?' he asked at one point.

'I write it when I'm asleep.' Holmes looked at him in disbelief, so Chris tried to explain. 'It's called automatic writing. I have the book and a pen by the bed, and while I'm dreaming the subconscious guides my hand. That's why it's in bits and pieces, and not proper sentences.'

Chris was questioned by Holmes for over three hours – as long as it took the DI to travel to the base, listen to the tapes, and get back. He stormed into the room, and threw a fax message at Chris.

'Read that,' he snapped. But as Chris tried to turn the paper on the desk so that he could read it properly, the DI snatched it back. 'I don't know who the hell you are, son, but I've been ordered to release you,' the DI snapped, screwing the message into a ball in his hand. 'And the message comes from God.'

Chris had just about managed to read the signature on the fax, and knew that the DI was referring to Commander George Churchill-Coleman, then head of the Anti-Terrorist Squad.

Had Paul Aylott really passed on his message? Was someone actually taking notice after all?

'Someone somewhere likes you,' snarled the DI. 'But just because they do doesn't mean that I have to. Go on, get out.'

Summarily dismissed, Chris was driven back to Bushey Heath High Street by two uniformed constables. They told him that despite the DI's hostility, everyone else at the station hoped there was something in Chris's story and that it would help avert a disaster. Word had come back from the RAF base – probably via the DI's driver – that the RAF officers had contacted Paul Aylott, as Chris had suggested. And the description of the green four-door saloon in Chris's dream had been sent out: police would be on the look-out for it. The constables wished Chris good luck as they dropped him at his car.

On his way home he couldn't help but think about the attitude of the DI. Chris was trying to warn people about a bomb threat, and all this policeman had wanted to do was arrest him on a trumped-up charge because he didn't like him. The whole situation seemed ridiculous.

When he got home Chris phoned Paul Aylott and told him about being arrested. Aylott, of course, knew all about it because the RAF and the Anti-Terrorist Squad had been on to him all day.

He sighed, 'I told you not to go. To leave it all to me. But you had to insist, didn't you. Feel happier now?'

Chris had to reply that he did. Now he officially existed, and was on record.

The attack on Stanmore took place on 21 June, just over a month later. During a routine check a bomb was found and detonated next to a disused photographic storehouse. It had been there only for a few minutes, as regular checks were being made. The base was evacuated before the detonation.

What happened to the car in Chris's dream provides an amusing side-light on the occasional misinterpretation of dreams – though it was not amusing for the person involved.

Shortly after Chris's visit to Stanmore (the following Monday), a green car was stopped in Wood Green, north London, after a cross-town chase. The occupant had been under surveillance and was suspected of being part of an IRA bomb squad. He was Kevin O'Donnell, who convinced an Old Bailey jury that he knew nothing of the Semtex in the back of his car. He was acquitted, and was later killed in a shoot-out in Belfast. This takes care of the references to Wood Lane and Green Lane and Chris's green four-door saloon.

The car was stopped at a roundabout, and the car in front – a red four-door Peugeot – sped away. Someone had obviously taken note of Chris's dream, as the licence plate tallied with some numbers Chris had provided. The car was traced to a pub car park in west London and the owner taken in for questioning.

Unfortunately, he was a doctor on holiday from Ireland. While someone high up had taken note of Chris's dream, they had forgotten that he was in the IRA car and had only described the car in front . . . something that the spirits had obviously meant to be taken as a reference point, but not an implication that the unfortunate doctor was involved.

Despite this misunderstanding, the startling clarity of Chris's information could not be denied.

CHAPTER NINE

Another police acquaintance of Chris, who had been interested in his dreams since the beginning but can, for security reasons, only be named as Andy, had remained low-key throughout the whole series of events surrounding Stanmore. His interest was re-awakened by Chris's visit to the RAF base. So it came as little surprise to Chris when, on the following Saturday, he answered a knock at his door only to find Andy standing there.

'Hello. I hear you've been a bit of a naughty lad,' said Andy with a smile.

The two men settled in Chris's mobile home and talked generally about things: Chris ran over the events at RAF Stanmore a few days before, and Andy told him that Paul Aylott had contacted him as soon as he had been called. 'You were lucky we were both in our offices – otherwise other people might not have heard about it . . . Know what I mean?'

He didn't have to say any more: without Andy, George Churchill-Coleman might not have known.

Then Andy changed the subject. 'Listen, that bloke who's studying you –'

'What, Keith Hearne?'

'Yeah, him. Does he reckon you could ask it questions, or what? You know, questions that are, shall we say, beyond the grave?'

'What do you mean, ask *it* questions?' Chris replied, bemused by the reference to part of him as 'it'.

'Well, could you ask it something by writing it down, and then get an answer?'

Chris pondered this for some moments. 'I don't know. I've never tried it, but I don't see why not. After all, I talk to people in my dreams, and they talk back.'

'Good. Because I've got something I'd like you to try.'

Andy outlined his plan. There were sections of the police and security services that were maintaining a discreet interest in Chris. Although unwilling to come out and admit that the powers of the unknown could be more efficient than conventional intelligence-gathering, they would admit – albeit grudgingly – that Chris got results. There was a school of thought within these sections that believed Chris to be an IRA man playing 'double' – playing for both sides. This was patently absurd: not only was Chris totally opposed to terrorism, but he wasn't getting any payment for his information.

Andy agreed with Chris that the idea was ludicrous: that was why he had come up with the idea of the tests.

'Let's be honest, it's a two-fold thing, right? First, if I can ask you a question and you get a positive answer, that proves that something weird is happening and you're not Gerry Adam's right-hand man. Second, if it can be asked questions, then it'll be good for us – you can tell us something we want to know rather than what we don't.'

This seemed reasonable enough. Chris contacted Keith Hearne, who believed that it would be a valid and worthwhile experiment. He warned Chris not to expect outstanding results, as the nature of dream precognition was always erratic. Chris agreed, but knew deep down that he was on the verge of discovering another facet of his powers: one that he would be able to use in order to channel his dreams in the future.

★   ★   ★

The tests would take place over three nights: 23/24/25 May. A Thursday, Friday and Saturday night. The questions were prepared by Andy, and were faxed to Chris during the day preceding the night-test. This way he would have no opportunity to tap into police contacts for any possible answers.

The first question was simple: who is Peter Darling?

It is impossible to use the man's real name as he is still at liberty, but suffice to say that he was someone the police were extremely interested in at the time. Chris had never heard of him before.

In his dream diary, Chris wrote:

W-Scrubs [43] should be
    [114]
      is it [VW] [Lies flat]   Ring xxx crossed.

None of this was a clear answer, but when presented to the police it made a lot of sense: 'W-Scrubs' mean Wormwood Scrubs, a prison in west London; '43' refers to Rule 43, which sections off prisoners convicted of child sex offences from other prisoners ... for their own safety. Chris had worked out that '[VW]' and '[Lies flat]' were connected by a line, and meant somewhere like Germany, only flatter: to him this meant Holland, as did the triple X phrase – from his years in the video trade Chris associated XXX with the certificates on pornographic films that had been imported from Holland.

Chris felt that he had failed, as there was no direct answer to his question. Andy, however, was delighted by the result. Peter Darling was an alleged child sex offender whom the police wanted behind bars, but he had fled the country. They had no idea where he was, but believed him to be in Holland.

The first test was therefore a success, if a qualified one. For instance, could Chris have known about Darling by

ESP (extra-sensory perception), picking things up from Andy? Perhaps. Certainly Andy now had some kind of proof. What would the next test show?

The next night there was more than one question. Andy wanted to know about Oscar Roberts and Andrew Arnold. Who were they, and where were they? He also wanted to know 'Is 11 June correct?' Chris had no idea what this question meant, and that was exactly how Andy wanted it to be.

Once again I have changed the names of the men Chris was asked about.

Chris wrote 'in side', connected by a line to '[out]'. He already had a feeling that the word out, when in a box, meant dead. So he said to Andy the next day, 'These two blokes – one of them is in prison, and he killed the other one.'

Andy whistled. 'How the hell did you know that?' he asked.

So Chris explained the code, then said, 'Look at this bit here – "sweetheart", "walked away", then "out" with the box round it again. I think that means that they had a row over a woman, and one of them got killed in the fight. I'll tell you something else as well – I think they're black.'

'How the hell do you work that out?'

'Look at this bit – "chocolate fingers in the cupboard". And I've underlined the chocolate. I saw biscuits, but that was just a symbol. At least one of them is black – and as the biscuits were in the cupboard, I think it's the one in prison.'

'They're both black, actually,' Andy replied shortly, not knowing what to make of Chris's accuracy. Things were going better than he had imagined – so well that it was beginning to frighten him. The only black spot on the tests so far was that Chris had got nothing on the question regarding 11 June. As Andy didn't enlighten him, Chris is still in the dark about that.

There were other messages coming through, jumbled up with all this – messages that were a warning to Chris. 'Have been tracked or bugged – listened 2', 'Did you hear that – everytime I talk.' Chris didn't elaborate on these to Andy, but had a nasty feeling that surveillance had started up again, perhaps to coincide with these tests.

Maybe Andy wasn't behind the tests: maybe he was the front man for another organisation, who were more interested in Chris than they wanted to let on. Chris had heard of the KGB developing psychics, trying to bring them on to the point where they could be used as intelligence weapons. He had also read books by other psychics, such as Uri Geller, in which they talked of their brushes with the CIA. It seemed like rampant paranoia and conspiracy theorising, but Andy had mentioned 'others' being interested in Chris. What if it was MI5 and 6, testing his capabilities? Part of Chris wanted to shy away from all of that – perhaps fake a few failures, so that the pressure would be off. The problem was, would the spirits let him?

With this preying on his mind, Chris made sure that he told no-one except his wife that he was going to New York that Sunday with Paul, his son from his first marriage.

He approached Saturday night's test in an unsettled state of mind. The questions he asked were: please tell me something I could not know about Andy; and where is the red French car like the one shown to me in the dream? The latter referred to the Peugeot that Chris had described after his dream concerning Stanmore.

Nothing much happened concerning the car, possibly because Chris's mind was preoccupied with what would happen when he tried to go to New York. He did, however, draw a detailed map of an office layout, with exact positions for a personal computer terminal, a fax machine and printer, and telephones. Beside it were the words 'Was he murdered? PNC check. Did Robinson know him? Fuck me, look where it was.'

By themselves they made no sense, but when Chris faxed them through the next day, Andy rang him immediately.

'How did you know what my office looked like?' he asked. 'And how did you know I said that?'

'What?' replied Chris, confused. So Andy explained: while he was going over Chris's fax of the night before, he had run a computer check on one of the men mentioned, and had come up with some additional information concerning the case. He had spoken those very words to another officer, and the occasion was etched on his memory by seeing them appear again on the fax sheet he held in his hand.

'You're too dangerous to know,' Andy told him. 'I don't know if I should have anything much to do with you.'

From that moment on Andy handed much of his contact with Chris over to another officer. The two men, who had been friends, have seen nothing of each other from that day on.

Paul, Chris's son from his first marriage, was eighteen, and he and a friend were going to New York on sponsored air tickets as part of a radio station fund-raising scheme, called a 'gaol-break'. The team who got furthest from Luton were the winners, and their sponsor money would be topped up by the station. Chris wanted a break, and was also a little nervous of his son being in New York, so he decided to go as well.

There was just one problem: Chris Watt had already told him that he didn't want Chris leaving the country. However, he was determined to go without having to get permission.

This would give him the perfect opportunity to see if his phone was tapped, as his dreams had seemed to warn him. He would also see if his movements were being followed.

For the few days preceding the flight, he was careful not to mention it over the phone, or even in the caravan, as he was certain that if the phone was bugged, then the rest of the caravan was sure to be. He did manage to tell his wife, when they were in the open, that he would phone her from the airport just before the flight took off. If nothing happened after this, then they could assume that the place was safe.

On Sunday Chris left the caravan as he would on any normal trip. Except that this time he made for Gatwick, and fifteen minutes before boarding he phoned his wife and told her that he was standing in the departure lounge, and he would see her when he got back.

Five minutes later the phone rang in the caravan. When his wife picked up the phone, a voice said, 'Has Mr Robinson left the country?' When she replied in the affirmative, the caller hung up in silence.

When Chris returned, he was greeted at the airport by two policemen, who warned him never again to leave the country without telling them.

While he was in New York Chris hoped that he would be able to find some clues as to the identity of a serial killer who had so far killed more than a dozen cab drivers. Trevor Kempson, Chris's friend on the *News of the World*, had a contact at a New York paper and so had arranged a few introductions for Chris, who was hoping that he might get a positive result and be able to claim a slice of the offered reward money. This would enable him to make other trips, and would finance experiments to try and validate his powers.

It wasn't successful: the dream writing included the phrases 'bungalow [overlooking the sea]' and '[dog] in back of the car'. The latter was pretty obvious: the dog was a killer – not IRA in this case, as it was in a box –

sitting in the back of the cab. All the drivers so far killed had been actually shot in their cabs. The bungalow that overlooked the sea meant Brighton. This was not so obvious, but stems from an association of ideas, as Chris has friends who live in Brighton, in a street called Wilson Avenue, in a bungalow that overlooks the sea. Therefore the killings were somehow connected with a place called Brighton.

Unfortunately there are many streets in the New York City area that have Brighton in their name, and there is also Brighton Beach in Brooklyn. If something was coming through, then it just wasn't clear enough. Looking back, this could be because it was something that had no real connection with Chris: even such seemingly unconnected events as the Philippine Airlines crash had some kind of link – Chris's wife is a Filipino, and he had been to the islands a couple of times and was in the process of planning a new trip there. The rail crash at Chorleywood also had a link, no matter how tenuous – it was an area he frequently drove through, many times crossing the bridge near the accident site.

But a serial killer in New York? Even if the spirits were trying to tell him something, there was too little in his own life for him to make strong enough connections.

On the other hand, there were dreams that related to things closer to home: on the second page of dreams, the '[dog] in back of car' made another appearance, this time linked to '[station] [leaving] [train]'.

When he read this back the next morning Chris felt a chill run through him. He could remember the dream clearly. Three soldiers, returning from leave, had been standing on a railway station platform when they had been shot down.

This haunted Chris for the whole day, as he moved on from New York to Niagara Falls. Once again he asked for information about the serial killer, writing down a question, as he now knew he could. There were some interesting results, if nothing conclusive. Beside a map showing an intersection of two streets, with five houses drawn down one side, the middle one asterisked, he wrote, 'New houses. Very cheap when built. Now very expensive. In New York.'

Underneath came: 'A person shown as [steve pearce] in the dream. Delivery to [Scotland] if we have enough. Put them in my garage until it is time to go. Do we have a driver? Yes.' On another page followed: '[chase] Manhattan [card]' and 'San Francisco. First visit. Killer lives in New York? Yes.'

The only thing he could really glean from this was that the killer lived in a house on an intersection like the one drawn, somewhere in New York. For some reason, he felt sure that it was Brighton Beach, but couldn't really explain why. He also felt sure that Steve Pearce – a friend – had appeared in the dream because he bore a resemblance to the killer.

There was something in it, but exactly what remained locked away, partly because there were urgent intrusions regarding the soldiers he had seen shot the previous night.

> Stop [train]. Gold bell.
> [campers 3]   1   2
>   3

This was followed by a diagram of a rail track switching-point on a single track. The two directions at the point where the track branched in two were both arrowed, and 'TRAIN TRACK. One comes down before the other can go up' was written beside it.

Analysing it, Chris felt sure that the single track and 'stop [train]' phrases were signs for a postcode: ST. '[Campers 3]' referred to three holidaymakers, or the three soldiers returning from leave. 'Gold bell' was another cipher – a simple one meaning G.B., as in

Great Britain. It was as if the spirits were re-directing his thoughts to home.

He left Niagara for Toronto, not really noticing what was happening around him. Instead he was focusing upon dreams that seemed to be warning of an attack on soldiers thousands of miles away.

Chris was with Simon Templar, the Saint. The popular hero had been stabbed, and was bleeding heavily after an attack from an umbrella. He told Chris that the tip of the umbrella had been poisoned, and that Chris must help him to get home.

Templar and Roger Moore, the actor who played him most successfully, were interchangeable, as Templar led Chris through the streets of north-west London until they got to the railway station at Stanmore. It was snowing heavily, and progress was slow. When they reached the station, Templar collapsed and died . . .

This was the point at which Chris woke. He had a feeling of foreboding: the message was so terrible and so clear. All he had to do was crack the code. He looked at what he had written while asleep. It read:

> The Saint – bleeding.
> Snowing – Died – at [Stanmore] station.
> Stabbed in the leg with a poison umbrella – a dart.
>   You follow him. I will follow her
> on [road to London]. Happens in the snow down
> a slope on a sledge on the [W]ay to [S]chool.

It was a comparatively short dream message, but there seemed to be little extraneous matter in it: it was heavily focused, and not as wide-ranging as other dreams Chris had.

As Toronto awoke and began to go about its regular business, Chris sat in his hotel room, hunched over the page, his thoughts once again thousands of miles away. He had dreamt about the Saint before, and knew it

was connected to Stanmore. The car number plate
was important. Previously he had figured that ST1 was
Stanmore. Now, with the new postcode map, he knew
that Stanmore was HA3. But there was an ST postcode –
Stoke, in Staffordshire. The way that the letters W and S
were boxed also suggested that they should be separated.
When Chris looked them up, he discovered that WS was
the postcode for Lichfield, also in Staffordshire.

It seemed that the dream was working on two levels
at once, warning still about Stanmore, but also alerting
him to something that would happen in Stoke: with the
recurrence of a railway station and someone dying there,
he was sure that this related to his dream of the three
dead soldiers.

But why was he dreaming of Stanmore station? Was
this just more confusion? Stanmore was in a box on
the page, so what if it just meant 'S' for station, as
in Stoke?

Chris sat back and looked out of the window at
the early morning sun, glowing over the bustling city.
There was a lot of information in the dream, and it
was obviously important; but May had been one hell
of a month, and he was beginning to feel the strain.
Perhaps he was seeing things that weren't there? Or
perhaps the dreams were becoming confused because
he was so tired?

No matter. He was on his way home today. Perhaps
the dream would start to become clearer when he was
back among familiar surroundings.

He was greeted at the airport by the police, angry with
him for leaving the country: but he found it hard to take
what they had to say seriously. He had hardly slept on
the plane and just wanted to get back home. It was a long
drive from Gatwick to the mobile homes park, longer
because of his fatigue. So it was with no little sense of
relief that Chris reached home in the early afternoon of

31 May. He went straight to bed, exhausted. He slept for several hours, and during that time recorded a mass of dream images.

[Canada] Murder Killer
Strikes 2 times   [New York]
Try to contact [Police] [log all thoughts]
 [Train] your mind. Follow all clues. They will come to you [police].
 Look at [golf balls] again. with holes in. drive [home] look and see.
 2 stations 1 old 1 new. 58[3]? [Stanmore] [Saint] blood soon? [snow on the ground]

He awoke in the early evening and read his writing back. Some of it seemed to be telling him that the serial killer he had little success with in New York would soon be striking again. Then there was some reassurance that the police would be taking notice of the information he gave them. After his recent problems with Wembley and Stanmore, this was an assurance he needed. Then the dream writing returned to its by now repetitious and familiar themes: trouble at Stanmore, and something to do with the shootings he had seen. Did '2 stations 1 old 1 new' mean that there would be two separate attacks? Or was that to tell him a specific postcode, like ST1 or ST2? Reference to his computer program showed those particular codes actually to be Lichfield, on the edge of Stoke, and not the town itself, as he had thought. The 'WS' in a previous dream had been a clue to this – there is an area that still carries a Stoke postcode, even though it overlaps with Lichfield.

Was this what it all meant? Chris was tired and confused, and wanted right now to forget about dreams. His sleep had been fitful, and the jetlag was still with him. He was about to go back to bed when something hit him, and hit hard: snow. He turned to the dream diary, and flicked backwards. On 28 May he had helped a dying Saint through snow, and in this recent dream there had been snow on the ground. The appearance of snow must mean urgency and great danger. Chris had to struggle through it in one dream, and it had sealed off the point of danger – the station where the dying Saint lay – in this last dream. Looking back to personal associations, Chris hated snow because it made his job difficult in winter, when he had to scrabble about on people's roofs, trying to repair television aerials.

He realised that the snow could only mean one thing: the shootings were imminent.

For the first time since he had the dream of the air crash Chris was afraid to go back to sleep. Just a few minutes before he had felt that he couldn't be bothered with the dreams, and that they were too jumbled to make sense. Now he felt a great obligation to get things clear in his mind. If the danger was imminent, perhaps he could help, perhaps he could save these soldiers from dying.

He had to understand whatever he dreamt that night.

Bomb warning. Now very soon.
Spit out blood. [houses] outside them. Train. Points. One on same track. Other runs out of track.
[AMBULANCE]   [INJURY]
Run away after [HA] still HA.
Funeral. Parked on drive at the place shown before. You can't rely on any other. The whole chain must be in our control. We will be caught otherwise.
Escape along the [track]. Trains each direction. Non stop. [Skoda car on track] between trains.

When he woke on 1 June Chris felt sick. Stanmore was still at risk, and the shooting at the railway station was imminent. Golf balls meant Great Britain – telling Chris to concentrate on these incidents. The blood had been awful: he had to do something about it.

He did all that he could: at 8.08 a.m. Chris began to fax the dream pages through to Superintendent Branscombe's office. But it was gone half-past nine when the last sheet went through, as the fax receiver at the police station jammed.

Chris could only hope that his dreams would filter through the police and intelligence systems in time to do some kind of good . . .

On the evening of 1 June 1990 three rookie soldiers stood on Platform Two at Lichfield City Station, in Staffordshire. All three were on leave from Whittington Barracks, which was situated near the station. They were on their way home to South Wales and intended to travel together. They were laughing and joking on the platform, waiting for their train, when two balaclava-clad gunmen walked up to them. They must have studied the barracks for some time, as all three soldiers were dressed in civilian clothes.

Before the three had a chance to notice, the gunmen drew handguns and pumped six shots into the soldiers from point-blank range.

The platform was busy with commuters on their way home from work, and it became a screaming mass of frightened humanity as the soldiers hit the ground. Men and women tried to take cover as the noise of the shots rang around the station. One brave railway worker advanced on the gunmen, but wisely backed off when they turned their guns on him: better to be alive and describe them to the police than be dead.

The gunmen turned and ran, sprinting across the tracks and into cover among the sidings.

The railway worker turned his attention on the soldiers. Two of them – Privates Robert Parkin and

Neil Evans – were still alive. One of them had wounds in the neck and shoulder, and had lost a lot of blood. The other was wounded in the right arm, and had been lucky.

The third soldier had been unlucky. Private William Davies had been hit several times in the head. He was already dead.

Chris had been on edge all day. When he woke up that morning his sickness had been accompanied by a headache and flashing lights. It had all the hallmarks of a migraine attack – except that Chris had never had a migraine in his life.

After finally faxing the last page through to the police, Chris went about his work, mostly for regular customers who were aware of his dreams, and he told all of them that there was going to be an IRA attack on three soldiers near Stoke.

At half-past five Chris was sitting at home, waiting for the early evening news with a mixture of anticipation and dread. So when a knock came on the door he expected it to be the police, as they had turned up after the Leicester incident. He was relieved to find that it was Keith, his brother.

'Here, you're a bit edgy, ain't you?' his brother said as he came in. Chris told him about the dreams, and how he was convinced there would be an attack. 'Leave it out,' Keith replied, laughing. 'You're mad or something. Look, old son, the only spirits you or me are ever going to see come out of bottles, so I should forget all about that old crap.'

'No, you say what you like, but I know it's going to happen,' Chris said.

'Oh yeah?' Keith decided that he would stick around for a while, just to see what would happen. He had a notion that he would be able to get hours of fun out of Chris if, as he thought, nothing happened . . .

News of the shootings was made available to the press at 6.15 p.m. and was broadcast on the BBC bulletin.

Both men sat and watched in silence. Chris really didn't know how to feel: on the one hand, he felt justified for continuing, and for putting up with the sleepless nights and having fun made of him; on the other hand, he felt incredibly depressed. Once again he had foretold an incident, yet hadn't been able to prevent a death. Why wasn't he given a clearer picture of what was going to happen? Were the spirits playing games with him? He recalled something David Bolster had told him months before, about the possibility of evil spirits using his dreams. Were they intruding, distorting the information? There was so much to learn: he was more aware than ever that he was sailing into uncharted waters.

Keith stayed with Chris while he checked the postcode on his computer program. The station lay in WS13. So ST1 had been misleading . . . all the time it was drawing him out towards Lichfield, but never quite getting him there: the actual postcode letters WS had turned up only once, in the phrase '[W]ay to [S]chool'. Why couldn't the dream have been more direct? One thing for sure: Chris had been right about the gunmen's escape along the track – there had been plenty of references to going up a track, away from a station.

The more Chris looked at it with hindsight, the more it seemed that the fault lay with him rather than with the dreams: it was his interpretation that was at fault.

It was something he would have to work at: and he would have to be patient. It could only be a process of trial and error.

June started with Chris asking the spirits to tell him the names of the gunmen who had perpetrated the Lichfield outrage. He was also working on ways of interpreting the dreams. Looking back retrospectively, he realised that there were references in the dreams to the way he had walked to school – W(ay to) S(chool) – when he was thirteen years old: it was a particular route that he never used again. So that meant WS13 – the postcode for Lichfield Station. He now began to reason that the postcodes themselves would appear in symbolic form. Again he asked himself why the spirits would present information in this way: but there is no answer, even all these years later. Chris just has to try and make the best of what is given to him.

Certainly the spirits were not going to help him any more with the names of the IRA gunmen. he had a dream about animals being let loose from a cage, and masked men swinging down from branches to free them. Perhaps this had something to do with a symbolic representation of their names; perhaps not. There were Animal Liberation Front raids on laboratories within a week of this dream, which would certainly seem to relate to their activities, but Chris was too preoccupied really to notice; once again there were repeated warnings about Stanmore, with the Saint and Gordon Avenue uppermost.

On 2 June there was the following entry in his dream diary:

Submarine – nuclear
　　　cutting through underwater nets.
Rescue　　*Radiation sickness*
　　　　　Mustard gas
IRAQ ATTACK　　　[fly by remote]　　　[USAF]

In his dream Chris had been in the middle of the desert, surrounded by US Air Force fighters as they bombed and attacked a group of Iraqi soldiers. There were chemical weapons in use, and many of the injuries he saw looked like radiation burns. When he woke, he was sure that there was going to be a major conflict in the desert, and that the Iraqis would be involved. It wasn't the first time he'd had this sort of warning – but previously he thought it referred to the long-running skirmish between Iran and Iraq. This time, because of the USAF presence, he felt sure that it would be something bigger than that – but exactly what was still a mystery.

It would remain that way for a while, as Chris was about to be sidetracked by events closer to home.

At the beginning of June he was approached by a journalist called Liz Phillips, who worked for the *Daily Star*. She wanted to write a story about a psychic, and had been given Chris's name by Stuart Winter, who worked on the news desk. Chris and Stuart had known each other for some time, as Chris was familiar with many journalists through his escapades with Trevor Kempson.

Phillips made a bargain with Chris: 'If you can predict three things that happen within a week – three big news stories – then I'll write about you.' Her tone of voice betrayed her scepticism.

'You're on,' replied Chris.

'There is one thing,' she continued. 'The police aren't too keen on this. They told me that what you're doing is remarkable, but they only have six months worth of dreams to go on – there's not enough evidence there to really attack any sceptics that come along. So we've got to keep the story fairly low-key.'

Chris wasn't too surprised about this, as by now Chris Watt had him reporting to Kilburn police station almost every day, and phoning in five times a day at pre-set times. This was partly an overt form of surveillance – there were still elements in the police who felt Chris must be in some way allied with the IRA – and partly a way of making sure there was no repeat of the Canadian escapade. The police wanted to know exactly where Chris was at any given time.

On the night of 3 June the first story came to him. A dog was among flowerbeds, planting a bomb outside a party somewhere in London. Robert, the soldier, was in attendance, telling Chris what would happen. Chris drew a map of a square with a building in it, steps leading up to the building, and a tube station at the corner. The name on the building was obscured: the last word was 'Company', but the first two were unreadable.

Saturday, 9 June: the IRA bombed the Honourable Artillery Company's London headquarters. At 11 p.m. a blast rocked the building from a bomb planted in a flowerbed outside, injuring fifteen people. An engagement party was being held inside at the time. That very afternoon Chris was in Kilburn station, explaining that the bomb would go off at around eleven, in either E1 or E18 . . . The Honourable Artillery Company is located on the edge of the City, where the district becomes postcode E1.

Chris was still puzzled as to why the Honourable Artillery Company had been unreadable in his first dream, but also excited that information about the attack had built up over the week. The repetitions were beginning to form cycles, and this was a new development.

First story complete.

During the week Chris began to get a lot of postcodes coming through to him, most relating to the Salisbury Plain area. There were also landscapes covered in snow. Chris was convinced that there would be a bomb placed under a vehicle on Salisbury Plain. There were numerous references in the dreams to 'sexy picture' and 'swimming pool'. Although these images were otherwise unconnected, they did represent a preponderance of phrases using the letters 'SP', the postcode for Salisbury Plain. He was also sure that there would be a bomb somewhere in Bristol, as he saw a repetition of '[bus] stop' in the dream. The initials, BS, are the postcode prefix for Bristol.

On Sunday, 10 June, a bomb exploded under a car in Bristol belonging to a scientist involved in vivisection experiments. The car was stationary and empty at the time, but a 13-month-old baby was injured when shrapnel from the bomb penetrated his buggy and lodged in his spine. The child's father, Jim Cupper, had no connection with the car and was simply unfortunate enough to be walking past it when the bomb went off. Animal Liberationists claimed responsibility, and the story made front-page headlines.

This was the week's second story, and it gave Chris a valuable insight into dream imagery: for the first time a bomb warning had been given that featured no dogs. This led Chris to the conclusion that dogs definitely equalled IRA terrorists, and no others. Animal Liberationists were given their own dream symbols: pigs, or bacon.

The third story was again connected with Animal Liberationists: this time it was the Salisbury Plain bomb. A Suzuki jeep driven by Margaret Baskerville, who worked at the Porton Down chemical research establishment on Salisbury Plain, was destroyed by a firebomb triggered by a Mercury tilt device. Fire swept through the vehicle, but the 49-year-old surgeon, who experimented on guinea pigs and mice, escaped with only minor injuries. The Animal Liberation Front expressed regret that she wasn't killed.

Although this happened second in chronology, on 8 June it was the third event to come to Chris in dream sequence, underlining once again the fact that – once out of the physical realm – time is no longer linear.

While all this was going on, other premonitions were still coming through: on the night of 9 June, Chris was sitting in an aeroplane when the fuselage opened – literally, like a zip fastener along the centre – and the pilot was sucked out of the plane. On Sunday morning – 10 June – Chris rang Liz Phillips to tell her about this dream.

'But where does it happen?' she asked him.

'I don't know,' he replied, 'but the plane lands at Southampton.'

During the day a British Airways charter jet took off from Birmingham Airport. Soon after take-off, at a height of 23,000 feet, the cockpit window blew out and the pilot – Captain Tim Lancaster – was sucked from his seat. His life was saved by Nigel Ogden, a steward who was serving tea in the cabin. Thinking quickly, Ogden grabbed the captain's legs and clung on desperately until another steward arrived to help. Between them they hung on to Captain Lancaster for eighteen grim minutes, until the co-pilot emergency-landed the plane . . . in Southampton.

Not only had Chris given Liz Phillips three out of three – he'd gone one better, and given her a fourth premonition that had come true. The story appeared in due course and was one of the first to feature Chris and his remarkable powers.

After May, any month would have seemed uneventful, but Chris was still getting information coming through to him, including symbols that he felt were important, although he could not crack them. One symbol whose solution constantly eluded him was that of cakes . . . three cakes on a plate, which went with three people in a café, and chicken on a plate. The multi-layering of meaning was obvious: first, it was significant that the letters PC were constantly repeated. And the fact that the number three occurred twice was also of significance. Yet what really worried Chris was the cake: he was sure that it had some important meaning, but it remained – for the moment – out of his grasp.

The spirits also began to show a distinct political bias during this month. They told Chris they believed the Tory Party to be intrinsically greedy, and that they would do little to prevent a forthcoming bomb attack on a Tory club.

'You can't do that,' Chris said in his dream, 'if I miss an attack at this point, it'll make me look like an idiot. Besides, you can't just let people die.'

So the spirits compromised. They told Chris they wouldn't tell him the name of the club, but instead would give him some clues, the main one being: Vauxhall cars in reverse. While Chris stood in front of a road, a procession of Vauxhall cars passed by him, starting with the earliest models and leading up to the very latest.

So what could the link be between cars in reverse, Vauxhalls and a Tory club in central London? Working with the police at Kilburn, Chris worked out that it might be the RAC Club, as this represents 'car' in reverse. The police searched the RAC Club and found nothing.

On 26 June, three days after Chris had the last dream relating to the cars, a bomb exploded at a Tory club in central London. Going off at night, at a time when many members were using the club to dine and for informal meetings, it was a miracle that only six people were injured as a blaze swept through all three storeys of the building, requiring 40 firemen to fight the rapidly spreading fire. It was a large bomb, and buildings up to 500 yards away reverberated in the shockwave, losing their windows.

The club was the Carlton Club. The latest model of Vauxhall car on the market was also called the Carlton.

In an attempt to understand the clues leading up to this bombing, it was easy to overlook the events already described of 21 June, when the alertness of a civilian electrician saved RAF Stanmore from a bomb disaster just two minutes before the timer exploded inside the hidden package.

Where did all this leave Chris, now nine months down the road from his first precognitive dreams? Certainly the police were now taking notice: Chris was faxing his dreams to three separate officers (Chris Watt, Paul Aylott and Watt's boss, Detective Chief Inspector Dale), was visiting Kilburn regularly and keeping in constant contact by phone. He knew that other agencies were keeping a close eye on him, and he had been told that his information was passed on to them – although he never knew exactly who they were.

He had proof, and witnesses, who could back up his claims: yet he still didn't have a result with which he was entirely satisfied. He hadn't, as far as he knew, helped to prevent any deaths or explosions. And the codes were becoming more and more complicated, always at the point where he thought he was just about to crack them once and for all.

June 1990 had been a quieter month than May. Previously the dreams had always been building in intensity. Now there were fewer of them. Was it all about to end?

CHAPTER TEN

The months of July and August 1990 were even quieter than June. For a while Chris began to worry that he was losing his gift because he was somehow not worthy of it, as though the spirits were punishing him for being unable to understand everything clearly.

It was only in later years, when this decline in dream activity occurred with regularity during the summer months, that Chris began to realise that it was due to something totally beyond his control. His own theory is that solar activity, which is always stronger in the summer months, interferes with the way he receives messages. If the spirits – or what he chooses to believe are spirits – use a kind of 'mental radio' to communicate, then it is feasible to assume that solar radiation might interfere with their 'radio' waves, in the same way that it interferes with radio and telecommunications signals during this period.

But all this was in the future for Chris Robinson, as he sweated out the months of July and August 1990, with the dreams becoming more and more confused. He did, however, get a few more clues and keys to his own personal Rosetta stone.

The dreams took a surreal turn at the start of July. Golfing umbrellas and hospital gowns filled his head; dogs ran around a house, but unlike IRA dogs, they didn't actually do anything except run.

On the night of 2 July Chris wrote: 'Gown not

sterilised', followed by '[DIED] YES [2]', with 'members of Parliament – going past in a [CAR]' and 'member of P election Tories do not get my vote'. At the bottom of the page were the words 'car in bits'. Most significant was the phrase 'Black Name 2[45]'. This could only be a postcode, and one of the most blatant he had seen for some time. Taking the letters, it read BN245. BN was Brighton.

He knew that this one would be a bomb: the dogs hadn't been terrorists, but had represented some kind of horror. But it was all too confused. Would it be an IRA bomb or one belonging to some other terrorist group? Recalling the dreams, he knew that two MPs died, but only one of them was murdered. He had written 'Hospital cubicles. [2] injured cardiac arrest.' The other MP would probably have a heart attack.

Chris faxed the material through as usual, but knew there was nothing there to go on. He knew it would happen when he was on holiday in his camper, as he had seen himself in the woods, but that was no good as an indicator, as he had no plans to go away.

On 5 and 6 July he saw lots of cups, large white ones and cups of coffee. Chris knew these meant dead bodies, but there were only one or two cups at a time. Still two people would die – but who were they?

Chris tried to impress on his police contacts that they must warn any MPs who lived in the Brighton area about the bomb attack – as for the heart attack victim, well that was just a stroke of fate that could hit anyone, and he couldn't work out the name from any of the clues he had been given.

Chris Watt's office phoned Chris later in the month and told him they had spoken to every MP who lived in the Brighton area. All precautions that could be taken were being observed. Chris asked Watt who these MPs were, but Watt refused to tell him: it would be a breach of security.

On 22 July Chris decided to take his family away for a few days, so they packed the camper and headed for the Cheddar Gorge camping site, a particular favourite of Chris's. One night Chris was talking to a man who owned the camper parked next to his. They were admiring each other's campers and got talking about a variety of subjects. Chris told the man about his dreams, as he told everyone. Everything always led to this subject, as it was taking over the whole of Chris's life, to the point of obsession. The man scoffed when Chris told him that an MP would die in a bomb attack that would occur in the Brighton area.

'You're having me on,' he said. 'Things like that don't happen.'

Chris was woken early the next morning by a banging on the camper door. Opening it, still half-asleep, he found himself face-to-face with panic and fear: the emotions of his new friend.

'It's just been on the news – some Tory MP has been blown up. In Eastbourne . . .'

Eastbourne lies only a few miles down the coast from Brighton. Ian Gow had been the victim of an IRA bomb placed underneath his car. His postcode was BN245. As far as Chris knew, from what he was told later, Gow had been warned but had dismissed the warning, as he didn't believe in psychics. He was also aware that he was a possible IRA target.

But that accounted for only one MP: who was the other? This question wasn't answered until two days later, when Mike Carr, the Labour MP for Derby, died at the wheel of his car. At first it was thought that the crash had killed him, but a post-mortem revealed that he had suffered a massive heart attack, and it was this that had caused the accident.

Looking back, Chris could see cryptic clues to the names of the MPs: hospital gow(n) and misspellings like '[Go]lf [U]mbrella' for Gow. Most important, in the case of Mike Carr, was the double clue of the MP in a car(r) – this being the type of vehicle in which both of them died. There was also a reference on 2 July to Derby, Mike Carr's constituency.

Yet in some ways the most interesting aspect about both premonitions was that they had arrived four weeks before the event, and then had ceased: there wasn't the increasing repetition of the Stanmore incident. Chris was at a loss to understand this: was it because they weren't – in the great scheme of things – as important as an attack on a military installation that could kill numerous people?

This theory didn't really hold up, as the start of July had also seen war warnings in his dreams. To Chris it seemed like World War Three, but when he told Chris Watt, the policeman laughed.

Nonetheless, almost a month to the day after Chris's last war dream – 7 July 1990 – Iraq entered Kuwait, and Operation Desert Storm was on the horizon. For a while it looked like a major war.

So here were two new aspects: the cycles between dreams and events could increase from a matter of days to weeks, and they seemed to run in three-night sequences: each of the three events just described ran for three nights in detail, although there were later 'reminders' to Chris if the spirits felt he wasn't really getting the message. The second major aspect was the addition of wordplay and puns in the clues: Mike Carr in a car, MP and a hospital gown for Ian Gow. Whatever you may think of the spirits' sense of humour, these were two new and valuable tools for Chris in his attempt to understand what was happening to him each night.

In August the dreams were non-specific, with a great deal of vague imagery thrown at Chris, associations of ideas that seemed to make little coherent sense. It was as though the spirits had decided to put him through a crash course in symbolism, and he was lost in a sea of signs.

One thing that did come through clearly, on 9 August, was that there was to be another bomb, and the postcode would be BH. On 10 August this was reiterated, as Chris dreamt of being in a house in Brighton – yet he knew the bomb wouldn't actually be there, as he woke to find he had written '[Brighton] [House]', which suggested that it was a cryptic clue rather than something literal. There was also a reference to Durdle Door, the only part of Dorset that Chris knew; this established the location as Bournemouth.

It was on the night of 11 August that something else became clear. There were very few dreams that night, and Chris couldn't remember any of them when he woke. There was very little written down; in fact, just a few lines:

> [FIRE WORK] – in the kitchen
> Tip out gunpowder
> Burn his hand.
> [Petrol station]   Fill to the top
> Long hair   cheating.

Some of this made no sense at all, but the symbolic meaning of firework was clear: it related to the bomb Chris had been dreaming about. This was reiterated by the phrase 'Burn his hand', which provided the initials 'BH – H'.

On paper, some years after the event, this all looks rather spurious, but Chris knew inside himself when he was on the right track, and he knew that the appearance of fireworks signified a bomb attack. He didn't have to see bombs any more, just this simple symbol.

From now on he decided to write in beside the dream the previous meaning of any symbol that he came across: by this kind of cross-referencing he hoped to find a few more answers to difficult questions. It was in this way that he discovered what the appearance of cake meant: it was the symbol for an important person.

This symbol had appeared when Prince Charles had a riding accident in June of that year. Falling from his horse while playing polo, he broke his arm. For some reason, when Chris saw this on the news it made him think of a dream he'd had a few nights before. He pulled out his diaries for that month and searched back through the pages. There it was, on 25 June 1990: the dream was about raspberry cake, which had fallen from a plate and the raspberry jam had spilled. Somebody had splinted the cake to hold it together, in much the same way that a broken arm is splinted. The words that clinched it as a symbol were 'HRH – DI' and '[horse] [race]' on the same page.

Now the cake was reappearing, but to whom did it relate?

The whole month was confused, and it seemed as though things were beginning to slip away from Chris. He was asking every night for information on the next IRA attack and getting nothing that was consistent.

He was still visiting Kilburn, and faxing his dreams through almost every day. When Paul Aylott asked him why there was nothing in the manner of a prediction that he was prepared to put his name against, Chris thought about it before answering.

'There's no repetition,' he said finally. 'They're what's really important. If you get something coming up just once, then you can make anything of it. If it really is some kind of message, then it has to come at least three times. That's something that I've learnt over the last ten or eleven months. And there's nothing that's coming more than once. It's just a mess.'

Chris was depressed by the month's dreams. He began to despair that he would ever again be able to predict anything. Yet in retrospect he would realise that

August 1990 was an important month, simply because
he received no solid message from it. Although he was
no nearer to knowing who the new cake was supposed
to represent, or whether there really was going to be
a bomb in Bournemouth, he had learnt that a dream
and its imagery were useless in themselves. They had
to be repeated and reiterated for there to be any point
to them.

He faced September with a growing pessimism. Yet
it was to be a month of surprises – not least of which
was the gradual return of his precognitive powers.

September started with a return to form. Chris wanted
to know about the next IRA attacks. The dreams told
him 'warning – getting hot'. There were to be two small
attacks involving a military base. There was also to be
a bigger attack, which, he was told, would easily be
carried out. 'Soldier' and 'gun' were placed together on
the page, and Chris knew that there would be a soldier
shot during the month. Interestingly, he didn't know if
the soldier would die. The shooting was also signalled
by a television with '1 [Russian] make' underneath. The
appearance of 'Russian' or 'Skoda' inside a box signified
a shooting: this was another of Chris's highly personal
symbols. He always thought of Russian-made AK47s
when there was an assassination. In fact, it was the
only make of machine gun or rifle whose name he was
familiar with. In the same way, Skoda cars always meant
something Russian or Eastern-bloc to Chris.

The first day of September had become the diary for
the whole month's activities. Whatever happened, Chris
knew there would be two major events in his dreams, as
the number two recurred with an alarming frequency:
'small television set [2]', '[2][2][k]', 'wire wound – G[2]
[FEED]', 'no [G] 2 volts', and 'High resistance [2]'.

The 'small television set' told Chris it was Stoke:
ST. There were two sets, so it was ST2. Would it be

IRA or Animal Liberationists? There were no dogs, but there was a reference to bacon. However, the two were nowhere near each other on the page, so they might relate to separate events.

Bournemouth came back into contention as a target, as there were references to '[BUY HOUSE]', and '[Back] of [house] to see [gardens]'. There were '[2] rooms downstairs' in the house, which was 'between [2] others'. This reiterated the idea that there would be two attacks.

Another postcode appeared in the frame: references to 'sacks of post' and 'safe place' gave Chris an SP postcode, indicating Salisbury Plain.

In all, there was more coherent information in this one night than there had been in the whole of the previous month. Chris was delighted: whatever had caused the flow of information to decline had now passed, and he was able to set about interpreting the information and passing it on to the authorities.

On the night of 2 September he asked the spirits to show him where the Bournemouth bomb might be placed. Bournemouth had been one of the few coherent details to emerge from the August dreams, and with the party political conference coming up, Chris was sure that any bomb attack would happen this month.

All he got were further repetitions of the postcode, as the night's dreams centered on postcode clues: '[Borrow] [hack][saw]', 'Balls hanging [out]', '[Husband] [back]', and 'Bought heart-shaped chocolates'. On the second page of dreams he drew a floor plan of a house, with a questionmark in one room. Was this to be where the bomb was placed, or where the shooting was to occur? At the bottom of the page was a message: 'Don't blame yourself, Christopher. Keep trying. Look into the Broken Hearts made of chocolate.'

On the nights of 3 and 4 September Chris was visited in his dreams by Ian Gow. They were walking along the front at Brighton, not far from where Gow had lived, and the dead politician wanted to impress on Chris that he was happy where he was now. He told Chris that he hadn't believed in the spirit world, but he now knew he was wrong, and should have paid more attention to the warnings when they came from the police. He wanted Chris to contact his wife.

'Well, what's her name?' Chris asked. 'I don't know anything about you, other than that you were an MP.'

So Gow gave Chris his address, and told him that his wife's name was Jane. He gave Chris the following message for her, which he wrote in the dream diary:

'Tell them Ian sends his love. Please keep trying Christopher. Jane I love being home here. You just can't see me, that's all.'

When Chris looked at the page the next morning, he found that 'Ian' was written '[I]an', and that 'being home' was '[Being] [Home]'. Again, this pointed to Bournemouth. Written further down the page was '[Two] in the [passenger] seat with [me]. Jane will remember.'

There were also references to 'Bourne and Hollingsworth', 'then Back Home' and 'She does not [?] in Bournemouth'. Finally there was the imprecation: 'please go and look, Christopher', along with 'Douglas Hurd – warn him' and 'Home secretary – warn him', both of which were underlined twice.

Chris was sure that Ian Gow had an important message to pass on, and so contacted Paul Aylott and Trevor Kempson. He reasoned that the police would be wary of telling a recently bereaved widow that her dead husband had left a message for her – but a journalist of Kempson's long standing would have no such qualms. Chris wanted Jane Gow to receive that message.

He was also convinced that the attack would come

at the Tory Party conference in Bournemouth, which was scheduled for the next month. It wouldn't be the first attack, as it hadn't appeared on the first page. More important was the shooting: Chris had an image of someone outside a house, bleeding from a tooth cavity – but the tooth hadn't been extracted, it had been shot out. Was this the shooting he had seen on the first page?

The welter of images was confusing in the cold light of day, and it was hard for Chris to recapture the true meanings, which had been much more obvious in the heat and intensity of the dreams.

On 4 September he wrote 'fly small plane – learn to fly.' This was the start of an image that was to recur over the years. Small plane could have meant Salisbury Plain (postcode = SP), but learning to fly? This was puzzling. A bit clearer was '4 volts [AC] from Radio Control. Find it.' This was an obvious message to Chris that he should work harder on the dreams. 'Radio control' signalled a receiver, and the initials reversed were CR – Chris Robinson. But how much harder could he work? In four nights he had received more information than he had had in any single month since May – and the strain was immense.

He clung to the postcodes and tried to make something out of the rest. For instance, there was the sentence 'Hamlyn Slowe – break into their offices sue them [2]'. Hamlyn Slowe was a firm of solicitors that Chris had been having problems with, but the crucial phrase was 'sue them [2]': ST2 – Stoke again. The box meant that the district concerned might not be the area covered by ST2, but was near it.

The next few nights told Chris that the Bournemouth attack would take place in a hotel, but he was still no nearer to getting a name or a date. He saw dogs in his dreams again, one watching television, another speaking Dutch to someone in a blue uniform who was on a boat.

On the night of 7 September he dreamt of the place where he used to work when he was younger – a shop on Wellington Street. The manager there was a man called Duggan, and Chris worked with someone called Fred Derby. Fred used to repair television aerials, which also appeared in the dream, and he was repairing one in Derby Road.

Four days later a 5-pound bomb exploded in an Army Careers Office in the centre of Derby. It was planted on the roof, and the soldiers inside escaped injury only because the concrete roof deflected the blast. Shoppers in the street up to 200 yards away were blown off their feet by the force of the blast.

Fred Derby, in Derby Road, on a roof: had it been a message that Chris hadn't been able to decipher correctly? Certainly he had written down all the salient points on the page where he had tried to interpret the dream.

It was the breakthrough: the first prediction for over a month, and he got it at least 50 per cent right. It was the morale-booster Chris needed. Now all he had to do was make sense of the rest of the dreams . . .

The dreams continued for the next few nights: once again the same places were reiterated: Stoke, Bournemouth and Salisbury Plain.

On the night of 15 September the Stoke postcode returned, with the added warning of very thick snow on the ground – Chris actually underlined the phrase 'snow on the ground' twice – and meat pies everywhere. From his experience of bomb warnings, Chris knew that meat pies meant dead meat, wounded meat – carnage and bloodshed. He also dreamt of a knight in armour, and of a girl called Christine Stokes, with whom he had been involved at one time.

He was now sure that the Stoke incident would relate to the shooting of a soldier, who might be a titled soldier, perhaps a retired or ageing General or Major. He duly passed this information on, but it was still a little vague.

On 19 September, just four days after this dream, Sir Peter Terry was shot nine times by the IRA at his home in the village of Milford, Staffordshire. The 63-year-old former Governor-General of Gibraltar was an Air Chief Marshal and had been Governor-General at the time of the 'Death on the Rock' scandal, when three IRA terrorists were shot dead by an SAS hit-squad in circumstances that even now are shrouded in a degree of mystery. This was significant, as Chris looked back over September's dreams and found that he had dreamt of an SAS squad killing three terrorists. At the time he had thought this related directly to the shootings that his dreams were predicting. In retrospect it could also be said that this was a clue to the identity of the man who was about to be shot.

Sir Peter was hit nine times by IRA hitmen, and yet he managed to survive. Interestingly, Chris hadn't seen any cups throughout this month – so he hadn't predicted any deaths.

Salisbury Plain was becoming more and more important, and it cropped up time and again. Chris also dreamt that it was connected with an Austin or Morris car – he dreamt of a red Mini, made by the firms of Austin and Morris at the time they were amalgamated.

This didn't come to a head until the beginning of the next month. On 3 October a dramatic police ambush on the edge of Stonehenge, on Salisbury Plain, led to the arrest of two men and a woman. They constituted an IRA cell, which was believed to be responsible for the death of Ian Gow.

A massive stake-out by the police caught the gang as they swapped information and explosives with a fourth man, in a grey Transit van. He escaped, but was later picked up on the road as the net tightened around the area. Meanwhile, the three captured terrorists were taken from their car and searched on the ground by armed police. It was a dramatic scene that amazed passers-by. The terrorists captured in the ambush were later tried and convicted.

That morning Chris had woken at 5 a.m. and faxed his dreams through to Hertfordshire police headquarters in a blind panic. He had foreseen the arrests during the night and wanted to make sure the dream turned to reality.

Chris was right about Salisbury Plain being the centre of activity, and he was also half-correct in connecting the red Mini with the scene. Although the car driven by the terrorists was a blue Ford Sierra, the car under which they had planted the bomb that killed Ian Gow was a red Austin Montego . . .

As September drew towards a close, the spirits had one last surprise for Chris: a surprise because it had nothing to do with the recurring dreams concerning Bournemouth.

On the night of 30 September the following information was contained in Chris's dreams:

> Gold lighter in a drawer. [Video tapes]
> Flat in London – radio equipment. [money
>   owed]
> Baby playing on the ground. Sale or return.
> [BOMB] in Kilburn. 2 informers in one street.
> Block of flats. Lamp stand. Leaded lights.
> Bamboo [cabinet]. [cocktail] cabinet.
> Machine gun – AK47. Russian Train.
> loser sight. 2 from Belfast. 1 man 1 woman.
> Gun is a bit rusty – shows me how to use it –
> change barrel bolt action.
> Underground station – hold doors open.
> Toilet underground. Water on the floor.
> Flat in London – girl on the floor.

near [Highgate] Point gun at them.
    Shall I shoot them
                    Wide open [attack].

Although it may appear rambling, this was in fact one of the most coherent pages Chris had written for some time. The annoying thing was that it had little bearing on the questions he had actually asked, which were to do with the disappearance of a young boy, Simon Jones. Simon was one of Chris's biggest failures, yet there was much to be learnt from this matter when it was finally resolved.

On the morning of 1 October 1990, however, Chris was not to know any of this. All he knew was that the spirits seemed to be wilfully ignoring the questions he asked, and were keen to impart information of another kind to him.

The most obvious part of the dream concerned the shootings and the reference to Belfast, as he found when he switched on his television and turned to the Teletext pages. As a source of up-to-date information, the Teletext service was quicker and more efficient than a newspaper, as it ran twenty-four hours a day and was constantly updated. Since he had become aware of his ability to predict the future, Chris had found himself becoming a Teletext junkie, and turning it on was the first thing he did whenever he came home: When he was staying in the camper, which had only a portable Television without Teletext facilities, he missed it desperately.

That morning's news carried a recently released story about two people shot in Belfast during the night: one male, one female. That explained the section of the page that ran from 'Machine gun . . .' to 'change barrel. Bolt action.' The fact that Chris had possibly been dreaming of the event as it actually happened also accounted for its clarity.

But there were other sections that seemed to be mixed up with it, and which related to something he had been discussing with Chris Watt at Kilburn the day before; something that related to events that had occurred a fortnight previously.

The day before Sir Peter Terry was gunned down outside his Staffordshire home, the IRA had mounted an attack in London, intending to strike at the heart of the then-Prime Minister Margaret Thatcher's constituency of Finchley. Colour Sergeant Bernard Cox was shot as he left the recruiting office in Finchley High Road. He was hit three times and hospitalised. He was released after a few days in hospital, but was left with a bullet lodged near the base of his spine.

The day before Chris had told Chris Watt that he thought the IRA would shoot someone in Hampstead. It was too imprecise for any action to be taken, but shortly afterwards Chris had asked the spirits for help in identifying the gunmen. There had been little response, except that he had drawn a map of a square, but he didn't know exactly where this square was located.

After the dream of 30 September Chris looked back through the diaries and found that he had made references to Kilburn on 18, 19, and 20 September. 'Chamber', 'Sidmouth' and 'Christchurch Avenue' were names that recurred.

That day he took an 'A–Z' map of London with him when he visited Kilburn.

'You know we were talking about finding an IRA cell around North London?' he said to Chris Watt.

'Don't tell me you know where they are,' laughed Watt.

Chris smiled. 'Maybe I do. Look at this.' He showed Watt the dream of the night before, and also the earlier references.

'Sorry,' Watt said after examining the pages, 'I can't say that it means much to me.'

'Yeah, well, you don't know what I do. You see this bit here about a gold lighter in a drawer, and then this bit about a bamboo cabinet and a cocktail cabinet?' He pointed out the relevant sections on the page.

'Yeah . . . so?'

Chris tapped his nose. 'Well, I had a look around here when I was on my way over, and there's a lot of nice blocks of flats around here. Old ones, look a bit like they were just pre-war, right?'

Watt nodded. So far he had no idea what this was leading to. 'Okay. But there's a lot of blocks like that all over London.'

'Yeah, but this bit about the cabinets is the real clue. Y'see, I used to have this girlfriend who lived in a classy block of flats. She had it done out really nice, had taste. It was one of these pre-war blocks, and it had a porter and everything. A bit like some of these round here would have done at some time. With me so far?'

'Yes . . .' said Watt slowly. 'I think I'm beginning to get the point. Her taste in furnishings wouldn't happen to run to bamboo and nice cocktail cabinets, would it?'

Chris smiled. 'More or less. She had this really nice cabinet that she used to keep the drinks in – it wasn't actually a cocktail cabinet, but she used it as one. And she had these bamboo screens. What's more, she had this really flash gold lighter – I don't know why, but I really remember that. In my dream last night it was her flat, but there were these dogs in it.'

'So you reckon that they're in a block of flats around these parts that looks like the one your old girlfriend lived in.' Watt laughed: 'I suppose that narrows it down a bit.'

'More than that,' Chris said, opening the 'A–Z' and producing his own sketch. 'I had a look in here, and around the streets as I came in. I reckon it's in this area here –' and he pointed to a block on the map, around

500 yards square. 'It covers a fair few roads, and a lot of flats, but I reckon it's there. You see: Sidmouth and Chamberlayne – just up the road.'

Watt smiled. 'You give me the creeps, old son. I'll pass this one on, see what happens.'

For over a month nothing happened and Chris had virtually forgotten about it until he bought the *Daily Express* on 12 November. The headline proclaimed: 'IRA Bomb Factory Smashed.'

The story related how a block of flats had been staked out since the preceding Wednesday, and how the police had finally raided it on the Sunday night. Over 100 pounds of Semtex high explosive was found on the premises, and it took army experts over ten hours to make sure the building was safe before the explosive could be taken away. Over 2,000 people living in the vicinity of the block were moved to a nearby community hall, in case of an explosion.

The police believed that the flat was a bomb factory preparing for a major Christmas blitz on the capital. Six people were arrested, and two cars were seized – both found to be full of guns and explosives.

The flat was located in Kilburn. The road in which the block was situated was Chamberlayne Road. The block was named Sidmouth Court. It was within the square drawn by Chris Robinson, who had also supplied the names Sidmouth and Chamber. Christchurch Avenue lay around the corner.

Unable to contain himself, Chris phoned Chris Watt. 'I told you they were there, didn't I?' he said.

Watt was silent for a moment, then replied that although Chris had told him, he didn't want anything further to do with Chris. They haven't spoken since.

The first year of dreams ended with an event that made Chris think long and hard about the manner in which he received them, and possible reasons why. It was a failure, but even in that there was much to learn. Chris discovered the truism that you can learn more in failure than in victory.

Simon Jones was a 4-year-old boy who disappeared from a park in the middle of Hemel Hempstead towards the end of September 1990. Chris felt this very deeply, as two of his own children were under five, and Hemel Hempstead lies not far from where he lives: it could easily have been one of his own children who was snatched.

Even though he had Salisbury Plain, Kilburn and Bournemouth running through his dreams, he was determined to try and help find Simon. He phoned Hemel Hempstead station, half-expecting to be treated like a crank – after all, he'd had no contact with this particular station, and there was no reason why they should know who he was. To his surprise, however, the detectives in charge of the Jones case were willing to see him.

'Look,' one of them said, 'you fax us your dreams every day, or bring a copy in, and we'll spend five minutes with you every morning going over them.'

From 27 September Chris began to ask the spirits every night what had happened to the child. The first night he had eight references to Stevenage, which led him to believe the child had been taken there: Hemel Hempstead and Stevenage are only a few miles apart in Hertfordshire.

He was also convinced that the boy was dead. The body had been dumped somewhere in the town, and Chris was sure that the killer was a vagrant, who had taken the boy with him on a bus to the town before killing him.

'Grass stains by his back door. Dig up the grass when [we] get set to move.'

The boy lay in a wooded, grassy area, buried rather than just hidden. The initial G and S of 'grass stains' were also important – together with 'smashed glass' the next night, they convinced him that Stevenage was right. The postcode prefix for the town is SG.

There were dogs in the park at Stevenage, but these were not IRA dogs – this was 'dog' in its original symbolic meaning of killer. The dogs were then inside a van, leading the boy away from a group of playing children. Chris also saw a fairground and was convinced that Simon had been abducted by a fairground worker.

For several nights, right into October, Chris saw the same things again and again. He reported them to the police in Hemel Hempstead, but they seemed to be losing interest. Then another psychic, Nella Jones, was brought into the picture by Simon's family and was reported by the *News of the World* newspaper. She believed the boy was still alive, and was being kept somewhere in the area.

Chris went to Stevenage at the start of October and drove around the town, hoping that this would help his dreams. Once again he asked the spirits where the body of Simon was hidden. They replied by telling him that the 'fair was at Stevenage, so was [I]'. They also showed him a gas leak in a loft, with loose boards all around, like those disturbed in order to hide a body.

This left Chris even more confused. Now the spirits were trying to tell him that the boy was hidden in the loft of a house, when they had already told him he was buried in some woods and that the killer was homeless.

The disappearance of Simon Jones was giving Chris the kind of anxiety he hadn't suffered since the very early days – not since the Special Branch had turned up on his doorstep after the Leicester bombing.

The police in Hemel Hempstead were sceptical about Chris's dreams – at least those that concerned Simon. The spirits had changed course yet again, and were now intimating that the homeless fairground worker with a loft was also a traveller: 'Been to fair. [out] Side going to see traveller site. Waiting near traveller site. Walk in entrance.'

This was followed by a sketched map of a footpath leading from a car park to a camping site, but it was so vague that it could have been anywhere. Then came: 'Car being driven in very deep snow. Snow on the ground under a car. [BOMB]. Christopher he will do it again soon. You will get him in court. [Waite] and see.'

Still there were no concrete clues. And the police were more and more convinced that Simon Jones was actually alive.

Meanwhile the Salisbury Plain arrests took place, and the policeman dealing with Chris in Hemel Hempstead, a DI Sparrow, was amazed by the dreams that had foretold this.

'Tell me,' he asked Chris, 'tell me how come you can get this right, but you're not any nearer helping us find Simon?'

Chris wanted to answer, but couldn't: he had an idea that the evil and mischievous spirits that David Bolster had talked of some months earlier had interfered with his dreams. Would a hard-nosed policeman want to hear that? Chris also wondered if the spirits were real: did they exist, or were they just inventions of his own subconscious? Were they as symbolic as the postcodes, cakes and dogs, and everything else he dreamt of every night?

The Salisbury Plain arrest gave him a confidence in his dreams that was drained by the Simon Jones débâcle: a confidence that was drained still further when Simon was found alive a few weeks later. He was still in Hemel Hempstead and had been taken by a man named May. He was unharmed. The night before he was found, Chris had dreamt that the boy was discovered – but there were still no clues as to where, or what had happened to him.

Several years later this still disturbs Chris Robinson: helping to find the child was something he was very keen to do, and the fact that he failed is still a sore point. Did he try too hard? Certainly, other psychics such as Uri Geller believe that wanting something too much can obscure any power you possess. This is why Geller generally refused to have anything to do with murder cases: he found that he began to care about the victims, and this would lead his conscious mind to block the unconscious, so that messages could not break through. Geller also discovered that being surrounded by detectives wanting to crack a case could obscure his power, as their will and determination would impinge on his own mind by ESP.

Did Chris want to solve this one a little bit too much? Did he block any powers that he had by willing a result too strongly? It's possible that what he saw was a mirror of his own fear about what might have happened to Simon – or to his own children.

Then again, if the spirits were real, as Chris had hitherto believed, it was possible that they were misleading him because they had work for him: they wanted him to concentrate on the other matters in hand. He had Bournemouth, Salisbury Plain and Kilburn running through his dreams throughout this period. Perhaps the spirits, and particularly Robert, wanted him to concentrate on the IRA and so misled him in order to prevent him from being sidetracked again in such a manner.

Kilburn and Salisbury Plain were successes; Bournemouth only partially so, as the bombs were firebombs and weren't found until they had caused a minimal amount of damage. This weighs up well compared to the one failure of this period: the lack of success in the Simon Jones case. But not to Chris.

October 1990: one year on from the time when the precognitive dreams began. In that year Chris had forged links with the police and security services, and was unofficially acknowledged as a source of information. Keith Hearne was still monitoring his progress, logging every success and failure for statistical analysis.

The only question now was this: how much further could it all go?

CHAPTER ELEVEN

During those first twelve months Chris had plenty of time to consider the wider implications of what was happening to him. There seemed to be three possibilities:

1. He was being used as a conduit for spirits to pass on messages. These spirits were human in origin, as they included people he had heard of, who came to visit him in the night: people like Fazad Bazoft and Dr Gerry Bull. But, confusingly, among them they also numbered Terry Waite, and Chris was sure at this time that Waite was still alive. There had been much speculation in the press during the preceding twelve months as to Waite's status as a hostage, but his spirit had actually told Chris that he was alive and hoped to get out soon.

   There were also spirits that he couldn't identify, such as the soldier Robert, who had been his first point of contact; and the spirits who had given him religious and quasi-religious messages.

2. The messages came from within himself. He had noticed that the best results were always obtained when he had some personal point of reference. The rail workers' accident in Chorleywood, for instance, had been on a stretch of line near which he frequently drove; the bomb warning concerning Stanmore had involved an area that

Chris knew well from his childhood and early work experience.

It was also worth noting that an event that was to happen just outside his own frame of reference often included some landmark that Chris knew. The clearest examples of this were the football hooligans rioting in Poole, and the bombs involving Bournemouth. Both occurred in Dorset, and the key that Chris was given involved the beauty spot of Durdle Door, the only part of Dorset with which he was familiar. Even something as seemingly unconnected as the Philippines air disaster could be accounted for by the nationality of Chris's wife, Bessie, and the fact that he had many times visited the islands with her.

If the messages about forthcoming events were coming from Chris's own mind, then it was highly possible that he could only see things with which he had some kind of link. Certainly psychic researchers and philosophers alike have pondered the idea of the subconscious mind reaching beyond time as we currently understand it: HF Saltmarsh, an early twentieth-century researcher, posited the idea that the mind works like two beams of light. The strong, focused beam is the conscious mind, taking in all that is happening in the here and now. The subconscious, however, is like a weaker, more diffuse beam that spreads over a wider area. As such, it observes things that will happen slightly ahead of what the conscious mind will see – that is to say, it can see into the future. It could be this that was happening through Chris's dreams, and the symbols and spirits were just his own mind's way of interpreting what he could see.

3. Time travel. In many ways Chris was willing to

admit that this was the most way-out of all the
ideas he had during the year: but who is to say
that it's wrong? Chris is the first person to hold
up his hands and say that he doesn't know what
is happening to him. So why shouldn't it be time
travel. He put it like this:

'Suppose, in the far future, they've found a
way of travelling back in time − but it isn't
physical. They can't send actual bodies back, but
they can send information. So they send back a
beam of concentrated message and information,
in the hope that someone back in time will be
able to pick it up. And that someone, just by
chance, is me. Why me? I don't know why. But
suppose that's what they're doing, and it's me
that's picking it up. That would explain things
just as feasibly as spirits from the dead, or me
seeing into the future.'

Ultimately, Chris believes that the messages come from
a spirit world − a dimension beyond death. The next
step of spiritual evolution, if you like: a version of the
Bhuddist Nirvana. But that is just his faith. He's quite
prepared to admit that he might be totally wrong, and
it could be any of the above explanations or one that no-
one has even considered as yet. For instance, the scientist
and researcher Andrija Puharich became convinced that
Uri Geller − whom he spent several years studying on
an on−off basis − gained his powers from alien beings
in UFOs. When I explained this theory to Chris he
laughed . . . and then told me that it might very well
be so. After all, who knows?

During that year Chris was able to ask himself why he
had been chosen. In truth, he didn't know, and when
he asked the spirits they refused to tell him. So he
began to look for answers himself. As he sat down to
consider his position, he began to write. What he wrote

is worth reproducing as one man's ideas about what was happening to him, and as a reflection of what was running through his mind during the year of learning.

Notes by Chris Robinson: 1990

Considering the amount of money spent on research into space and astronomy, I think it's incredible that no-one has ever written a book or undertaken any exhaustive research into dreams. Dr Keith Hearne has done a little into 'signalling' – the transfer of thought from one person to another during dreaming – but nothing appears to have been done on content or meaning. Millions of people all over the world are dreaming every time they sleep, thousands of millions of dreams every day, yet not a single study has been published. If they have, it can't be found in any library I've tried. Is there some law about studying precognitive dreams that I don't know about? Or am I the first person to have enough precognitive dreams to be able to say that what is happening is beyond mere chance and warrants further study?

So far as the police I've spoken to are concerned, I'm the only person that they know of who has repeatedly had dreams that appear to foretell unforeseeable occurrences. I'm alone in uncharted waters, yet not on my own. I have the police, Dr Hearne and David Bolster on my side. My own doctor has told me that I'm not mad, nor do I need any medical treatment. He has said that there is still a lot to learn about the human brain and the way that it functions. He says it is possible that I am more developed mentally, or perhaps I have been affected by the high number of near-death experiences that I have had over the years, or by the prolonged periods of anaesthesia that I endured during my open-heart surgery, when I was a child.

I have had a number of surgical operations, the most

serious being one for the rectification of a defect to the aorta. I was nine years old when this was carried out and was in hospital for four months. The operation was performed by the top heart surgeon of the time, Mr Donald Ross, at Guy's Hospital in London on 3 August 1960. I still have the most vivid memories of my time in hospital, and can remember the names of most of the nurses who looked after me.

Dr Hearne believes that this may be a key factor in my ability to have psychic experiences: he told me that a high proportion of people he has studied have had prolonged periods of anaesthesia. His theory is that the mind is somehow expelled from the body and so the out-of-body experience (OOBE) makes you more inclined to accept psychic experiences like precognition when they happen to you: most people cannot let go enough to accept them, but those of us who have had numerous out-of-body experiences are more receptive.

When I was sixteen I was involved in a very serious accident on my motor scooter. I was very seriously injured, and almost didn't make it. It was then that I had the first OOBE that I can remember. I remember vividly looking down on the ambulance that was transferring me from Edgware General Hospital to Mount Vernon in Northwood. It was as though I was travelling on top of the ambulance, and could see it speeding through the streets. I could also look down and see through the ambulance: see my body inside.

By coincidence, Mount Vernon was the hospital where my nan would pass on some twenty years later . . .

Why do we dream what we do – the content of dreams? I have a friend who has suggested to me that we do not exist on a physical level. We live in a mentalistic universe: everything is a dream; one we call asleep, and one we call awake . . .

If you gaze up at the sky at midday you will see,

clouds permitting, the sun. An enormous, bright, round ball of fire, a swirling, seething mass of hydrogen, helium and countless other components. You are looking across ninety-three million miles of almost empty space.

If you look up at the same position at midnight, again into a clear sky, then you will see millions upon millions of suns. Many are exactly the same type of fireball that we see in the daytime; the only difference is that they are much further away from us. Of course, we are surrounded by these suns – we call them stars. Because of their great distance away from us they appear as tiny pinpoints of light. But don't be fooled: some of them are more than a thousand times bigger than our own sun, millions of miles in diameter.

Not all the twinkling objects in the night sky are balls of fire: some are cold, equally hostile worlds that shine by the reflective light of the suns. We call them planets, moons and comets, etc. The use of a telescope enables us to shrink the vast distances and see these heavenly bodies in more detail.

If you took a microscope instead of a telescope, and pointed it at yourself instead of the sky, then you would see a similar picture – if the microscope is capable of a magnification equal to the shrinking powers of the telescope. The atoms and molecules that you then observe, the ones of which you are comprised, look remarkably like the solar system. A universe in miniature.

As above, so below. Microcosm, macrocosm, worlds within worlds, but at the end of the day all you have are objects spinning around each other at phenomenal speeds. At the minuscule end of the scale you have atoms, at the other end galaxies and maybe other universes. Who knows what else is out there or in there?

Mankind and everything else we see is made up of them, but are the atoms that make you really you? Maybe not: we are continually taking in 'new' atoms from our surroundings and at the same time shedding 'old' atoms back out into the environment. My reasoning says to me that if this is the case then we are not our 'physical' or 'material' body, as this is never the same from one minute to the next. We are continually exchanging atoms with our surroundings and with each other. Some of the atoms that at this very moment make you were yesterday part of somebody else, and millions of years ago those same atoms helped to build a dinosaur. Where were those same atoms a billion or ten billion years ago? They did exist, and must have been somewhere out there in the universe.

Any A-Level physics student will tell you that you can't destroy matter, but it can be changed from one substance to another. At the time of conception, a child is just two cells, but those cells go on to grow into a new human being made of old atoms – atoms as old as the universe. Atoms that have perhaps been in hundreds of other plants and animals.

If you are not what you are made of, then who are you? I think that we are constructed of an unknown substance: sub-atomic, particles smaller than the ones that make up atoms. Science will, I am sure, discover the answers to these questions in due course, for now all we need to do is prove that the seemingly impossible happens.

Nothing seems more impossible than foreseeing events before they occur, especially if those events are outside human control . . .

I was brought up as a Christian in the Church of England, and as a child I went to Sunday School. I do believe that there is a God, and have no problem in accepting a man called Jesus. Equally, I believe in the existence of Mohammed, and in many – if not all – of the other prophets of whom there is historical evidence.

There are some stories in the Bible that I find it impossible to accept, mainly because what we call scientific facts seem to rule out these events as being impossible. But that would not cause me to dismiss the teachings of the Bible and I think I understand how and even why it was that people of 2,000 years ago wrote in the way they did. Today we would write using modern words and symbols, but the basic meaning would go unchanged.

It would naturally follow that we would today dream in modern symbols too, and so far as I know we would use in our dreams the symbols that were most familiar to us as individuals. The symbols that occur in my dream language are in many instances personal and would only have any meaning to me. Some are more general and have a 'universal' meaning, a meaning that many people would understand . . .

The Big Bang: the beginning of time and all things known to man. If it started with a big bang, and all ends with matter contracting back into one lump – a singularity – then it will surely start all over again. The question must be: how often has this cycle repeated itself? It is estimated that one cycle lasts thirty billion years. Could this be one of God's days?

If a form of life could develop during this cycle to a point where it could escape the continuum, then that life form would develop and continue to develop unaffected by the changes brought about by the destruction of its creative cycle: the first cycle, the birth of God.

The events of the second cycle must be identical to those of the first, if all events start from a single act, a single particle – assuming there was no God.

It must be that, if a life force was created and did escape from the influence of the physical cycle, then that would be the first cycle. If the first cycle lost something at some part of its cycle, then we would expect to see a change in the second cycle with no relation to the first. But if no further loss or escape of something occurred in the second, then no further changes would be brought about, no matter how many times the cycle repeated itself.

As we are here now, and some of those among us are able to see into the future, then we could not be on the first cycle, as there would be no future to observe.

What could be happening when we glimpse the future is that we are seeing what has happened on the cycle before. Without interference the same will happen again, but by seeing or being shown the forthcoming events we are given the opportunity to make changes. Those of us who can see the previous cycle and predict our future hold enormous power, and I feel that what we claim to see is not actually what we see by chance, but what is shown to us.

I believe that there is a God. I also believe he would keep a strict control over the seeing, and only allows to be seen what he needs to show in order to show that the changes he desires us to make can be made.

Our eternal spirit is not physical and is not affected by material actions and is in this sense indestructible. It can only cause physical change by controlling a physical body. Spirits cannot harm us, only cause us to harm ourselves and others. These are the conclusions I have made so far, but are they correct?

This is what I was directed to write one night by Robert, the soldier:

> For every action there is a reaction. Before this can be related to, you must first discover if you are looking at an original act or a reaction to an act or chain of acts. It can, of course, be argued that every action is, in fact, a reaction, and there must have been only one original act.
>
> It has, so far, been impossible to isolate the original act. There must only have been one.
>
> It can therefore be assumed that everything that happens is the direct result of the previous action, or the result of the combined previous actions.

If this is all true, then it must be possible to calculate the actions that have yet to occur.

Time: what is time? Well, that is another difficult question to answer.

Time is the interval between two events or a series of events. If there were not an action or event, time, it could be argued, would not exist. It must follow from this that the gap is also an action or event as it does and must exist.

Try to imagine a gap between two events that is small enough that no other action or event, however apparently unrelated, could have occurred. This gap or unit of time is time itself. It can be argued that this gap could not exist, and if that is correct, time cannot exist either. As time is something that we could not deny must at least exist in our minds, it could then be argued that everything that has existed, or will ever exist, must have existed at the same time.

It is worth at this point trying to consider this: everything that has existed, or will ever exist, must exist now and have always existed, and will always exist.

If all things exist always, then travel between one event and another could be a possibility. Try to imagine it as a sideways, rather than a forwards or backwards, step.

The thoughts put forward so far are, of course, assuming we exist at all . . .

PART TWO

MORE THAN A COINCIDENCE

CHAPTER TWELVE

One of the strangest things that happened to Chris started in the early December of 1990 and stretched out over the next eight months until the July of 1991. It wasn't a major media news story and wasn't earth-shattering in its consequences. For all that, it did help make a few people happy, and helped bring a killer to justice – although in an extremely oblique manner.

On 9 December Chris had a variety of dreams. There was a lot of activity and a great deal written down. But one part particularly stayed in his mind and Chris went to tell Paul Aylott about it: a man was being drowned in a bucket of water. Chris could feel his pain as the breath seared through the drowning man's lungs, bursting to escape from under the water; and he could feel the relief when the man managed to gasp a few deep breaths when his head was momentarily raised above water.

His killer was playing with him, and finally he plunged the man's head below the surface one last time, holding him down until there was no life left.

Somebody was calling the killer by name and Chris strained to catch it . . .

When he woke up, he had written:

[Urqhy] Baby – drown him in a bucket of water
            Hold him under

Further down the page was written:

Black [Hairs] on a plate   [Chicken or fish]
    or eyelashes

Chris was convinced that the killer was a man called Urquhart, and that he was going to kill a man called Patrick Frater. Where the second name came from, he had no idea: it had popped into his mind as he looked over the dream pages, trying to make sense of them. He also knew that Frater was a black man – again, this had just come to him after the dream. It wasn't often that he got intuitive flashes like that, post-dream. Were they left-over dream images that he hadn't recorded and couldn't remember, slipping into his consciousness before finally being lost? Or did they represent some kind of precognitive power that didn't rely solely on dreaming?

At that point it didn't matter, and Chris didn't care. He already had a dream sequence running that required him to fax his dreams to Cambridge Special Branch as well as to Paul Aylott, so he got on with the task in hand, and pushed the drowning man to the back of his mind. But only temporarily . . .

Later in the day, when he had a chance to think further about it, Chris decided that he really had to tell Paul Aylott about this part of the dream in more detail. It was still imprinted firmly on his mind and had worried him throughout the day. So he sat down and wrote to Aylott, detailing everything he could remember about the dream and the fragments that had come to him afterwards.

Paul received the letter, and rang Chris.

'What's this about some black guy getting killed by a bloke called Urquhart?' he asked, puzzled. 'I mean, when's it going to happen?'

Chris shrugged at the other end of the phone, and paused to consider his answer. Finally he said, 'I don't know when, only that it is, and that this bloke Patrick is the victim. I couldn't tell you what it's all about, but I do know that it's not some run-of-the-mill dream.'

'How come?'

'Because I've had a look back through all the dreams since last October, and there's not a single mention of the name Urquhart. It's never come up before.'

'So what does that prove?'

'It proves it hasn't just come out of my head . . . look, Paul, I don't know anyone called Urquhart, and I've never even heard of anyone with that name – I mean, it's not common, is it?'

Aylott admitted this, and said that he would keep the letter on file. After all, there was nothing in it to indicate when the killing would occur and Patrick Frater had no criminal record to make him known to the police.

It was the middle of December 1990, and in the Hockwell Ring area of Luton a man was sitting in his car. He looked out across the road and saw a man coming towards him: a man he recognised as the boyfriend of a girl he had once dated. The man was carrying a bag at an odd angle, and the man in the car felt a cold tingle shiver down his back. He had been waiting for his brother, but that was out of the question now: all he could think about was getting away before something terrible happened to him.

He fumbled with the ignition key, trying to shake the car's engine into life. It coughed, but the key caught on the way round. He looked up: the man with the bag was hurrying now, seeing that he was trying to get away.

The key turned again, and the engine spluttered into life. He revved it desperately and began to draw away. The man with the bag dropped it, revealing a shotgun. He fired at the car as he ran towards it.

The driver was hit as he pulled away. Not seriously, but enough for him to drive to the nearest casualty department, where he was detained and the police called.

It was not a major incident, and Paul Aylott didn't get to hear of it for some days. But when he did, it made him wonder about the letter from Chris . . .

The man who had been shot was called Danny Frater.

Nothing further seemed to come of this line of dream, and Chris had almost forgotten about it when his dreams of 19 January brought it back into sharp relief.

There were dreams of snow, connected with an on-running sequence relating to a bomb warning. Then suddenly everything changed. Chris could see himself back in Hockwell Ring, a large council estate on the edge of Luton built within a ringroad. He knew that something was going to happen, and also that it was connected to the dream of Patrick Frater, which was something he had consigned to the past. When he woke, he found that he had written:

[Marsh Farm] Flats across the road –
[lee bank] or Hookers Caught
Phone police

Further down the page was written, 'Ring – [diamond] or junk'.

A ring that he was selling – or pawning. In fact, it was being put 'in hock': Hockwell Ring. The names Marsh Farm, Lee Bank and Hookers Court were all blocks on the Hockwell estate. They prescribed an arc around a road called Acworth Crescent.

Chris knew that the murder would take place here, and that it would involve Patrick Frater. He phoned Paul Aylott, who was mindful of the event concerning Danny Frater when Chris mentioned the name. But there was little concrete for them to act upon:

'But when is it?' Aylott asked.

'Soon,' Chris replied, as frustrated as his friend.

'So what am I going to do – set a cordon round the Ring until some bloke comes along? You know I can't do things like that.'

'I know . . .'

For both men it was a frustrating experience. Aylott knew that Chris was right at least 50 per cent of the time, and after the shooting of Danny Frater there was some reason to assume that Chris was on the right track. At the same time the Bedfordshire Police had to struggle with the same low levels of manning as any other force, and Aylott couldn't commit men indefinitely.

They left it with Paul promising Chris to try and sort something out. Perhaps this eased Chris's mind, because he didn't dream of Patrick Frater on the night of 20 January.

The following night, however, he did.

On the morning of 22 January he woke up to find, among the writings of the night, the phrase 'Plane-[2]-America – Spirits'. He knew immediately what this meant and phoned Aylott.

'Has anything happened to that guy Frater?'

'Not that I know of,' Aylott replied. 'Why?'

'Because I've just dreamt that he's dead, that's why.'

'I'll check up on it, but I don't think anything's happened to him . . .'

Aylott found that Danny Frater's brother Patrick was still alive and well. He phoned Chris and told him. It didn't make Chris feel any easier: something was about to happen.

On the night of 22 January Chris had a disturbed sleep, with a lot of dreams. Most of them made little sense, until at one point a West Indian appeared in front of Chris and grabbed him by the arms. He started to talk, wildly and incomprehensibly.

'Colin did it, he killed me,' the spirit babbled. 'It was horrible, man. There was the burning, and the things under the skin on my face. But it was Colin – he was the one.'

There was something more real about this than the dreams that surrounded it. There was a tangible taste of fear, and it jolted Chris out of his sleep. When he looked at the clock it was a little after three in the morning.

Eventually he went back to sleep for a few hours, finally waking up to be confronted by '[Colin] – spirit – [keep out]' in the middle of the page. He knew what this meant and called Aylott immediately.

'Pat Frater's dead,' he said when Aylott came on the line.

'How the hell did you know that?'

'Come on, Paul, do you really have to ask?'

'No, I suppose not,' Aylott sighed. 'There's not much chance of getting anything else on it, is there?'

'You know better than that,' Chris replied heatedly. 'I gave you the information I had. I've told you that the spirits – or whatever they are – don't like being ignored.'

'I didn't ignore them – or you,' Aylott said angrily. 'There just wasn't the time –'

'It's a bit late now for us to be arguing over it,' Chris sighed. 'So what did happen?'

Aylott told him.

Pat Frater was a West Indian who lived in Acworth Crescent with his girlfriend Laura Jowett. He liked to drink, smoke and party, but kept himself to himself, and was not a man to court trouble. The ongoing feud with which his brother Danny had become entangled worried him: he had a strong sense of family and so backed his brother, but he had two small children to worry about, and was inclined to wish the matter was all over.

Danny was in the middle of a feud over his ex-girlfriend, Tracy Woodcock. She had left him for another man, and Danny had chased after her. There had been a fight with her new boyfriend and Danny had beaten him. The man had friends, and matters had begun to escalate.

It was a month since Danny had been shot. Patrick knew what had happened and there was talk of revenge attacks. He was still willing to back his brother – but only so far. He didn't know that he had already been dragged in too far.

It was late at night on 22 January before Pat and Laura finally got to bed. So to be woken by a hammering on the front door only a couple of hours later was not the best thing that could have happened to them.

'What time is it?' Pat groaned as the hammering penetrated his sleep and pulled him into consciousness.

'Dunno,' Laura replied sleepily.

Pat Frater looked at the clock by the side of the bed. It was a little after two in the morning. He swore softly to himself.

'What sort of a fool goes around waking people up at this time?' he asked himself, dragging his legs out of bed.

Laura grabbed him. 'Don't go down,' she said.

'Why not?'

'Don't take chances – it might be to do with Danny.'

Pat laughed. The last thing he was expecting was either his brother, or people looking for his brother. Still, if it made her happy . . .

'Okay, I won't go down,' he said to her with a smile. 'I'll just stick my head out of the window, see who the hell it is.'

All the while the hammering continued. The children had woken up. One was a toddler, and the constant noise had made her start to cry. Laura left the bedroom to see to their children.

Pat walked over to the window and looked out: there was a car by the kerbside, engine still running. In the cold

January night he could see the plume of the exhaust as it billowed into the air. The driver was revving the engine to keep it ticking over.

'Damn fool,' Pat muttered, thinking that the engine would soon give out if it was treated in that manner. He looked down, flattening his face to the glass, but was still unable to see who it was hammering on the door.

He swore again softly and sighed. He had hoped to see who it was without having to open the window and let in the chill night. If it was Danny down there, then he'd have a few words to say to him, all of them obscene.

Pat Frater flung open the window and leaned out.

'Oi, what d'you think you're doing, man?' he yelled to the shadowy figure below.

Whoever it was stopped hammering on the door and stepped back. In the light of a street lamp Pat could see that it wasn't his brother. The figure looked up, and the light caught his face.

Pat recognised him, and in the same instant took in the shotgun that he was carrying. Took in that the gun had been raised.

'Oh God –'

He had no time to say anything else. The explosion of the gun was deafening, followed by an immense and cavernous silence. He felt the pellets from the cartridge rip into his face like molten pebbles, penetrating the first layer of skin so quickly that the pain was like a brief burn. Then the nerves were gone, and there was only the fire inside his head.

The sound of the shotgun brought Laura back into the room. She screamed, not believing what she saw.

Patrick Frater lay dead on the floor of his bedroom, thrown backwards by the impact. The front of his head was missing, blown away by the shotgun charge.

In the distance a car screeched away.

Chris knew nothing about this when the spirit of Patrick

Frater came to him, shortly after his death, trying desperately to communicate some information about his killer.
Why Chris was chosen to be the one Patrick came to
is something that has puzzled him ever since, just as he
cannot tell why other spirits approach him. In this case
he assumes that it was because he lived in the area, and
that the spirit of Frater, desperate to capture his killer,
sought out the nearest living person who was somehow
in touch with another plane of existence. Chris was –
in physical terms – just down the road from Luton.

Whatever the reason, Chris knew that the message
given to him was genuine, and that he must tell Aylott
everything. The afternoon of 23 January saw him at
Dunstable Police station, talking to Paul Aylott.

'I've passed on your letter to the investigating officers in Luton,' Aylott began. 'The date on it proves
something – well, to me it does. But we really need
to get something on paper about what you told me this
morning.'

Between them, the two men compiled a defini-
tive statement of what Chris had dreamt concerning Patrick Frater. The information was then passed on to Luton police, who were dealing with the
murder.

In Chris's evidence, there were two names: Colin,
and Urquhart, or 'Urquhy Baby', as Chris had heard
him referred to in the dream. Did these names mean
anything to the investigating officers?

They certainly did: Tracy Woodcock, the girl over
whom the whole affair had blown up, had left Danny
Frater to go and live with another man. This man had
a friend called Colin: Colin Nicholls.

Nicholls was known to the police, and had a reputation as a man with violent tendencies. He had been
under suspicion after the shooting of Danny Frater a
month before, but there had been no evidence to make
anything other than suspicion stick to him. And Nicholls

had a friend called Andrew Urquhart, also known as 'Urquhy-baby'.

Was it possible that Chris Robinson had seen the murder of Patrick Frater in a dream, and that the spirit of Frater had come to him, naming his killers?

It was a proposition that would seem outlandish to anyone but Chris himself, or Paul Aylott, who now found nothing surprising in anything Chris told him. The question was: would the Luton police, and the officers investigating the murder, make something of it, or would they reject it out of hand?

At the time Chris had no idea: however, more than three years later, when he was asked by his then-contact in the Bedfordshire police, Detective Chief Inspector Alex Hall, to assist in the investigation of a man killed in a fish-and-chip shop, Chris came face to face with one of the officers who had investigated the Frater killing.

Asked to visit the site where the murder took place – a man had walked into a chip shop and simply blown away someone standing in the queue – Chris introduced himself to the officer in charge.

'You don't have to tell me who you are,' the officer replied, 'I worked on the Pat Frater case. That letter you wrote is in our office, in a frame on the wall.'

So what did happen?

Chris's information was passed on to the team investigating the murder. The names Colin and Urquhart meant something to the police concerned, who had already connected the murder with the shooting of Danny Frater and the long-running feud between what had become rival gangs. They also knew that Pat Frater had little to do with this. If he had been shot as part of the feud, it was quite probably a mistake.

Further investigation ensued. It became apparent that neither Colin Nicholls nor Andrew Urquhart had an alibi for the night concerned. They were pulled in for questioning.

One thing soon became apparent: neither man had anything to do with the earlier shooting of Danny Frater. This made the detectives begin to question whether they were on the right track. Was it possible that Chris had led them down a blind alley?

A search turned up the shotgun, which could be linked to Nicholls. And the police were able to hold Urquhart on a lesser charge, pending further questioning, as he had been driving while disqualified.

The circumstantial evidence became too great and witnesses came forward who could identify the two men. It was a slowly built case, with no major breakthrough but, rather, a good example of persistent detective work piecing together a case: a case in which Chris's evidence had played a very real part.

Eventually there was enough to charge both Nicholls and Urquhart. Nicholls was charged with murder; Urquhart with manslaughter and the secondary charge of driving while disqualified.

The case came up before the Inner London Crown Court, where it was heard in front of Judge George Shindler, QC. At the trial it emerged that Nicholls believed Danny Frater to be staying at his brother's house. He went there with the express intention of shooting him, hammering on the door at 2 a.m. When the window was raised, and a head peered out, Nicholls assumed it to be Danny Frater and fired wildly.

Although there was murderous intent, in the dim street lighting and at that time of the morning, with a shotgun he was firing above his head, it was more by luck than good judgement that Pat Frater was hit full in the face. It was a cruel stroke of fate that he should be hit in such a random manner, and in mistake for his brother.

Both Nicholls and Urquhart denied the charges against them, but both were found guilty by the jury. The judge made a recommendation that Nicholls serve a minimum of fifteen years for what he described as a 'brutal, cruel, callous and cold-blooded murder'. He was also given concurrent sentences of two years and four years for firearms offences.

Urquhart, who had acted solely as getaway driver and so charged with the lesser offence of manslaughter, was convicted and jailed for a total of four years. For driving while disqualified, he received a five-year ban.

The judge also ordered the confiscation of the firearms and Urquhart's car, which he ordered to be sold, the cash raised to be kept in a trust fund for Patrick Frater's children.

In many ways this was a pleasing result for Chris: the evidence of his dreams had helped to find the killers of a man whose spirit had come to him in great distress, crying out for help. In another sense, Chris would have preferred it not to have happened: if having no dreams meant that Pat Frater had not died, then that would have been a far better result.

It was at times like this that Chris began to feel the strain of having his strange gift. The night he had seen Frater die was etched on his memory. Even though it had actually happened more than a month earlier, he had carried around the feelings aroused that night. Curiously, his first dream had occurred around the time that Frater's brother Danny was shot.

In his initial dream, in which he had seen the death of Pat Frater, the method of murder had been by drowning. Although, in reality, Frater had been shot, his moment of death must in many ways have been similar to death by drowning: the shortness of breath and sudden molten inrush into the lungs giving as much burning pain as the shotgun pellets ripping into his face.

When Pat Frater had come to Chris shortly after his death, these intense emotions had been re-awakened and re-doubled: Frater was a soul in torment, only just departed from the earth and in search of someone who could not only share his suffering but also try and help catch those who had perpetrated it.

Chris had been able to help, but at the cost of immense personal stress and anguish. Throughout the affair he had also been having dreams concerned with bomb warnings, which had been less emotionally anguished but still intense. Now he hoped that the spirit of Patrick Frater would rest in peace.

So he would: but not before he asked Chris for help one more time.

Between the first appearance of Pat Frater and the actual event of his death, Chris left the country and spent some time in the Philippines. While he was there something happened that showed the lighter side of being psychically gifted.

While he was staying at a bungalow, he was approached by a Sergeant Major in the Filipino army, who was acquainted with Chris's uncle and knew of his powers.

'I wonder if you can help me,' he said.

'I'll try,' Chris replied, wondering what was coming next.

'I've got this problem with one of my men. He's lost his rifle, he claims . . .'

'Then you don't think that he has?'

The army officer shrugged. 'He says he has, but I don't believe him. I think he has another motive and something in mind. Something that could get him into a lot of trouble. I don't want that to happen. He's not a bad man, but a bit headstrong.'

'So what do you want me to do?' Chris asked.

'Maybe you could dream about what has happened, then tell me?'

Chris laughed. 'Maybe I can. I don't know – I can't guarantee results. But I'll give it a go.'

So that night Chris wrote a question at the head of the sheet of paper he was using to write down his dreams.

He asked simply for the spirits to show him what the
soldier had done with his rifle, and why.

The dream that night was crystal-clear, and literal
rather than symbolic.

It was a small village, and the evening had crept on.
The air was still and humid, and an old woman sat alone
in her hut. The soldier came into the hut and greeted
the old woman: his mother, perhaps. The relationship
wasn't clear.

What was perfectly clear was that the soldier had the
rifle hidden under the floor of the hut. It was an M-16,
easily identifiable. The soldier took the rifle and went
out of the hut. Chris followed: it was as though he was
an invisible tail, moving as he would in so-called reality,
yet hidden from the eyes of the soldier.

As he followed, the idea behind the disappearance of
the rifle became obvious: the soldier intended to frame
a love rival for murder. He reached the home of the
person he was going to kill.

Chris woke up, knowing what he must do. The
next afternoon he met the Sergeant Major at a bar, as
arranged.

'So,' the Sergeant Major asked, 'did you dream anything?'

'I certainly did,' Chris replied, before telling the story
of his dream. The Sergeant Major listened avidly, and
when Chris had finished he said, 'I suspected as much.'

'So you believe me, then?' asked Chris with a
wry smile.

The Sergeant Major nodded. 'I've been around a long
time – it's not the first time I've seen something like this
and it won't be the last.'

As he rose to leave, Chris stopped him. 'Why did you
believe me so readily?'

'Sorry?'

'Most people don't take what I say at such face
value.'

The Sergeant Major smiled. 'You told me that the missing rifle is an M-16. That's not a common service issue here, only certain units have it. How else would you have known that?'

Several days passed before Chris saw the Sergeant Major again. This time it was by chance. He greeted Chris in the street and suggested that they have a quick drink.

When they were in the bar the Sergeant Major turned to Chris with a grin. 'You were right.'

'What – about the missing rifle?'

The Sergeant Major nodded. 'I confronted him with the whole story, and he broke down and confessed. He couldn't work out how I knew all about it.'

'What did you tell him?'

'I told him the spirits were on my side,' the Sergeant Major said with a broad grin.

Back in England, after the conclusion of the Patrick Frater case, Chris thought that he would see no more of the restless spirit.

He was wrong.

CHAPTER THIRTEEN

The connection with Patrick Frater came back to haunt Chris – in more ways than one – in June 1991.

By this time Chris was no longer sending his faxes to Paul Aylott, who had moved on to another position in the Bedfordshire force, although he was still talking to Chris on a social level. Chris's contact was now Detective Chief Inspector Alex Hall, who had only recently taken over the job of handling Chris's dreams. They had already established a good rapport, and Chris was now in the habit of spending a certain amount of time each day at Bedfordshire Police Headquarters, cloistered with Alex as they tried to make sense of the dreams.

At one point, the dream page read: '[Premium Bond] 2QB – [9999] 2 one.'

At the side of the page, when he awoke, Chris had written 'ERNIE – random number generator – computer', followed by '2 [QB] 999 call?'. He felt sure that the first four 9s inside a box meant that there should only be three, signalling a call to the emergency services. He was also sure that in his dream he had seen the computer whose acronym was ERNIE, which was used to select the winning numbers for Premium Bonds.

Further up the page he had written, 'Why [Eaton Bray]? Or is it THE AVENUE?'

At first Chris assumed that this was something to do with another bomb warning that he had running: yet

it didn't fit with the rest of the information he had
received.

It was an incredible night for dreams: Chris had
produced six pages of writing, and at the top of the
fourth page he had written, 'Pat Frater – I am here –
watch.' This was followed by a drawing of a watch face,
with 'two doors on front – no strap'. Underneath was
written:

Trouble – [£25]
In a [spirit] – is it Colin?
   [Nunnery Lane] I promise I would not lie about
that – [sweets]
   Chocolate cups in a [sandwich] box
Lots of baby bees in the street.

And on the last page was written:

Are the chocolates after [8] mints?
I do not like chocolates any more – you can have
all of them.

Beside this was drawn a broken chocolate bar. It was
all incredibly cryptic when viewed on the page, but Chris
could distinctly remember certain aspects of his dream
that helped everything begin to make sense.

The random number generator had been shown to
him by Patrick Frater, who had returned to Chris's
dreams in order to introduce another spirit to him.
The spirit was that of another black man, who came
forward to Chris.

'I didn't commit suicide. Whatever happens, tell them
that I didn't.' His voice was confused and garbled, and he
was obviously in some distress. 'It's really cold – they've
got me in a freezer,' he continued.

All this came flooding back as Chris and Alex Hall
went over the dream page.

'That's incredible,' Alex said, 'how do you get all that from it? I mean, where does it tell you that he was black?'

'For a start, I remember seeing him – but look at this . . .' Chris drew Hall's attention to a section of the dream diary for that night. 'Right here, it says "chocolate cups". Chocolate is a sign for black people, right? And you should know already what cups mean: they signify dead people. Don't ask me why,' he added, seeing that Hall was about to ask. 'They just do. And you see this bit here about baby bees in the street?' He pointed out another of the key phrases. 'Bees are always black people – like a gang of them in this case. When they're angry and buzzing about it means there's going to be trouble for someone black. Then, if you go over the page, there's this bit here about –'

'About chocolate, and not liking it any more,' Hall said, noting the drawing of a broken chocolate bar.

'Right – it's going away, being sent away – "you can have all of them". It seemed like it was being pushed away from me, going away . . . like a spirit dying.'

'What about the chocolates being After-Eight's?' Alex asked, noticing the cryptic reference to chocolate mints.

'I wouldn't swear to it, but I bet that was about the time he died.' Chris paused, deep in thought. 'Have there been any dodgy deaths lately?'

'What do you mean by dodgy? Anything we have to look into is dodgy,' said Hall wryly.

'Well, this bloke claimed that he didn't top himself, so I suppose I mean any suspicious suicides in the last few days.'

'Not that I know of,' Hall replied. 'I can look into it, see if there have been any reported that look a bit strange.'

They moved on to the coded bomb warnings that might have been contained in the dreams, and the matter was temporarily forgotten. When Alex Hall looked into the matter there had been no suicides in suspicious circumstances in the last few weeks.

Chris and Alex decided to concentrate on more immediate matters. But the suicide, Ernie, was not to go away.

Ernie stayed away until 6 July. There was a bomb warning in Hayes and the escape of two IRA men from Brixton prison: these were the subjects that occupied Chris's dreams at this point (and will be dealt with in a later chapter). There was little time and space in his dreams for anything other than this.

But by 6 July things were beginning to calm down, and Chris had the mental capacity for Ernie to make a reappearance. He signalled his presence by the metaphorical use of a spade: perhaps in many ways an insulting term when used to refer to black people, it was nonetheless one in common use, and Chris had long since found that his dreams drew from a language that ranged far and wide and were no respecter of political correctness.

In the dream, a woman called Maria had been made pregnant. Chris knew several women called Maria, but this particular one lived in a road in Luton called Arrow Close. Chris was sitting on her bed, talking to her and two other people. He heard about another girl – Lisa – who had also been made pregnant. When he asked who was responsible, he was shown a spade, such as is used for digging up a garden. When he asked where it came from, he was told that it was kept in another house in the road.

Looking at the dream page in the morning, Chris knew that the spade was a symbol for the black man – Ernie. He was also sure that Ernie lived in Arrow Close: and Chris had been told that the spade was kept in the same road as Maria's house.

Chris knew that Ernie desperately wanted to tell him something about the way he had died, and where he came from: he wanted Chris's help. And Chris would be only too glad to help a spirit in distress, if not for the fact that he didn't know exactly what Ernie wanted from him. The messages he was receiving were still too garbled. Perhaps it was because there were other things that he had to concentrate on; perhaps the spirits weren't letting Ernie come through properly because his need wasn't as great as that of the people threatened by bombs.

It was a thorny question and just part of a bigger puzzle that had often kept Chris awake: what was the purpose of his dreams? To what end was he shown all these things? Obviously to help someone: but who? An individual or some amorphous mass of 'the public'? Why not both? Why shouldn't Ernie be able to come through as clearly as the spirits who were guiding Chris in his dreams about bombs?

It may have been this confusion that clouded his mind on 7 July, as nothing came through concerning Ernie. The following night, however, Chris had a startlingly clear message.

There was terrible trouble ahead: Chris knew this because he was surrounded by snow at every point in his dream. He carried a fridge down towards a stream, and it was heavy, as though it was full. Snow was falling and lay all around. He was camping in the country, and snow fell on the bare branches of the trees – even though it was really July, in Chris's dream it was winter.

He was chasing after an airline ticket that had fallen out of his pocket. It blew along the ground, and Chris chased it through the billowing clouds of snow, picking it up as it came to rest near his camper.

Looking up, he could see there were copper pipes on the roof of the camper, lashed to it as though on a roof-rack. Although he hadn't seen them appear, he knew – as a kind of dream-memory – that they had been put there by a traveller. He went inside the camper to get away from the snow, which lay all round.

Inside the camper was a machine. He'd never seen anything like it before, but he knew its function. He switched it on, and it began to measure the snowfall outside. It had a counter on it that actually recorded the number of snowflakes falling in an hour.

The counter whirred around, out of control. Chris looked out of the window and could see that the snow was falling as in a blizzard.

Abstractedly, even though he was actually dreaming at the time, there was a part of Chris that was conscious enough to know that terrible danger lay ahead for someone. Snow always signified danger, and it was months since he had seen it this bad.

In the camper there was a flap that held up one of the beds, and masked it from view. Chris felt that he had to let the bed down: as he did, Ernie appeared, sitting on the bed.

'It's cold here, just like in the fridge. I'm still there, y'know, still waiting. You just ask them about the fridge. You've really got to help, because I want them to know that it wasn't suicide. I didn't kill myself, it was someone else. It just looked like I killed myself.'

'What do you mean?' Chris asked. 'You keep turning up telling me this, but you don't really tell me anything that I can use. I don't know who you are, or what this is about.'

'Of course you do. You know I'm Ernie, and that I lived in Arrow Close. And you know that I'm supposed to have killed myself. I didn't – I did not commit suicide. It was two guys – they took me and made it look like that.'

'Then tell me who they are. If I knew that –'

'You could do what you did for Pat,' Ernie said, referring to Patrick Frater. He shook his head. 'No, that won't do me any good, man. It can't take me back, can it? Why should they suffer? They know they did it, they've got to live with it. I just want them to know that I didn't commit suicide. You just ask them about the fridge.'

With that, the dream dissolved and Chris woke with his heart pounding. It was almost half-past three in the morning, and the whole page was a description of the dream. The last two sentences on the page particularly caught his eye:

Who committed suicide   not long ago?
ask about the fridge.

Chris wrote another two pages when he went back to sleep, and analysed these the next day with Alex Hall as he always did. But it was the dream with Ernie that really bugged him: there had to be something he could do to help this spirit. It was a very similar situation to the one with Pat Frater, inasmuch as there was a disturbed spirit from his physical locality who needed his help. Pat had wanted his killers named, whereas Ernie only wanted people to know that he had not committed suicide: he was refusing to name his killers, saying this wasn't important to him now.

But Ernie wasn't as forthcoming as Pat in other ways: although Chris knew that he lived in Arrow Close, he still didn't know Ernie's other name, or how he could contact anyone who knew him.

When he went to bed on the night of 9 July, Chris's main concern was with the escaped IRA men, and the question he wrote at the top of the clean page was about them. Yet he also wanted Ernie to come to him again and provide a little more information.

Ernie did appear again and the dream was so chilling that even now, almost half a decade later, Chris still shivers when he talks about it.

*   *   *

The first part of the dream was a confusion of jumbled images. Then it changed, and Chris was in a room with Graham Bright, then Parliamentary Private Secretary to John Major and Chris's local MP. The two men had been in touch frequently because of Chris's dreams, and it came as no surprise to see Bright represented in the dream. At first, Chris thought this would be a bomb warning, but it soon moved off at a tangent.

Chris handed Bright a steaming mug of coffee. He knew from previous dreams that a mug of coffee was another representation of a dead person – a mug being a large cup. And because it was coffee, he knew that it was a black person.

As he was dreaming, Chris knew that this was connected with Ernie.

Bright was sitting in a room at Chandos, a school that Chris used to attend. Chris walked along the roads surrounding the school, partly re-tracing his old route, carrying the steaming mug. There were school-girls walking along the road, and he stopped to look at them.

When he reached the school, and tried to hand the mug to Bright, the MP asked him to leave it outside for him and said he'd attend to it later.

Chris left the mug and walked off down the road. He came to a house and went inside. He could hear struggling from upstairs, and as he went up he could see three men on the top landing. There was a hatch leading into the loft, with a long ladder partly hanging down from it. While Chris watched, two of the men tied a noose to the third and hanged him from the ladder.

It was unusual for Chris to have this sort of dream: when he had seen a death previously, he had felt it and woken in distress. Not this time: this was like a re-enactment, a reconstruction. A play put on for his benefit. This was something that Ernie wanted him to see.

Chris was no longer in the house. Now he was walking around the streets with a bunch of school children. He was one of them, yet he was his real age. He had a hood over his head to try and cover this up. He knew that he should be looking for the name of the road where the house was situated: the house in which Ernie was hanged.

He was outside the school and saw the name Broomfield Road, which lay near Lyons Meade, both familiar names from his past. The school's headmaster got out of his car.

The dream changed again. Now Chris was with Graham Bright once more, and they were making a bet for five pounds about how long Bright would last in his job. They went up in the lift at a hotel with two other men and knew they were waiting for one more. Would he come?

The dream faded into nothing, dissolving as Chris woke up in the morning. It was then that he looked at the two pages he had written that night and felt his blood run cold.

Mug of [coffee]. Take it 2 Graham Bright.
He is at Chandos. My old school.
    I walk along the road 2 it – mug in my hand

That was at the bottom of the first page. Overleaf the dream continued.

Ladder in [2] the loft
too long to fit without being dropped down. in 2
the stairwell and then straight up into The Hatch.

There was then a sketch of a house, with a staircase and a ladder drawn leading from the top of the stairs into the loft. Two arrows indicated the area covered by the ladder with the words 'ladder is longer than this'. Underneath, Chris had written, 'Look at the map. What road did I walk up when I went 2 school.'

Chris was sure that he now knew how Ernie had died. He had been hanged by two men, who had made the killing look like suicide. There was also a clue as to where it had happened, in the names of the roads along the route to Chandos School. As the only names he had noticed were Broomfield Road and Lyons Meade, Chris knew that it must be either one of these names or names that sounded like them.

The one thing that puzzled him more than anything else was when Ernie had died. Alex Hall had checked for him, and there had been no suspicious suicides around the time that Ernie had first appeared. Did this mean that it had taken time for Ernie to come through to Chris? Or – and this was something that he found highly disturbing – was this some kind of precognition and Ernie hadn't yet died?

It might seem strange to consider someone's spirit contacting a medium about their death before it had actually occurred, but there is a possible explanation for such a curious phenomenon.

If the current theories about time are correct, then time is not linear: that is to say, we don't start at point A (say 1900) and proceed to point B (say 1999) in a straight line. It seems this way to us, because of the way that we perceive time. In fact, everything that has happened or will happen is here right now. Time is more like a point than a line. It is therefore possible to see the future, as it lies all around us: it's just that our brains filter out everything except that which we need to survive. We live in what is called 'the information universe', and if we took in everything, we would experience a kind of sensory overload and would be unable to function.

Chris wonders if time proceeds like a series of curves and, as a medium, he is able to see across the troughs to each peak – this would account for the way in which his dreams seem to run in cycles of days and weeks, rather than be totally random.

If he was right, then was this what was occurring between Chris and Ernie? Was Chris able to see across one of those troughs to another peak in the curves of time? A curve where the dead Ernie was crying out to Chris about what had yet to happen?

Chris went to see Alex Hall as usual that morning but wasn't too forthcoming on the subject of Ernie and his supposed suicide. There were other matters that were more pressing: Chris's main purpose in reporting to the police was still to reveal his dreams about bomb threats.

It was an uneventful morning and the subject of Ernie was playing on Chris's mind when he reached home. He had only been in for a short while when the phone rang. When he picked it up, there was an unfamiliar female voice on the line.

'Hello – is that Christopher Robinson?'

'Yes?'

'You don't know me, but I've read a lot about you. My name's Jeannette, and I advertise in the local paper – that's where I've seen you. You might have seen my ad.'

Chris made encouraging noises: he hadn't seen her advertisement and had no idea who she was. He had, however, been in the paper quite a bit over the last year and a half with his predictions. He asked the woman to continue.

'I've got a couple of people here who you might be able to help. You see, I practise alternative therapies and give Tarot readings, but I'm not a medium or psychic in any way – and I think that's what they need. It's about their brother.'

As she spoke, Chris felt a shiver run down his spine: could they have anything to do with Ernie?

'Can I give them your phone number?' the woman asked.

'They can come over and see me if they like,' Chris replied. 'I've got to go out in a little while, and I won't be back until around seven, but if they want to come over then, they're quite welcome.'

'I'll tell them that – shall I get them to ring if they are?'

'No need – just tell them to come. You've got the address?' Chris's address had been printed in the local paper, so he was sure that she would have it if she also had his phone number. Jeannette confirmed this and rang off.

Chris was expecting to hear nothing further until the evening and was surprised when the phone went again, a minute or two later. When he picked it up, it was Jeannette.

'Hello, Chris? They're really grateful – their names are Dulcie and Paul, and they'll be over around seven . . .'

Chris had only just got home when there was a knock at the door. It took him by surprise, as it was exactly seven o'clock. Whoever these people were, they were certainly keen. It would be an amazing coincidence if they were related to Ernie, but then again, Chris was used to the improbable happening to him.

When he opened the door he was confronted by a man and woman of Afro-Caribbean origin.

'Thank God you're black,' he exclaimed, unable to suppress his surprise. The couple looked at each other in bemusement, and Chris felt that he had to explain further. 'Don't get me wrong: I'm not prejudiced, it's just that I've had a black man coming to me in my dreams, asking for help. I'm wondering if he's your brother.'

The couple looked nervous and confused: whatever else, they obviously hadn't expected a reaction like this.

'Look, come in and sit down. I'll put the kettle on and you can tell me all about it,' Chris said, doing his best to put them at their ease.

He led them into the sitting room and left them there while he went into the kitchen to make some tea. When he went back he was carrying the dream diary, which he had opened at the previous night's page. He put it on the coffee table and sat down opposite them. But he took care to keep the page with the drawing of the house turned towards him and partly masked with a newspaper, so that they couldn't see it yet: if Ernie wasn't related to them, then it might be distressing if they saw the sketch and jumped to conclusions.

'I only know what that Jeannette woman told me on the phone this morning,' he began. 'You're looking for your brother, right?'

'No, we know that he's dead – well, he was my girlfriend's brother, really, but –' began Paul.

'Was his name Ernie?'

There was a silence, as Dulcie and Paul sat staring at Chris. Finally Dulcie nodded. There were tears in her eyes.

'I've had a man called Ernie come to me recently, telling me that everyone thinks he committed suicide. But he says that he didn't. He also keeps talking about being cold, and being in a fridge. Has he been buried yet?'

'No.' Dulcie shook her head. 'He's still in the mortuary. They haven't had the inquest yet. I know they say that he killed himself, but I don't believe that. I know him too well for that – he wasn't that type of man, you know? Sure, he's been down, and said that he might, but . . .'

'There's a big difference between saying and doing,' Paul added.

'Well, he's come to me and said that two men killed him and made it look like a suicide. But he won't name them. He says that it won't do anybody any good, but he just wants you people to know that he didn't kill himself.'

Dulcie began to cry.

'D'you know, I don't even know his surname,' Chris said softly. 'I know he's called Ernie, because another spirit told me – did he know Patrick Frater?'

Paul nodded. 'Yeah, we all knew Pat.'

'Well, he's the one who brought Ernie to me. Look, let's make sure we've actually got the right man. Would it be too upsetting for you if I told you how I thought Ernie died?'

Dulcie wiped away a tear and shook her head. 'No, tell us what you know.'

Chris took a deep breath before beginning. He didn't want to upset them any more than was necessary – any more than they already were upset.

'I think that Ernie was found hanged from a ladder in a loft, coming out from the hatch. Can I show you something?' He waited until they both nodded, then uncovered the dream diary and turned the page towards them. 'I drew this in my dream last night. Ernie showed me what had happened. The house is in a road called Broomfield, or something that sounds like that. Does this make sense to you?'

Dulcie looked at the page, then continued to cry. Paul comforted her, then looked at Chris and nodded.

'That looks like the house. It's in Bramingham Road. That's where we found him.'

Ernest Bandoo was thirty-six years old and had disappeared from his home in Arrow Close, Luton during the first week of April. He worked as a painter and decorator, and had recently been working on a house in Bramingham Road, Luton.

The house had been empty for some time and it was a large-scale job to get it in habitable order. There had been other men working on the property with him, and all of them were discontented with the conditions under which they were forced to work: it had been several weeks since they had last been paid.

Bandoo had four children, and to go this long without pay had been a severe financial strain. He was a man given to emotional extremes, and had been depressed about the situation regarding his employment and the resultant pressures on his family life. The lack of money was getting him down. In fits of temper he had talked about taking his own life, and had even claimed to his wife, Medina, that he had tried to hang himself with a belt. But no-one took him seriously: those who knew him said that he was prone to such outbursts, either of joy or depression. He blustered, but didn't act.

Bandoo and another worker had daubed graffiti on the walls of the downstairs rooms at Bramingham Road – among the graffiti was a hangman, which led to a strengthening of the suicide theory, as far as the coroner was concerned. It's much more likely, however, that the hanged man in the drawing was their elusive employer, abusively referred to in the rest of the scrawlings. Attempts to trace him and get the monies owed to his employees had so far proved fruitless.

When Bandoo stormed out of his house, his wife had a feeling that he would go and stay at the house in Bramingham Road. At first she did nothing about this: he was a man of quick temper, who had previously walked out after rows. He had always returned home within a few days.

But a few days turned into a week, then into two weeks. Finally, on 19 April 1991, Medina called Bandoo's sister Dulcie, and asked her and Paul Jacques, her boyfriend, to look for Ernest. She told them that she had a 'cold feeling' that he had gone to the house in Bramingham Road, and that something awful had happened to him.

Dulcie and Paul went to the house on the evening of 19 April. It was dark and deserted. They let themselves in with one of the keys to the property that Ernest had left at home, and explored downstairs. There were several crushed beer cans and evidence that somebody had been drinking heavily.

With a feeling of dread they mounted the stairs to the first floor, where they could see something moving in the darkness: it was the hanging body of Ernest, already beginning to decompose and stirring softly as their footfalls moved the floorboards and walls of the house.

The coroner, Dr John Harte, called in the Home Office pathologist for an independent autopsy and ordered Luton CID to carry out a thorough investigation into the death.

This was still going on when Ernie turned up in Chris's dreams.

'You've got to ask Ernie, if you can,' Paul told Chris. 'We must know what happened. I know that Medina and Dulcie couldn't stand it if someone else was responsible for Ernie's death and no-one did anything about it.'

Chris looked at Dulcie, who was still crying. 'I can't promise anything,' he said slowly, 'but I will try.'

That night he wrote the following question at the head of the page: 'Ernie – show what happened to you and tell me who did it.'

That night, Ernie came to see Chris again.

'I didn't kill myself,' he repeated, 'but there's no reason for me to tell you who did. What good is it going to do me? Look, if my brother and my family really want to find out who did it, they need to look for two guys who were at the house the day I walked out. That's all really. And remember the fridge. I'm in the fridge . . .'

Chris felt sure that the fridge was a cryptic clue that

meant more than just being in a mortuary, but exactly what, he just didn't know.

On the pages of dreams he had written:

and I was murdered – when Glen comes back he will help you.

if Harry want him [2] catch them The Fridge is an important clue – so is [Ernie Bandoo]. Maps are spread out all over [his] bed

HAND PAINTED colour blue –

READ MY FILE at the police station – then you will understand – then I can come back to your friend and you – Rohip has made a hit.

Some of this was extremely confusing: Glen might refer to Glen Clemence, who was Alex Hall's driver and had worked with Chris on some of his dream translations at the police station. He had been in the dream earlier, concerned with another matter. Did this mean that the next time he appeared in a dream it would be concerned with Ernie?

HAND PAINTED was a postcode clue: where was the HP postcode, and what did it have to do with Ernie? And who on earth was Harry?

This was less than Chris had hoped for. He rang Paul and Dulcie with a heavy heart, telling them that Ernie had once again said that he would not identify the men who had killed him, only that they should ask about two men hanging around the house the day that Ernie stormed out of his home.

He read them the rest of what he had written – and was stunned to hear that Ernie had a brother called Harry, who lived some distance away and would shortly be visiting Medina for the inquest.

Paul and Dulcie thanked Chris for his attempt to help

them. He heard nothing more about the case until the inquest.

The inquest was held some time later, under the auspices of Dr Harte. The evidence of the Home Office pathologist showed that Ernie had been hanged with his own tie. In the opinion of the pathologist, he had done this himself – there was no evidence of struggle. He had been drinking heavily before he died and the corpse – which was naked from the waist up – had been hanging in the house for at least a week before it was discovered.

In her own evidence, Medina Bandoo claimed that Ernie would not have been alone in the house, as he hated to drink on his own: there must have been someone else there.

The investigating officer from Luton CID, Detective Inspector Garth Pestell, told the coroner that 'a medium called Christopher Robinson' had told the family to 'speak to a woman in Bramingham Road about two people who visited the house on the day that Mr Bandoo was found'.

Somewhere between Chris and the CID the message had been distorted. This was not what Ernie had said to Chris in his dream, so it came as no surprise to hear that DI Pestell had eliminated from his inquiries a woman and child seen knocking on the door of the house on 19 April.

Despite the evidence of the pathologist, there was enough uncertainty surrounding Ernest Bandoo's death for the coroner to record an open verdict.

To this day Chris believes that Ernie was murdered, but that he was able to rest happily knowing that his family was not stigmatised by his alleged suicide.

About a month after the inquest Chris was driving through Luton, on a route that he didn't usually take.

It took him past the cemetery, and as he approached the entrance a voice came over his shoulder.

'Come and see me, Chris.'

He recognised the voice as Ernie's. It was a request he didn't want to ignore, so he indicated and turned into the cemetery.

It is the main cemetery for the Luton area and covers a large area of land. Chris got out of his car and began to walk: he didn't know where he was going, only that he should follow his instinct. Eventually he came to a patch of recently dug graves. They were all unmarked. Without hesitating, he walked up to one.

'Hello, Ernie,' he said, sitting down by the grave. He had only been there a few moments when Paul and Dulcie came towards him.

'What are you doing here?' Dulcie asked, astonished.

'I was driving by and I heard Ernie's voice. He asked me to come and see him. I hope I'm not intruding, or anything.'

'Of course not,' Dulcie replied. 'You can come and see him any time – but how did you know where he was?'

'I don't know . . . I mean, it's not marked yet, is it? I just came here automatically.'

'The stone won't be ready for a week or two,' Paul said. 'Did you know that Patrick Frater's buried here?' he added.

Chris shook his head. 'No, I didn't. Whereabouts?' Paul was about to speak when Chris stopped him: 'No, don't tell me – let's see if Pat does.'

They were in the middle of a series of graves, some of which had headstones, and some of which were too fresh. They stood in the middle of a row, and it was impossible to see much further than two or three rows either way.

Chris started to walk, trusting the spirits of Ernie and Patrick to guide him. He walked back five or six rows from the spot where Ernie was buried, followed by Dulcie and Paul. He didn't look at any of the headstones until he stopped in front of one. He couldn't say why he stopped: he just felt that he should.

'This is it,' he said, looking down.

The headstone had a name on it: Patrick Frater.

CHAPTER FOURTEEN

During the February and March of 1991 Chris had his first brush with the world of television. The experiment conducted was so effective and so accurate that it caused him a great deal of anguish, and also led to him being dropped from the programme for being too good.

It's not often that a psychic will be called upon to demonstrate their powers for the camera, and all too frequently these occasions are intended to debunk what is happening and to expose all psychic phenomena as fake. This was the situation in which Chris found himself.

On 28 February Chris was at home when the phone rang. He picked it up and found himself talking to a woman called Sue Walls, who announced herself as a researcher for Granada Television.

'We're doing a show on psychic phenomena, and your name was passed on to us by a policeman who says that you're really good.'

Chris wondered who the policeman was, since most of the forces he had worked with so far were understandably nervous about public reaction to the regular use of a psychic by the police. However, he let this go and asked her what the show would be about.

'The show is hosted by James Randi, and we want to study and test the effectiveness of psychics under experimental conditions.'

'Well, look,' Chris replied, 'I'm quite willing to do

this, but I won't be happy if you make up the test without consulting me about how it's done.'

'What do you mean?' Sue asked, no doubt expecting some outlandish condition of secrecy, which is the stock of many fake psychics who wish to preserve their secrets.

'It's like this,' Chris began. 'I have dream premonitions. They only really come to me in dreams. I don't hold seances, or anything like that. And I don't really practise psychometry – I might be able to pick something up from holding your watch, or whatever, but that's not really how it works with me.'

'Well, what do you do then?' Sue asked, puzzled.

'I just dream. When I go to sleep, I keep a piece of paper by the bed and I write things down on it. In the morning I look at them and try to interpret the symbols. Sometimes I remember the whole dream, and it's very literal. And occasionally the spirits of dead people come and talk to me in my dreams. But it all happens when I'm asleep, and then comes the hard slog of working it out. It's not exactly going to be riveting to watch, but that's how it goes.'

'Would you do any other kind of experiment for us?'

Chris sighed. 'That's what I've been trying to tell you. If you make me try and hold a seance, or hold someone's watch, then you're not going to get any result. I've had this happening to me long enough to know that most experiments try to impose themselves on the psychic, rather than testing them in the way they work. If you want to see if I'm genuine – which I assure you I am, but I don't expect you to believe me out of hand – then you're going to have to test me the way I actually work.'

There was a pause, while Sue considered whether she could actually do this for the show. Finally she said, 'Okay, I'll tell you what. Can you tell me tomorrow what will be on the front page of Monday's newspapers.'

'Which one?' Chris asked. 'There's a lot of dailies. I don't think I could do all of them – y'see, I actually write a question on the paper before I go to sleep, so I need to have something a bit more exact.'

'Um . . . tell what will be on the front of *Today* – that's the paper I get anyway.'

'All right. I'll fax you what I've written first thing tomorrow morning – both the paper with the dream writing and my interpretation.'

'Even if you don't get anything?'

'Even if I don't get anything. It doesn't always work, and I'm not hiding that. It's the fact that it happens at all that gets me.'

Chris put the phone down, intrigued by his first brush with television.

The dreams that night were unclear: he was in a restaurant with swing doors, and read a horoscope to a friend called Barry Grayson – except he didn't read it straight, he paraphrased it.

There were glasses of milk on all the tables in the restaurant, and on a round table near the door somebody had left a carrier bag.

Things changed, and he was standing under a bus shelter, with a hail of penknives falling from the sky, talking to somebody he couldn't quite recognise about it being their birthday.

The knives became rain, and caused a flood. He explained to someone that the flood in the middle of the road was only rainwater, not a sewage pipe bursting, as they had proclaimed.

There was a young girl, getting into a Mini – but it wouldn't start and the gear lever was tight, jamming as he tried to get it out of neutral for her. So they took a scooter, and followed a car driven by a friend of his called David.

The car stopped, and they ran into it. When he picked

himself up, he saw that she was putting something into the back seat of the car. He turned the scooter round, asked her if she was all right and if she wanted to be taken home.

He was looking into the Mini – there was something wrong with the exhaust, and there was a black leather cover on the steering wheel that was in two parts. It came off the wheel, but the lining remained.

He took the driver of the car on the back of his scooter, and they had to push the machine to keep it going. Eventually they made their way to a police station, where he was asked for his driving licence. As he produced it, his teeth fell out. Since he was sixteen he has had false teeth on a bridge, replacing those he lost in a motorscooter accident. These were the teeth that fell out. He tried to put them back in, but they were covered in oily fingermarks, and three of them fell out again. He tried to piece them together as they left the station.

Suddenly he was outside a shop with glass double doors. They had been left open, even though the shop was empty, and he could see some strawberry cream cakes inside.

He sneaked in with his friend David, who had been in the dream since the scooter crash. As they started to eat the cakes, the shop manager appeared from the back of the shop, dressed in a brown coat. He had come to lock up, and was surprised and angry to find them there. He threatened to call the police unless David paid for the cakes . . .

When Chris woke, he showered and had some coffee before turning to the task of working out what his dreams meant. Looking at what he had written there didn't seem to be much that made any sense.

Although it had been more of a continuous and coherent dream than usual, the actual writing he had produced during the night seemed to reveal little. The name of his friend Barry Grayson had been boxed, and he had written beside it 'read him his horoscope from a book – para phrase it.' The misplaced gap in the word paraphrase was perhaps significant: did it stand for Paras, as in Paratroop Regiment? It might be another IRA message, as 'Birthday Today' at the bottom of the page proclaimed by its capital letters that it was a postcode – BT for Belfast.

On the second page he had written 'Main Pipe underground', which he could interpret as MP or PM – Prime Minister underground. This might tie in with the codes for Special Branch and the postcode for Cambridge that appeared further down the page. There was also a cryptic reference to Chris's friend Bob Monkhouse, whom he had known since helping to install his private cinema in the 1970s. The girl in his dream had been putting what might have been a video tape on the back seat of the car, and he knew that Bob was having problems with tape that had been stolen from his car.

There was little on the third page apart from another reference to Belfast, and one to his friend Gary Simpson. But then Gary often turned up in Chris's dreams, as the men were very close. From the three teeth that had fallen from his bridge, Chris felt sure that three people would be hurt in Belfast, but there was nothing more definite than that.

Finally, the shop on the last page and the colour of the manager's coat suggested Sainsburys (whose employees wear brown uniforms) and that something being locked up was connected to them. What it was, Chris just didn't know.

It hadn't been a successful night. Chris reflected wryly as he faxed the pages to Sue Walls that it *would* turn out to be a quiet night the one time that he wanted it to be spectacular. There was little chance of the television company wanting to use him now.

So he was more than a little surprised when he received a call later that day from Sue Walls.

'We found your fax very interesting and want to use you on the show,' she said.

'Really? There wasn't anything in it that I'd call particularly brilliant,' Chris replied.

'Oh no, we all found it all very interesting. Would you be interested in doing another test for us?'

'Well, of course I would – I might actually get a better result this time.'

'When you have a dream that you think will come true, and is outside your control, call us and fax it, too. Is that all right?'

'That's okay by me – I have some kind of dream every night.'

'Good . . .'

When Sue hung up, Chris sat down and wondered what was going on: as far as he was concerned, the previous night's dreams had been of little use, either to himself or as an experimental study. He considered it a failure.

What he didn't know at the time was that failure was exactly what the programme makers were look-ing for . . .

James Randi is an American magician who has made a career out of debunking psychic phenomena. Starting as an illusionist, working on his own and for rock stars like Alice Cooper in the 1970s, he built up a considerable reputation. Like Harry Houdini before him, he became obsessed with the idea that all mediums and psychics are frauds, taking advantage of people's gullibility with their cheap tricks. He set out to expose them for the cheats they were.

The irony is that genuine psychics like Chris feel that people like Randi perform a valuable function. There are many fakes and frauds who purport to have psychic powers. Many of them do take advantage of people, charging high fees to deliver faked messages from deceased loved ones. These people need to be rooted out, for two main reasons: first, they are preying on people's grief and misery; second, they are obscuring the study of those psychics who do have a genuine gift.

Most fakes have a complete mythology and belief system to back up their frauds, be it a perversion of the Spiritualist faith, a reincarnation myth, or something they have cobbled together from a variety of sources. Genuine psychics, on the other hand, tend to have beliefs but are willing to admit that they don't know what is really going on. They are too busy trying to find out what is happening to them to set up as a small business.

So the prescience of a James Randi, rooting out the fakes in order to help recognition of genuine phenomena, is a good thing. However, like Houdini before him, Randi has let his obsession overtake him, to the point where he now believes that there are no genuine phenomena whatsoever, and that all so-called psychics are fakes. His stock-in-trade is to resort to even the weakest rationalisation to try and disprove everyone he comes into contact with – even when, as with Chris, there are numerous other people who can attest that something genuinely unusual is happening. The sad fact is that Randi really wants to find genuine phenomena, yet cannot accept anything less than 100 per cent accuracy in a result – and such a perfect result is never achieved in any experiment, psychic or otherwise.

It was therefore not surprising that Sue Walls – a researcher on Randi's show – was pleased that Chris's fax to her was so inconclusive: it was a perfect set-up for the show.

It was the second week of March 1991 when Sue rang Chris again.

'Are you still willing to take that second test for us?' she asked.

'Sure. In fact, I've got one for you right now.'

Chris prepared photocopies of his dream diary to send to Sue, and also to one Clive Seymour and his working partner S. Laws. They were members of the Association for the Investigation of Anomalous Phenomena, or ASAP. They had contacted Chris after reading about him in *Psychic News* and had agreed to monitor this experiment as part of their study of him.

The previous night Chris had written a simple question at the top of the page: 'Next IRA attack, please'. There had been a strong thread relating to bomb attacks running through his dreams during this period, so Chris thought this was what he would get for the Randi programme.

He couldn't have been more wrong.

He was sitting in a plane, in the passenger cabin, watching a hostess demonstrate how to use the oxygen mask. It was something he'd seen a hundred times before and his attention was wandering. He got up from his seat and walked up the aisle towards the flight deck.

When he got there the pilot was waiting for him: Chris recognised him as the pilot of the plane involved in the Papa India crash at Heathrow, nearly twenty years before. It had always stuck in Chris's mind, because he had taken his mother and sister to the airport that day and had just been driving away from the airport car park when the plane came down in flames on the runway.

'Sit down, we're ready for take-off,' the pilot said.

Chris took his seat next to the pilot, and found himself taking control of the plane as it taxied to the runway and turned to begin its take-off run.

The noise in the cabin was intense: a roar that penetrated through the earphones he was wearing. The plane began to thunder down the runway, gaining speed. Chris watched the dials on the instrument panel: even though he had never flown a plane in his life, the situation didn't seem strange and he knew exactly what he was doing.

The nose of the plane began to lift, and Chris gave the engines full throttle, feeling the sticks buck in his hands as he pushed them forward, the plane protesting at being forced upwards. He had to push with all the force he could muster, sweat gathering on his brow.

The plane had full power and was beginning to lift off the ground: but there was something wrong. The engines were stalling, and he pushed forward even harder, trying to give the engines his own strength – for what it was worth – trying by sheer force of will to lift the plane off the ground.

It was in the air, but wobbling and veering danger-ously. He couldn't hold it steady, and it began to dive towards the earth.

'The engines . . . it's a flame-out,' he heard someone yelling through the headphones.

There wasn't enough power to lift the plane, or to keep it on an even keel: something had happened to one of the engines, and the entire cabin turned on its side as the plane came back down towards the runway at an angle too acute to land. Inside there was chaos: paper and cups flew around, the instruments went crazy, with lights blinking on and off; the pressure in the cabin changed, and Chris felt as though he would black out.

The plane missed the runway and crashed down on to the grass alongside a main road.

The cabin exploded into flame and heat, a deafening roar and rush of air filling Chris's head until it reached a point where a vacuum was reached, and there was an eerie silence as the plastic and leather on the seats melted into the glass and metal of the cockpit windows, the heat bubbling his skin as it began to fry in the crash conditions . . .

Then he was outside the plane, watching it burn. It was a British Airways jet, like the Papa India plane. Yet he knew that this was not right: the plane that would crash would not be a commercial flight. The pilot was standing beside him, gesturing at the crash and yelling into his ear above the noise of the burning wreck.

'There wasn't enough power. There was a flame-out,' he yelled – using the same words Chris had heard in his headphones.

'Who are you?' Chris yelled.

'I'm the pilot,' the flyer screamed in reply. He was wearing an RAF flying uniform.

'No, I mean what's your name,' Chris shouted back, struggling to make himself understood over the roar of the fire.

'You know who I am, Christopher,' the flyer said, suddenly in a very quiet voice. Despite this, Chris was able to understand him over the noise of the crash. 'I'm Steven,' he said softly.

Then an incredible thing happened. Chris was used to the unbelievable in his dream worlds, but this was all the more remarkable for never having happened again since.

The RAF pilot standing in front of him suddenly metamorphosed from an adult into a small boy. It was as though his shape changed in front of Chris's eyes, shrinking in stature, his clothes becoming those a child would have worn thirty years before.

'I'm Steven from next door,' he said in a boy's voice that Chris recognised.

Chris closed his eyes and shook his head, trying to make sense of what he had seen. When he opened them again, the flyer was once again a grown man.

'Who are the others,' Chris yelled hurriedly, 'and where is this going to happen?'

The flyer looked down the runway and pointed to it. 'His father built the runway,' he said cryptically. 'Remember that – his father built the runway.'

The dream began to break up and become garbled – there were random images, but one in particular stuck in Chris's mind: he was a boy again, sneaking past the house of an old neighbour called Mrs Swan. She was looking out of her window, and he got past without her seeing him, heading for the back door of a nearby house.

The dream began to fragment again and everything became confused . . .

When he woke up, Chris was sure that there would be an air crash, and he thought he knew where it would be. The runway so close to the main road, with a few houses nearby, seemed familiar.

He looked at what he had written down:

> During take-off – watch [Hostess] – oxygen mask demo
> Plane take-off – full throttle
> Push both sticks forward – full power
> Crashes back on to? [Airport] Road
> Runway – fire – MELTS – Buildings
> Engine – flame-out –
> Sitting in plane – British Airways
> Stall – push sticks
> Forward – not enough power – fire –
> His father built the runway.

There were other images, relating to later dreams that he couldn't recall, and at the bottom of the next page he had written:

> Past Mrs Swans House – she is looking out of the window Go round to back door.

The dream of the air crash was so vivid that it became Chris's one overriding concern: he must work out what it meant – where and when the crash would happen.

Analysing the phrases he had written down, he could see a couple where the letters S and P began adjacent words. This was the method by which he received postcodes. So which part of the country had a postcode that was either SP or PS? Looking on his postcode maps he could see that it was either Swansea or Peterborough.

He was pretty sure that there wasn't an RAF base in Swansea, but there was one near Peterborough. RAF Wyton lay near Huntingdon, and Chris had travelled that way recently: first, he had been to Huntingdon because of premonitions he had received concerning attacks on John Major, whose constituency was in the area; second, the local passport office for Bedfordshire was in Peterborough, and Chris had needed to renew his son's passport. To expedite matters he had gone there in person. On the way he had driven near Wyton, and he could remember the way in which the main road ran parallel to the runway, with a small clutch of houses nearby.

It was exactly as he could remember it in the dream. Now he thought he knew where the attack would occur. But when?

That was harder to answer. Some events came to him weeks before they happened. These re-occurred in repeating patterns over successive nights. Yet other events turned up three nights before they were due to happen, or even the night before. The only way he would know for sure was if the crash either happened during the day ahead or he dreamt about it again that coming night.

One thing Chris was sure about were the names of the men involved in the crash: 'His father built the runway.'

This cryptic clue had something to do with the material the runway was constructed of: the flyer had pointed to it when he gave Chris the clue. Most runways and roads are built of tarmacadam – so Chris was convinced that the name of at least one of the flyers would be Adam, or Macadam, or have Mc or Mac in it.

The identity of the pilot who had spoken to him was another thing of which Chris was certain. The pilot had changed into a small boy and said 'I'm Steven'. Then Chris had received a dream image of the place where he used to live as a boy. Thirty years before he had had a friend whose name was Steven – Steven Wilkinson. It was this boy that the pilot had changed into. What's more, Steven had lived next door to Chris, near old Mrs Swan.

It wouldn't be the same Steven Wilkinson – but it would be someone of that name.

Chris completed his notes to attach to the dream sheets and faxed copies of them to Sue Walls at Granada, and to Clive Seymour at ASAP.

This was on Sunday, and he spent most of the day wondering what would happen in his dreams that night. Would he get another clue concerning the crash? He hoped that it would not be like the actual dream of the crash, which haunted him all day.

Perhaps it was because the dreams of Saturday night had been so intense that he dreamt very little on the Sunday. Most of it was inconsequential, but there was one segment that made Chris think of the air crash when he woke up. Looking at what he had written, it said:

Half sunk – orange in colour. Rowing boat.
Police launch – bring back a rowing boat
Bottom cracked in half – no good for him now
   Size of him he should have a bigger boat.

There were also several references on the page to words that began with C and B – a Cambridge post-code. By themselves they didn't have any particular significance, but the dream of the rowing boat had a personal association that made Chris think again. He had a friend named Alan, who had an orange boat. This was moored at Hartford Marina, which was located at St Ives in Cambridgeshire.

Cambridge – RAF Wyton was in Cambridgeshire, and as Chris looked at his map of the area he could see that the road running along the runway would be the route he would usually take when he visited Alan on his yacht.

That was where the plane would crash.

Sue Walls rang him during the morning.

'When is this plane going to crash, then?' she said.

'I don't know,' Chris began. Then something made him change his mind – call it a hunch, a feeling . . . perhaps a premonition was penetrating his waking mind for once. 'I say that, but you just watch the nine o'clock news tonight.'

Sue's tone had been light when she first spoke to him, almost as though she thought him another of the fakes she had been directed to find. But there was something in Chris's voice when he said this that made her change her mind.

'You really think it'll happen today, don't you?'

'Well, it might not be today, but . . . yes, I really think it will.'

'Then why don't you do something about it?' she asked.

'So what am I going to do?' Chris threw back at her. There was a weariness to his tone: he'd had this asked of him so many times, and it always made him think of RAF Stanmore.

'I don't know – tell the police or something.'

'I do. All my dreams go to the police every morning. I fax them, like I do to you. But what's going to happen? Are they going to ring up the RAF at Wyton and say,

'Don't send up any planes today 'cause we've got this psychic who says one of them will crash'? They know as well as I do that the station won't listen to them out of the blue. It'd have to come from some RAF high-up, and how long is that going to take?'

'Then go there yourself.'

'You think I haven't tried that?' he replied. 'I've been there, and I know what they're like. I'm not going to get them to listen just by turning up.'

'But if the plane crashes –'

'I've learnt to live with things like that,' Chris replied shortly.

Chris sat down to watch the nine o'clock news that night with a sense of foreboding: it was soon justified, when one of the headlined items was an RAF Canberra vintage jet that had plunged to the ground just after take-off. The jet came down on the road at the side of the runway at RAF Wyton. Wreckage was strewn across nearby fields, but no vehicles or buildings were hit.

The crew of three were killed.

The phone rang as soon as the item had finished. When Chris answered it, he heard Sue Walls at the end of the line. She was in tears.

'You were right. You said it would crash and it did. Have you seen the news?'

'Yes, I've just been watching it, too,' said Chris quietly, trying to keep the emotion out of his voice. It was hard for him to know that this had happened – that he had known it *would* happen – yet he had been unable to do anything about it.

'I've got to tell my producer about this,' she said, beginning to calm down. 'We've got to have you on after this.'

'Yeah, that'd be good . . .' Chris replied distantly: the last thing on his mind was a television appearance.

'I'll call you tomorrow, and see if you dreamt the names of the flyers,' she finished.

Chris put the phone down and was unable to concentrate on the rest of the news.

The dreams on the Monday night were confused and of little consequence. It was as though the anguish surrounding the plane crash was too much for Chris, and he couldn't focus on anything. When Sue rang him the next morning he was too confused by the dreams to give her exact names.

She asked him to look at the Teletext reports of the crash. He was astonished when he came to the names of the crew: the plane was piloted by Group Captain Reginald McKendrick, aged forty-five. Also on board was Flight Lieutenant David Adams, aged forty-eight. One name with a Mc in it, the other Adams . . . if you put them together it gave you Macadam, as in tarmacadam . . .

'His father built the runway.'

But it was the name of the other crew member, a 30-year-old Flight Lieutenant, which immediately caught Chris's eye. His name was Steven Wilkinson.

He read out his dream diary to her and she was astounded by the result. She promised to phone him back about the show.

A couple of days passed and there was no call. Still, Chris reasoned, it was a busy production office, and there was probably a very good reason for her failing to ring.

There was: the brief of the researchers on the Randi show was to be concerned with debunking all aspects of the so-called paranormal, from astrology to psychic activity. An inexplicable result like this, which couldn't be explained away in terms of trickery, was going to tie Randi in metaphysical knots.

The call came a few days later. Sue Walls was on the line and she sounded embarrassed.

'You see, it's like this,' she said. 'We don't think we can use you after all.'

'What?' Chris was astounded. 'But I told you there was going to be a crash. I told you where. I didn't say when, although I did suggest a day over the phone. I gave the complete name of one of the crash victims, and supplied you with the partial names of the other two. What more do you want?'

He was annoyed that they had asked him to take part in a test, expected him to fax them his dreams as they happened, got an extremely impressive result . . . and then decided to drop the whole idea.

There was a pause while Sue drew in her breath before speaking again. 'That's the problem, you see. You gave us too much.'

'How the bloody hell can I give you too much?' Chris raged.

'It's the producer,' she replied. 'He's told me that our brief is really to find people who are crap, so they can be shown up. What you've done is just too good.'

Chris was stunned into silence: he'd been accused of being many things in his time, but this had never been one of them.

'I'm really sorry,' Sue continued. 'Speaking personally, I hope that someone does a documentary on you at some point, because I've never come across anything like this before. What you did was truly remarkable.'

It was scant consolation. As soon as she had put the phone down, Chris rang ASAP to see what they made of the fax he had sent them. After some time he was finally able to talk to Clive Seymour.

'Well, what did you think?' Chris asked him.

'It was mildly interesting,' Seymour replied.

'Mildly interesting?' Chris parroted in amazement.

'Yes. Quite a few coincidences in there. I suppose it might be worth having a look at it.' His manner was offhand and disinterested.

'No, don't bother,' Chris said angrily. 'If you don't believe me, and think I plucked those names out of the air by chance, then just forget it.'

He slammed the phone down: he wanted what was happening to be investigated, but by someone who was actually showing a positive interest in what was going on. That didn't seem to be ASAP's attitude.

Since then Chris has been tested on numerous television and radio shows. He's never again been rejected for being 'too good'.

CHAPTER FIFTEEN

The dreams have been recurring with frequency and accuracy for over half a decade now. During this time Chris has established a rapport and understanding with the various police officers who have been appointed as his liaison officer. Other officers he has encountered have also taken easily to the truth behind the precognitive dreams. Yet despite this there have been certain forces, or individual officers, who have shied away from the idea of using a psychic, and have displayed a degree of scepticism that borders on the ridiculous. This is perhaps understandable: when initially confronted by a man claiming to be a psychic and to have dreamt about future events, many of us would probably be inclined to wonder, at the very least, about the man's credentials.

And yet there is one branch of law enforcement with which Chris has never had any problems. They listened to him from the very first time that he contacted them about a dream, and have always acted upon what he has told them. This is the department that enforces the laws of HM Customs and Excise.

The actual point of contact between Chris and Customs came several years before the dreams began. In the early 1980s video piracy – both witting and unwitting – was rife. Not only were there video pirates at work in Britain, there were also individuals and companies reproducing video titles that they believed they had obtained legitimate licences to copy. These licences were, in fact, fake, and several people were swindled out of huge sums of money and also put in the unwitting position of being law-breakers.

At this point in time Chris Robinson was in a position held by relatively few people in the industry: he was both a retailer and distributor, via his small chain of shops in the Bedfordshire area; he was also a licence holder for various titles. Many of these licences emanated from Holland, where the bogus licences also originated. Because of his contacts, Chris was in a position to help the Customs and Excise department in their investigations when they asked for his assistance.

During the course of the investigation, Chris became friendly with the officer in charge, named Pete. After the successful conclusion of the case, Chris stayed in touch with Pete and the two men often saw each other socially. So when Chris began to have precognitive dreams, he told Pete about them – as he told everyone who knew him – in an attempt to gain support for what was an intially difficult situation.

As Pete knew about the dreams, and no doubt had followed up through his own channels what had happened about the dreams Chris had reported to the police, he was only too willing to listen when Chris came to him with dreams that involved what appeared to be shipments of drugs, or offences that would be of direct interest to his department.

More than that: Pete knew Chris as a man and knew that, whatever Chris was, he was no liar.

Pete is not the officer's real name. He and his department have given us permission to include the following two cases in this book on condition that names are changed and no dates specified. This is because some of the people involved are still serving prison sentences, and officers are still working on cases that arose directly from the arrests made.

Despite this, the contents of this chapter are, in essence, as true as those of the rest of the book.

★   ★   ★

It was one of the most literal dreams he had ever had. So real that he at first thought he had woken on the plane and had suffered some kind of amnesia.

The stewardess was shaking those passengers who were still asleep, and when she got to Chris he asked her what was going on.

'Time to disembark, sir,' she replied softly, 'this is Heathrow.'

Chris stirred himself, stood up and stretched. He had no hand luggage and was soon walking down the metal ladder towards the bus that would take them to the terminal.

It seemed strangely old-fashioned: Chris hadn't disembarked from a plane in this way for some time. And as he looked around, Heathrow seemed to be incredibly spartan compared to the bustle with which he was familiar.

He realised that this really was a dream and got on the bus with his fellow passengers, most of whom were Asian. As the bus pulled away, he looked back at the plane: it was an Air India flight. All these Asians, and a plane from Air India: that had to be significant.

The babble of voices on the bus made it impossible to make out any particular conversation, until Chris suddenly heard the driver refer to the flight number quite clearly – and then he told a man standing next to him that it was Thursday.

A flight number and a day: there was a reason that Chris had heard these, and part of his mind that was always conscious hoped that he had written it down in the dream diary.

The bus arrived at the terminal and the passengers filed in to collect their luggage from an old-fashioned baggage carousel that slowly wound its way round the room.

Chris stood there in the crush of passengers, suddenly aware that he had no idea what sort of case or holdall he was looking for. So he simply stood and waited while the other passengers collected their motley assortment of old and new, battered and sparkling luggage, until there was just the one case left.

It sat on the carousel, a new case in leather with dark brown panels and tan surround. Even though it was the only one left, Chris also knew by instinct that this was the one he had to pick up. He walked towards the green channel, as he was sure he had nothing to declare.

'Excuse me, sir,' said a Customs official as he walked through, 'could I have a look at that?'

'But there's nothing in there,' Chris protested.

'I'll be the judge of that, sir,' said the official in a dry tone, as Chris put the case on the Customs counter and opened it.

There was a top layer of clothing, badly packed. It looked as though it had been thrown on top of a small mountain range, as the clothes in the case formed hills and valleys.

'Well, well, what have we here, then?' muttered the Customs official, as he removed some of the clothes. Underneath were a series of transparent plastic bags, filled with a brown powder. Chris knew what they were straight away: heroin.

'That's nothing to do with me,' he said, shaking his head as the Customs official advanced on him . . .

Chris woke in a sweat. It seemed so real that he half-expected to be in a cell. After taking a few deep breaths, he looked at the dream diary: as he had hoped, he had noted down a flight number and the day mentioned, and had also jotted down a few phrases about drugs and Air India. Best of all, he had written something about the suitcase, and had even drawn a sketch of it.

It was one of the clearest dreams he had lived through, and he was so excited that he rang Pete straight away.

'I hope you know what time this is,' said a sleepy voice at the end of the line.

'I don't, actually,' Chris replied, 'but you're going to love this.'

'Robinson? Christ, this had better be good.'

Chris described his dream to Pete, and read out to him what he had written. By the time he had finished Pete was fully awake.

'I want you to fax all that to my office now, and I'll want to see you later. This could be very interesting.'

Chill winds blew across the fields that separated the runways at Heathrow. In the crisp morning air, they made Chris shiver in his baggage-handler's uniform. He turned and walked back into the building where Pete and his men were sitting. Pete handed him some coffee.

'Thanks,' Chris said, sipping the scalding liquid. 'I still don't see why the hell you want me here all week. I told you it was Thursday and the flight number. What more do you want?'

'First thing is this: sometimes your dreams are a bit out. They get the substance, but not the detail, right?' Pete waited for Chris to agree before continuing. 'Second thing, then: you might be out on the day, and also out on the flight number. There are flights with similar arrangements of digits in their numbers all week. So we look at all of them, okay?'

'Well, yeah, I can understand that – but why do I have to be here?'

Pete grinned. 'If we're going to freeze out here all week, then so are you, my son.'

In actual fact Chris found that he was working too hard to feel the cold on the long stretches of open space out to the planes: loading the baggage proved to be strenuous and soul-destroying, as there was little sign of what they were looking for.

Monday, Tuesday and Wednesday all passed in a blur

of shifting luggage. It was on Thursday that Chris arrived to be greeted by a smiling Pete.

'You look pleased with yourself,' Chris said, knowing what Pete was about to say.

'You're the one that should look pleased, my son. It's Thursday, the flight number you wrote down is due in this afternoon, and although it's not an Air India plane, it is coming from Bombay.'

'I told you,' said Chris peevishly. 'I needn't have come here until today.'

'Maybe I just like making you work,' grinned Pete.

When the passengers had disembarked from the plane, the Customs men moved in to unload the baggage.

'My God, I've seen some things this week, but this lot tops it all,' Chris said, amazed at the junk that was in the plane's hold. There were the usual array of old and new cases, along with canvas holdalls. But there were also wicker baskets, parcels tied with string and plastic carrier bags. Many of these hadn't survived the turbulence of the flight, and foodstuffs were scattered across the floor of the plane, running into odd-smelling liquids that congealed in pools.

Picking their way around the detritus, the Customs men unloaded the baggage and took it to their temporary base. There they set about the task of trying to find the type of case described by Chris in his dream.

There were over 800 cases on the flight, and after a solid hour's work the team had narrowed it down to nine, which they put in a circle around Chris.

'Come on then,' said Pete, 'do your stuff, my son.'

'You what?' Chris replied.

'Tell us which one it is.'

'How the bloody hell am I supposed to know that?'

'Well, you're the psychic . . .'

'Leave it out – I saw this in a dream, didn't I?' Chris looked around at the nine cases. All of them were dark brown leather, and some of them had a tan trim. But was there one that looked exactly like the one he had carried in his dream?

There was: it was almost new, and he was sure that it was identical to the one he had carried through Customs. He pointed to it.

'That was the one I carried. It's almost identical.'

'You sure that's the one?' Pete asked. Their next step would be to open the case: that was something he didn't want to do without being certain.

'That's the one in the dream,' said Chris, 'but I reckon the drugs are in the one next to it.' He changed the direction of his arm, and pointed to an old battered case that stood beside the one he had seen in the dream.

'You sure?' Pete frowned. 'Why the change of mind?'

'I don't know – instinct, I suppose. But that's it. I'm sure.'

Pete shrugged and directed his men to take the case and open it. They placed it on a trestle table and used a skeleton key to pick the locks – not that this was really necessary, as one of the locks was broken, and the only thing really holding the case together was a piece of twine tied around it.

'Doesn't look a likely candidate, does it,' Pete sniffed, as he turned over the pitiful collection of clothes and belongings inside. 'But then again, you wouldn't expect it to be signposted . . .'

The contents of the case were emptied on to the table. They seemed too few for a case that had appeared so full. Looking at it closely, Chris could see that Pete had located a false bottom to the case. Carefully he lifted it up.

'Jackpot. Do not pass Go, do not collect two hundred pounds – go directly to jail,' Pete muttered to himself, as he pulled out several plastic bags filled with a brown powder. Making a small hole in one, he took some out, placed it in a glass tube and poured in a chemical. It turned green.

'Smack. Nice one, Chris.'

The Customs officers were now left with something of a dilemma. The owner of the case was waiting in the terminal for his case to arrive, so that he could take it through Customs and enter the country. Out here, on the airfield itself, the case was not legally in England until it had been checked through Customs and its owner had walked through Arrivals and into the airport's main building.

They could earmark the case, and let the owner be caught going through Customs, in which case they would leave the heroin in the case. Or they could substitute bags of sand of a similar weight and colour, and let the smuggler walk out of the airport. The chances were that he was just a courier, and if they gave him a free hand, then they might be able to follow him to his rendezvous and snare part of a larger network.

Of course, if he was arrested at the rendezvous he would be carrying bags of sand, and this was hardly illegal.

Pete had to think fast. There are no hard-and-fast ways of handling such cases: there are, of course, guidelines, but officers in his position are given a free rein to use their own experience and judgement.

'Swap it for sand and let him walk,' he finally decided. 'I don't want anyone taking their eye off him for more than a second. He's got to be heavily tailed. There's a chance that we may be spotted, and he'll be left to take the rap on his own, but we've got to play those odds. I can't let that smack get away from us without being able to recover it, or at least giving us a chance to nick someone higher up.'

The case was passed through, and word sent to Customs at the airport to let the courier through unchallenged. It was hard for them to be unobtrusive and also keep a tight tail on the courier in such a crowded place, but somehow they managed.

The courier had obviously received instructions over the phone: he went to the Underground station and bought a ticket that would take him to the other end of the line. The Customs men followed at a distance, one always making sure that he was in the same carriage as the courier.

He changed at Covent Garden and finally alighted at Finchley. The Customs men followed him to a park, where he waited for several hours.

No-one came to meet him.

The Customs men were in radio contact with Pete, who finally conceded defeat and ordered that the courier be arrested. The people he was working for must have had an observer at the airport, who had spotted the Customs officers tailing the courier or had at least become suspicious. He was only a courier, and he was expendable.

He was also little threat to them: he knew little English, and via a translator it soon became clear that he was a poor man who had been offered a sum of money that seemed enormous, simply to deliver a suitcase. In Britain he would have been paid and joined members of his family who were resident in this country.

The courier stood trial and received a heavy prison sentence. He had been caught thanks to Chris's dream. It was just a shame that no other members of the gang were netted in the operation. But perhaps Chris had helped to dry up one line of supply for drugs being smuggled into the country.

Some time later Chris was in Cyprus on holiday. The night before he was due to fly home he had a dream in which three men carrying suitcases were arrested for trafficking drugs. The three men were all dressed in soldiers' uniforms.

It was only a brief part of the dream, and soon it was out of focus, the dream having moved on to tell him something else.

When he woke in the morning he found a reference to the soldiers and the drugs in his automatic writing, but it was only the briefest of references in an otherwise full night of images and symbols. He was momentarily puzzled by the idea of soldiers carrying drugs, but thought no more of it and put the book to one side as he carried on with his packing.

It was only later, when he was at the airport, that it came back to him. The flight he was taking was a charter flight, and the passengers were all part of the same package holiday deal. Before they embarked, and the flight was ready for take-off, they all shared the same departure lounge.

Most of the people in the lounge were either married couples or families. There were only one or two people on their own. In such a setting, three young men travelling together stood out perhaps more than they would otherwise have done. Especially as the three men were fooling around, and being noisy.

Everyone's attention was drawn to them at some time, but Chris's more than most . . . The three young men were all in their middle to late twenties, quite tall, and had cropped and crew-cut hair. They looked uncannily like squaddies about to go on leave.

They were seated together, at the end of a row of chairs. As Chris watched in amazement, a man not in the charter party wandered into the departure lounge, carrying a holdall that was identical to one carried by one of the boisterous young men. Without apparently noticing the man who had just entered, the crew-cut man slid his holdall to the end of the row of seats, where it stood slightly apart from the other baggage in the row.

The strange man sauntered past the end of the row and then put his holdall down on the ground in order to take something from his pocket. It was an air ticket. He looked at it and seemed to indicate to anyone looking that he had somehow wandered into the wrong lounge. He smiled to himself, put the ticket back in his pocket, picked up his holdall and walked out.

It was the kind of thing that could happen to anyone: an honest mistake, all executed in the blink of an eye with a natural calm.

Except that the man had not picked up his own bag: Chris had been watching closely, and had noticed that he picked up the wrong bag. At first Chris thought that it might be a simple mistake: he was disabused of this notion when the crew-cut man reached out just a little too casually and pulled the strange holdall towards him. The giveaway was a slight glance around, to see if anyone had noticed.

Chris couldn't believe it: was it just his imagination? He looked round – no-one else seemed to have noticed anything going on. He turned to his wife.

'Here, did you just see that?' he asked her.

'What?' she countered, her attention momentarily distracted from the book she was reading.

'Over there,' he said, indicating the three young men. 'They've just switched bags with some bloke who wandered in and out.'

His wife looked at him askance: 'Are you sure about that?'

'Of course I am.'

'Well, I didn't see it. It was probably nothing.'

It may very well have been, but Chris wasn't so sure. He kept watching the three young men while they waited to board the plane, but nothing else suspicious happened while they were in the departure lounge.

When the time came to board, Chris was still trying to persuade his wife that the men were dubious characters.

She was convinced that his imagination was getting the better of him. However, he couldn't help remembering the soldiers in his dream.

The plane had been in flight for a couple of hours, and several of the passengers were asleep, including Chris's wife. But he was still wide awake, wondering if he should do something about what he had seen. Looking down to the front of the plane, he could see that the three young men were seated near the cockpit. That would make things difficult if he was going to carry out the plan now forming in his head.

As a stewardess passed by, Chris stopped her.

'Can I see the Captain?' he asked.

'I'm sorry sir, I'm afraid that while the plane is in flight –' she prepared to go into the little speech she had prepared for all nervous fliers who wanted to see the Captain. Chris stopped her with a gesture.

'All right. But will you do something for me?'

'I'll ask, sir,' she said doubtfully, probably wondering if Chris was going to be awkward.

'Can you ask him to get through to Customs at Luton and give them a message?'

'I'm not sure he'll want to do that, sir,' she said.

'Right.' Chris nodded, and wrote down Pete's phone number on a piece of paper. 'Try and get him to do that, and get them to phone this man and verify who Chris Robinson is. I've got reason to believe that drugs are being smuggled on this plane.'

The stewardess's eyes popped out of her head. 'Are you with MI5 or something?' she asked.

Chris suppressed a laugh. 'No, I'm not. I have had some dealings with – shall we say – certain agencies. Just ask him to do that, will you?'

The wide-eyed stewardess took the piece of paper and went off to the cockpit. Chris settled back into his seat to await developments. Even if nothing happened, at least he had tried to get something done.

It was almost half an hour before the stewardess returned.

'Can you come up front, sir – the Captain would like to see you.'

Chris looked towards the front of the plane. The three young men all seemed to be asleep, but he couldn't be sure. Someone – anyone – just going to see the Captain might seem a bit suspicious, and if Chris was right, then the last thing he wanted was for the young men to become suspicious.

'I don't want to alert the people I suspect,' he began, deliberately being circumspect. 'Is there some way that I could get up there with a legitimate reason?'

The stewardess pondered this for a moment. 'If I go up there now, and you follow in a minute or two, you could ask me for an orange juice. Then I could take you behind the curtain, because that's where the fridge is kept. That way you could slip in to see the Captain without anyone knowing.'

'Okay, we'll do that,' said Chris, and he settled back to wait as the stewardess walked back up the aisle.

When she had been up front for a minute or two, Chris got up and went to join her. On the way he cast a quick glance at the three young men who were his suspects: two of them were asleep, and the other was looking out of the window, listening to his Walkman and paying little attention to what was going on around him.

'Excuse me, I wonder if you've got any orange juice,' he asked the stewardess, feeling faintly ludicrous. He hoped he didn't sound too false or loud, or that it didn't look like something from a bad spy movie.

'Certainly, sir,' the stewardess replied and led him into the Captain's cabin when the curtains were safely drawn across, hiding them from view.

The Captain turned to greet Chris as he entered the cockpit.

'Ah, pleased to meet you, sir. I was wondering if you'd like to use the radio.'

'Sorry?' Chris felt bemused at this treatment: it was as though James Bond had stepped into the cockpit.

'I just wondered if you'd like to use the radio to contact Customs at Luton yourself. I can get you patched through.'

'Have you actually spoken to them yet?' Chris asked, a little confused.

'Oh yes,' the Captain replied. 'It was their suggestion that you call them yourself.'

Chris shrugged. 'Okay, then. If you can get me through to them.'

He waited while the call was patched through to the Customs department at Luton airport.

'This is Chris Robinson,' he said when the mike was handed to him. 'Have you been told of my suspicions?'

'Yes,' came the disembodied voice. 'There's someone who wants to speak to you about it. Hang on while I patch you through.'

Chris stood in the cockpit, mike in hand, feeling rather foolish while he waited. The Captain was watching him with interest, but Chris wasn't too sure what the pilot expected of him. He supposed that it wasn't every day that a charter-flight pilot ferrying package holidaymakers across the globe came across a situation like this: it was probably the greatest excitement the Captain had ever had on a flight. That was certainly true of the stewardess, who had hung around in the doorway to hear what was going on.

Finally the radio crackled into life again, and Chris heard a familiar voice.

'Robinson – what the hell are you up to now?'

Chris grinned. 'Hello, Pete. You're not going to believe this, but I'm on my way home from holiday –'

'– and you just happen to have run into a trio of drug traffickers?' finished Pete's amused voice.

'How did you guess?'

Pete sighed audibly. 'All right, my son, run this one by me and see how it sounds . . .'

So Chris explained to him about the soldiers in his dream, and how the three young men in the departure lounge reminded him of them; and then how he had seen the bag switch executed.

He could see the Captain looking at him in disbelief. It seemed he was astounded to have put through a call to Customs because of one man's dream – and that they were taking him seriously.

'What do these three bozos look like?' Pete asked.

Chris described them as well as he could, then waited while Pete disappeared from the end of the line. After a short while he came back.

'Yeah, they sound very familiar, and very interesting. Can you do me a favour? Can you keep an eye on them while you're on the plane, just in case they get wind of something and try to dump the bag? I'll organise something down here for when you land.'

'Okay, I'll do my best,' Chris replied.

He handed the radio back to the Captain, who was looking at him with an expression that didn't know whether to be respectful or disbelieving. Chris wasn't surprised: it was a reaction he was used to encountering.

The stewardess, on the other hand, was plainly excited about the whole thing as she led Chris back to his seat. By now, his wife had woken up and wondered where he had gone. Chris whispered a hurried explanation to her as the stewardess disappeared. She came back a few minutes later, carrying a bottle of Champagne.

'If there's anything else you want, just ask,' she whispered, leaving him with the bottle.

The rest of the flight proceeded uneventfully and

before long the approach to Luton airport began. The three young men strapped themselves into their seats without a care in the world, little knowing that Chris was keeping an eye on them from the back of the plane.

When the plane had landed and taxied to a halt, the passengers prepared to disembark. Chris and his wife gathered together their hand luggage, Chris all the while watching to see if the three young men were preparing to switch their holdall with someone else's.

The three men were first off the plane, with Chris not far behind. They were still clutching their original hand baggage, and Chris breathed a silent sigh of relief when they touched the tarmac. They were no longer his responsibility.

He and his wife checked their baggage through Customs and went to collect his car from the car park. They didn't see what happened back in the Customs hall.

The three young men had collected their luggage and were going through the green channel when they were stopped by a Customs official.

'Anything to declare, sir?' he asked politely of one of them – not the one with the switched holdall.

''Course not,' the young man said belligerently. 'I wouldn't come through here if I did have, would I?'

'Then you won't mind me having a quick look at your bags, will you,' the official said with a smile.

The young man sighed heavily but consented to having his luggage searched. He had no real choice in the matter, and besides he was not the one carrying the drugs. He submitted to the search with an ill grace, and smiled slyly when his baggage was passed clean.

The three men were about to leave when the Customs official called them back.

'What is it now,' sighed the man whose baggage had just been searched.

'Since you're so clean, you won't mind me searching your mates, will you?' the official said.

The three young men suddenly became nervous, the tension beginning to crack. As they looked around, they could see that there were several men and women hanging around the Customs hall whom they didn't recall seeing on the plane.

They didn't want the bags searched, but they had little option. All the bags were opened, until finally the Customs official reached the switched holdall.

He removed some of the contents and then found a wrapped package at the bottom.

'Well, well, what have we here?' he said with a smile.

Pete rang Chris a couple of days later.

'Did you get a result?' Chris asked.

'Did we?' laughed Pete. 'I'll say so. Not only was that holdall stuffed with gear, but these three jokers are guys we've had our eye on for some time. It's a nice little scam that some traffickers have taken up, using package holidays. After all, who'd suspect innocent families and holidaymakers of harbouring smugglers in their midst?'

'I would,' laughed Chris. 'At least, I would now.'

'Tell me, was it the switch or the dream that really put you on to them?'

'To be honest with you, I don't really know,' Chris replied thoughtfully. 'I don't know if I would have taken that much notice of the switch if I hadn't had the dream of the soldiers – they really did look like squaddies, and that's what made me notice them in the first place. I think otherwise I either wouldn't have noticed the switch, or would just have put it down to an accident.'

'Instead of which you helped nail three nasty little pieces of work. I hope you keep dreaming.'

'So do I,' said Chris. 'So do I.'

CHAPTER SIXTEEN

In September of 1990 Chris began to feel that very few people were taking notice of what was happening in his dreams. He felt that he had to get some results: so he decided on a bold course of action. He wrote to Graham Bright (his local MP), Scotland Yard and the Ministry of Defence. In each letter he outlined what had happened to him so far, and asked each party what they intended to do to help further research into his dreams and also to put the dream results to good use.

On 8 October he received a letter from the Ministry of Defence that was so non-committal as to be almost offhand. It read:

> I have been asked to reply to your letter of 21 September to the Secretary of State for defence in which you claimed to be able to foresee the time and location of terrorist attacks launched against MOD bases and senior public figures.
>
> As I believe you already appreciate, this is a matter more properly dealt with by the relevant Police Force; you appear to have had a number of contacts with the police regarding your predictive powers already. Clearly if you have any knowledge that an attack is to take place, it is your responsibility to make the relevant authorities aware. Nevertheless you have to be certain that any advice you give is well-founded and could not be regarded as an attempt to waste police time.

I hope this is helpful.

Read in a more sardonic mood, this last sentence could almost be construed as satire: on the one hand, the letter told Chris to keep going to the police with his dreams; on the other, it tried to disclaim any responsibility for acting on them. This was something Chris knew to be false, as his encounters with Special Branch and the Anti-Terrorist Squad over the past twelve months had proved.

So there was little joy to be had there: Chris could supply the information, but he would get no help in studying why he dreamt, and no feedback on whether or not his premonitions were acted upon.

Graham Bright did, however, reply more positively. In fact, he wrote several times and telephoned Chris about his premonitions. The two men arranged to meet at Parliament, but commitments on both sides caused this to be postponed. Chris was then put in touch with Special Branch in Cambridge, and Mr Bright began to take particular notice of Chris Robinson.

Why? Because Graham Bright was John Major's Parliamentary Private Secretary, and Chris began to have dreams about an attack on Major.

The first time that Cambridge entered Chris's dreams was on 18 October 1990. He was in a car with an Irishman in a blue suit. He could see the man's face clearly, with its pointed chin, classic pear shape, and thick shock of red hair. The man was talking about the IRA, and although Chris could remember no details about the conversation, he was sure that it had something to do with an attack.

The car was a white Mini, and they arrived at a garage where the front of the car was changed: the old front wings were chiselled off and replaced. Then the car was re-sprayed silver after a welder had welded the new parts in place.

There were pieces of car all over the place.

When he woke Chris could see that he had written 'Car in Bits' and '[mini] change front'. From this he knew that the next IRA attack would utilise a vehicle – not necessarily a Mini, which was why the word was boxed – that had been altered in some way. And from the way he had written the former phrase, he knew that the postcode would be CB – Cambridge.

This was reiterated by a later part of the dream, where Chris dreamt of '[2] Childrens Bikes laying on the ground'. Again, the use of capitals by his subconscious mind indicated a Cambridge postcode. The same could be said of the phrase 'Clip Board on a trolley', which occurred at the very end of the dream.

There was then a long gap before the next intimation of an attack came to Chris. On the night of 14 November 1990 he dreamt of a white transit van, which was being used by the IRA. Two nights later, on 16 November, there was a reference in the dreams to '[Philip] Lawson', followed by 'I tip off police'. The box around the name Philip suggested that this should be discarded – which left Chris with Lawson . . . the name of the then-Chancellor of the Exchequer, Nigel Lawson.

Chris began to feel that the next attack would take place on Downing Street itself: he had Cambridge postcodes running, which indicated John Major, whose constituency lay in Cambridgeshire. But now he also had Nigel Lawson indicated in his dreams. The Chancellor's official London residence is 11 Downing Street, next to the Prime Ministerial residence. John Major was not yet Prime Minister, but Chris had a feeling that this would change: for some time he had been receiving dreams that told him Margaret Thatcher would soon be replaced. Put together with the preponderance of references to John Major, Chris felt certain that he would be the replacement. At any other time this would have been a premonition noteworthy in itself, but right now that was the last thing on Chris's mind.

There was nothing actually to give a concrete attack date, but the dreams were starting to filter through some sort of warning.

Chris wrote to Graham Bright again, telling him of his fears. Bright responded by inviting Chris to meet him at the House of Commons to discuss his dreams. The meeting was set to take place within the next couple of weeks.

In the meantime, the dreams began to come through with a stronger message. Chris dreamt of IRA men getting away from a scene of crime on a big motorbike. This turned out to be correct – after the Downing Street attack to which this was a lead-up, the IRA men who had perpetrated the attack made their escape by motorbike. But the dream had a double meaning, as Chris wrote the phrase 'Big Old Motorbike' in his dream diary, which was becoming a way of indicating a bomb: Big Old Motorbike.

He also began to get postcodes for SW – Downing Street, of course, is SW1. Along with this came a vision of being in a large house, with plaster shaking off the walls. The house was beginning to crumble.

Chris was beginning to get worried by the increasing frequency of these images. By 23 November Cambridge had begun to figure again in the equation. There were more postcodes coming through.

Graham Bright had to change the date of his meeting with Chris and postpone it until the New Year. He had commitments that made it impossible to hold the meeting, and Chris was due to fly off in December to the Philippines. With some regret on both sides, therefore, the meeting was postponed.

Bright was, however, sufficiently concerned by what had happened to pass Chris on to the Cambridge Special Branch, from where he was contacted by a Sergeant

Peck. Peck gave Chris his fax number and requested that he forward all his dream diary sheets with his translations.

The MOD may vacillate, and Scotland Yard may have kept its own counsel, but Graham Bright was taking Chris very seriously indeed.

On 2 December Chris asked the spirits to show him the next IRA attack in England. He needed to know so that he could leave the country with a clear conscience and warn whoever he needed to with an ease that wouldn't be possible if he suddenly had a message while in the Philippines. For his pains, he was rewarded with a series of images that left him in no doubt about the target.

The dreams of 2 December were extremely confused, and made no sense as a series of images, but when translated the next morning there were repeated references to 'PM' and 'CB' – the Cambridge connection coming up again and again. Chris dreamt of a river, and this remained a strong image: was there a river running near Major's house? He faxed the dream, and his questions, to Sergeant Peck.

More startling still were the dreams for 3 December, when Chris actually wrote the postcode SW1 in his dream, without it being symbolically represented. More than this, he dreamt of a massive Old English Sheepdog, which chased after him. In his book, he wrote, 'Dulux [dog] after [ME]' . . . The dog was obviously an IRA symbol and the 'me' in the dream, as it was boxed, seemed to infer that a target was close at hand.

Further down the page was written:

> Watching TV – Whole House shakes
> Did the outside walls [shake]
> switch on the wall [stays still]

It was yet another indication that the attack would

be on a house, and that it would severely damage it in some way. 'switch on the *w*all' was also a postcode clue. The house would appear to be in an SW postcode. Put together, this had to mean an attack on Downing Street.

While this had been happening, the expected coup in the Tory Party had occurred and since the first warnings had come to Chris, John Major had been installed as Prime Minister. Thus it was no surprise that Chris wrote on 3 December:

> Halt at Major Rd ahead
> Phone call warning to [police]

Later in the dream Chris had been at a pub in Thrapston, which is on the main road to Northampton. He was with two Irishmen, drinking beer and eating. When he awoke this worried Chris, as Thrapston is near the town where Major lives – his house is located on the other side of the A1, the main road Chris had seen. In case this was a clue for a military target, Chris checked on the nearest military installation, which was the Simpson Barracks in Northampton. But there had been no direct military involvement in the dream, and the barracks were located several miles from the dream's locale.

The meaning was pretty self-evident: there was danger ahead for John Major.

On 4 December Chris wrote again to Graham Bright. He received a reply dated 14 December, which read:

Thank you for your letter of 4 December listing all the various incidents that you have foreseen. As you know, I have been in touch with the police and have spoken personally to the Chief Superintendent at Luton. The Cambridgeshire police are aware of you and of the fact that you have information to give to them.

If you would like to let me have any additional detail, particularly of what you are predicting for the future, I will ensure that the appropriate authorities are fully aware.

The letter was signed personally by Graham Bright.

In the period between the two letters, more information had been coming through strongly. On 6 December Chris had once again written 'Halt At Major Road AHEAD'. At the top of the page was 'Northampton – at a [House] watching a tape'. Again the reference to Northampton, which seemed to be Chris's own personal geographical indicator for John Major's home.

Was the attack actually to be on Major's home rather than on Downing Street? Was it possible that attacks were planned on both locations? Certainly the dream seemed to be inferring this.

Chris had also written 'J [MORGAN]' and 'open to car [MORGAN]'. This was another of Chris's personal clues: almost twenty years before, Chris had worked at a place called Bar Hill, as an engineer. Bar Hill lies less than ten miles from the Majors' home. The company that Chris had worked for was Phillips Electrical Engineering Services, and his boss had been a man named Jim Morgan. The open sports car had been an old-fashioned racer – a Morgan. Taken together, Chris felt that the location was being given to him by the spirit of his old boss.

John Major now began to flit in and out of the dreams as a real person. He didn't do anything that was worthy of note, but he was always there, lurking in the background. His presence made Chris certain that he was now a prime target.

On 14 December – the day that Graham Bright replied to his last letter – Chris flew to the Philippines, leaving behind him as much detail as he could: the dreams hadn't given him as much as he might have hoped, but certainly enough to put Special Branch in Cambridge on their guard.

While he was away the dreams became scrambled, and there was little in them that related to home: Chris has noticed time and again that his dreams seem to shift their reference to wherever he is located. It is rare for him to have precognitive dreams relating to England when he is as far away as the Philippines.

During this time he was out of touch with what was happening at home and had no idea whether or not an attack had occurred.

Things started to hot up for Chris just a few days before he came home. On the night of 1 January 1991 he began to dream of trouble.

> Firework – [Roman Candle] 2 close
> [fountain] – blows up in the air and all over us
> – try to run away.

The firework was a new symbol for a bomb – and the fact that it was a Roman candle meant that it would be a rocket. There was heat and fire over the people who tried to run away. There were two of them, and Chris knew this meant that there would be two IRA men who made the attack.

Another reference to rockets came with the mention of Chris's friend Bob Monkhouse – a mention of Bob also meant a bomb, although it took Chris some time to work this out. Eventually he realised it meant 'I see Bob Monkhouse', or 'ICBM', therefore: intercontinental ballistic missile.

The night of 2 January was even more intense: there were numerous references to SW and SW1 in the dream and on the page. There was a long section of dream when Chris was in his camper. The particular camper he had at the time was a white transit van, and this tied in with one of the very early dreams in which a vehicle was being re-sprayed silver. The location was also being fixed by a more personal reference at the beginning of a long written section:

> Tomato sandwich with salt – alternate in rows – park on a hill – brakes not very good – snow on the ground outside a phone box – make a phone call. Phone Churchill Coleman – on allocation.

When Chris worked in London he often used a sand-wich bar in SW1, a few minutes' walk from Downing Street. He would always order a salt beef sandwich, but would horrify the Jewish owner of the bar by requesting tomato with the salt beef. This reference gave a clue to location. Snow on the ground was the long-standing sig-nal for danger. And the final part of the writing was pretty clear: Chris was being told to ring George Churchill-Coleman, then head of the Anti-Terrorist Squad. In the dream he couldn't get through, as the Commander was 'on allocation' and couldn't easily be contacted.

The meaning of this, too, was obvious: Chris would have immense difficulty getting through to anyone from his remote location in the Philippines. He would have to wait, and be patient.

There was one other thing, which didn't make sense at the time: at the top of one of the pages was a mention of being in the camper – the white transit van – and lighting the gas. Further down the page was a drawing of three gas rings on top of a stove. It was the design of stove his mother had had over twenty years earlier. What this had to do with anything Chris just couldn't work out. Except that it bore an uncanny resemblance to the kind of mortars the IRA used to fire rockets.

It was only a couple of days until he returned to

England, and Chris wondered what the future held in
store for his dreams.

Back in England the important dream came on Tuesday,
8 January. It was so explicit in many ways that it
prompted Chris to send it directly to Graham Bright.

The dream revealed codes for the SAS, SW1, BT
– the postcode for Belfast, and a sure sign of IRA
activity in Chris's universe – and Cambridge, signifying
John Major.

Part of the dream read:

> Very complex – [WH Smith] can you get the
> card back – what do you press.
> 2 cards. 2 machines.

To Chris, this meant that two attacks were planned,
both in the SW1 area. The second target would be a
branch of WH Smith. But why? It wasn't that Chris
distrusted the spirits, but he couldn't work out why a
branch of Smiths would be attacked. Even as what was
termed a 'soft' target – one with little strategic importance – it seemed a waste of effort. Especially when there
were much bigger fish for the IRA to try and fry.

But Chris had no doubt that a branch of WH Smith
would also be bombed, as he turned the page of the diary
and began to translate. For there, on the top line, was
'sex on the floor', which had come to represent the term
'soft target'. Like many of Chris's dream codes, the real
meaning was once again obtained by taking the initial
letter of each word, which in turn spelt out the word
that was the real message.

Also on this page was a drawing of a house, with the
word 'MALL' written up the side of the house, as though
along a road running in front of it. Underneath was 'not
up 2 roof', and '½ way up only'. The real clincher was
'S. Wall', obviously another SW postcode symbol.

There was only one thing which, again, did not make sense at the time. At the top was written 'New World [43X]'. Taking this as a postcode symbol, Chris came up with NW3 and NW4 – Swiss Cottage and Hendon.

Was this an indication of another target, or some kind of clue as to the whereabouts of the cell that was about to perpetrate the attack?

Later, of course, much would become clear to him: 'New World [43X]' referred to a make of gas cooker, and was another reference to the gas rings he had seen a few nights before. And the word 'Mall' was written beside the house because the attack was launched from a van parked in London's Mall.

Now, years after the event, it's hard to imagine how Chris must have felt as he tried to make people listen to him, and feverishly translated the dream to send to Graham Bright. These dreams had visited him with an intensity and emotional impact that he hadn't experienced since the Stanmore affair. He had hoped that he would be able to control the way they pulled on his emotions, but now he found that this was impossible: they haunted his every waking hour.

On 10 January he saw a white transit van being re-sprayed by the IRA. He knew the van that would be used in the attack would be white – as indeed it was. Throughout the rest of the month he was still getting postcodes, and lots of dreams in which snow littered the ground: there was imminent danger.

However, things began to get confused, as the Gulf War was on the horizon, and Chris found his dreams being filled with visions of Iraq and war in the desert. It wasn't the first time that he had encountered such visions in his dreams, but he was inclined to put them down less to precognition than to the fact that the imminent war was ever-present on the television and in the newspapers and was a favourite talking point among the public. Everywhere he went, he heard something to do with the forthcoming conflict – would it happen, wouldn't it, would it be World War III, or merely a local conflict . . . The subject was inescapable, and Chris felt that this was starting to leak into his subconscious and obscure the real messages.

But just to let him know the attack was still imminent, he had a dream on 25 January 1991 that told him the SW postcode was connected with the IRA and the number 2 – two attacks. The following night he dreamt of being at Victoria Station: he hadn't been to the station for many years, not since he had a girlfriend who lived in Brighton. He would travel into London to catch the Brighton train from Victoria.

Victoria Station is at the other end of SW1 from Downing Street and the Mall. That much Chris knew. What he didn't know was that there are two branches of WH Smith located in the station complex.

February began with a bang, as Chris saw ICBMs (Bob Monkhouse again) attacking in London.

On the night of 3 February the dreams became stronger. Chris was at a roadblock, and asked the driver of a white van if he had seen the reason for the roadblock. The driver replied that he had seen the crash leading to the roadblock, they were driving too fast ('2 fast'), and they killed themselves. The car was a write-off.

This could only mean that two people would be behind the attack, that the vehicle from which the attack was launched would be a write-off, and that it would be a white transit. All the clues were adding up, more and more of them. But was anyone listening? By this point Chris was beginning to wonder: Chris Watt had little to do with him; he was sending things to Graham Bright, but who was he passing them on to? At the end of the day all he was left with was Paul Aylott. And, as Aylott said to him, 'You've written to the Prime Minister, his private secretary, the Ministry of

Defence – what more can I do, or what can you do? Go and knock on the door?'

The increasing intensity and frequency of the messages was pushing Chris close to the edge of madness. He was telling everyone he came across about the imminent attacks, and how he couldn't make anyone believe him.

Wednesday, 6 February, saw the most blatant dreams yet: three rockets firing into space, with postcodes for SW1. There were more re-sprayed cars like those he had been seeing for so many months. When he woke in the morning he knew what was going to happen. At this level of intensity, the attacks would happen either that day or the one after.

It was early morning: 4 a.m. Chris knew that he wouldn't be able to go back to sleep, as the dreams were far too intense for him to rest from them.

His wife was still working at a hotel, and she was due to start an early shift at half-past five. Chris made her breakfast, then drove her to work. When he got home it was still early and he couldn't rest. For something to do, he took his children to school and told a couple of their teachers about his dreams.

By the time he got back home it was close to ten o'clock. There was no way he was going to ring Paul Aylott, or fax Cambridge Special Branch or the number he had for Chris Watt – or even contact Graham Bright. By this time Chris had become resigned to the fact that no-one was taking any notice of him.

He had to make himself relax somehow, so he ran a bath, hoping for a long soak with which to ease the stress. It was not to be.

He had been in the bath only for a few minutes when the phone rang. At first he wasn't going to answer it, but a voice in his head said, 'Answer it, Chrissy, it might be important.'

If there was one thing he had learnt by now, it was

never to ignore the voices that occasionally came into his head. He got out of the bath and wrapped a towel around himself. Covered in shampoo, and freezing in the February weather, he answered the phone.

It was Graham Bright. He told Chris that there had been a mortar attack on Downing Street at ten o'clock that morning. Three rockets had been fired from a white transit van that had then exploded in the Mall. Two men were seen making a getaway.

One of the rockets had landed in the garden of No. 11 Downing Street, the other two had hit No. 10, but had caused little damage, apart from the falling plaster dust that surrounded Bright as he spoke.

'What can I do to help you?' he asked Chris. 'I now know that you were utterly correct.'

'If you really want to help, the first thing you can do is write me a letter,' Chris replied, 'and in it you can tell me about all the things I sent you. Because when I go to people, the biggest problem I have is that they don't believe me. If I had verification from somebody in your position, that would make things so much easier.'

'Well, you write to me again, detailing all that you have done, and I'll reply, affirming it all. I have to be very careful because of my position as the PM's private secretary – but I do believe you. And all the police I've spoken to who have dealt with you believe you. The problem is that all the ones who have no experience of you think that you're mad, and think that I'm mad to believe you.'

It wasn't until Chris put the phone down that something remarkable struck him: within an hour of a major attack on Downing Street, the PM's private secretary had found time to ring a psychic in a small Bedfordshire village.

What kind of powerful feelings had motivated him to remember what Chris had said in the midst of all that mayhem?

★   ★   ★

The first attack, and the one that had really occupied his thoughts, had occurred. But what of the other attack? The dreams had been very specific about there being two attacks, and one of them involving a branch of WH Smith.

On 10 and 13 February 1991 he dreamt about Victoria Station again, and was certain that the attack would occur at Victoria. A soldier came to tell Chris about the IRA attack. It wasn't Robert, his usual contact, nor was it anyone else he knew. But on 13 February the visions were much clearer.

There were killers on a station platform, and while they stood there, Chris looked upwards and could see World War II planes criss-crossing the skies, firing at each other. He was witnessing a dog-fight – did this signify the IRA? Were they the fighting dogs somebody was trying to tell him about? He was at the station waiting for his friend from Brighton.

On 14 and 15 February he again saw railway stations – the dream on 15 February could have been London Bridge station, as Chris recognised parts of it – on the other hand, was it just because he remembered so little of Victoria that his subconscious was drawing on images of London Bridge, a station he knew so much better? He bought a ticket to Gatwick, and the only stations he knew on the route were Victoria and London Bridge.

By Sunday, 17 February, he knew that the attack was imminent. When he woke up on the Monday morning he was certain the bomb would go off that day.

The first thing that greeted him on the news was an announcement that a small bomb had gone off at Paddington Station, at about half-past four. There had been some damage, but no-one had been hurt.

Naturally, Chris was relieved to hear this but at the same time he felt confused: he was sure it was Victoria, and his dream of the night before had been distressing, as he had been in the Underground at Victoria after a blast, with many people who had been injured.

Why had the spirits misled him about the station? The answer lay in the fact that his dreams had started to warn of two bombs in the next attack . . . and Paddington was only the first.

The second bomb went off three hours later, at the peak of the rush-hour. The shrapnel bomb was placed in a litter bin outside WH Smith on the station concourse. It erupted with savage and bloody violence, killing 34-year-old David Corner, the father of a 16-month-old child, who was on his way to work. A piece of shrapnel gouged a massive hole in his chest and pierced his heart.

Three children were among the injured, one of whom was a 12-year-old boy who was hit in the buttock by a piece of shrapnel as he waited to catch a train on a day out with his father.

One eye-witness described the scene:

'I was standing watching the world go by and waiting for my platform to be announced. Suddenly there was a loud bang and a big yellow flash about fifteen yards to my left. People were screaming, 'It's a bomb, it's a bomb', and there was organised chaos.

'Windows were broken. There was shrapnel, pieces of metal and a lot of blood.

'One man was very badly injured. His whole stomach was exposed. He took the whole impact in his stomach.

'There was a cyclist with him, doing a very good job calming him down, talking to him and checking his pulse.

'I went to the man nearest me. His jaw was broken and part of his lower leg was gone. He said his name was Geoff and he was an engineer. He was in quite a bit of pain. I didn't think it was a good idea for him to look at his leg, so I talked to him.'

In all thirty-nine people were caught in the blast as the bomb exploded at 7.40 a.m. Deadly showers of glass and debris ripped into commuters as they arrived at the station, into people buying tickets, and into people using the payphones.

The IRA claimed that they had telephoned a warning, and that it was a cynical act on the part of the police not to clear the station. The police, on the other hand, countered that the warning had been given using a new codeword that they could not verify in the midst of a spate of hoax calls following the Paddington explosion.

The phone call had been logged at 7 a.m. leaving the police less than three-quarters of an hour to clear a mainline railway station at the beginning of a weekday rush-hour. It is extremely doubtful that a busy station could have been cleared in the time given before the explosion.

The carnage at Victoria resembled that seen by Chris in his dream the night before. It was the culmination of a long-running series of dreams relating to attacks in the centre of London.

Once again Chris had tried to make the police listen to his premonitions. He was having success in helping the police at a local level, as his experience with Patrick Frater was demonstrating; this was happening concurrently with the Victoria and Downing Street warnings. Yet once matters got beyond a local level Chris kept running into a wall of silence.

Were his reports really being acted upon? He didn't doubt that Graham Bright had passed on information that Chris had sent him: the fact that the clearly rattled Bright had telephoned him so soon after the mortar attack on Downing Street certainly showed that he took Chris seriously. But what happened to that information afterwards?

Chris felt that the intelligence services, and the higher echelons of the police, didn't seem to take him as seriously as those who had actually met him. It was as though there was a level at which the apparent outlandishness of the manner in which he derived his information outweighed – for them – his past accuracy.

That was why he was glad that Bright had agreed to help him: without back-up of this kind Chris wouldn't be able to get his dreams logged and the process by which he dreamt investigated. Then, perhaps, he would be taken seriously. He would be able to stop an outrage like the one at Victoria, instead of sitting, crying, in front of the television, knowing that he had done all he could to prevent it but that, because of other people, it had not been enough.

CHAPTER SEVENTEEN

During the years since the dreams started to take over Chris's life, he has had several spirit guides: that is to say, the apparent spirits of dead people, who have appeared in his dreams and have either guided him through forthcoming events or have given him information that he has been able to translate into everyday sense.

Whether or not they really are the spirits of the dead, entities that appear to take on this form, or indeed manifestations of Chris's subconscious is ultimately unimportant. What is significant is the information they pass on and the fact that Chris is able to accept these 'people' in his dreams and relate to them. In this book they have been referred to throughout as 'spirits', simply because it is best at this stage to take Chris's word that they really are deceased people.

Most of the spirits who have visited Chris are either people who have been in the news – such as Fazad Bazoft, the journalist executed in Iraq – or have been friends. After his death in December 1990, a frequent visitor was the journalist Trevor Kempson, who had worked with Chris on a number of stories for the *News of the World*. On the other hand, the spirit who came to Chris in his first precognitive dream was an unknown soldier who only once revealed his name as Robert, and then only in passing.

Possibly the most contentious name to have emerged from Chris's spirit world over the past few years is that of Yvonne Fletcher, the woman police constable who was shot down by a sniper's bullet outside the Libyan Embassy in London in 1984. One of the most active spirits to have visited Chris, she was involved in a number of foiled IRA attacks and in predictions of IRA hits.

Such a high-profile spirit presented its own problems to Chris. Even now, several years after her first appearance, the mention of Yvonne Fletcher is still inclined to raise the hackles of police officers who have little knowledge of Chris and his record with the security services. As recently as 1994, on a cable television show in Bristol, a phone-in guest who was an ex-policeman raised objections and insulted Chris on air when the question of Yvonne Fletcher was raised.

Even Chris was a little bemused when the spirit of Yvonne first identified herself to him. However, the circumstances surrounding her description of how she came to find Chris were so convoluted and particular to himself that he was left in little doubt that she was a spirit – after all, she knew things about his friends that he didn't know himself . . . This might sound mysterious, but will become startlingly clear later.

By a strange act of synchronicity, Yvonne entered Chris's life at around the same time as Detective Inspector Alex Hall, who has already featured in an earlier chapter. Paul Aylott was promoted and moved to a position at a training school; Chris Watt had little to do with Chris any more. For a while it seemed that there was little interest in Chris and that nobody was interested in monitoring his dreams any longer.

All of this changed at the beginning of June 1991.

The night of Saturday, 1 June, had been disturbed. Chris had slept only fitfully, and the welter of dream images had made little sense to him.

He had been engaged on a repair job, connecting wires. Then he had driven off with a man in a big black car, which had been following another car, driven by a woman. They had tailed this car round a maze of streets and down an alleyway that stopped in a dead-end.

The driver told Chris that his name was Ben Holloway, and they then picked up two young girls who were looking for a lift. The next thing Chris was aware of was that Holloway was getting out of a taxi, and Chris was dropping the girls at a filling station, asking them to get out of the car . . .

None of it seemed to make much sense and when he woke Chris felt terrible: his head was muzzy, and there was a sour taste in his mouth. He got up and had a bath before making himself some coffee and trying to sort out what the dreams might mean. He was astonished to find a reference to writing a letter to Chris Watt – he hadn't been in touch with, or even thought of, Watt for some time.

He was still puzzling over the dream diary when the phone rang. He answered it to find Sergeant Glen Clemence on the other end of the line.

'Can I come and see you this morning?' Clemence asked.

'Yeah, I'm not doing anything much,' Chris replied cautiously. He vaguely knew Clemence, but had had no real contact with him over dream matters. He wondered what this could be about.

'Good. I'll be up in about half an hour,' the Sergeant replied.

Before the half-hour was up there was a knock at the door, and Chris opened it to be greeted by Clemence.

'All right, let's not play games,' said Chris, 'what's all this about?'

'I'd like you to come down to the station for a bit. There's someone down there who wants to have a word with you about your dreams.'

'Okay – I suppose it can't do any harm,' Chris replied. It may have sounded offhand to Clemence, but inside Chris was relieved: someone actually wanted to talk to him. That meant that they were still taking him seriously.

Clemence drove Chris to the Bedfordshire Police Headquarters in Luton. Chris was familiar with the building, and knew several of the officers they passed on their way to a quiet office. Clemence opened the door without knocking and ushered Chris into the room.

'Sit down,' said the man sitting behind a desk, his back to Chris as he stared out of the window. When Chris was seated, the man swivelled round in his chair and looked Chris full in the eye.

'Would you like a drink?' he asked. Chris nodded, so the officer took a bottle of whisky out of a desk drawer and brought it down onto the desk top with a loud bang.

'Let's get this straight from the start,' he said with a smile. 'The only spirits I believe in are these. It's up to you to convince me otherwise. All right?'

He took two plastic cups from another drawer and poured two shots of the whisky, pushing one towards Chris.

'Have a drink – and tell me all about it.'

Chris took the cup. Where would he begin? So much had happened in the last twenty months that he wasn't quite sure. Taking a deep breath, he decided to start at the beginning with the first appearance in his dreams of the soldier Robert.

Two hours and half a bottle of Scotch later, the story was complete. Along the way the man opposite Chris had asked him numerous questions, and had sidetracked Chris away from the main story in order to check up on minor details. At last he seemed satisfied.

'I'll make a deal with you,' he said finally. 'There's a lot in what you say that's really interesting. If you keep sending your dreams to me, and there are things in there that get results, then I'm prepared to monitor you indefinitely. Can't say fairer than that, can I?'

'As long as you'll be reporting to someone, and you haven't just done this off your own back,' Chris replied.

'You know better than to ask stupid questions like that.'

And so ended Chris's first encounter with Alex Hall.

It was only afterwards, when he got home and looked again at the diary, that Chris realised that this meeting had been shown to him in his dreams. The writing concerning Chris Watt read:

[Stanmore] – Tell Chris Watt – Write a letter [2] him – he may be allowed [2] talk [2] you again – outside Stanmore station.

It seemed strange that after an 8-month gap between his last official liaison and this sudden meeting with Alex Hall he should have had a dream the night before about Chris Watt in which the figure 2 was so prominent – two policemen, perhaps?

Whether or not he was searching for a meaning that wasn't there, Chris now felt that he was being taken seriously again.

Three days later, on the night of Wednesday, 5 June 1991, Chris dreamt that he was in Hemel Hempstead, a town just over the county boundary in Hertfordshire that he knew well. He kept passing a road called Fletcher Way. In fact, he seemed to be going round in circles, as he passed it several times. What Chris couldn't work out was why he should keep passing it.

In the dream he was talking to Sergeant Sparrow, who was the officer he had dealt with during his attempt to help find Simon Jones in the October and November of the previous year. They were discussing Simon, and then Chris noticed that there was a uniformed woman police constable with Sparrow. She was trying to break into the conversation.

'Listen,' she was saying urgently, 'there's going to be something about me in the paper tommorow. I was with the Met until I died, and there's going to be a large cheque.'

She went on to talk about a plane going down, but the dream began to get muddled and Chris lost the sense of what she was saying.

When he woke, he looked at what he had written. Among all the usual verbiage that he couldn't decipher were the phrases:

> Large cheque –
> Front page – I died from the MET
> PLANE DOWN – Bless you

This all related to what the police constable had told him, but what 'PLANE DOWN' meant Chris just couldn't work out. He came to the conclusion that a policewoman from the Metropolitan Police Force would be killed, and that it would make the front page of the newspapers. It was a feeling reinforced by the appearance of another woman police officer – this time a woman Detective Constable – in a later portion of the dream, where she was questioning a prostitute.

Chris phoned Alex Hall. 'There's going to be a front-page story today about a dead policewoman and a large cheque. She's going to be from the Met.'

'I haven't seen anything in the papers,' Hall replied, 'but on the other hand I haven't actually seen all of them.'

Chris went out and bought as many of the daily papers as he could find, but there was nothing on the front pages that could possibly fit with what he had seen in his dream. He was despondent, and more than a little confused. It had seemed so definite in his dream, and yet there was nothing – not even on the inside pages – that seemed connected.

There was one more chance for him to be proved right: the early edition of the *Evening Standard*, the evening paper for the London area, hits the streets around midday, and Chris was at his local newsagent when it arrived. The headline took his breath away:

YVONNE'S MURDER: GADAFFI ATONES
Huge cash payment.

To the right of the headline was a grainy black-and-white photograph showing the head and shoulders of a young woman in police uniform. The photograph was captioned: 'WPC Yvonne Fletcher: she fell dying into the arms of her fiancé Michael Liddle. People still leave flowers at the spot.'

Chris stood in the middle of the pavement staring dumbstruck at the front page. He instantly recognised the photograph as showing the WPC who had spoken to him in his dream the night before. He had almost forgotten about WPC Fletcher, who had been in the headlines seven years ago.

As he read the story it all came back: 25-year-old WPC Fletcher had been policing an anti-Gadaffi protest outside the Libyan People's Bureau – the name given by the left-wing dictator to his embassies – when a shot rang out from the first-floor window. It hit Yvonne in the back and she fell dying against the garden railings in the centre of the square, where she was comforted by her fiancé, who was also policing the demonstration.

From inside the building a Libyan official with a machine gun was peppering the square with shot. Eleven protestors were also hit in the hail of fire. Yvonne was the only fatality.

The country was outraged at the killing, and the Libyan People's Bureau was under siege for eleven days, but despite Britain severing all diplomatic ties with Libya, none of the Libyans was ever charged with the murder: the thirty officials claimed diplomatic immunity and were simply expelled without arrest. Among them was the man who had fired the shot that killed Yvonne Fletcher.

The Libyans had left a cache of arms inside the building, and a legacy of hate. A pavement plaque was later placed in St James's Square, reading simply 'Here fell WPC Yvonne Fletcher, 17 April 1984'.

As Chris read on, he realised that the spirit who had spoken to him the night before had belonged to Yvonne Fletcher, and she had been trying to tell him about the six-figure offer of compensation that Colonel Gadaffi was offering a police charity under the auspices of Conservative MP Teddy Taylor.

When Chris phoned Alex Hall, the policeman was more than impressed by what Chris had told him: 'After all,' he said to Chris, 'it's not often that a dead woman police officer makes the front page of a newspaper – especially in connection with large sums of money.'

It was only afterwards that Chris looked back and realised that she had also tried to tell him her name in the dream – after all, he had met her in Fletcher Way.

But why, when she had been dead for over seven years, and Chris had been meeting spirits in his dreams for almost two years, had she chosen that moment to visit him? Chris believes that it was precisely because he had a new police contact who had started to monitor his dreams that week. It was, in effect, the most opportune moment for her to appear.

Years later, I asked Chris why he thought WPC Fletcher had come back at all – had she ever given him a reason? He told me that she hadn't, but he believed she wanted to carry on her work. When she was alive she was a conscientious police officer who loved her job. Now that she was dead, she had a chance to carry on her work in a different way: she could, as it were, act undercover and find out things that it would be physically impossible for anyone else to discover. Having done that, she was then faced with the problem of relaying that information to the physical plane. Chris just happened to be there: able to pick up her signals from some other plane.

And those signals were to prove extremely interesting.

Chris was looking through his telescope, with Yvonne standing beside him. There was a full moon in the cloudless sky, shining brightly. As he looked, it was almost as though he could see every detail of the moon's surface. While he looked at the shining orb, Yvonne spoke to him, 'There's going to be a bomb. A bomb on the full moon. You must tell them that.'

The postcodes that were contained within the dream told Chris that it would explode somewhere on the M4 corridor, near Heathrow. But, frustratingly, he could get nothing more accurate than that.

On Tuesday, 11 June 1991, Yvonne came through with another message and a new set of symbols and codes for Chris to decipher: 'Bolt the [doors] – no, I will do it [4 YOU].'

4 You = Four You: an initial-letter code. A Y and an F, for Yvonne Fletcher. Either way round, this was how her messages would in future be prefaced on the pages of the diary. This did present a bit of a problem for Chris, as FY was also a postcode – for Blackpool. In future it would always be quite difficult for him to differentiate between a message from Yvonne and a message about Blackpool.

In the dream she was showing him a series of clocks, and telling him that there would be a problem connected with them.

The next night she was back – and Chris was looking through the telescope once again. Yvonne was trying to

tell him the date of the bomb – it would be on the full
moon, but which full moon? The one forthcoming, or
the one after, or . . . 'June [21st] mid-summer – soon –
is it summer [or] winter.'

The next full moon wasn't on 21 June – it came a
week later, on 28 June. But Yvonne hadn't been trying
to tell him that it would actually occur on 21 June –
after all, the date had a box round it. Chris could only
surmise that she was trying to tell him that it would be
on the next full moon – in sixteen days' time.

The next night he saw more telescopes and found
himself at Jodrell Bank. He began to realise now that
a telescope didn't just refer to his own telescope: it
was another symbol. Because Yvonne was trying to tell
him information that wasn't in the immediate future –
the next two or three days – she was showing him a
telescope to indicate that it would happen a bit further
on than that. It was remote information, something that
Chris had to look some distance to see – like looking
through a telescope to see a far-away object.

On the night of Monday, 17 June, Yvonne and Chris
were looking through the telescope once again. The
moon was out, and she told him that there would be
a bomb on the occasion of the full moon – and she
was getting worried as that time was fast approaching.
As if to emphasise this, the moon began to move, and
as Chris watched it through the telescope it began to
move towards him at speed, filling the whole of the
lens, coming closer and closer, faster and faster, until he
could see every crater in incredibly close detail . . .

He woke up sweating, his heart pounding. He looked
over at the page he had been writing, to find:

A bomb is planned for the [Strand]
[Full moon] is fast approaching

The reference to the Strand baffled him – it didn't fit

with anything he had previously written. On the other hand, it had a box round it, and so might be a cryptic clue to something else. Yvonne was new to contacting Chris and it was rather like a bad phone connection, where some of the words get lost.

Later in the morning he rang through to Alex Hall's office and spoke to Glen Clemence.

'This bomb is definitely going to be on the full moon, wherever it is – but I'm not sure when the next full moon actually is. Can you find out for me?'

Clemence glanced at the wall behind him. There was a calendar hanging up, and by chance it was of the type that marks the stages of the moon each month.

'Yeah, that's easy,' he said. 'The full moon this month is over the night of the twenty-seventh and twenty-eighth.'

'I thought so. This one isn't going to go off, you know. Yvonne's going to do something to stop it. But I'd feel easier if I knew what.'

'What about the Gulf Parade?' asked Hall, suddenly coming on the line. 'What about any bombs there?'

Chris had to think about this one: for some weeks there had been concern that the IRA would attempt to bomb the parade being held for the forces who had returned from the short and savage Gulf War. Operation Desert Storm had taken the spotlight away from terrorism for a few weeks, and the parade for returning soldiers would be an excellent target for the IRA propaganda machine.

Could this be what the reference to the Strand was all about? Chris didn't know the route of the parade, but it would certainly be through the City and the centre of London.

'I don't know,' Chris muttered, as he thumbed through the pages of the dream diary. 'I don't think – no, I don't think there will be.'

A random phrase in the diaries had triggered a

memory: very thick snow had carpeted the ground, and there had been dogs. As Chris had stood looking at them, the dogs had turned around and slowly walked away. The snow meant danger, and the dogs were the terrorists: they were walking away from the danger, turning their backs on the opportunity to create havoc.

He explained this to Hall and finished by saying: 'I don't know why they won't do it, I just know that they've changed their minds.'

For whatever reason all their energies were to be concentrated on the attack that Yvonne had vowed to stop.

A dream on Wednesday, 19 June, gave Chris a clearer indication of the cryptic direction that his dreams were destined to take.

> Subway train – [american] [coins] all over the floor – stuck in chewing gum
> Indian [head] on coins

Chris had drawn four coin shapes, with '25c.' written on them. American 25-cent coins, with Indian heads on them: what did this mean? Further down the page, things became even stranger.

> [I] am a policeman now – they have given me a job – when do I start Tomorrow – morning – put [2] trains in my bag
> Who's passport is that in there – you are not supposed to have someone else's passport. Better put it back.

In the dream Chris had been in Petty France, the part of London where the main office for the issuing and administration of passports throughout the country is housed. He couldn't remember the last time he had been there, so it struck him as extremely odd that he should dream of it now. And why had he been made a policeman?

Sitting down to decipher the dream, he began to write on the blank sheet opposite the dream page. The first thing he wrote, concerning the coins, was 'Indian heads – Head Quarters'. Then, further down the page, he wrote the initials 'PF', to remind him that he had been in Petty France. It struck him that, although this wasn't a postcode, when the letters were reversed he could get Finsbury Pavement – would the Gulf Parade be going down this part of the City of London?

After puzzling over the page for some time Chris decided that it must just be one of those nights when everything was coming through garbled. He faxed the dream and his interpretation, as usual, then forgot about it.

It was two days later, on the afternoon of 21 June 1991, that the dream came back to him with a jolt. While flicking though the Teletext service to try and catch the news, an item caught Chris's attention: there had been a bomb at the Indian Army Headquarters in Colombo.

Indian? Head? Quarters?

Chris scrambled to his feet and fetched the current dream diary from the bedroom.

There it was: Indian heads on quarters. That bit was right . . . but why did Colombo ring so many bells in his head? Looking down the page, he could see that there were lots of references to police. Suddenly it leapt out at him: 'PF' might stand for Peter Falk, the actor who plays a policeman called . . . Columbo.

So Chris could easily claim to have seen this attack in his dream two nights before, yet it was only with hindsight that he was able to piece it all together. What's more, he worried that perhaps he was reading something into the dream because he could make it fit, rather than because it was genuine.

He had experienced similar doubts when the dreams began, but a steady system of code use and a number of very literal images had laid those doubts to rest. Now they were flooding back: this dream did seem precognitive, but there had been a new type of code in use, one that was much more cryptic than before.

If this was going to become the norm then it would involve a lot more work on the dreams than Chris had put in recently. He could only hope that the work would reward him with even better results.

Yvonne returned again on the night of Saturday 22 June. She left Chris with another clue as to the whereabouts of the forthcoming bomb, which tallied with his earlier feelings.

> Paddington – goes west – other stations – Direct
> Can the river be opened [2] Bigger [Boats] –
> there is a campaign [2] do it.
>   [7 Railway Bridge]

Looking at this, Chris could remember what Yvonne had told him in the dream: 'Draw a line along the M4, from Paddington to Wales. The bomb will be on this line.'

Later in the dream he was back in familiar territory: 'Telescope at the moon – Full Moon in the sky.'

Over the page Chris had written about looking through the telescope, and then 'Do not touch it, Just look', which brought home to him that Yvonne had promised to look after this one herself.

Chris was left in a quandary: did he trust her spirit to stop the bomb, or did he simply assume that this was some other part of a code? In the final analysis he couldn't let himself take a risk like this, so he contacted Alex Hall again.

'I'm sure there's a bomb on the full moon, and

I'm sure it's along the M4 corridor. I think it's near Heathrow, but I don't know why.'

Hall considered this. 'Come into the station. We'll go over everything again, in case there's something you've been missing.'

The two men spent some time poring over the dream diaries, Hall throwing questions at Chris concerning obscure entries that might have some deeply personal meaning. There was nothing new that could be deduced from what had already been written.

It was now Monday, 24 June. According to the dreams, the bomb was due to go off on the night spanning 27 and 28 June: three days away.

Monday and Tuesday yielded nothing: despite Chris's requests, Yvonne failed to appear in his dreams and he was beginning to get despondent when something finally happened on the Wednesday night.

Chris went to bed early: he was tired, and also hopeful that he might get a relevant message in his dreams. He was not to be disappointed.

Yvonne came to him in the dream. As usual, she was wearing her uniform, and she was looking pleased with herself, patting the breastpocket of her tunic.

'I've got the fuses,' she said with a smile. 'I've got the fuses here in my top pocket. The bomb can't go off without them, can it?'

'I'm not with you,' Chris said. He was confused, because the whole of his dream before she turned up had been concerned with his past as an engineer. He had been working in a repair shop and had taken the van out, when he had been attacked by a swarm of bees. When he arrived at the job he had been assigned, he had found that he had no fuses for the television among his box of diodes and other spare parts. He searched through the cardboard box he was carrying, but had been unable to find any.

And then everything had changed, and he was standing on a piece of waste ground, talking to Yvonne.

She was laughing. 'The fuses on the timer. I've got them here.' She patted her pocket again. 'No bomb's going to work if the timer isn't set, is it?'

'But how did you manage that? I mean, what happened?'

The thought of what had occurred made her start to giggle again, and she had to compose herself before beginning her story.

'I haven't been able to get through to you exactly where this bomb's going to be, right? But that's all right, because I've already told you that I'll see to it myself. So I followed these scum when they set out to plant it. They came round here –' she gestured at the waste ground around them. Chris wished that he recognised it, but it was unknown to him. Yvonne continued, ' – and left their van. The guy who was supposed to set the bomb brought it over here, and started to set the timer. Well, I was going frantic, because I didn't know exactly what to do to stop him.

'He was about to set it, so I knew I had to do something fast: I did what any spirit would. I crept up behind him and went "boo" in his ear.' She burst out laughing. 'I've never seen anyone run so fast in my life – or whatever you call this now. He was so shocked that he just dropped the fuse for the timer and legged it out of here, right over that fence –' she pointed to a distant wire fence ' – and into the van. They shot off like the proverbial bat out of hell. And I just scooped up the fuses and put them in my pocket.'

She smiled broadly. 'I'd like to see him explain that to the rest of the cell.'

Chris could remember this vividly when he awoke. There were also several parts of the night's writing that backed up his memory:

Take out a fuse − 2 fuse
Taken out − 1 put in a box
I put in my top pocket.
   The [HT] fuse in My Top Pocket

There was also something else, which he couldn't recall figuratively from the dream, that he was sure was of some importance:

[SKIRT] − Home Made − Waist Band
it is 2 tight − will it fit over my head − YES it will
but it is still 2 tight −

He couldn't immediately work out the significance of this, but didn't want to waste time on it at the moment: he had to phone Alex Hall.

'Look, there definitely is a bomb. It is on the M4 near Heathrow, and it is planned for the full moon. But it won't go off − Yvonne's got the fuses.'

'Are you sure about that?'

'Positive . . . trust me.'

Chris believes that Hall passed his information on to military intelligence, but in the meantime something unconnected but also quite astounding happened.

The actual question Chris had written in his diary on the night of 26 June had nothing to do with the forthcoming bomb. Instead it concerned one of two traffic wardens who had come to see Chris that day. They had heard about his abilities, and one of them had a twin with whom she had lost contact. She wanted to know if the twin was all right, and possibly where she was.

In the excitement of Yvonne's message, Chris had forgotten about the traffic wardens until they returned to see him that evening. It was then that something came back to him: Yvonne's uniform was very like that of the wardens, and at one point she had told him that her father had worked in Canada, and that he was either a doctor or had something to do with the navy – this became hazy, as he hadn't paid much attention to it at the time, and his memory was playing tricks on him.

When the two wardens were seated, Chris turned to the one who had asked about her twin. 'Your father was a doctor, wasn't he? And he worked in Canada?'

She was speechless for a second, then replied, 'Good lord, how did you know that? As a matter of fact, I was born in Nova Scotia.'

Chris was able to tell her something about her twin, something too personal to repeat without permission. She was, however, glad to hear what he had to say. Talk turned to the bomb and Yvonne's warning. The wardens left Chris's home more than satisfied with what they had heard.

The night of the full moon – 27–8 June – there was no sign of Yvonne and nothing in the dreams about the bomb. Instead Chris's dream was occupied by Patrick Frater and the first appearance of Ernie Bandoo, as recounted in an earlier chapter.

With no bomb and no Yvonne, Chris wondered if anything had actually happened along the M4 corridor. At 3.10 a.m. he had woken up and known immediately that the bomb had been planted. But this interpretation might have been false; when he woke again at 9.45 he immediately phoned Glen Clemence and asked him if a bomb had been found.

'Not that I know of,' the officer replied, 'but I'll check.'

The next couple of hours were nail-biting for Chris: not only did he want to know whether his prediction had been accurate, but there were a number of matters riding on this dream precognition that would determine the way he looked at his dreams for the foreseeable future.

The way in which some of the clues had been presented to him revealed not only a new set of symbols to be learnt, but also a twist to the cryptic manner in which some of the information was conveyed. If the dreams had been correct, then he had to get to work on cracking this new code – if not, then he could disregard it as an aberration.

Was Yvonne 'real', or was she just a dream figure talking rubbish? He had to know, as she had been a frequent visitor. If she was 'real', then the dreams were continuing as before. If not, then he would have to watch for his own subconscious playing out dream fantasies on a field that had previously been used as an information channel.

Finally, the big one: if a defused bomb were found, then could it be that Yvonne – a spirit – had caused this to happen? Did she just tell him in a roundabout way that it would be defused, or did she actually appear to haunt the bomber?

The last question could not really be answered satisfactorily – but if the fuses were missing from the timer, then Chris knew what he would believe, even if others found it hard to accept.

Chris phoned Clemence three or four times in the next couple of hours, asking if he had found out anything: each time the policeman told him that no reports had filtered through to him.

The morning had been written off in worrying: Chris hadn't even looked at his previous night's dreams yet. Feeling unsettled and on edge, he turned on the television in the hope of finding something to take his mind off the morning's anxiety.

It certainly did that: it was coming up to noon and the midday news started. The first item was about a bomb that had been found in Hayes. It had been found defused – and Hayes lies in Middlesex, less than a mile from the M4 as it runs past Heathrow.

Chris ran to the phone. Clemence picked up at the other end. 'What about this bomb in bloody Hayes, then?' Chris was almost shouting with frustration. 'Why didn't you tell me about that, then?'

'Because I've only just found out about it myself,' Clemence replied calmly, before telling Chris all that he knew.

The bomb had been found at the Beck Theatre, in Hayes, during a routine check: routine because the Band of the Blues and Royals – a military band, and therefore a likely target – was due to play the venue.

The bomb had been planted at the back of the theatre and had been primed to explode: it was a fully functional bomb in every way. Yet it was perfectly safe.

Chris asked why.

Clemence laughed and told him that the start button on the timer hadn't been pressed: a digital watch was being used and the stopwatch function used to time the bomb. A time had been set, but the button to start the countdown had been left unpressed.

'God knows why they forgot that,' Clemence said, 'unless . . .'

'Unless it was Yvonne,' Chris finished.

When he put down the phone and returned to the dream diary for a few nights before, he could still clearly remember Yvonne telling him how she had scared the terrorist planting the bomb. Could it really be that she had broken through to the physical world sufficiently to frighten away a bomber?

Suddenly the significance of 'waist band' in the section of dream about the tight skirt became apparent: this was a coded warning that a band would be involved. If Chris had deciphered that, then it might have been easier for him to trace the exact location of the bomb.

Conducting a small experiment with himself, Chris looked back through that year's dream diaries to see how often he had written the word 'band'.

It didn't occur at all: the only time it had been written was on the night of 26 June.

Shortly afterwards, when he saw her in a dream, Chris asked Yvonne why she hadn't told him exactly where the bomb was planted.

'If I'd told you then there would have been people chasing around all over the place, looking for it. I wanted this one for myself. You see, Chrissy, the future was set: that bomb was going to be planted, and you couldn't stop that. What you could do was stop it going off. But I wanted to do that: I wanted to scare this monkey – and did he run when I whispered in his ear. Over the fence, into his van, and away. I don't know what he told the others, but he better have had a good reason why he didn't set the timer – after all, who'd believe that it was a ghost?'

CHAPTER EIGHTEEN

In July 1991 two IRA prisoners escaped from Brixton prison and were on the run for several weeks. Chris Robinson not only foresaw their escape, but was also able to track their progress through his dreams. Was he instrumental in helping to catch them?

At this point it's hard to tell: certainly he was faxing his dreams to Alex Hall every day, and Hall was passing on information contained in them that may have been of use. Perhaps the truest thing to say is that, as with all his activities, Chris's dreams were treated on a par with information coming in from all kinds of informants, and were assessed as to their individual worth on a daily basis.

The story really begins on 4 July . . .

Dr Keith Hearne was staying with Chris at the time, carrying out one of his periods of in-depth study. During these sessions he would stay with Chris and assess the information with him on a day-by-day basis. He would also observe Chris while he slept, noting how he moved in his sleep, his REM and the manner in which he recorded information by the process of automatic writing.

Although he has his own facilities, Dr Hearne is one of the few parascientists in Britain to realise that studying subjects outside their own environment can be counter-productive: the kind of forces and energies concerned in precognition are not yet quantifiable, and could be easily upset by the stress of strange surroundings and the tension of a laboratory atmosphere. It is actually more productive to study the subjects in their own environment, and just as easy to apply the controls that can prevent fraudulent – or even unintentionally false – results.

The dreams of 4 July were extremely interesting to both Chris and Keith Hearne:

Bird [in a] cage
   Don't let it fly away.
      Fireworks or rockets.
Chain – does it go to a foot or boot or plug

Analysing it the next morning, Chris told Hearne that the birds in a cage meant that there were prisoners about to escape – 'don't let it fly away'. He was also sure that they were IRA prisoners.

'How do you get that?' asked Dr Hearne.

'Look at this,' Chris replied. 'Where it says birds in a cage, the "in a" is boxed, which means that it's not quite that. If you change one letter, then you get IRA.'

'But that's a bit spurious, isn't it?' Hearne asked, playing Devil's advocate.

'I suppose you could say that . . . except that I've had this before, and experience has taught me how to read it.'

It was another example of how Chris has learnt to decode messages that may seem nonsensical to anyone else. Going on with the analysis, Chris told Hearne that he believed the prisoners would escape on foot – hence the part about a chain, meaning prisoner, being attached to a foot or a boot. He was also sure that there would be two of them, as the number 2 was a recurrent feature of the night's dream writing. Now they had to determine where the escape would occur.

Looking at the dream, he could see that there

were postcodes for SW, and also for Central London. However, the SW ones were more prevalent, so Chris went to his computer and punched up the postcode map for the SW area of London, part of whose codes cover Brixton.

On Brixton Hill stands Brixton Prison.

Chris faxed this to Alex Hall without delay, and both men were excited by the prospect of the following night's dream results.

On the night of 5 July the number 2 was again spread all over the page, and Chris knew this referred to the two prisoners – the birds in the cage – of the previous night's dream. In this dream he saw them getting on the Metropolitan Line at Baker Street, and also saw Detective Sergeant Holmes – one of the policemen who had interviewed Chris over the Stanmore affair. There were also several references to Harrow: and the Metropolitan Line goes out past Harrow.

Looking at the dreams with Keith Hearne, Chris again attempted to analyse them in depth.

'Look at this: "they both have gold lighters in Harrow or Wealdstone", then there's this bit about "2 in my camper – in Harrow" over on this page,' Chris said, turning over the two pages he had written during the night. 'Back here we've got something about "Detective Sergeant Holmes will get a shock soon", only the word sergeant is boxed, so I think it means just a detective called Holmes – Sherlock Holmes. He lived in Baker Street, right? And this bit immediately after it says "Met line 2 Baker Street". So I reckon these jokers will get on the tube after they escape – and if they don't get out to Harrow, then Harrow police station will have something to do with their arrest.'

Once more, the material was faxed to Alex Hall, along with the proviso that both Chris and Dr Hearne believed that the escape would happen some time on Sunday. This was a conclusion they had arrived at because the dreams concerning the escape had occurred two nights running.

After nearly two years they had established between them, by careful study of those precognitions that had come true, that there were different cycles of dream frequency, dependent on how far away the actual event was and how major it would be. For instance, an IRA bomb attack would build up over a period of weeks, possibly months, and the dreams would come at increasingly frequent intervals – from once a week to every night. Small, everyday events would crop up in dreams the night before. But events like this – where it would be a big news story but not particularly life-threatening – would occur in three-night cycles: three nights, and then it would happen.

Saturday 6 July was the third night.

In the dream Chris was camping out in a bell-tent. Two killers with guns came looking for him, then decided to try and get away quickly when they couldn't find him. They had a hire car, but it refused to start, and they were left desperately looking for another car in a blizzard, with blankets of snow covering everything in sight – more snow than Chris had ever seen before in a dream.

From this, he was sure that the escapees would be trying to get away in a hire car, and that the car wouldn't work. They would have to take another one, and in so doing would put someone in danger. He also had a definite postcode: '2 See Who is' on one line. Taking the capitalised initials, you get SW2 – the postcode for Brixton.

Chris was awake at 5 a.m. and couldn't get back to sleep. Yvonne had visited him and shown him all of this happening. In his diary he had written:

In a hire car Very thick snow on the road – car

can't move – gets stuck – have 2 get out and walk
– 1 goes one way one the other

It was all so vivid still. He woke Dr Hearne and told
him about it. Hearne could see for himself how agitated
and unsettled Chris became when a dream premonition
was that vivid, and suggested that he fax it through
right then.

The two men waited all morning, occasionally glancing at the Teletext service on television to see what was
going on.

It happened at 10.30 a.m.

Convicted IRA terrorists Nessan Quinlivan and Pearce
McAuley escaped from Brixton Prison after morning
service in the prison chapel. It was 9.40 a.m. and as
they left the chapel McAuley bent down as if to tie a
shoelace. As he straightened up warders were astonished
to see that he had a gun in his hand. Somehow he had
secreted a smuggled pistol inside his shoe.

Firing four shots into the air to discourage would-be
heroes, he and Quinlivan grabbed the prison officers'
keys and rushed through several sets of security gates
leading to the prison yard. Once there, they stacked
a wheelbarrow on top of a dog kennel and scaled the
perimeter wall.

Once the other side, and down into Jebb Avenue,
they threatened a prison officer who was just getting
into his car, and after warning him off with the gun,
screeched away.

Jebb Avenue is, however, actually more of an alleyway
than a road, with the looming shadow of the prison on
one side, and the prison officers old quarters on the other.
There is barely room for two cars to pass, and so it was
easy for another prison officer to use his car to block the
road before the escapees had a chance to speed past.

The two fugitives dumped the car where it stood and

ran out onto Brixton Hill, where they tried to flag down passing vehicles.

In any area of London two men trying to flag down cars would be an indication for drivers to speed up – even more so in an area with a reputation for violence and crime. But there are always those motorists who worry that they might truly be passing someone in need.

The driver of the red Vauxhall Cavalier that pulled in to assist Quinlivan and McAuley won't make the same mistake again: McAuley wrenched open the door on the driver's side and yelled at him, while Quinlivan opened the passenger door and dragged the driver's wife onto the road.

The terrified driver was too scared to move. McAuley did just what one might expect of him: he shot the driver of the car and dragged him from his vehicle. Fortunately he was too hyped-up to take aim and the shot passed through the man's thigh. Painful, but not life-threatening.

Leaving the distressed and wounded couple in the road, the gunmen roared off.

Two miles from the prison, at Lambeth Town Hall, the fugitives abandoned the car in Porden Road before calmly walking into Acre Lane and hailing a black cab. They told the unsuspecting driver to take them to Baker Street Underground station and even had the audacity to give him a £12 tip.

There they entered the station and disappeared temporarily from view.

As the drama unfolded over the Sunday, both Chris and Keith Hearne watched the reports, astounded. The events of the day had been mirrored in Chris's dreams of a few nights before.

Both men looked back over the dreams of the nights preceding the appearance of the birds in a cage. In one of them there was a reference to Shooters Hill and

Shooters Road: there is a Shooters Hill not that far from the prison, but Chris was loath to accept this, as he believed it was more likely to refer to Shooters Avenue, in Harrow. Chris had an aunt who lived there and although he hadn't seen her for some time, he was sure that the dream was more likely to refer to her than to the forthcoming escape.

About six weeks later Chris actually had cause to visit his aunt, and in the course of their conversation he mentioned that he had dreamt about her, and that there had been an attempt to tie her in to the Brixton escape.

'It's funny you should say that,' his aunt began – and Chris felt a familiar shiver run down his spine. The long arm of coincidence or synchronicity was about to reach out to him again. 'It's a pity you didn't come and see me sooner,' she continued, 'because on the Monday after they escaped, they came into the shop.' She worked in Littlewoods department store in Harrow, which is, of course, on the Metropolitan Line from Baker Street. She continued, 'I recognised them, and said to my supervisor, "Here, that's those two who got out of Brixton yesterday." But she wouldn't let me phone the police or anything, as she was frightened of Littlewoods becoming a target – well, it might, I suppose, if they were recaptured there. Anyway they went out of the shop and that was that.'

After this there was something of a quiet time for Chris throughout the rest of the summer. Yvonne was still around, but her information wasn't getting through clearly. For instance, he knew that there would be bombs in Blackpool, which would be planted at around the time of the Labour Party conference, but that they wouldn't go off until afterwards. He also knew that they were hidden under something.

That was all. Perhaps, for some mediums and psychics,

that would be enough to trumpet as a prediction, but Chris was unsure and as a result was none too happy when the editor of his local paper splashed it across the front page as a 'local psychic predicts' story. It was basically concocted from an aside that Chris made to a reporter on the paper, and although there was nothing false in the story, it wasn't the type of insubstantial claim that he would have liked to see on any front page.

At the end of October a series of firebombs, which had been hidden some time before, detonated in department stores throughout Blackpool. Ten stores were damaged by fire.

When this made the national news, the editor of the local paper rang Chris and said, 'You really can do it, then, can't you?'

'Oh yeah, I can really do it,' Chris replied with as much irony as he could muster. He could do it all right – but with much better results than those that had impressed the newspaper's editor.

As November arrived the messages began to get clearer in Chris's dreams and the build-up started for another major bomb warning. Chris would also find out how Yvonne Fletcher had first come to him.

In his unusual and varied career Chris had met many people who flirted with the wrong side of the law. This had brought him into contact with police officers several times before the dreams began, and he's convinced that sometimes everything was laid out for him, enabling him to contact the right people at the right time when the dreams began.

As may be recalled, Chris first met Paul Aylott when he was approached about a blackmail plot against Graham Bright.

On 12 November 1991 he had a dream that began, 'Write a note 2 Glen.'

This meant Glen Clemence. In the dream there were

two dead people. They had been blown up, and Chris was sure that they were terrorists. There were also two banks, next to each other, and these had also been blown up.

Chris was walking down a road called French Road. It was in St Albans, a market town in the commuter belt of London. He crossed the road and came to the banks.

He was following two dogs . . .

CHAPTER NINETEEN

The first intimations about St Albans had come to Chris
eight days earlier on Monday, 4 November 1991, when
he started to receive postcodes in his dream. He dreamt
about driving a car down the central reservation of a
motorway, then being in a classroom. Later on he was
telling someone that he couldn't remember the phone
number of his friend Philip.

Looking at the dream diary in the morning, he saw:

> Drive on *Central* Reservation
> Ina Class Room – make a phone call
> Can't Remember Philip's No!

The preponderance of CRs signified a St Albans
postcode. Also interesting was the way he had written
'in a' as 'ina' in the second phrase: previously the use
of 'ina' had been confined to a box and was a code for
the IRA.

Did this mean that a bomb attack on St Albans was
being planned?

On the night of 6 November Chris dreamt ceaselessly
about dogs – they were chasing him across a farm,
almost catching and biting him. Three dogs waited
for him, two in one room, one in another. One
of the dogs went after him, and he found himself
grabbing a man's wife and threatening her if the dog
wasn't called off.

Then he was talking to someone, saying that it was

worth serving six months in prison for killing a dog if it taught the owner a lesson.

He woke up sweating: were the dogs after him? He looked at his diary: teach the dog owner 'a lesson' – AL was the postcode for St Albans town centre. Were the dogs massing for an attack there?

But why? It was only a small town, with little real significance. As a target it was almost too soft to bother with.

The next night he dreamt of his son Aaron and his friend Curtis: they were trying to fly, and when he woke Chris found that he had written, 'Aaron and [Curtis] try 2 take off And Fly.'

So now he had a postcode for AL2. St Albans again.

On the night of 11 November he was looking out on a field where it was snowing heavily, and there were dogs running through the field. He was in a house belonging to a friend of his, who lived in St Albans.

Something big was brewing.

The next night he dreamt of writing a letter to Glen Clemence. Yvonne was telling him to write it, and she handed him two cups of coffee – signifying two dead people.

Then he was in St Albans again, walking up French Road, crossing at the lights and continuing towards two banks, one of which stood on a corner. He was following two dogs, which were also walking along this way.

The dogs turned into people: so now there were two people in front of him, one of them carrying a package. They walked up to the banks and put the bomb through the letter box.

As it went through it exploded, and they were both blown up in front of his eyes.

When Chris looked at the dream diary, it read:

2 banks – blown up in St Albans last night
Put through letter boxes – after [MT]
[3] bombs in Holland or is it 2

The reference to bombs in Holland were somewhat confusing, as he could remember nothing of this: the vision of St Albans was too clear in his mind.

It was only when Chris scanned the Teletext pages that he discovered some bombs had gone off in Holland during the night. They were nothing to do with the IRA, but it was possible that he had picked up something about them because they were current.

He was relieved to see that there had been no bombs in St Albans. His diary might have said 'last night', but Chris had no doubt now that this was a prediction. Later in his dream he could recall that he was in a police station talking about what he had seen: a clear indication that now was the time to act.

He was prompt in faxing the dream through to Alex Hall and Glen Clemence. There was, however, one problem that he had to face: as yet, he had no real time frame for the event.

Wednesday night saw him standing outside a branch of the Midland Bank. To Chris, this was confirmation that the bomb was imminent. But still no actual time . . .

Thursday, 14 November, saw him back in St Albans in his dream. He was with Yvonne Fletcher, in his car, and they were driving into town. Chris knew that he was heading for a shop called Video Viewpoint, in the town centre, where he used to buy equipment and supplies during his days as a video dealer.

They went past the shop and continued on towards the banks, where Chris saw meat pies scattered on the pavement. He recognised these as a symbol for badly butchered corpses – meat from a butcher's shop, or in a pie, always meant the same thing.

Yvonne turned to Chris. 'Don't worry about this,'

she said. 'It's not like the other one, but it's in my pocket.'

'What do you mean?'

She smiled and pulled out a coin. 'Like this,' she said.

When he woke, Chris had written the following:

> [Video] recorder – black front – [brand] new £150 – trade price – Video Viewpoint – repair it today.
> [Meat] pie
> [Yvonne] Fletcher
> coin in my pocket – [Hole] – gone in 2

There had been other aspects of the dreams that Chris found to be of possible significance. There were the two people that he had seen approaching the banks – the two who had been dogs and were then blown up. They were now in bed, and there was snow all around the bed. He had also written a reference to a 'Terminal 2'. Ordinarily he would connect this with an airport, but under the circumstances he was sure that it referred to the two dead people he had seen – the two dead people that there would be that very night.

On Friday, 15 November, he phoned Glen Clemence and told him that he was absolutely convinced that the incident would happen in St Albans, and that it would happen that night: the dream had come to him this strongly three nights running and he had little doubt now about the timing.

Clemence took this in and could see how concerned Chris was by what had happened to him during the night.

'Okay,' he said, 'the best thing you can do this evening is stay in all night. Don't go anywhere, and for God's sake don't disappear. Just in case we need you.'

Chris agreed. If Glen was prepared to ask him to do

this, then it meant they were taking him more seriously than they had for some months.

He was on edge for the rest of the day and found it hard to settle to anything: come the evening, he was stretched out on the floor of the caravan, going through the back pages of the diaries, to see if there was anything that he might have missed.

It was about quarter to ten when the phone rang and Chris answered, half-expecting it to be Clemence or Hall. In fact, it was a friend called Tony Centrachio, who had been interested in Chris's dreams for some time and had given him a photograph in the summer: the photograph was of a girl he had met in Italy. She was a small girl with long, dark hair, and there was a strange white blur in the foreground of the picture that had not been there when the picture was taken and could not be attributed to a reflection. Interestingly, the night before Tony had shown Chris this picture, he had dreamt of a photograph featuring a small girl with long, dark hair. It was shown to him by a spirit who claimed to have been there when the picture was taken. Tony had been astounded when Chris told him this, and since then had called regularly to talk about both Chris's dreams and his own.

Chris spent some time talking to Tony and when he put the phone down he heard a shout behind him, 'It's gone off.'

'What –' Chris looked round, expecting to see his wife . . . and then he remembered that he was on his own that evening. Besides which, he recognised the voice: it was Yvonne Fletcher's.

It was unusual for him to hear a spirit's voice outside a dream: the last time had been when he had driven past the cemetery where Patrick Frater and Ernie Bandoo were buried. He had no doubts that the bomb had just gone off in St Albans, and that the two terrorists had just died.

Chris was now on edge, pacing about the floor and waiting for Clemence to ring. The suspense was killing and at ten-past ten he decided to do the ringing himself. He put a call through to Clemence's paging service and within a few minutes the policeman had rung him back.

'Have you heard anything yet?' Chris demanded.

'No – why?'

'I've just been standing here, and I heard Yvonne's voice – I wasn't even asleep. I actually heard her, and she told me that it's gone off.'

'Well, look,' Clemence said, thinking on his feet as he spoke, 'I'm in the middle of Bedfordshire at the moment. Let me ring through to St Albans and see what they say. Don't go anywhere – just wait for me, okay?'

Chris agreed and waited by the phone. Each second seemed like an eternity, but it was in fact only a couple of minutes before the phone shrilled in the silence and Chris snatched up the receiver.

'All hell's broken loose in St Albans,' Clemence said. 'They want you over there – now. Just get over to St Albans as fast as you can.'

'Right.' It was only when he put the phone down that it occurred to Chris that getting over to St Albans might prove a bit difficult, as earlier in the week his car had broken down. All he had in the way of transport was a battered old moped.

It was 15 November – freezing cold weather, and it was now half-past ten at night. The prospect of travelling from just outside Dunstable to St Albans on such a machine did not fill Chris with joy. But it was something he had to do.

Dressed in reflective yellow clothing for the quiet country roads and ill-lit A5, Chris felt a bit of an idiot as he set off for his destination. Even more so when he reached the turn-off that would take him onto the A5 –

the main road to St Albans – and the moped spluttered to a halt.

He got off the machine and looked at it in the dim light. As far as he could see there was nothing wrong with the engine. Then he looked at the petrol gauge . . . Of all the stupid things to do, he had run out of petrol.

Cursing to himself, Chris began to push the machine towards the nearest filling station, which was about a mile and a half away. In the bitter night air, with the hint of rain, it seemed to take him hours.

After he had filled up the moped and set off again there were no further delays on his way to St Albans, but the moped wasn't fast and his detour for petrol had eaten up a fair amount of time. So it was nearly a quarter to twelve when he reached the outskirts of St Albans.

A complete security cordon had been thrown around the town by this time, and Chris came up against it as he rode towards a bored policeman leaning against his car. The policeman held up his hand to stop Chris as he approached.

'This is really important,' Chris said as he slowed to a halt and got off the moped. 'My name is Christopher Robinson, and I'm a psychic. I've been told they want to see me in there.' He gestured towards the town centre.

The policeman eyed him sceptically. 'Yeah, and I'm Father Christmas,' he said slowly, 'so turn your bike around and go back home. You must be joking.'

'No, look,' said Chris desperately, 'You've got to understand. I've been talking to a police officer and he told me to come here. They want to see me.'

The policeman sighed. 'And I'm telling you that I'm Father Christmas, right? Just get on your bike and get out of here before I arrest you.'

'Well, you can do that if you want,' Chris replied, knowing the results that had come from being arrested in such a situation before.

He dug into his coat and produced a crumpled bundle of papers, which included some of his press clippings and a few letters: the letter from the Ministry of Defence and one from Graham Bright among them. He had grabbed them before leaving, just in case he needed to prove what he was saying. With hindsight, perhaps he should have mentioned Glen Clemence by name, but the attitude of the policeman on duty was such that he probably wouldn't have bothered checking.

Chris handed the bundle to the policeman, who started to read them by the light of his car. He wasn't particularly interested in them and made that clear, but he was bored and cold, and it gave him something to do on this quiet stretch of road.

Nearly half an hour passed, and Chris felt frozen to the bone. The policeman had finished reading the clippings and discarded them. He was now beginning to get irritated that Chris was still hanging around.

'Look, mate,' Chris said to him, time and again, 'if I have to try and get in, and get arrested, then I will – because they want to see me in there.'

'Yeah, of course they do,' the policeman replied dismissively, with more than a hint of annoyance in his voice.

The sparring went on a little longer before another car rolled up to the checkpoint. It was occupied by a uniformed Sergeant, who got out and came over to the patrol car.

'Who's this?' he asked the policeman on duty, casting only the barest glance at Chris.

'He says he's a psychic,' the policeman replied, his voice weary, 'and he says that they want to see him inside. He's been here ages, and he won't go away. I'm going to have to arrest him at this rate.'

'They want him, do they?' The Sergeant's eyes narrowed, and his mouth set firm. 'We'll soon see about that.' He returned to his car, where Chris could see him talking over the radio. Obviously he hadn't wanted to speak in the open, where Chris could hear him.

'Your number's up, boy,' said the policeman with a chuckle.

It was a chuckle that died in his throat as the Sergeant emerged from his car and walked back to where the policeman and Chris were standing. In the reflected glare of the car headlights he looked completely white, and his voice was shaking as he reached them. He addressed the policeman.

'They only want to see him, don't they,' he said in a quiet voice. 'They've only been standing around waiting for him.'

'You see? I told you,' said Chris, unable to keep a triumphant note out of his voice. He was tired and fed-up, not to mention cold to the bone after standing around in the cold November night. He was bundled into the Sergeant's car and rushed through the streets of St Albans to the central police station.

To Chris, coming in out of the night, the station was a hive of activity and light – and, most importantly, warmth. He was taken down a corridor and left in an interview room, given tea and biscuits, and shortly two plainclothes officers came in. They didn't introduce themselves, and to this day Chris has no idea who they were: CID, Anti-Terrorist Squad, Intelligence services, or whatever.

But they knew plenty about him, and about his dreams. He spent a couple of hours in the interview room, going over the dreams that had occupied him during the last fortnight, particularly those of the last three nights. The officers had copies of the faxes he had sent to Alex Hall, and they kept returning to points in the dreams, going over and over them to try and extract more details from him.

From their questions and their demeanour, Chris eventually deduced that one of them was probably a military man and the other a police officer of some sort.

'Look,' Chris said, 'you've got to believe me about this, I'm not just making it up –'

He was cut short by one of the men. 'Christopher,' he said slowly, 'you don't have to sell yourself to me. I believe you. But can we ever do anything about this?'

It was something Chris had often wondered: was the future pre-ordained and he was merely seeing snatches of it? Or was it possible to alter events, and it was simply a matter of the right action being taken quickly enough?

'I don't know,' he said finally, 'but if we don't try we're never really going to find out, are we? I don't know if I'm seeing what's going to be, or whether Yvonne really is there and playing tricks: she said she was going to sort this one out. Maybe she did – maybe as the bomb was going through the letter box she blew it up, just as she went 'boo' behind the guy planting the bomb at the Beck Theatre. I don't know – all I really know for sure is that the circumstances of the dream exactly fit the circumstances of the reality.'

'Okay,' said one of the men, 'so this is what we want you to do. We've got some bits of body –' he smiled grimly as Chris went pale '– yeah, that's all that was left. But that's all there is. Just bits. What we really need to know is who they were, and how many of them.'

'Well, I'm perfectly happy that there were two of them, and that they were the bombers –'

'Going by your record, I'd say that's probably right,' the man replied. 'But what we really want you to do is go home now and get hold of Yvonne. Ask her who they are.'

'I'll try – but I don't think you'll get much change out of it yet,' Chris replied, looking at his watch: it was now 5 a.m.

The police took Chris back to his caravan and left him to get on with things. He tried to sleep, but

after the tension of the night before it was impossible,
and any dreams that there were became lost in an
almost-waking state.

He spent most of the Saturday feeling tired and
depressed: lack of sleep always made him feel like a
zombie, and today was no exception. When he finally
did go to bed in the evening, he wrote down the
question that had been requested of him and hoped
that he would get an answer.

He didn't get one. He did, however, get some
interesting messages from Yvonne:

> [Remote] [Control] are you pointing it in the
> right direction − if the LED's are at the front
> I will make sure it is when the time is right −
> But the police are still not ready [2 BE] give any
> more − what would have happened if I told you
> more at St Albans − 2 dead or property damaged
> − I decided [WATTS] best [4 You] but you must
> try to rest more

Further on down the page, he had added:

> send it all if you want but they still don't talk it
> [THROUGH] With You.
> *Ask Him* 2 interview all the people you told
> about St Albans − he can't be bothered − why −
> Ask Him that

Yvonne had appeared to Chris throughout that night's
dreams − there were three scribbled pages, mostly
meaningless nonsense − and she seemed determined
to lecture him about the way he was treating his
dreams. 'Remote Control' referred to Chris: anything
electrical with the initials CR or RC is a code for Chris
Robinson, the ex-engineer. Yvonne obviously felt that

Chris was receiving the information, but that it wasn't being treated with respect by the police who were handling Chris. Her coded references to Chris Watt – the boxed 'Watts' – and Alex Hall – the initialled 'Ask Him' – showed a certain contempt for the way they had handled the dream information. It was a view that Chris didn't share: from his own experiences with officers who turned up out of the blue to question him, he knew that his dreams were definitely being passed on to a higher authority.

Yvonne was also concerned that Chris was not devoting enough time to his dreams: her imprecations 'but you must try 2 rest more' and 'go 2 bed at nine o'clock' were commands that she felt he should take notice of. She even signed herself, by telling him that she would decide what's best '[4 You]' – FY, or Yvonne Fletcher reversed.

So, an interesting night's dreams, but Chris was still no closer to getting the information he wanted to know.

The night of Sunday, 17 November, he asked the same question, and this time he got five pages of dreams, which told him the names he had asked for. Whether or not they were correct, he didn't know – but they were names.

The first clue was the appearance of a girl, who looked like the girl he had followed to the bank. She was in a flat in Chesham, and there was no running water. Instead, Chris had to take the kettle outside the flat to fill it from a tap.

The girl was called Pat – tap backwards – and she was dead. This was certain, as the tap was outside, and 'out' meant dead.

The next section that related directly to the names came a little later, when Chris was looking at a baby in a pushchair. It looked like his son Paul when he was small, but the child was covered in gravy. He drew a box around the word gravy, and knew that this meant the colour was important, not the gravy itself, a feeling backed up by the next section:

> She says his Father is [Mick Brown] From Harlington. Does he still live in Lincoln Road – I bet it's not his – a blood test will prove it.

Could one of the names have been Mick Brown? But this section also contained a reference that was entirely personal, and to do with people Chris knew. From the writing he could also get the name Ryan. The use of the word Father triggered off another personal reference point, as Chris remembered a Father Ryan he had once known. Could his name have something to do with it?

Underneath he had written 'Don in a van' – but he knew instinctively that Don wasn't a forename, but part of the surname belonging to one of the terrorists.

At the start of the next page was the fragment of dream that caused him the most puzzlement:

> 4 bar electric fire – don't touch the electric while is switched on – electric drill, handle broken – council house – is the [drill] powerful enough to keep turning

The only make of drill with which Chris was familiar was a Black and Decker, and this was what he saw in his dream. He was holding it, with the handle snapped away from the main body of the drill. He knew that the make of drill was important, and also that the handle being broken was significant – but why?

A broken handle – handle as in name? Did this mean that one of the terrorists had a broken name? Double-barrelled, perhaps?

There were two references to the name Duggan within a few lines of each other: 'Duggan in another tram' and 'Duggan tells her' at the end of a long section concerning Chris being on a tram in Holland, trying to speak Dutch to a young girl and not making himself understood.

From this he was sure that Duggan was an important name, but that it didn't refer to one of the dead terrorists. If anything, Duggan might have been the man who sent them to plant the bomb. Certainly there were a lot of IRA cells that used Holland as a base, and there had been a strong Dutch theme to this part of the dream.

Most of the fourth page of dreams made little sense in the cold light of day, but there were snatches that he could remember that seemed to be significant. He filled a glass from a Coke bottle, and also dropped a glass ashtray. Glass had been associated with the girl Pat, at the beginning of his dreams. Why glass?

Further down the page there was a reference to a television crew filming. Except that Chris had written it as 'TV Crewe' – a very particular spelling error. There was only one thing that Crewe meant to Chris: his friend Frank, another ex-video dealer who lived in the Cheshire town. The two men had become very close as they each fought a court action against the same company. The 'Crewe' spelling was such a strong clue that it had to signify the name Frank.

On the last page there was a section of the dream where he was being investigated by private detectives who had newspapers all over their office floor. The investigation was connected with video films, and they had a series of cassettes on their desks. There were girls on the covers of the videos, and Chris wrote, 'Video tape covers – what has it got 2 do with Donnelly?'

The figure '2' signified that this was connected with the two dead bombers, and there were girls on the covers of the tapes: the surname of the girl Pat must be Donnelly.

He now had the following names: Patricia Donnelly for the girl; for the man, there were several possibilities:

Mick Brown, Ryan something or something Ryan, and Frank something. Looking over the dream writing and his attempts to translate and decode, he could see that Ryan had meant Father Ryan to him; was it too much of a leap to assume that the 'F' was supposed to be an initial, and that Frank went with Ryan, giving him Frank Ryan?

So now he had three names to give to the police in St Albans: Patricia Donnelly, Frank Ryan and Mick Brown. One of them also had a Black in their name, as part of a double-barrelled name. He suspected it would be either Frank Ryan or Patricia Donnelly, as Mick Brown was a name that Chris believed simply led him to Frank Ryan's name – it was a signpost, but he included it on the grounds that exclusion would be a dangerous omission.

One puzzle remained: what did glass have to do with Patricia Donnelly? That was something he would have to worry about later.

On Monday morning Chris met Alex Hall and Glen Clemence. Also present was a reporter from the *Sun* newspaper, Keiron Saunders, and Ron Fairley, the owner of the Bedfordshire news agency, who regularly put stories about Chris on the wires to the dailies in London. Chris had requested that the latter two be present when he met Hall and Clemence to go over Sunday night's dreams: if he was right, he wanted the world to know about it. He might still want to help the police, but his primary objective, as always, was to gain recognition for the phenomena he was experiencing, and hopefully to encourage research and experiment on what was happening to him. For this, publicity was essential.

The five men went to a Chinese restaurant for lunch, as it was the middle of the day by the time they had all assembled. Chris waited until the food arrived before he began to explain to the two newspaper men what had happened: he started with his dreams leading up to the bombing, and then revealed what had been requested of him.

'This is the first time any of you will have seen this,' he said, primarily addressing Clemence and Hall as he took the dream sheets out of a bag. He laid them on the table for all to see.

There were some minutes of silence while all four men pored over the scribbled sheets of paper.

'So what's the conclusion?' asked Hall finally, as the men sat back.

Chris took a deep breath. 'I'm convinced that the girl was called Patricia Donnelly, and there may be something else in her name – Black, maybe. Yvonne handed me a Black and Decker drill in the dream, and I was holding it with a broken handle. That's CB language – slang, right? Means name. So maybe there's a Black in there – I'd be surprised if it was Decker.' He laughed, and a ripple of amusement ran round the table. 'As to the man – I think it was Frank Ryan. I've got Mick Brown down here, but really that had other associations, and I think it's just a sort of leftover on the way to these names.'

'That's pretty far-out,' said one of the newsmen.

'You think I don't know that?' Chris smiled.

A few days later the IRA released details of the terrorists killed in the bungled attack on St Albans. The woman was named Patricia Black-Donnelly and the man was Frankie Ryan. The police in St Albans already knew that: they had been told by Chris Robinson.

Ron Fairley also knew, and as soon as the news story came through to him on the wires he phoned Chris.

'How the hell do you do that?' he asked. It was the one question Chris was always asked, to which he had only one answer.

'I don't know, mate,' he sighed. 'I only wish I did

know – then I might be able to do something about it, control it better, find out what causes it.'

'But aren't you frightened that the IRA are going to catch up with you?'

'No, not really . . .' There was silence at the end of the line, but it was something that Chris had thought about long and hard. He continued, 'I look at it this way. The spirits keep giving me messages, they want me to do this. It's not like I can really ignore it – well, I could, but I just think I'd never sleep properly again. I'm not like that. Anyway, they keep giving me messages because they want me to pass on all this information. So they're not going to let me get hurt, and cut off their way of getting it through. I think that they'll let me know if someone's coming after me and protect me in some way.'

'You really believe in this afterlife, don't you?' said Ron.

Chris laughed. 'If a few of these terrorists believed in an afterlife, then things might change – because it's only if you believe there's nothing after this life that you can go around being greedy, and selfish, and harming people. If you realise that you're going to be judged in the next world on what you do in this, then you're soon going to buck your ideas up and stop being stupid about things.'

Over the Christmas of 1991 there was one final bomb warning that showed Chris that his fate was in the lap of the Gods – or, rather, the spirits. He actually tried to see a bomb go off, and missed it by fifteen minutes.

It began in the third week of December, when Yvonne was telling him about a bomb that was going to be planted, and that this would occur in Central London. The postcode was SW1 or WC1 or 2, which would make it the Trafalgar Square area, and he also saw himself shopping in Sainsbury's. He actually wrote down 'Sainsbury's shopping trolley'.

When he checked, he found that there were no branches of Sainsbury's in that part of London. However, he still passed the information on, reasoning that he had misinterpreted the visit to Sainsbury's and that it must mean something else.

The warnings continued for three nights, and on the third Chris decided to see for himself what actually happened when a warning was passed on. So in the late evening he got into his car and drove up to London. Parking where he could, he walked through to Trafalgar Square.

It was Saturday, 28 December, and even late at night it was still fairly busy. Chris felt uncomfortable sitting on a bench in the middle of the square. He dislikes London at the best of times, but on this night it seemed to be particularly oppressive. He found himself continually checking his watch, but there was no sign of anything happening as the time crept round into the early hours of the following morning.

At half-past two, tired and cold, Chris decided to go home, chalking the trip up as a failure.

Fifteen minutes later, at a quarter to three in the morning, a bomb went off in the Sainsbury Wing of the National Gallery.

Perhaps he's just not supposed to see these things actually happen. If he did, it might prove just too horrific to contemplate, and the dreams might stop, as his subconscious blocked them out.

One thing that had always puzzled Chris was how Yvonne Fletcher had found him, and why she had chosen him to give her messages to the world. At first he hadn't really wanted to question her, but one day he asked her outright. She told him to look back at his diary for June, then she would reveal all.

Looking back over the June 1991 diary, he found an entry for Saturday, 29 June, when he had been visited

by the spirit of his old friend Trevor Kempson, who had
this to say:

> Look in the *News of the World*?
> 2 pages – Chrissy – why are they the same?

He had gone out and bought the paper the next day.
There weren't two pages the same, but there was a two-
page story that had caught his eye because it concerned
Prince Kahled, nephew of the Saudi King Fahd, and
his affair with the actress Brigitte Nielson. Particularly
interesting to Chris was the paragraph that ran:

> Kahled was also in the headlines when two of his
> British bodyguards were fined for illegal possession
> of machine guns, revolvers and ammunition.

The story had a particular resonance for Chris because
one of those bodyguards was a man called Gary – he
doesn't want his full name used – who was very close to
Chris at the time. The weapons with which they were
found belonged to the armoury of the Saudi royal family
and were in Britain without an appropriate licence.

But this still didn't explain why Yvonne had chosen
him. So the next time she appeared in a dream, he asked
her again. Her answer was quite astounding.

Yvonne Fletcher was shot in April 1984. It was around
this time that the bodyguards of Prince Kahled were
being investigated by the police following the discovery
of the illegal weapons.

After she had been shot Yvonne Fletcher was shocked
and frightened to find herself a spirit. However, being as
practical in death as she had been in life, she decided to
find out what was going on, and so followed members of
the Anti-Terrorist Squad back to Scotland Yard. There
she had the novel – if not unique – experience of seeing
her murder investigated.

As it became apparent that the investigation had reached a dead-end – the Libyans had claimed diplomatic immunity *en masse* and were simply waiting to be deported without further action being taken, in the meantime living in their embassy in a state of siege – Yvonne became bored and decided that she would have to search around for something else to do.

In her new-found spirit state, she was able to wander freely around Scotland Yard, looking in on anything that took her fancy. And it was here that she came across the name Christopher Robinson.

One of the offices into which she wandered was devoted to the investigation into the firearms offences committed by the bodyguards of Prince Kahled. Because of the amount of weapons involved, and also because of the delicate situation that always existed between the Israelis and the Arab nations, the men involved were being closely monitored.

One of these men was, of course, Chris's friend Gary. And there, on the blackboard in the operations room, was chalked the name of Christopher Robinson.

Yvonne knew that Chris was the one she must find. She never explained to him why she knew this, but he speculates that it was because she somehow knew that he had psychic abilities: although the dreams didn't start until 1989, Chris freely admits that he had several experiences previously that could be classed as premonitions, or examples of mediumistic ability. Until they began in earnest, however, he was always too busy actually getting on with his life to take full notice of them, and what their consequences might be.

Yvonne followed the surveillance team that was keeping an eye on Chris, and settled down to wait until his abilities were developed enough to receive her messages.

When he woke from this dream Chris was dumb-struck. It seemed such a ridiculous, convoluted story.

Yet it might be true: the only thing that didn't ring true to Chris was Yvonne seeing his name on a blackboard at Scotland Yard.

He had to check out if this was possible. If he asked Hall or Clemence, there would be no way that they could give him a straight answer, even assuming they could find the answer out themselves.

There was only one person to ring. He immediately picked up the phone and dialled, biting his lip impatiently while he waited for an answer. Finally a sleepy voice came on the other end.

'Gary, I've got to see you today,' Chris said.

'Christ, do you know how early it is?'

'Never mind that, can I come over later?'

'Yeah, sure . . . now let me get back to sleep.'

Later that morning Chris drove over to Gary's house. The two men hadn't seen each other for a few weeks, and there was some small talk as they caught up on each other's lives. Finally there was a lull in the conversation, and Chris decided it was time to broach the subject.

It was something he was nervous of doing. Not because of the nature of his dreams: everyone who was close to Chris was familiar with his dream precognitions, and most were comfortable with them. They knew him, and they knew how honest and also confused he had been about them. Rather, he was nervous of raising the subject of Prince Kahled. Gary had done many things in his time skirting the edge of the law, and being a bodyguard was one of those. Walking around 'tooled up' with guns from the Saudi armoury was one of the more illegal moments in his career. It was also the closest he had come to being jailed. The Prince had gladly paid his fines, but as Gary was a British citizen diplomatic immunity could not have been claimed, if the sentence had been imprisonment. It was something Gary was still sensitive about.

Chris explained to Gary about the dream in which

Yvonne had told him how she had tracked him down. Gary listened in silence. Finally, Chris said, 'So, do you really think that my name was on that blackboard?'

Gary exploded into laughter. 'On it? I reckon they must have written it three or four times at least.'

'But why would they do that? I wasn't a bloody body-guard – Christ, I can't think of anything less likely.'

'No, but you think about it . . . back then, you and me were like brothers, always in and out of each other's houses. So if they've got me under surveillance, then they're sure as hell going to be keeping an eye on you. What? They see me going in and out of your place and they're going to be thinking: who is this geezer Robinson, and what's he got to do with it? Of course you were on that bloody blackboard – I'd be more surprised if you weren't.'

Chris thought about it, and had to admit that Gary was right: the long arm of synchronicity had reached out and grabbed him yet again. If Yvonne was real, then it would make sense for her to follow him up from a name on a board at Scotland Yard.

If, on the other hand, she was not real, then how had Chris managed to concoct this story to explain whatever he saw as Yvonne? The revelation that his name had been on a blackboard at Scotland Yard came as such a shock that he didn't think his subconscious could have pulled it out and presented it to him as a rationale.

In the final analysis it brings Chris back to the conclusion that the spirits – or whatever outside force presents itself in this way – have been grooming him for this role throughout his life. The out-of-body experiences, the occasional flashes of psychic insight, and now the years of precognitive dreams: they had to be planned for him in some way. Otherwise, how could a television-repair-man-turned-video-dealer end up being validated by the then-current Commander of the Anti-Terrorist Squad, George Churchill-Coleman, when he was in a police cell after his arrest at RAF Stanmore? If not for the web of coincidence that surrounds him, would Chris have met Paul Aylott, and would that policeman have known Chris well enough to believe him when Aylott was first approached about the dreams?

All that can finally be said is that even Chris doesn't know exactly how or why these things happen. But the results speak for themselves, and as long as they continue Chris will keep trying to find the answers.

Answers to something that is far more than just coincidence.

CHAPTER TWENTY

Although this book ends as 1991 draws to a close, that isn't to say that the dreams have ceased to happen, or that they have ceased to mirror real events to a degree that goes beyond mere coincidence. All it really says is this: the first two years of dreams contained amazing stories – so many that they fill this book. There are more, but there is simply not enough room in this volume to do them justice. Chris still faxes his dreams to Alex Hall, who remains his liaison officer.

As the years have passed Chris has become a minor media personality, as newspapers and magazines have heard about his incredible predictions. He has appeared on radio and television shows discussing his dreams; he takes part in tests, and is always scrupulous to dismiss anything that isn't accurate enough. In many ways this makes him unique, as numerous psychics who have appeared on television and failed then compound their error by trying to make tenuous links between the truth and their predictions, or by trying to explain away their sudden failure.

Chris Robinson doesn't do this: he asks researchers whom he knows are sceptical to study him and help him understand what is going on. He makes no great claims, other than that he gets results and doesn't really know how . . . Compared to a whole field of mediums-for-money, this approach tends to floor most sceptics, who can't for the life of them work out why he should be faking. But he must be, they say, because isn't everyone?

There are, however, a growing number of hard-nosed journalists, television and radio producers who can attest to the fact that when Chris gets a result, it's spot-on.

It was this ability that led to Chris's appearance on British television three times in one day while this book was in progress. And in that synchronistic way in which things happen to Chris, an appearance on one show led to his involvement in the search for a body.

28 October 1994 was an amazing day for Chris Robinson: he would be on three separate television programmes throughout the day. It was only the wildest of chances that could schedule two pre-recorded programmes on the same day as a live show in which he was to take part – all three on different channels, and none of them clashing in any way.

Perhaps the least important was *Esther*, a chat show helmed by Esther Rantzen, which was shown on BBC2 at five o'clock in the afternoon. The viewing figure would be relatively small, and the show itself was something of a disaster.

Esther introduced a psychic who charged by the hour and made the appalling claim that she would tell people when they were going to die – if that was what she saw. To do such a thing is dangerous in the extreme, whether or not the psychic is genuine: the phenomenon of the 'self-fulfilling prophecy' is well-known. This occurs when someone believes they are going to die, and as a result they have accidents caused by their carelessness, as their minds are on other matters; or they will themselves to death by believing that the slightest illness will develop into something serious; or – in extreme cases – they commit suicide.

This psychic – who may or may not have been genuine, but could produce no real evidence either way – was followed by a supposed psychic who performed a first-class piece of trickery before revealing himself as an illusionist. The point of this was supposedly to demonstrate how easy it is to fake a psychic result. However, the illusionist ruined his case by claiming that he could not reveal how the trick was executed: surely this was a golden opportunity to inform people how frauds can deceive, so that they can be detected?

Also on the platform was Dr Susan Blackmore, a psychologist who has made a career out of being a sceptic. Unfortunately, like James Randi and his ilk, she ruins a good standpoint by being vehemently opposed to any kind of psychic phenomena.

Chris was in the audience: although he had been invited to speak, he was given only a few seconds, and when he began to talk about his experiments at Hatfield College, in which he had been studied under test conditions and had achieved interesting results, Dr Blackmore cut him short with a curt 'I've heard differently', before going on to something else. In refusing to explain herself, and refusing to let Chris explain himself, she cut short an intriguing argument.

Also in the audience was Professor Arthur Ellison, who has spent many years studying phenomena for the Society for Psychical Research, a parascientific body established in the 1880s for the investigation of mediumistic and other phenomena. When called upon to speak, he said briefly that statistical evidence proves that there are some kind of phenomena within the broad area of extra-sensory perception, but he was suitably sceptical about psychics who make claims and have no evidence to back them up. He was also cut short, to allow someone in the audience to rant about how this was all rubbish because we live in a set universe . . . itself nonsense, as quantum physics has proved otherwise.

The aim of the show was obviously to disprove psychic phenomena, but unfortunately no-one came out of it well. The only positive thing to emerge was that Chris publicly challenged Dr Blackmore to test him, and she accepted. This was confirmed in print in the issue of *Psychic News* dated 12 November 1994. These tests were to prove inconclusive for varying reasons, as will be explained.

In order of importance, the next programme to feature Chris was the first episode of *Strange But True*, a networked ITV show made by London Weekend Television. The format of the show is simple: each week Michael Aspel wanders around the Harry Price Library (Price was a noted psychic researcher in the early years of this century) and introduces two ten-minute films. Each film features a psychic, or a group of people who have had encounters with anomalous phenomena. The show covers everything from poltergeists to alleged UFO abductions.

The first film, in that first episode, was about Chris. Interspersed with interview film of Chris, describing what happens in his dreams and recounting some of the things that have occurred to him as a result, were reconstructions of some of the incidents that have followed his dream precognitions. The actor who played Chris was excellent and captured his mode of speech well. The most notable reconstruction was that of Chris's visit to RAF Stanmore.

The film was made earlier in the year and its timing alongside the *Esther* show, recorded a week or two earlier, was coincidental. The same cannot be said of the most important appearance that Chris made on television that Friday.

This Morning with Judy and Richard is ITV's daytime flagship show and is broadcast live from a studio in Liverpool. Using a magazine format, and hosted by the husband-and-wife team of Richard Madeley and Judy Finnigan, it is one of the most watched daytime shows in Britain. Chris was appearing on the programme to promote the start of the *Strange But True* series later that day. In the process, however, he managed to do

something on live television that not only stunned
the studio audience – particularly Richard Madeley –
but also validated everything that was later broadcast
on film. I am only sorry that the *Esther* show was
recorded, as it would have been interesting to see what
Dr Blackmore made of the events that occurred on the
Friday morning.

It began a few days earlier, when Chris was invited to
appear on the programme, and was asked by a researcher
to perform a test for use on the show. I had seen a similar
test done once before, when Chris was due to appear
on the cable channel Wire TV. On that occasion Chris
had not been happy with the result when the sealed box
was opened, and so had not wanted the test used on
television.

This time there was no such chance for him to assess
the evidence beforehand: the sealed box – the contents
of which were his to dream – would be opened on air.

Chris would be travelling up to Liverpool on Thursday, and arrangements had been made for him to stay
the night at a hotel in the city. That one night was all
he had in which to dream about the contents of the box.
As must be obvious from the preceding chapters, Chris
usually prefers to dream for at least three nights before
drawing firm conclusions: the frequency is an important
establishing factor in divining the precognitive elements
of his dreams. However, he felt that the show would
be important for him and so agreed to the test, trusting
to the spirits and to his own powers of judgement in
translating the dreams.

That night the dreams were vivid and clear. He was
walking down a road until he came to a phone box.
In the phone box was his friend Raymond, making a
call. Raymond's nickname is Dolly, so Chris wondered
if this was significant. This was confirmed by the sudden
appearance of Chris's friend Trevor Kempson, who
stood behind Raymond, waving a small doll at Chris.

'This is what it's all about, Chrissy,' he said.

The dream changed, and Chris was watching Trevor empty a post-office sack onto the floor. A lot of boxes came tumbling out of the sack, wrapped up as Christmas presents.

When he woke Chris was left with some pretty clear ideas about what lay inside the sealed box.

After a leisurely breakfast he was taken to the studio. The show begins at half-past ten, and Chris wasn't scheduled to appear until after eleven, so there was no rush for him to be made up. The production team did, however, force him to wear a tie, a hideously patterned affair, and it was this rather than anything connected to the dreams that made him feel nervous. After all, who wants to look like an idiot when he appears on national television?

He was shown into the studio and came face to face with a burly security guard, who had stood over the sealed box all night. It was faintly absurd: Chris is all for precautions and controls in experiments, but did they think he was going to try and break into the studio just to get a look inside the box?

While they were waiting to go on, Chris tried to make conversation with the guard, but the man was uncomfortable. Perhaps he was afraid of unwittingly giving something away and being accused of wrecking the show. Chris was announced as a guest who was 'coming up after the break', and a camera focused on both Chris and the security guard – before zooming in for a close-up of Chris, who looked understandably startled at this sudden movement, as his face filled the screen.

There was a brief moment of relaxation as the advertisement break gave everyone a few moments' respite from the tension of live television. Then there were the cues, and the show was back on air.

Richard and Judy went through the link, and there

was an excerpt of the *Strange But True* film as Chris was led onto the set, accompanied by the security guard and the sealed box.

Film clip over, Richard explained what the box was doing sitting on a table, and Judy asked Chris a few questions about himself. She also asked the guard if the box had been in sight all night. Quietly and nervously he affirmed this. Finally came the moment of truth, and Chris was asked what he believed to be inside the box.

Chris began to explain – wisely leaving out the references to Trevor, as mention of spirits can easily sidetrack a conversation of this kind.

'In my dream I saw a man in a phone box. This man was my friend Raymond, but we always call him "Dolly". So from that, I'd say that there was a dolly in the box. But where I've written down the word dolly as I sleep, I've put a box around it, and that usually means it's "not quite" what I've written.' Chris had the dream diary sheet with him, as proof of what he was saying. He continued, 'Later on in my dream, I was with a man who was emptying a post-office sack, and this sack was full of boxes. They were wrapped up like Christmas presents. Boxes again, and like presents . . . I'd say that there was a children's toy in the box, possibly a dolly.'

'Well, we don't know what's in there, so let's open it up and see,' Richard said.

When the box was opened, Richard pulled out a teddy bear – small, old and battered.

'I bet that's either called Trevor or Edward,' Chris added promptly. He didn't explain why on air, but was thinking of Trevor Kempson holding up the dolly in the phone box – Kempson's full name being Trevor Edward Kempson.

'Hang on . . .' Richard paused as he received a message through his earpiece from the producer. 'Yes, right . . .' He turned to the camera, and was obviously amazed at what he had just heard. 'The teddy bear belongs to our

producer, Helen Williams, and it is called Edward.' He
turned to Chris. 'That was remarkable.'

'Well, I did say a dolly, or like it. I didn't actually
say a bear.'

'But Helen's just told me that her parents used to run
a post office when she was a child, which could be where
the post-office sack comes in. What's more, she was born
on Christmas Day, which would account for the presents
in the sack. And you knew what the name could be.'

He was still a little stunned as he introduced the next
item. And no wonder: Chris had forecast that a child's
toy, like a doll, would be inside the box. A teddy bear
is a figurine, like a doll. There are many other types of
toy that could have been used, from a model car to a
football. He also knew that the bear would be called
either Trevor or Edward, because of the link with his
friend Trevor Kempson.

Perhaps most interesting of all is the fact that he
perceived a link between Christmas, a post office and
the contents of the box – without even being aware of
the connection until someone else told him.

Statistically, the amount of information contained
within the dream and translated from symbols by Chris
is phenomenal. The odds of him simply guessing this
much about the contents of the box are stratospheric.

This was proof, if it were needed, that something
strange and unusual is happening to Chris Robinson.
What is important now is that his powers are investigated
and that attempts are made to help Chris understand
what lies behind his dreams.

After the show Richard and Judy were eager to talk
to Chris and find out more about him. It's not often
that presenters on a show are touched in this way: so
much passes by them on a five-days-a-week basis that
it's difficult for anyone to keep track of who is on the
show on any given day. Chris, however, made such an
impression that they made a particular effort to speak to

him, inviting him to come and stay with them, as they had friends they wanted him to meet.

Psychic News reviewed the show, and quoted Richard Madeley as saying, 'We didn't believe Chris could do this, which is why we arranged the test. And yet it just about worked.'

In the same review Chris also told the journalist that he had been contacted by a woman living on Merseyside who had seen the show, and wanted Chris to help her in the search for her missing daughter.

What he didn't mention was that the daughter was already known to be dead. A man had been convicted of her murder and was serving a prison sentence. What the woman dearly wished for was to find her daughter's body – the location of which the killer refused to divulge – and lay her to rest.

What Chris didn't realise was that the spirit of the daughter had already visited him, and had also asked him for his help.

Marie McCourt is a middle-aged housewife from Liverpool. Her daughter Helen disappeared one night and was never seen again. An investigation ensued and a man was arrested for the murder of Helen McCourt. He stood trial, was convicted and sentenced. Throughout the investigation he refused to tell police where he had buried the body. Even when he was in prison, and had nothing to lose by revealing the location of the corpse, he still kept silent.

For Marie, this was torture: it was strain enough to know that her daughter had been brutally murdered, without the added burden of not knowing where her daughter lay. All she wanted was to give her daughter a decent burial, but even this had been denied her.

It was now six years since the murderer had been convicted.

While her daughter was missing Marie had appeared

on *This Morning* and knew exactly who to ring when she saw Chris Robinson on air. She knew that if anyone could help her achieve the impossible, and find Helen's body, then it was Chris.

What Marie could not know was that two days before Chris had travelled to Liverpool to appear on *This Morning*, he had a dream in which he was visited by a young girl. She was lost, and had been murdered. Her spirit was not in torment, but she wanted her mother to know that she was well, and to help her mother find where she was buried.

For Chris, this was somewhat alarming, as only rarely does he dream of a straightforward murder, such as that of Patrick Frater. Usually his dreams are to do with events that may or may not end in death, such as bomb warnings. To see a murder victim close up, and to talk to them in his dream, is an experience of such emotional intensity that it tends to leave him drained. What made this situation even more alarming was that he had had a dream two nights before his appearance on *Esther*, in which he had seen a friend who was a used-car dealer shot and killed by a hitman. He told Professor Ellison about this when they were chatting after the recording, and later phoned a stunned Ellison to report that his friend was actually shot in a nearby village the day after the recording – thus exactly mirroring Chris's three-day window for events.

The girl hadn't told Chris her name – the dream was rather unclear, and the connection between them was prone to interference from other dream factors – but she did reveal some personal details about herself.

So when Marie McCourt wrote to Chris, following up her phone call to the *This Morning* production office, he was able to ring her immediately and talk to her about the girl he had seen. By the time he had finished describing her, and relating some of the details she had told him, Marie was in tears. She had no doubt that the girl was her daughter, as there were things Chris told her that only Helen could know about.

'You've got to help me find her,' she told him. 'I won't be able to rest happily until she's properly buried.'

Chris could see that Marie's desire to see her daughter given a decent burial was not just due to religious conviction, but was part of her grieving process: in order to grieve properly, she had to see that her daughter was dead and her body carefully laid to rest.

It broke Chris's heart to hear Marie on the end of the phone, so he agreed to help. He told her that he would write down some questions and invite Helen to talk to him again. He also warned Marie that he might not be able to get much more detail from the spirit: sometimes they could only say so much in the dreams.

It's difficult to describe exactly why the messages can be so erratic, and why seemingly inconsequential details may emerge when the sought-after, more important details may be kept back. Even Chris finds the manner in which communication happens hard to put into words: perhaps the nearest analogy is to say that the dream communication with spirits is a little like using a mobile phone – sometimes the transmission can break up because of an imperfect connection, and parts of the conversation may be lost.

Marie was overjoyed that Chris was to try and help her, and even had a suggestion of her own.

'Why don't you come and stay up here?' she asked. 'You could sleep in Helen's bed – her room hasn't been touched since she died, and it may be that the vibrations are stronger there.'

Chris thought about it. His dreams were constant wherever he was at any given moment, but he did wonder if an aspect of psychometry might enter into it if he stayed in Helen's room. Psychometry is the gift of holding an object and being able to divine from it impressions and scenes from the life of the owner. If he slept in Helen's bed, surrounded by her belongings, was it possible that some kind of psychometric powers would infuse his dreams, and perhaps make it easier for her to communicate with him? Certainly, Chris has an aptitude for psychometry.

He agreed to travel up to Liverpool within the next few weeks and stay with Marie. In the meantime he would continue to ask questions of Helen, and hope that she was able to communicate with him.

Chris knew that this had something to do with Helen McCourt, but she was nowhere in sight. Instead, he was sitting in a prison cell. There was one man with him, but he didn't seem to know that Chris was there: he sat looking at the wall in silence, every muscle in his body poised.

It must have been ten o'clock at night, because the lights suddenly cut off – Chris knew that ten was the time for 'lights-out' in prison.

As soon as the darkness descended, the man rose to his feet, a shape uncoiling in the darkness. He stood facing the door of his cell, and with a voice that rang in the sparse confines of the four brick walls, he began to quote verses from the Bible in a declamatory tone.

The voice was deafening in the darkness, and Chris couldn't follow the sense of what the man was saying, as his voice took on a sing-song tone, becoming almost a meaningless chant. He was intoning Old Testament verses, about begetting and begatting, going on and on, into the night.

Helen appeared one night and took Chris to a piece of waste ground, where there was a steep incline. Together, they climbed the incline, and when they reached the top Chris could see five ponds, stagnant and still, like small gravel pits.

'I'm in there,' she said, indicating them.

But which one?

When Chris woke, he looked at the dream diary. He could see that there were recurring letters, which must be giving him a postcode, but arranged either way, it was not one he was familiar with. Using his postcode map on the computer, he found that it covered the area around a small Lancashire village called Billinge, near St Helens.

It was some way from Liverpool, but not so far that it was impossible to suppose that the killer had taken her there.

He had something to tell Marie.

A few days later, when the telephone rang, Chris found himself talking to a police officer named McKay.

'I understand that Marie McCourt has asked you to help her find her daughter,' the policeman said.

'Yes. I said I'd help, and I may have something.'

'That's good. You do know you'll have help if you need it?'

'What do you mean?'

'I mean that we're willing to help you look for the body. I can't go too far, as our part in things is really over and done with – the killer's in prison, and that's the end of it. But it must be awful for the mother. If we can help her get her daughter's body back, then it'll be a lot better for everybody.'

Chris was pleased to hear this. He's found, time and again, that it's hard for him to get a result if the police are unhelpful or uninterested. By far the best results have been on those occasions when the police have trusted him and given him co-operation. He thought it politic, however, not to say this in so many words.

'I'm really pleased you feel like that, because I've got a few ideas. For instance, I work on postcodes a lot, and I've got one that fits a place near St Helens called Billinge. Does that mean anything?'

McKay thought about it. 'It may,' he said finally. 'Anything else?'

'Well, yes – I've got an idea that she may be buried in or near these ponds – a bit like gravel pits. There are five of them. Are they anywhere near this place Billinge?'

McKay whistled softly. 'There's a place called Moss Bank, which is just a couple of miles from Billinge. They've got five ponds there. And we know that this guy used to hang around near the village.'

Chris was encouraged by this and felt confident enough to broach a subject that had been worrying him.

'Look, I know this is going to sound really strange, but I've had this peculiar dream that I feel has something to do with Helen – but I just don't know how or why. Can I tell you about it?'

'Sure, why not?' McKay said after a pause.

Chris took a deep breath and began: 'In the dream I was in a prison cell, and there was this guy in there. When the lights went out, he stood up and started ranting and raving. It was some sort of biblical nonsense . . . It might not even be actually from the Bible, but it sounded like all that Old Testament stuff about Isaac begetting Jacob – or was it the other way round? Anyway, you know the sort of thing. Does that ring any bells?'

There was silence on the end of the line.

'Hello?' Chris said after a few moments. 'Are you still there?'

McKay's breathing told him that the police officer was still on the end of the line. Finally, he said, 'How on earth did you know that? How the hell could you possibly know that?' He laughed shortly, and said after a brief pause, 'The man we've got banged up for the murder – you know what he does? Every night, at lights out, he gets up in his cell and starts shouting verses from the Bible. It drives all the other prisoners mad, and most of the staff. He shouts so loud that they can't ignore him, and he does it every single night, without fail. He has done so ever since he was convicted.'

Chris was silent. Now it all made sense: Helen had been showing him the face of her killer. Except that he had been caught, and didn't help Chris at all in his attempt to find her corpse.

After half a decade of the dreams, Chris had become used to the unusual seeming commonplace, but this stunned even him. To be able to tell the officer who had been on the team investigating the murder exactly what the convicted killer did every night, without ever having seen or heard him . . . At least he was sure of the police's co-operation.

'Look,' said McKay finally, 'you just get yourself up here, and we'll try and help you find that body.'

Less than two weeks later Chris was in Liverpool, staying with Marie McCourt. He slept in Helen's bed, and spoke to her in his dream. Still she showed him the five ponds, but there was no additional information.

In some ways the idea of staying in Helen's bed was counter-productive. Chris felt there was a pressure on him to succeed that perhaps inhibited his faculty to dream. It was not a conscious awareness, but studies into those people who score highly in ESP tests have shown that they perform less well when they have been told that they are able to do it. It seems as though the subconscious rebels at the idea of being forced into a position where it is precognitive.

Uri Geller has a view on this: in his work with the police he has felt that the more his success has been willed by those around him, the more of an inhibiting effect it has had upon him. This also explains why, when he was performing on the show business circuit in the 1970s, Geller sometimes resorted to faking in order to produce results for the cameras. Interestingly, he was always caught out when he did fake. Since retiring from public life, Geller has made a fortune dowsing minerals on a freelance basis. He is paid no fee, only commission on what he finds. He is now a millionaire: the conclusion is obvious.

Chris had previously experienced no problem when asked by the police to perform certain tasks: the way in which he obtained the names of the terrorists killed in the St Albans bomb attack is ample proof of this. However, there's a world of difference between going home and trying to get a result and trying to obtain the same result when someone in the next room is willing you to succeed.

Should he have stayed at home?

While he was in Liverpool Chris met McKay, and the two men travelled out from the city to Billinge. It gave Chris an opportunity to see a place that had otherwise been no more than a postcode to him. Afterwards they went to look at Moss Bank.

When they reached the desolate and derelict area, Chris felt a shiver pass through him: a strong feeling of déjà-vu. He had never been here before in his life – yet he had in his dreams. This was the area Helen McCourt had taken him to; this was where she claimed to be buried.

Chris got out of the car, and looked up the grassy incline.

'Do you recognise it?' McKay asked, seeing a look cross Chris's face.

Chris nodded. 'Yeah. She brought me here and showed me the ponds. They're up there, right?' He pointed up the slope.

McKay acknowledged this. 'That's right. Want to take a look?'

Chris took a deep breath. 'Might as well, while we're here.'

They set off up the slope. It was a much steeper gradient than Chris remembered from his dream, and he was puffing by the time they reached the top. What he saw made the breath catch in his throat.

The five ponds were laid out as in his dream. And he was standing at exactly the same point he had stood with Helen: the perspective was identical.

'This has got to be them, right?' McKay queried. 'There aren't any other ponds around here.'

Chris sighed. 'This is them, all right. Five ponds. And Helen's in one of them.'

'Which one?'

'That's the sixty-four-thousand-dollar question, isn't it? I know it's here, but I don't know which one. She either won't – or can't – tell me.'

'Can't?'

'She was dead, just. Her spirit must have been confused, right? Everything is going to be confused. I mean, she must have been terrified.'

'I guess so . . . well, I guess we'll just have to drag all of them,' said McKay.

'How long will that take?'

'By the time I get the manpower together – and let's be honest, the killer's locked up, so I can't make it a priority – I'd say it'd be too late to do it this year because of the winter. We'll have to wait till spring.'

Chris looked at the ponds. He was sure Helen was buried in one of them, and he just wished that he could be of more help. Now Marie McCourt would have to wait for the seasons to allow her daughter to be found.

Chris Robinson returned home. Home to more dreams. More and more people are accepting that there is something paranormal about his dreams, and that he does have powers of precognition.

Chris firmly believes that we can all do this if we

train ourselves to remember our dreams, and learn how to interpret them correctly.

He will keep on studying his dreams until such time as they cease, and until he has the help to research properly the reasons why this strange power has touched his life.

However long that takes.

CHAPTER TWENTY-ONE

The Hatfield Tests that Susan Blackmore had been so dismissive of had come about as a result of an approach made by Sadie Holland, a researcher for *Arthur C. Clarke's Mysterious Universe*, a series of half-hour documentaries linked by the scientist and science fiction writer from his Sri Lankan home. Considering his scientific background, Clarke is refreshingly open-minded towards anomalous phenomena, and although he does little more than link the shows, this attitude permeates throughout the production team. Thus, when Chris was asked to participate in an experiment to be conducted by Dr Richard Wiseman at the University of Hertfordshire in Hatfield, he had no hesitation in accepting.

Sadie told him that the tests were designed so that a series of psychics would be called into a room and shown three predetermined objects. These were the responsibility of Dr Wiseman, and only he would know what they were until the day.

'Well, you do realise that I don't actually work like that, don't you?', Chris said over the phone. 'I may be able to dream about them in advance, but I won't just be able to look at them and give you an instant history. It doesn't work that way.'

Time and again, he found himself having to explain how it worked, getting the feeling that people thought he was making excuses.

Sadie seemed a little doubtful about the manner in which he wished to work, and was insistent about the tests being carried out according to Dr Wiseman's method. She was, however, keen for him to participate, and there were no real problems anticipated.

'Is there anything you particularly need?' she asked finally.

'The only thing I ask is that you put the objects in boxes, and label the boxes A, B and C. Then I can ask the spirits questions about box A on Friday night, box B on Saturday night, and box C on Sunday. I can then fax you the dream notes the next morning, and you can compare them later to the history of each object, and see if there is any correlation.'

Sadie Holland agreed to this, and Chris put down the phone trusting that the experiment would accommodate his methods of working. He did exactly what he had said and repeated the method the following week. This way he had two sets of dream notes and a chance to find any recurring patterns.

On the first night, the dreams were confused. Chris slept more fitfully than usual, and the only really memorable thing when he awoke was that a woman had been attacked and murdered. He knew that she was acquainted with her killer, and that she had been killed with a gun, but beyond that was nothing concrete.

The second night was better. Chris was visited by PC Keith Blakelock, who was killed in the Broadwater Farm riots of 1985. On that evening, Chris had been in North London, only a few miles away from the Tottenham location of the riots, and so had been near enough for the spirit of Keith Blakelock to search him out. As with Yvonne Fletcher, it had taken some time for the spirit to establish contact, but now Blakelock (or something that purported to be Blakelock, and represented itself in this way) was a regular visitor to Chris's dreams, and sometimes worked on dream solutions in tandem with Yvonne.

This night, Blakelock was on his own. He told Chris of two murdered policemen. One death was his own and the other related to the second object – box B. Like Blakelock, this constable had died of wounds to the head. However, these wounds had been caused by a gunshot.

So, things were beginning to get clearer. On the third night, the dreams were equally vivid. Chris and Blakelock sat on a grassy bank, watching a steam train pass in a leisurely way. That part of Chris which is always in touch with his conscious mind was aware that Blakelock's presence was an indication of a clue about the third box.

As if this realisation was the trigger, Chris found himself in a change of scene. He was observing a woman preparing a bottle for a small baby. Yvonne Fletcher appeared by his side, and said words which he wrote down in his diary:

KEEP YOUR FINGERS AWAY –
BOILING OVER – TURN HEAT OFF

With this, the scene melted, and Chris found himself standing in a flat which he knew was in London. The room caught fire, and it began to spread around him.

As he was beginning to panic, the scene changed yet again: he was sitting at a desk, writing a book about murderers. This changed before he had a chance to really take much in, and he was now in a plane which had a fire in the right engine.

The shock of this made him wake up: he looked down at the diary and saw what he had written. As he looked, the name of the powdered milk came back to him. It was called Progress – would this be significant?

Eight days later, Sadie Holland rang again: the test was to take place next day in Hatfield, at the CP Snow Building.

This was the location of Dr Wiseman's lab, and Chris was to report at 9 a.m. The TV crew hoped to start filming at 11.30. Chris told her that he felt confident about two of the boxes.

On 13 September, a group of four psychics, a TV crew, and Dr Richard Wiseman assembled in his lab. Wiseman told the psychics about the design of his experiment: they would be taken individually into the room used as a studio for the day and shown the objects. They would then have to tell the camera and Dr Wiseman what they thought each object pertained to, and answer a questionnaire. On this document were eighteen statements. The psychics had to tick six which related to each object. All of them were a little surprised by the questionnaire – after all, what if the statements couldn't exactly fit in with what they were saying? For simple semantics, would their observations be discounted?

However, all four had agreed to the test, and to back out now would look like admitting they were frauds, so all four agreed.

An associate of Wiseman's came in with a large box. The objects were contained within. The man, accompanied by Dr Wiseman and Ms Holland passed into the studio room and there was an uneasy pause. Then they returned and informed Chris he was the first to go in.

When he entered the room, he received a shock: the objects were laid out on a table. They were neither boxed nor labelled, as he had requested. Chris felt a familiar sinking feeling: the experiment had been designed to suit Wiseman, and not any individual variation in the way the psychics received their messages.

'Can these at least be labelled, as that's how I've worked,' requested Chris.

Wiseman seemed put out: 'Very well,' he sighed, and asked a student to label the items A,B and C. This the student did in a manner that seemed somewhat desultory.

Chris sat down in front of the table, facing the camera. He looked at the yellow labels, only just stuck on, with a heavy heart. Finally, he picked up object A, a lady's shoe. In an almost perfunctory manner, he told the camera what he had dreamt and that he expected the shoe to have belonged to a woman who had been shot. He had been expecting to see the gun which had killed her.

Object B was the projectile part of a bullet, without the shell casing. He told the camera about his encounter with Blakelock, and how he expected that this was connected to the murder of a police constable.

Object C was a red woollen scarf. As he picked it up, he experienced a rare flash of psychometry. As soon as it was in his hands he could see a woman being strangled: he put the scarf around his neck, and as he did he could see milk bottles. It was his opinion that the scarf had been used as a murder weapon, and that the murder was in some way connected to milk.

After this came the questionnaire. It was a sheet of eighteen statements, many of which bore little relation to what Chris had dreamt. Ergo, he had to leave many of the statements unticked. However, there was no space for him to record his own observations. As a foolproof device for testing psychics – or the veracity of anything – this leaves a lot to be desired.

Interestingly, Wiseman's questionnaire showed the psychics to have a worse success rate than chance would have given them. His control group of students, however, did much better than chance. I leave the reader to draw their own conclusions about the efficiency of such an experiment.

It is, however, worth recording what the psychics were then told about the objects, which all came from the Essex Police Museum, based at the County Constabulary Headquarters.

The shoe belonged to Miss Camille Cecile Holland, a 57-year-old woman shot dead by her common law husband, Samuel Dougal, at their remote farmhouse in Clavering. She was missing for four years before a digging party found her body at the farm. She was identified by her shoes, and Dougal was hanged on the evidence of a London cobbler who made the shoes. Miss Holland's dog Jacko had assisted in the digging party, and it was because of his sense of smell that the body was located. He was later stuffed, and is still on display at the museum.

The bullet was that used to kill Police Constable George William Gutteridge at Stapleford Abbotts in September 1927. He was shot in the head on the Romford to Ongar Road by Frederick Browne who was later arrested with a gun in his possession. William Kennedy confessed to being with Browne when he committed the murder and the gun was proved to be the same as that which killed PC Gutteridge by the use of ballistics evidence – the first time it had been used in a murder trial in this country.

The scarf had been used in a recent murder. The victim's name was not revealed, but she had been killed by her milkman in a row over her milk bill. He had reported finding the body on his rounds to try and cover his complicity. When he finally confessed, he claimed that it was an accidental killing, and that she had been strangled by the scarf when he had grabbed it to prevent her running away.

Chris Robinson may not have been able to answer the questionnaire correctly, but what did he say to camera?

Sue Blackmore, who had challenged Chris on the *Esther* programme, finally agreed to a series of tests over the Christmas of 1994. They proved inconclusive, even though they were designed to Chris's specifications.

Unlike Dr Wiseman, Dr Blackmore agreed to place

an object in a box on an agreed date. Chris would
then try and dream about this object, and keep the
usual records of his dreams. This would be carried out
over the six-week period that Chris was to spend in
the Philippines. Dr Blackmore would change the object
twice a week on predetermined days – a Friday and a
Monday.

Chris obtained two correct results out of seven.
Although this may not sound impressive, these were
the only two sets of notes that he actually brought
home with him. The other five were left behind in
the Philippines due to the confusion caused by a murder
case in which he became involved.

Hopefully, Chris will be able to recreate the experiments with Dr Blackmore at a later date – always
assuming that she hasn't already obtained the result she
was after . . .

Chris and his family arrived in the Philippines, at Cavinti,
Laguna, on 15 December. On that night he had an
appalling dream.

As he was about to fall asleep, a tremendous jolt
rocked him, as though someone had grabbed him by
the shoulders and spun him around. He was wrenched
back into full consciousness, and lay there sweating. A
jolt like that could mean only one thing: when he fell
asleep something terrible would happen either to him
or nearby.

Finally, he did fall asleep . . .

The river was shallow but flowed fast, carrying debris and
leaves on its rushing surface. A young man and a young
woman stood in the water. They were still, and the man
held a stanley knife. In almost slow motion, he started to
attack the woman, hacking at her body viciously. The
attack was so horrific that Chris woke with a start.

★   ★   ★

On the corner of P Burgos Street lived a police constable. This was near where Chris was staying, and he was acquainted with the young man. The next day he approached him and asked him if a young woman had ever been killed in the river. When the baffled constable asked why, Chris explained to him about his dream.

In the Philippines, such matters are treated with less scepticism than in England and everyone in town was aware of Chris's abilities. The constable asked if it were not possible that the murder had been a dream symbol, and that the woman in the river had not actually been murdered, but been washed away in a torrent of water from the mountains, which usually followed a rainstorm. He asked because his own wife had been killed in such a manner the previous July. When her body was found, she was covered in vicious cuts which had been caused by a fall over the Pagsanjan Falls.

It made sense, yet Chris felt that this was a real murder he had dreamt of, not just a symbolic representation of death.

On Sunday 18 December the dreams seemed to continue the story of three nights previously. This time Chris dreamt of a woman's body, face down in the river. A search was being conducted for a man and police questioned Chris about what he knew. More significantly, a girl in the river came to him. She told Chris that the man who had killed her would run away from home.

The woman came again on Christmas Eve. She told Chris the murderer lived in the same street as her, and that after the killing he would run away from home. He had known her since childhood: they had attended the same school and he was jealous of both her and her husband. She pleaded with Chris to look after her child now that she was gone.

When he awoke, Chris knew that the murder would

happen soon, and that because of what he had said the police would want to interview him. To be in a foreign country and at the mercy of their police, no matter how innocent you may be, is a daunting prospect, and Chris went out of his way to be surrounded by people until such a time as the murder would take place.

On Christmas day, Chris had a surprise visitor: the constable he had discussed his dream with some days before. He came with his immediate superior and they took Chris to a nearby bar where they sat for three hours drinking and discussing the dreams.

Mr Deleon, an ex-mayor of the village, joined them. He was still a man with influence, and he, too, wanted to hear about Chris's dreams. Once again, Chris went over them: the concensus among the men was that Chris had symbolically dreamt of the death of the constable's wife.

'Besides,' one of them added, 'even if there is a murder, what have you to fear? You won't be the culprit.' He laughed. 'Our police have never arrested the wrong person.'

Somehow this was not reassuring.

On Boxing Day Chris went to a resort called Paradise Mountain with a group of people. He didn't arrive back in Cavinti until 7.30 p.m., where he was greeted by a roadblock at the entrance of the village. He discovered that there had been a murder: Billy Jean DeLeon Vamenez, a local girl of twenty-two, had been found in the river at lunchtime. She had been killed by multiple stab wounds.

It took about thirty minutes for the police to realise that Chris had arrived back in the village. Because of what he had already said, they believed that he may have vital clues as to who was responsible. The local police sat with him and went over the pages of the dream diary with him.

However, when the city detectives from Manila

arrived at the village, they dismissed Chris's dreams. They had already decided that the killers (they believed it may be more than one) were out-of-town drug addicts. Chris maintained that it was a local boy who knew his victim and had been to school with her.

The funeral was held a week later. Chris walked the half mile to the cemetary with Rollando Mesina, the local police chief, and Mr Deleon, the former mayor, who was the murdered girl's uncle. Chris felt helpless and sad. Despite his offers of help, he had been unable to be of any practical use.

After the ceremony, Mr Deleon asked Chris to meet the girl's family. He wanted Chris to see the young child that Billy Jean had left.

As he sat with the family, Chris remembered that Billy Jean had asked him to look after the child. Almost as if he had known Chris was thinking this, Billy Jean's father asked him if he would like to adopt the boy, named Dadrick. Chris declined, but agreed to become *ninong*, which is the equivalent of becoming a Godparent. He would send money to the child, and his status as *ninong* meant that Billy Jean's family would be able to ask for help from Chris's family in the village without any stigma being attached.

The following day, a young man who had attended the funeral ran away from home. He had known Billy Jean all her life and had attended the same school. His mother reported his disappearance to the local police, who placed this against what Chris had told them.

Within a couple of days the young man had been traced to a neighbouring village. He was arrested on suspicion of murder and confessed under questioning.

However, there was one final twist: two days after this the young man escaped from custody, and has so far eluded his pursuers.

★   ★   ★

Back in England, it was a matter of business as usual as Chris tried to demonstrate his powers to those who would listen. However, it sometimes seemed as though he was up against an army of sceptics determined to bend the rules to suit their own ends.

Such was the case with the *James Whale Show*, for whom Chris had a slot in April 1995.

The production team had agreed to a box test for Chris, and had placed some objects in a box. When Chris asked the spirits to help him, this is what he got:

He was looking at a map of the Bristol Channel with someone he didn't recognise. They tore the map in half and gave the pieces to a woman who stuffed them in her bra. Because of rhyming slang, he wondered after if perhaps Bristol was the key (the map, and Bristol City = titty).

The remainder of the dream was concerned with Chris driving a car. There were more maps and the car keys were prominent, as were some batteries.

Chris turned up for the recording: the show was recorded about a fortnight in advance of transmission, which is in the early hours of a Saturday morning.

Whale's show is known for its acerbic and somewhat contrived air of satire and pseudo-anarchy. Chris should have known he was being set up.

Chris detailed his dreams, and showed pages from his dream diary. The box was then opened: there were four items. The first were two screwed up pieces of paper which Chris had mentioned. There was a piece of cardboard which had not been mentioned. Finally there was a toy car. Chris had been in a car in his dream.

However, because there were no maps, batteries or keys, Whale denounced Chris as a charlatan. Angered by this blatant manipulation, Chris left the studio.

When the programme was broadcast, most of the

analysis of the dream diary was left out, and only Whale's rancour was left intact.

If nothing else, it taught Chris to stick to live tests in future, and to make sure that there was only one item in any one box.

This contrasted heavily with his experience on *Dial Midnight*, two years previously. On the night before the show, on 1 October 1993, Chris had been visited by Yvonne Fletcher and Keith Blakelock in his dreams. They had warned him not to go near the studio, as a bomb would explode in Finchley Road which was on his route. The producer had naturally been upset when told that his guest was pulling out at the last minute, but had rapidly been on the phone when five bombs detonated along the Finchley Road on the evening of 2 October. That time he had been taken seriously.

The same is also true of Wire TV, the now defunct cable channel, who invited Chris back on 7 March 1995 – a much better show for him than the James Whale débâcle of a month later. Chris received a call from Sarah Dunn, a researcher at Wire TV, asking him if he would appear on a live lunchtime show in a fortnight's time. He would be asked about his dreams and they wanted to do another box test with him.

Chris had appeared several times on Wire and was only too pleased to agree. He put no stipulation on the box – size, contents, etc – other than it be one item only.

When he put the phone down, he realised that he might have already started to dream about this, as his dreams for the previous night had been strong, to say the least:

Tape – Disk
Must not let it stick to the spinning disk – so it stops turning.

Below this was a drawing of a record in its sleeve. The

dreams woke Chris at 3.55 a.m., and it proved impossible to get back to sleep.

Tuesday night's dreams followed a similar pattern, being about computer program disks and driving on an uneven road surface with no shoes as he punched at the brake and accelerator.

Although he wrote nothing at all on Wednesday, he framed the following question at the top of the dream diary page: What will be in Sarah's box, please?

Chris was sitting in a cafe when two men came in. They sat down near him and began to discuss him in a manner that showed they wanted him to hear. He recognised one of them as an actor and the man was condemning Chris as a fraud and a fool, saying that his dreams were nothing more than a delusion. Chris got up and hit the man around the head . . .

Then he was standing on a bridge, looking down a river or canal.

The rest of his dream was concerned with the steering wheel of his car and how easy it was to turn now that he had power steering. Yvonne Fletcher was with him, and she was showing him steering wheels, and also compact disks.

When Chris woke, he felt pleased with the night's dreams. In his book were written the words 'BOXED HIS EARS', followed by 'steering wheel' and 'compact disk'.

The first was obviously a signal that the dreams concerned the Wire box. And as the latter had been shown to him by Yvonne Fletcher, whose messages generally needed little interpretation, he felt sure that the box would contain something to do with spinning.

To this end, he wrote the same question on Friday night. When he woke, he had written:

★   ★   ★

Resolution – Window. Settings change them back and forth.

Return equipment – make sure you go to right house.

Telescope. Point it at the sun. Gets very hot. Can burn paper.

Don't look through it – just move it around.

More round objects that could spin, but still nothing definite. He repeated the process on Saturday, and came up with:

Train – models – Comes off the rails – gramophone motor.

The dreams had seen him standing by a railway, looking at the wheels of the trains. After this he had been in a TV studio, with cameras pointing at him. Someone pointed a starting gun at him, and then at an old gramophone, which only played 78s.

This he singled out as important, as a common link between many of the disc objects had been that they could be used for recording.

Would something like this be in the Wire box?

The journey from his home to Wire's Bristol studios and offices took less time than he expected, and even this seemed to fly by. Returning his radio on the way, Chris had tuned into Terry Christian's show on Talk Radio UK. A popular phone-in programme, the show had been – by chance – about psychic phenomena, and Chris had used his mobile phone to call in and discuss his dreams.

It was by now quite late in the evening, and when Chris and his son Aaron – who was with him on this trip – arrived at the hotel, there was little time to eat. So Chris ordered some sandwiches and they ate in the bar.

It was deserted when they arrived, but before long a man whose face was familiar walked in. Aaron recognised him as a former breakfast TV presenter and got quite excited. Chris, too, recognised the man, but was unable to put a name to the face. Urged on by his son, Chris introduced himself, and the two men soon fell into conversation.

The man was Mike Morris, now a presenter with Wire – and neither knew that they would face each other over the cameras the following day: just another touch of synchronicity.

The next morning, Chris took Aaron into the centre of Bristol before being picked up by taxi and taken to the old Georgian house used by Wire as a studio.

Both men were surprised to be facing each other in a more formal setting, but it helped to break the ice, and the interview went well until finally Morris announced that it was time to guess what was in the box.

Chris mildly admonished him: he wouldn't be guessing so much as interpreting the dreams to help him see what was in it.

He continued: 'I started dreaming about a particular object even before I knew about this show, and I started to draw a particular shape. I'm still drawing a similar object over and over again. Last night I drew something similar.

'It's some kind of circle, possibly with a hole in the centre. It could be either a telescope mirror – which is a round, reflective circle – or it could be a compact disc, or recording disc of some kind. I have drawn discs constantly throughout. It's some kind of recording disc or mirror . . .'

Mike Morris reached down beside his chair and drew up the box. When he opened it, the object inside was an old 78 in a paper sleeve . . . just as Chris had actually drawn.

★　　　★　　　★

Even after all these years, the dreams still have a habit of getting Chris into trouble that he's not looking for. Take, for example, the dreams of 4 July 1995, which landed him in the middle of a riot the following day . . .

In his dream, Chris was near the house of his friend Maria, who lived on an estate near him called Marsh Farm. Her car was on fire, and she was in danger. He could remember no more, woke up at half-past three, and when he finally managed to get back to sleep, the dream had vanished.

The next evening, Chris decided to drive over and see Maria. He wasn't sure that the dream would come to anything as the months of July and August are always erratic. However, he didn't want to risk it.

When he reached the estate, he noticed that the road layout had changed since his last visit a couple of months before: there were new mini-roundabouts, and some barriers had been erected to prevent joy riding. When he passed three blocks of flats, he noticed several groups of youths milling about. Perhaps it was the wrong time to visit: he swung round at the next mini-roundabout and headed back the way he had come.

One of the groups of youths had moved and they were now milling around the newly erected barriers. He slowed, and called out to them, asking what was going on. A youth in a ski-mask, disguising his face, told him that the barriers had to go. Almost on cue, the mob began to batter the barrier with sledgehammers.

Chris accelerated, wanting to leave as quickly as possible. He slowed beside a young man who was walking away from the mob.

'What on earth's going on?' he asked.

The youth replied: 'They're going to smash all the barriers. It's been planned for tonight. I'd get out of here, mate. They've got petrol bombs, the lot . . .'

Chris did get out, but not before he had put through a 999 call on his mobile phone and reported about a hundred armed and masked youths damaging the road signs and steel barriers.

'This isn't a hoax call,' he continued. 'There's going to be a serious disorder incident. I've been told they've got petrol bombs.'

He had time to give his name and address before leaving the estate quickly.

Over the next two nights 500 police and 250 rioters clashed on the estate. Cars were left blazing, three schools were burnt down and a policeman was stabbed.

Once again, the dreams had put him on the spot when it came to trouble.